Mr. Wicker

Published by Raw Dog Screaming Press
Bowie, MD
First Edition

Illustration & Jacket Design: Ryan Rice
Book Design: Jennifer Barnes

Printed in the United States of America

ISBN: 978-1-935738-66-4

Library of Congress Control Number: 2014945129

www.RawDogScreaming.com

To those who've been embraced by The Void
and are afraid it won't let go

and

To Rebekah
who lived with
unspeakable childhood memories

...memories materialized through the strength of implacable evocation and walked like human beings through the cloistered rooms.

Gabriel Garcia Marquez, *One Hundred Years of Solitude*

Mr. Wicker

Maria Alexander

**RAW DOG
SCREAMING
PRESS**

Chapter 1

The blood welled vermilion. *A lovely color.* It reminded Alicia of a picture she'd painted as a child for her grandfather. She then pressed the razor into the other vein.

The blood—no longer hers, but a free thing—ran from her stinging wrists and dribbled over one side of the bathtub to the black and white tile. A few drops bruised the sleeve of her emerald silk robe. Her legs stretched before her under the water. Even as a child she could see the veins in her legs creeping deep beneath her skin. She clenched her fists, nails digging into her palms, and the blood ran faster.

Alicia's career lay in pieces, shredded by the fits of fortune. As her wrists bled, the books she'd written, old and new, burned in the fireplace. Her husband had run off some time ago, leaving her the house with a double mortgage. Relationships, family—they, too, had run out, some sooner than later. She'd waited for the good things to come, nature abhorring a vacuum, but things continued to leave.

She'd been no longer able to summon the strength to believe it would ever get better, despite what therapists had told her over the years. The idea that it was her responsibility to hope as the cold void kissed her cheeks angered her against God Himself, and after the doctor's call that morning, that's when she'd decided she would take the last thing that could be taken. She'd prove God was an asshole for expecting her to hope while He took everything else.

God had repossessed her car last week. As she'd watched the tow truck haul it away, the black waters washed over her head. With nothing to look forward to and no hope of retrieving her life, she had one option. If she'd had pills, she would have used them to escape the pain because they are surer by far. But being the sort that hated taking pills and rarely even had prescriptions, she hadn't any. So she'd propped a copy of Gray's Anatomy (what better way for an author to learn how to turn characters into cadavers?) on the bathroom counter surrounded by burning candles. She'd wedged it open to Chapter 5, "The Wrist and Hand," and marked her own wrists where she should best cut. All the while, a gothic anthem blasted from her office stereo, vibrations tickling the floor.

Alicia slid further under the water, the glistening warmth lapping at her chin. The blood swelled like the delicate tendrils of a jellyfish around her breasts and under her arms. The water eased the pain of the incisions, just as she had read. Her head swam with shadows as her sight faded. Fucker. Taking, hiding. Keeping. No more. She sobbed. Shuddering. Breath shallow. Her reason flew with the winds of departure. *Whatever is beyond, it must be kinder. But if there is nothing...*

...nothing...

Nothing but an inky hallway...widening...to a tunnel.

Alicia cried as she walked, sorrow blossoming in her chest. The tunnel air was still and damp. She stepped forward, her wrists bleeding, soles scraping gravel and rough wooden boards.

A train tunnel.

A pinprick flickered so weakly in the distance that at first she questioned its existence, much less its momentum. But it fled toward her at high speed—a mass of howling, gyring light.

Wind buffeted her robe.

She turned and ran, shadows wavering across the tracks. She screamed as the howling splintered and fanned at her back, a monstrous chorus of shouts and shrieks. Her foot struck a broken board. She fell, the train's lights spilling over her shoulders. She started to rise. It was too late.

Instead of roaring iron, a scented wind—cotton candy, hot cocoa, and cut grass—billowed over her. A joyful, swirling throng of laughing, squealing sprites. The souls of children. They clambered over her miserable form, happy and loud and ghostly white, as if she did not exist. Their faces pressed through the vapor. "Marco...!" "Polo..." "Doooon't tickle me!" "He likes you." "Ring-a-round the rosie, a pocket full of posies..."

It all felt so...familiar.

Alicia reached out to them, the vapors trailing between the fingers of her open hands. The wind carried away what she longed for, everything that had escaped her in life. "Come back!" She cried, unheard. "Help me—please!" But they disappeared into the darkness as swiftly as they had overtaken her, playground banter echoing.

"Goddamn you!" She considered following them, but they were too fast. Perhaps there were more like them further down the track? She needed the company of angels, especially since she didn't feel like one. She stood and turned forward again, eager to find new companions, but now found a wall of heavenly light, pure and warm, within arm's reach. Amazed, she placed her hands into the warmth. Soft. Soothing. She stepped into it.

Although she'd expected to be weightless and formless as her consciousness shifted, she emerged among dusty library stacks with her flesh and form intact. She heard nothing but the gentle cacophony of timepieces. *Tick-tock, click, click, tick-tock.* Grinning bronze imps cradled gas-lit lamps, faces protruding between towering bookcases. The lamps cast a dim gloss over the swayback shelves burdened with black, hardbound tomes.

As she squinted at the stacks, Alicia noted that the bindings of many books were freshly woven, a name inked in gold with gothic pen strokes on each spine. The names of artists. Celebrities. Common folk, like her next-door neighbor from childhood who had been arrested in college for selling cocaine. And a girl she'd hated in her dorm at NYU who slept with the professors.

Alicia's sticky, pallid fingers traced the spines. She'd loved libraries even as a child, spending endless hours pouring over old ghost stories and Agatha Christie mysteries. Nostalgia heated her lifeless heart. The skin of her wrists gaped at the wounds, blood crusting the edges. She'd upturned her wrists to examine them when the creaking of wood elsewhere in the library startled her. Terrified, she held her breath as she listened.

"In a time and out of time, in time the ink shall sing."

The words drizzled icily over her skin as a deep voice sang. She peered down the aisle. A scratching picked up where the caroling left off. The presence invited some sort of meeting, but she wasn't sure it was the kind of meeting she wanted.

Whatever lies beyond, it must be kinder. That was, indeed, her last thought in life. Perhaps she was right.

She continued down the aisle toward the voice. As the aisle drew to an end, the floor cleared and widened into a vast study. Here hung the many clocks that were ticking, clacking, whirring. Some were round with black-numbered faces and hammered silver borders, while others were square with teensy doors and eaves housing heralds ready to spring forth on the hour. None of them had been set at the same hour, and nothing indicated if they represented an hour anywhere at all. Here and there stood thick-legged oak tables piled high with dark books. Tarnished candelabras dripping with blazing candles crowned the literary heaps. She moved around the tables that obscured the scratcher and caroler, if indeed they were the same person.

Scritch, scritch, scritch. Scritch, scritch, scritch, scritch...

"Blood and trust they turn to dust, each secret that they bring."

A window smoky with lavender twilight arched over a desk littered with books and weeping columns of burning wax. Over the desk hunched a sooty-headed character. The scratching paused as he dipped a quill into an inkwell that sat beside an old-fashioned black telephone with large finger holes for dialing. The scratching resumed with vigor.

Arrested by fear, Alicia stood beside one of the tables. She was trying to accept death as it came, strange as it was. She was unsure of her role in it, as death so far defied any concept she'd heard in life. But now, as this begrimed creature turned to face her, she dropped any pretense of ever hoping to understand. If in life God had taken from her, He now gave like a mad uncle tearing pages from a fairy tale book and handing them out like banknotes. A thick char covered the man's otherwise well-formed body, which was draped with the burned rags of a gray robe and cowl. His sea green eyes were wet with humanity. He smiled jaggedly, his lips flaking obsidian. At last, he spoke.

"Alicia Baum." He sunk his quill in the well. "The once-beloved horror writer, no less. At last you've come to see...Mr. Wicker." He seemed fond of his name, smiling as he said it. His eyes recorded the contours of her body, and his expression softened. He said nothing, however, and watched her with even more interest than before.

A raven cawed, sliding through the air to alight on a nearby stack of books and preen its oily feathers. Soon another raven landed next to it, strutting back and forth along the edge of a large tome as it cocked an eye at Alicia. More feathers rustled elsewhere in the cavernous library, but the beasts that shook them remained hidden.

Alicia stepped back, putting the table corner between her and this blackened man-thing, this gentleman incubus. "Is this hell?" The depression and anger that drove the blade to her veins was rekindled.

"Only for me," he replied. His eyes wandered from her body to the heights of the repository shelves. "And those who wish to remember."

"I don't understand. Aren't these books of people's sins?"

"Sins?" He laughed, examining the book he'd just penned. Hands with long, crisp fingers crouched like tarantulas on the page. One of the ravens leapt with a squawk from its book-perch and landed on Mr. Wicker's shoulder. "Perhaps, in a way," he continued. "This is the Library of Lost Childhood Memories."

"I see. Gauging by how grim this place is, I don't suppose these are the lost memories of when a child went to Disneyland and ate his first churro, or fell asleep apple-cheeked and adorable during church."

"No."

"Hmm."

"What did you think you would find?"

"Here?"

"In death."

"Oh," she said. "Well, I figured it had to be better than life, which was unbearable. It had to be either blank like a chalkboard or full of fuzzy amber light beings I'd read about in New Age books who want me to evolve or something." She looked him over a moment. "Not that I want to evolve. And not that you're exactly a fuzzy amber light being."

He rose from his chair, the ornately carved legs scraping the wooden floor, and closed the distance between them. Alicia found her fear and heat in his dour, half-lidded eyes and dominant advance. One hand raked into her blood-and-bath-soaked hair and the other caught up a slit wrist, bringing her death's bouquet to his nose. His touch left ash on her arm. Everything that had repulsed her about him sweetened as he slowly inhaled. An incubus was he, and more. She also took in his scent, a smudgy amber smell instead of the burned flesh she'd expected.

As the scent blossomed in her nose, she never wanted anyone like she wanted him.

"You slipped into the light because you love the darkness," he said. Those sea green eyes—embers, damp and direct—slid from hers to the sagging line of her emerald robe as it sank from her shoulders, caught between her breasts.

"I don't love darkness," she stammered, half-drunk with him. "I don't even like the shades drawn." It was true. Not the literal darkness, anyway. She had even died in a well-lit bathroom. What disturbed her was not his accusation, but that this scribe of pain could spread her legs as easily as he palmed open pages of a book.

"Take off your robe."

With a pull of her sash and a shrug of her shoulders, the bloodstained robe slipped to the floor, unveiling her waxen skin. He touched her chastely at the shoulders as he surveyed the continent of her alabaster flesh. "Perfect," he breathed with a moan, his look hardening her nipples. "Absolutely perfect. It will do well."

She cooled when she heard that last phrase. "*It* will do well?" She pulled away. "What's that supposed to mean?"

He sighed. "What it means is that I want your skin." He placed a hand on her neck, more lover than assassin. "I'm tired of being the keeper of memory, and I want to leave. You don't want life. I do. To be human again, I will need your skin."

"Look, I'm not giving anyone *anything*," she growled, swiping her robe from the floor. "I've had too much taken away already. Besides, I don't have living skin anymore. I'm dead. Or haven't you noticed that?"

He retreated to his chair, facing the room. "Perhaps you are now, but I could change that." He dug an elbow into the armrest as his hand propped an ebony cheek. "What if I told you that I could explain everything that's happened in your life?" He leaned forward. "What if I told you that everything terrible in your life happened because of these missing memories? That they've controlled you from the day you gave them to me. That someone died for them."

"I'd say you're mad."

"I'd say, suicide girl, that you're hardly in a position to argue."

A rush of realization. "Oh, crap." She knotted her sash. "Is this one of those near-death hallucinations?" She threw up her hands. "How stupid of me. Of course." Even the dim library seemed to brighten a shade with this insight. The tunnel, the lights: common imagery to the myth of modern mortality. The rest—well—an LSD flashback, no doubt.

At that thought, a howling maw of shifting light opened from between two stacks. The candle flames bowed from its palpable hum and flux. Mr. Wicker winced. The ravens shrieked as they fled the portal.

"Ha! The Afterlife Express has arrived!" Her eyes moved over Mr. Wicker with the same half-lidded, impassioned look he used when he studied her naked body. "You've been a stunning hallucination, but I must find eternal peace before God takes that, too. The miserable bastard." As she turned toward the light, he reached behind to the desk and raised something before him.

"Don't you want to read your book?"

Her fingers twitched like live wires and she shook, a hot bolt of fright riveting her spine. She looked back, curiosity compelling her. His eyes burned as he held the tome, her name branded on the cover. Mastering her delusion—for this was what it must be—she forced its face into the waters of improbability until it stopped kicking, and she entered the light.

As soon as she was gone, Mr. Wicker sighed and grinned, pleased with himself. Facing the window, he picked up the black telephone, and spoke into the receiver.

"9-1-1 please."

Chapter 2

Dr. James Farron winced and backed away as five-year-old Jesse pointed the laser gun at his crotch. "Bow to me, you Raffabarf!"

He certainly felt like a Raffabarf at the moment, whatever that was. Black circles and bloodshot eyes—no amount of espresso could supplement his sleep deficit from conducting research. Dark brown hair and a boyish face revealed his Irish ancestry, but his party habits (or lack thereof) did not.

As the child stood fast in his aggressive stance outside the therapy room, Dr. Farron beseeched Jesse's mother. "Mrs. Flemming, I can't let him into the room with *that*." He indicated the laser gun with a nod of his head.

"It's *play* therapy, isn't it?" she snipped. She wore yoga pants and a stretch camisole. Hair the color of root beer in sunlight and skin overly tanned, she was soaking in the vapors of some expensive perfume. Her cell phone bleated out an electronic merengue and she flipped it open. "Those are his toys. Play with him, for Chrissake!" She threw a skeptical glance at Dr. Farron's Marvin the Martian tie. Then, she spoke sweetly into the cell: "Namaste!"

The parents were so often worse than the children.

Resigned, Dr. Farron opened the door to the therapy room and Jesse ran inside, the laser gun flashing as it sputtered and rattled like the back end of a Harley. Dr. Farron rolled his eyes and followed the child, slamming the door behind him.

He pulled up a stool while Jesse ran around in circles, blasting the "Raffabarf" dollhouses, dinosaurs, dolls, puppets, and crayons into tiny plasmatrons. "How are you, Jesse?"

"I'M MASSIMUS BLASSER!"

"Wow. You are very angry today, Jesse. You seem like you want to hurt somebody with that gun."

Jesse's mother had reported that Jesse was having nightmares, was defiant, and could not concentrate on anything for more than a few moments. He was also biting adults. He obviously wanted to hurt somebody.

"MASSIMUS BLASSER WILL KILL YOU!"

"I see. Why don't you play with some of the other toys here?" He picked up a bucket full of dinosaurs. "We've got lots of new dinosaurs and soldiers." He encouraged children to use anything but guns to express their rage as they played out their emotional dramas. He learned that children would often tell their own stories if they were allowed to express themselves in a safe environment.

This was not always true, however. Not lately. The children's stories had been drying up, leaving vast dunes of empty memory. One child after another had stopped talking to him. Stopped playing. With great concern for the wellbeing of his tiny patients, he'd turned them back to their parents with unsatisfactory explanations for their behavior. These failures sometimes crippled him with doubt as to his abilities as a doctor. At the age of thirty-five, he'd already had his share of tragedy and he wondered if his difficulties were interfering with his work, which in turn fed his self-doubt. All this sent him sliding along a Möbius strip of despair.

Then one night at the bedside of a boy lying unconscious from trauma, he'd heard a name. A whisper in the darkness from the bloodied lips of innocence.

"Mr. Wicker."

The boy mumbled to "Mr. Wicker" a frightening tale of his alcoholic stepfather swinging a wrench at his head as the child turned the TV channel. When the boy woke up, Dr. Farron asked him about Mr. Wicker, but the boy was puzzled and had no idea what he had even told Mr. Wicker in his sleep. Dr. Farron then kept vigil with other children, using voice-activated recording technology. Time and again, he was rewarded with the mysterious name, if not the traumatic incident itself.

"Who is Mr. Wicker?" It was the question of the century. His research grant was to explore exactly that.

While employed part-time at the Bayford University Hospital in Berkeley, Dr. Farron had spent many long hours researching libraries, professional journals, periodicals, and especially the web as he tried to find the source of this phenomenon. He'd thought perhaps a children's book or television show held a key to the mystery, but he found nothing.

He'd eventually concluded that the abused children had some kind of universal imaginary friend. Someone suggested that they might have created a folktale like the "secret stories" that the homeless children of Miami purportedly tell each other. The problem was that he'd never seen any research confirming such a thing even existed beyond a single news article. These stories included tales of Bloody Mary, also known as "La Llorona," the Crying Woman who weeps blood from ghoulish empty sockets and feeds on children's terror. And the Blue Lady, who has pale blue skin and lives in the ocean, hobbled by a demon spell. Supposedly, you could interview waking children about these secret stories, about how demons travel through the gateways from Hell: abandoned refrigerators, mirrors, a cemetery in Dade County, and Jeep Cherokees with "black windows." You could ask them and they would respond, if you had earned their trust, or so the news article said. But not the children who spoke to Mr. Wicker in their sleep. They were unaware they had done or said anything. It was no wonder Dr. Farron had earned the epithet "Whisper Chaser."

Or worse: "Mulder."

None of his colleagues took him seriously until he received the research grant, and even then, he knew they didn't appreciate his work. It made no difference. He had to find out what was happening with the children. Never mind that the measures he took to capture the nightly confessions were making him unpopular with—or at least a spectacle to—the rest of the hospital staff.

Not everyone found him strange. Although he was single and straight, he dreaded another awkward situation in the cafeteria as he declined the company of female staff.

At least, the newer female staff. The more senior women knew not to ask. And why.

Today he decided to abandon play therapy and try a more traditional method of treatment. As Jesse continued a peppery monologue of cybernetic destruction, Dr. Farron walked to his desk fringed with Crayola masterpieces and withdrew a stack of Rorschach blots.

He sat on the stool with the cards lying facedown on his lap. "Hey, Maximus, can you look at something for me? I need to know what you think."

Jesse reached into the bucket of dinosaurs, grabbed a handful, and threw them against the wall. "Maybe."

Dr. Farron sighed and picked up a card. "What do you think this is, Jesse?"

The child paused a second. "DRAGGAMASSER OF THE EIGHT DIMESSHON!" The laser gun rattled at the card in an explosion of flashing lights.

"Okay, how about this one?"

"DRAGGAMASSER OF THE EIGHT DIMESSHON!"

"And who am I again?"

"RAFFABARF OF THE EIGHT DIMESSHON!"

A moment of silence.

"Jesse?"

"Yeah?"

"Do you have any special television shows or movies or cartoons you like that you want to talk about?"

Jesse ran to the corner of the room and grabbed an anatomically correct doll, leveling the laser gun at its head.

"JESSE!"

"Don't move or the nasty doll gets it."

Stacks of papers towered on Dr. Leonard Dulac's desk like stalagmites, stalwart against the long exhalations of the air conditioning. The accreditations and accolades of a psychiatric department chairman spackled the dingy walls of his office, the epitome of adulthood. Dr. Dulac sat without speaking for a moment as Dr. Farron struggled to understand what his mentor and superior was saying. He'd guessed something was wrong when Dr. Dulac had closed the office door and asked him to have a seat.

"James, I understand your frustration, but you need to rely more on drug treatments."

"My ADHD cases are *not* under-medicated!"

"But then that leaves one answer as to why your patients are not responding. You."

Silence.

"Have you been seeing Stanley?" Dr. Dulac asked.

"Of course! I've done everything that's been suggested." That last phrase bit so acridly that he crossed his arms and looked away. The therapist was considerate, professional, and perceptive, but the weekly sessions were discouraging, especially when they dragged on to a third year. He should know better, he told himself. He should not need this. Every principle of healing stood monolithic in his intellect along the road to recovery. But the same way skyscrapers are invisible to New Yorkers, he had ceased to notice the principles as he hurried toward a destination that never arrived. Why did it seem so hopeless?

"I have to put you on probation, James. It's just a thirty-day formality. I have to do it because of the parental complaints."

The words slipped under his skin like a clumsy injection and stung with unfairness. "You can't do this," he said. "It's not my fault that they're talking to him and not me!"

"To him?" Dr. Dulac leaned forward and adjusted his glasses.

"You know who I'm talking about."

"Humor me, James."

Dr. Farron crumpled. "To Mr. Wicker."

Dr. Dulac shook his head and settled back in his leather chair. "Why don't you pick up an extra shift tonight in ER?" he suggested.

Goodbye support or protection from Dr. Dulac for grant work! He was on his own. The ER gig wasn't an unusual practice. Some of his psychiatric colleagues moonlighted in ER from time to time, all having been through the rigors of a medical degree and residency. Dr. Farron had done it more often when his practice was just starting. He just thought he was way past that in his career, that he'd never need to do it again.

"Just see how it goes," Dr. Dulac said, pushing the probation paper toward Dr. Farron.

The younger doctor signed it. Thirty days of humiliation. ER could not be worse than this.

"Suicide, fifteen minutes!"

The radio room PA system beeped with the paramedic call for the latest trauma patient. Triage ushered the gurney through the double-layers of automatic glass doors and into the trauma room. Dr. Farron scrambled to swap out her I.V. alongside nurses in blue cotton scrubs. He examined her wrist wounds: this woman had drawn in ink where she needed to cut lengthwise on her wrists. "She'll need a bilateral unit laceration repair," he told one of the nurses. "And a transfusion."

The woman's lips moved ever so slightly. Another nurse gathered her matted blond hair and swept it aside. If it weren't for her dire condition, she'd look something like a Botticelli painting. She was certainly not an anorexic fawn that had limped into her mother's bathroom in a miasma of teenage angst to swallow a bottle of pills. Usually older women ended their lives as an angry statement. Suicide was a last "I told you so" to whoever they wanted to get back at—husbands, families, the Universe. Her mouth worked in silence to communicate with her inner demons. Nothing audible. She swallowed hard, and then her jaw stopped moving.

"O-R?" the nurse asked.

"Nah, do it here," he replied. The wounds weren't that deep.

Sidelong would she bend, and sing a faery's song...

A line from a Keats poem drifted through his thoughts. He grabbed the chart clipped to the gurney. Name: Alicia Baum. Age: Unknown. He guessed she was in her mid to late thirties. He replaced the chart, and nurses rolled her into another room to be anesthetized.

Alicia Baum.

Why was that name familiar?

ER was exhausting. Almost, in fact, enough so to make him forget the forlorn morning he'd spent referring his patients to other doctors so they could continue their care on his probation. He'd been busy intubating another patient two hours later when an orderly pushing a gurney toward him mouthed, "Nice tie," and gave him the thumbs up. Dr. Farron smiled. Today it was SpongeBob SquarePants. When he realized the gurney held—what was her name? Alicia Baum?—he finished up what he was doing and checked on her. Nylon restraints lashed her to the gurney. A loosely woven white nylon blanket was pulled high over her chest. Leaning over her gurney, he once again examined her chart. She had been clinically dead in the emergency vehicle for a couple of minutes. Rubbing his chin, he tried to remember how he knew her name.

"Celebrity crush, eh?" the orderly said, patting him on the back as he passed.

Mortally embarrassed, he tugged his tie loose with one hand and replaced her chart. "What celebrity?" he asked, but the orderly only winked.

The woman gasped, neck twisting as if avoiding the sight of something. Her mouth opened with fright, and her fingers flexed as she grasped the air. Then, she relaxed, and with the voice of the wind she sighed as if reciting a terrible prayer:

"Mr. Wicker."

Icy floes of fear slid through Dr. Farron's veins as she repeated the name, a mantra of madness.

No grown man or woman had *ever* spoken the name "Mr. Wicker" in his or her sleep as this woman did. At least, none of which he'd ever known.

He snatched her chart from the bed and wrote in it.

She stirred and opened her eyes.

"Ms. Baum? Ms. Baum, can you hear me?" he asked, hopeful that her faculties were intact.

She nodded, tugging at her restraints. Tears leaked from her eyes.

"Ms. Baum, my name is Dr. Farron and we have you restrained until you are medically stable. We can't have you trying to hurt yourself here. Do you understand?"

She whispered.

"I'm sorry, what did you say?"

"Did you save my life?"

"Yes."

"You...BASTARD!" A geyser of rage erupted behind her eyes. "What is wrong with you?"

"I'm a doctor. I'm sworn to save lives."

"Promises are made to be broken."

Dr. Farron made notes in her chart. It wasn't unusual for patients to react strongly. He just hoped that she'd be amenable to talking to him later. "So, if we let you go, will you try to kill yourself again?"

More tears. She rubbed her cheek on the pillow to dry them.

"Do you plan to do this again?" Dr. Farron asked.

Her eyes drove a look deep into his that revealed not just keen intelligence but bottomless heartache. "You think I'd tell a fuckwit like you? Fuck—OFF!"

He made another note in her chart. "Okay, Ms. Baum, you have the right to representation at your first inquiry."

"What?" Her head lifted off the pillow.

"As soon as you stabilize, you're going to lockdown."

Chapter 3

Brooding at his antiquated desk in the lavender twilight of eternity, Mr. Wicker recalled the unspeakable delicacy of Alicia's skin as he'd inhaled the fragrance of blood on her slashed wrists. Her book sat before him. He stroked the cover as he reminisced about how his fingers had left ash on her skin where he'd held her. As always, one taste of her had inflamed him more than any opiate.

Perfectly composed if not completely collected, he'd tried not to show how powerful the encounter was for him, that it had shaken him to his core. He'd been expecting her. He'd spun the whole act as an erotic joke lest she remember what happened a century or more ago. She remembered nothing. After the 9-1-1 call, he'd collapsed in his chair and hadn't moved until now.

"Muninn!"

A pother of rustling feathers. A squawk. The raven alighted on his shoulder, an obsidian creature with glassy eyes, big beak, and claws that curled sharp as thorns.

"Muninn, it's her. You remember, don't you?" Mr. Wicker had not seen her since she was a child. Even then he had suspected, but it was difficult to tell for certain the identity of another's soul when looking at the eyes of one so young. Besides, he hadn't been ready to see her again at that time. Every time he'd encountered her in previous incarnations, it had meant catastrophe for him of one sort or another.

He closed his eyes and once again waltzed with her as Eliza in that New England ballroom as he wore the skin of that loathsome dream thief who had broken into the Library with his even more loathsome cohort to steal her book. The heady swirl of the dance gave way to an even more ancient memory of her. And then another. The memories went on like a snowstorm, obliterating everything else in his mind.

Since his imprisonment, he had only once been in the waking world. It was nearly impossible for him to escape this prison of memory and sin. He wept tears of blood that splotched the inkblots and raven scratches on his desk.

All he knew was that she had come back.

Never was an enticement this strong not mutual, and even as he was in this terrible state, her shade responded exquisitely to his blackened touch. And when she'd dropped her robe, the urge to consume her was almost unbearable. All he would have to do was lick her neck, touch her just *so*. Of all the times he had tasted her before, none had been either as toothsome or winsome. As if a wind blew a flaming seed into his parched fields, she ignited a fire that roared through every stalk and stem of his tormented existence.

He could not have let her die without taking her book. If he had, he might not ever see her again. So, he'd had her rescued, even if it meant risking her ire. He had to have her back. Such bliss. So pure. Nothing could come close.

He stroked his servant Muninn's sleek head and wings. Huginn slept somewhere in the rafters, her massive beak tucked into her wing. She seldom minded him, although when he needed her most, she was useful. And right now what he needed was the most effective course of action. He didn't know how Alicia might bring about his devastation, but he had no doubt that she could. And it wouldn't be out of malice, but rather her unfailing curiosity and integrity.

The gods who had bound him in that infernal repository had whims beyond understanding. Before the telephone had appeared, he tied notes to the legs of ravens and let them fly from the Library into the crossing light, but he no longer wanted to risk losing another raven in the waking world. That risk would be a calculated one, indeed, for the last incident almost brought horrendous consequences. The telephone was a bizarre yet welcome development. He knew what a telephone was from talking to his many visitors, but he had never seen one before. As demonstrated by a young boy with a harelip and bloodied cornea, he held the receiver to his ear like a conch shell and listened to the dry echoes of ubiquity. He had learned that he could request to speak to specific people with varying degrees of success. Hopefully, he would never need to send a raven into the other world again.

He opened Alicia's book on the desk. Golden fairy tale calligraphy. Sooty cover. His desire for her rose like broken glass in his throat, a thousand gashes in his lungs as he inhaled the ink, which warbled a sweet song of anguish, a lament of two female voices echoing through the rafters. Mr. Wicker often marveled at how human beings are both alive and dead, suffering an incomplete death over the lifetime. Death tainted the flesh to serve this odd communion of opposites. The bitter soup of the soul. The hardened crust of the body. Oh, how he could devour her, soup and crust.

He had her book. She could still return.

Was that the answer? To lure her back to the Library? What would he do then? Keep her? And how then would he do this? She was too happy to leave when she was here, and would be less happy to be here again. If he could bring her to the Library and the light were to come for her, she could leave as easily as she did before. And what if bringing her to the Library was the means of his devastation?

Which brought up another question: did he care if he was ruined?

The yoke of his curse crushed him at times but he had managed to cultivate a certain satisfaction over the centuries. At first, he'd found the ceaseless stories of malice soul crushing, but he eventually learned to savor human depravity and destruction. He grew to appreciate the service he performed for humanity, even if it caused people serious problems later in life.

Brooders weep and brooders keep
Their misery at hand
Let Mr. Wicker wash your sicker
Memories in sand.

He had purpose. He took away crippling distress and later restored it to each owner. And there was no way she was going to take that from him, too.

He slammed the book shut and the madrigal ceased. To his surprise, the pages of Alicia's book ruffled between the hard covers and the ink mewled from the pressed pages. The spectacle could mean only one thing: in the waking world, she was trying to remember. It was not a daydream or musing but rather a concerted effort to recall specifically what was in her book. That meant she remembered him and the Library.

She might not bother him again. Simply because she'd caused him trouble in the past did not mean she'd create future trouble. So why was he worried? He had vowed he would never leave the Library again, which meant a repeat of the nineteenth century near-apocalypse would be avoided. If for some mysterious reason someone stole her book, this time he would let them take it and let the consequences be whatever they would be—although why someone would want to steal her book this time, he could not imagine. He didn't even believe magicians of any real power still existed, anyway, much less one that could find the Library.

Yet he worried. He rested a hand on the rustling pages of the mewling book, pressing them together. It muted the sound. Why would she want to remember? If she were to recall what had happened, she would kill herself outright, perhaps by far surer, more violent means. For despite the roses, this was no garden-variety memory.

Perhaps he could watch her. And if it seemed anything was amiss, he could intervene, but only in extreme circumstances. It meant making a significant sacrifice but one that was temporary.

He looked up to the rafters. "Huginn! Here!" After a moment, Huginn emerged, strutting to the edge of a book stack and peering down at him. She was smaller than Muninn, and owned herself in a way Muninn never did.

"Huginn. Here. Please." He hated saying "please." It felt demeaning. But it seemed to work and Huginn alighted to his forearm without a squawk. She kneaded his arm, pacing excitedly.

"Huginn, I want you to do something for me. You will enjoy it, but you have to promise that you will return. Because I need you. Do you understand?"

The raven eyed him and opened her beak, a throaty rattle escaping her gullet. She then coyly tipped her head toward the wall through which Alicia had disappeared.

"I want you to follow her and relay back to me what you see. Don't enter any structures or dwellings whatsoever. Do you understand? All you need is to be able to see her. See her yet do not be seen."

Huginn gave no indication that she even heard him but rather seemed intent on the wall until the heavenly light tore open its surface. She launched from his arm with such ferocity that her talons ripped his robe sleeve. Her excited cawing stirred the other ravens in the Library, inciting a cacophony of clicks and screeches.

Mr. Wicker shielded his eyes. He already missed his Huginn as she sailed into the ethers. But as the light faded, he realized that the one he truly missed was Alicia...

...Eliza...

Sirona.

Chapter 4

DAY 1—BAYFORD PSYCHIATRIC UNIT

With the orderly at her elbow, Alicia shuffled from the elevator to a white door with a small window. She grasped the cold metal handle, but her hands were too weak to turn it.

"Allow me," the orderly said. He waved a card at a security pad, cranked the handle and swung open the door.

Her hands were fucked up. Just how badly, she didn't know. She was fine with using the restroom this morning and eating grape gelatin with a plastic spoon, but there was residual damage from her careful cutting job. She had not intended to survive it. How on earth was she found? There was no way anyone could have known. If someone had been worried because they hadn't heard from her and called the police, the timing was incredibly suspect. No one knew that she had been leaving the world at that one moment.

No one but that odd character in her death dream, Mr. Wicker.

"Here you go, Ms. Baum!"

The orderly escorted her down a long hall lined with dirty sodium lights to the nurses' station. A tall, thin black woman, probably in her fifties, helmed the high counter. At her direction, nurses raced to-and-fro. A hall broke to each side of the station.

"How ya doin', Ms. Baum?" said a young, white man, emerging from behind the desk with a chart in hand. He chewed a piece of cinnamon gum she could smell clear across the room. His tanned skin wrinkled in places with bulging veins, particularly the backs of his hands. "My name's Arnie, and I'll be your charge nurse." The orderly surrendered her to Arnie's care and left. "This is Rachelle. She's our top dog."

Rachelle waved him on as she walked into an adjacent office. "I'll top dog you all right."

He led Alicia down the hallway that reached to the left of the nurses' station, explaining that this side of the unit was for women and the other for men, with the activities room in between. Above that was the ward cafeteria along with rooms for group therapy and administrative offices.

They stepped into what appeared to be a miniature hospital room. The grayish green tiles flecked with black caught the russet haze of twilight filtering through the curtains. The bed looked like a cot.

"And this is where you'll be sleeping, Ms. Baum. Just so you know, someone will be checking on you every fifteen minutes or so."

"I thought there would be a common sleeping area," Alicia said, thinking back on the movies she'd seen.

"Nah." Arnie smiled, snapping his gum. "We'll often double up on these rooms, but never more than three." He grew serious. "Now, Ms. Baum, your grandma is here, but she doesn't know you're *here*—that is, in lockdown. She just knows you're admitted to the hospital."

"Why doesn't she know? Why doesn't someone tell her?"

"'Cause we can't tell her without your permission," he said. "You up for it?"

She nodded.

"Great! Normally we encourage patients to leave the rooms, but I'll let you have a visit here for now."

Before he could turn away, she asked the question that had been beating its way out of her head. "Who found me?"

He shrugged. "Don't know," he replied, a fresh wave of cinnamon from between his lips. His compassion dimmed to worry. "Do you want me to ask?"

Her heart pounded to the affirmative, but fear overtook curiosity. "No, not yet. Thank you. Will you open the curtains?" He did. And, promising to return, he left.

The voice outside her door twenty minutes later was pastel, crocheted, and perfumed. When she entered, Alicia's grandmother stopped in the doorway, puckered her coral lips, and patted her chest. She was short and pear-shaped, golden-bangle laden, a silver-haired whirlwind in a blue jogging outfit. She descended on Alicia, Nordstrom's bag on her arm, and held her granddaughter's head against her chest.

"Leesha!" She pulled back to assess Alicia's face, and then covered her forehead and cheeks with kisses. Alicia smiled. In that bathroom, the void was the last thing to kiss her cheek, and it had never baked her a pumpkin pie. In the arms of her dear grandmother she felt regretful, embarrassed, irritated. And more than a bit foolish.

The elderly woman sat next to Alicia, placing a hand on her shoulder. "I never thought you'd do it," she said. "Your mother..." her lip trembled. "Why, honey? Was it Eric?"

Alicia's gaze wandered to the window. At the mention of her ex-husband, an angry silence widened into the moment as her grandmother waited. She felt the words, the anger, and the void become the masonry of her body. They were part of the architecture in which she dwelt, not blueprints on display to explain her every step and stair.

"I went to the house. All you had is that dreadful black clothing, so I bought you some new things." The Nordstrom's bag slid off her wrist over her clattering bracelets, and she opened it to show Alicia the contents. A toothbrush in a baggie. A lavender sweater. Red velvet slippers. Exercise pants. A t-shirt and some panties. A peach silk dress. The last felt smooth and cool as Alicia dipped her hand into the fabric. "I have to take them up front. I'm told they have to keep everything."

A thin smile. "Thanks, Grandma."

"I wish you'd have come and stayed with me a while," her grandmother said. "But now it's too late. The house is in escrow. It's just too much for me these days, you know."

Sold! Alicia remembered every detail of the house that nurtured her after her mother's tragedy: the bar in the den where she had hidden in the cupboards; the sprawling butterscotch kitchen that smelled of honey and coffee; the upright piano in the family room, on top of which her grandfather had kept a carousel of crystal shot glasses and a prismatic decanter of whisky. She used to climb up on the piano and sneak whiffs of the whisky. Her mind assembled the rest of the house, planting every gardenia bush around the border. It had been her home.

Her grandmother sighed. "What are you thinking, Leesha? Sweetheart?"

"Nothing," she said, picking at the dried blood under her French manicure, which was now pink, not white. "I was thinking of the house, the parts I loved best," she said at last.

The old woman's smile was sweet yet fiery like ginger drops. "You loved the rose garden until..."

"The rose garden?"

A cold chasm sprawled within Alicia's memory. No rose garden. She shook her head.

"It's for the best," her grandmother said, looking away as she patted Alicia's knee.

"What? Why? Grandma, please remind me."

Alicia's grandmother shook her head and bit her lower lip. "Sorry I brought it up," she said. She kissed Alicia on the cheek and left.

Don't you want to read your book?

"Mrs. Rains!"

Dr. Farron hurried after the elderly woman as she hustled down the hallway to the elevator with an orderly. He pulled a card from his pocket. "I'm Dr. James Farron. Do you have a moment?"

"A moment only," she replied, taking the card. "What do you want?"

The slap of attitude reddened his cheeks. "I understand you're busy, ma'am. I just wanted to speak with you a moment. Does she have anyone? A husband maybe?"

"Oh, heavens, no!" the grandmother snapped. "She drove off the poor man. And now her memory! What are you going to do about that? She can't remember a thing!"

"Memory loss is normal with severe depression," he said politely.

"Well, I don't care!" The powder, perfume, and crochet gave way to wooden hairbrushes and early bedtimes without supper. Her eyes narrowed to dark, wrinkled fissures, and she raised a gnarled finger to his face. "You people did nothing for her mother." Then, with a sniff: "You'd better take good care of her."

Chapter 5

Alicia examined her prison.

The room had a door that opened outward and was propped open by a spring lock. No chance of anyone barricading themselves in. She had heard stories of agitated crazy people being put in isolation; she suspected the room served a dual purpose. Fold up the bed, close the bathroom, and restrain the patient: *voila!* Isolation. The miniscule restroom had no shower or mirror, just a toilet and sink with a retractable sliding door with no latch.

As her eyes swept the sterile room, her mind kept returning to Mr. Wicker. Why had she been so attracted to him? Something in his eyes perfumed his appearance. He was revolting, yet so familiar and provocative that it was paralyzing. Like the boyfriend who was not only bad for you, but from whom you could not get away because the sex was both insanely hot and as powerful as religion. *That* boyfriend, but in a Halloween mask. She wanted to figure out why she was attracted to Mr. Icky and get over it pronto but wasn't sure how.

She brushed her teeth and tried not to think about it. Instead, her thoughts turned to writing. How for the first time in a while she felt like writing but had no means. She could use a voice recorder if not a laptop—*Will my fingers be able to type again?*—but she doubted they would let her have either. About three years ago, her creativity had fled as the Godzilla foot of depression eclipsed her. When her words left her, she was at such a loss because she'd always defined herself by her writing. What was she now? A sad crazy woman? A pathetic loser with no life skills whatsoever? That's what her husband had called her.

"Ms. Baum!" The cinnamon gum nurse leaned into the doorway, checking his watch as he spoke. "You got a therapy appointment now."

She'd just had some boring talk with a therapist whose skin reminded her of desiccated oak. Questions about her suicide. Questions about her failed marriage. Questions about work. Questions, questions, questions. These people asked the same damned questions. They even wore the same clothes. So many of them had turned out to be crazier than she was that she'd given up on them. There'd been one good one, but she moved to Connecticut. There was no winning in this department. "Another one?" she asked.

"Another doctor," Arnie replied, initialing a box on the front sheet of her chart. "We've got to leave the ward. So, come on now."

She would go but not cooperate, no matter what they wanted. Her damnation belonged to no one. Her guilt, should she be able to conjure any for her deed, would remain firmly in hand. She didn't want those fucking know-it-alls to get their analytical bullshit all over her dream, the one thing God saw fit to give her. Even though the previous therapist had explained to her that suicide was not necessarily an indication of mental illness, she didn't want to give them any further reason to detain her. Especially since she could, at odd moments, still feel Mr. Wicker touching her. Still *wanted* to feel Mr. Wicker touching her.

Yeah, that couldn't be healthy. She'd have to keep mum. It was her best bet if she wanted out. What she really wanted, though, was her memory.

The missing memory.

What if I told you that everything terrible in your life happened because of these missing memories?

It seemed to her the reasons for her suicide attempt were obvious: unbearable depression brought on by a series of significant misfortunes. But "Mr. Wicker" had said she'd died because of her lost memories. Or did he say the things that had happened to her were the result of her lost memory? She supposed they were one in the same. But if there was a deeper explanation for what had pushed her life off the ledge and into a swan dive, she wanted to know. It made her crazy thinking an invisible hand was not only steering her life, but straight toward another cliff—a cliff that was no longer comforting.

If only he hadn't seemed so real. That library. Even the ravens. It didn't feel like a dream but rather something that just happened in the other room.

Mr. Wicker haunted her. She couldn't think for more than a minute without his face, his hands, that voice welling up in her memory with baffling clarity. And since she'd stabilized in the medical ward, the black waters had fled. She no longer felt a stone lodged in her chest but rather a lightness of being, as if she'd just emerged from the mists into sunlit shafts strafing the ground. Her encounter in the Library seemed to cause some kind of essential shift within. She wanted to liken it to being a survivor on the *Titanic*, but then thought better of it because those survivors were cursed.

After exiting the high security elevator, they entered a hallway decorated with Disney characters and anthropomorphic fire engines. Just past a large room where children played—some together and others alone with blocks, books, and toys—a blond woman in a white cotton skirt led a girl with wide eyes from one of the office doors. Alicia felt far too big for the hallway, as if she should stoop or hunch like Snow White in the dwarf house.

Arnie halted before a door plastered with children's drawings. One had fallen over the office nameplate. He pushed up the drawing, pressing the corners to reinforce the Scotch tape, to reveal two black birds scrawled with black crayon on white construction paper. The nameplate that had been hidden read: "James Farron, M.D. M.F.C.C."

Alicia stared at the drawing of the ravens, the eerie coincidence slipping between her ribs and prodding her insides.

"Are you all right, Ms. Baum?"

She nodded.

Arnie knocked on the door.

"Come in," said a man on the other side.

They entered to find a white, middle-aged man scrubbing the wall with a sponge, removing the crayon scribblings of his last patient. It looked as though the marks had run over the edges of giant, self-adhesive poster paper he had stuck to the wall. The man dried his hands on the towel and stood as the cinnamon gum nurse opened the door to admit her. He extended a damp hand to her. "Hi. I'm Dr. James Farron. Please call me James."

Arnie winked at Dr. Farron, who smiled back. "Thanks a bunch, Arnie," he said, and the nurse closed the door.

They were alone.

Alicia's eyes wandered over the play therapy room. Toys of every description, including some bloated dolls that appeared to be handmade sat on a gargantuan beanbag. Each doll wore a different expression on its swollen face. The rest of the office was strewn with trains, planes, balls, Barbies, dollhouses, Legos, dinosaurs, militiamen, and space rockets. A half-washed wall of rainbow scribbles loomed over a sudsy bucket full of water with a dirty sponge floating on the surface.

"Won't you please have a seat, Alicia?" he asked, gesturing toward a metallic desk with a white skirt of crayon portraits taped around the sides. Beside the desk sat an overstuffed loveseat, just big enough for a parent and child. After rifling through the papers of what looked like her file, Dr. Farron wheeled his big black desk chair out from behind the desk and turned it to the loveseat.

Looking around his office, Alicia thought about how she had never wanted children, never had the desire. She'd learned years ago that the whole biological clock thing was nonsense—a media creation by *Time Magazine* journalists from an undercooked behavioral study. Thankfully, she had not had any with that bastard Eric. Her novels and stories were her children. They grew up and moved out, one by one. Some did better than others and occasionally younger siblings outshone their elders. She could never predict. But those were her children to groom to maturity and then let go. Real children made her nervous. They seemed fragile and beastly at once.

He waited for her to cross the room and didn't take a seat until she sat across from him. She noticed Blossom the Powerpuff Girl staring at her angrily with big inky anime eyes. His tie. Great. A cartoon geek. Either that, or a lame attempt to connect with the kids.

"Why am I here?" She then realized that this was the man she'd told to fuck off a few days ago. He was the one who'd threatened to put her into this god-forsaken lockdown. She had been furious that he'd saved her. Did he interpret her behavior as childish, thus warranting some kind of remedial treatment as punishment?

"I'm a child psychiatrist," Dr. Farron replied. "And, although I don't normally work in the psych unit, I've been assigned to your case. I have some expertise that might assist you in your recovery."

"Expertise? In what? The Cartoon Network?"

A thin smile spread on his face—or was that a smirk? "I know you've spoken to Denise—or *not* spoken to Denise, as it were—about your suicide. So, why don't we instead talk about the person you were speaking to while you were unconscious?"

She darkened. "What are you talking about?"

"Someone named Mr. Wicker."

Heat and shock flooded her eyes. The child psychiatrist's face whitened with surprise. He handed her a box of tissue from his desk, which she hugged in her lap. She noted his unsteady hand as he offered her the box. Something about this was rattling him, as well. He was sensitive. Her heart opened a little to him.

"Thanks." She smiled through the deluge and blew her nose before proceeding to recover her composure. "You're the one I called a bastard, aren't you?"

He flashed her a sympathetic smile. "That would be me. Doctor Bastard. And you? Any relation to L. Frank?"

"Great niece, twice removed," she said. "Normally I tell people to fuck off when they ask that question."

"You've already told me to fuck off once. It's not so bad. I can take another hit."

Alicia wiped her face with a fresh tissue. "Voluntary target practice. Not nearly as fun."

Dr. Farron seemed to enjoy the joke, but clearly had another agenda and wasn't going to let her distract them. "What did I just say that was so upsetting?"

Alicia said nothing, terrified that he was going to tell her she was crazier than she already knew.

Dr. Farron shifted in his chair. Eons seemed to pass before he spoke. "You know, it's only fair that I tell you what's going on. I'm doing a study as part of my research grant. Over the years, I've discovered that gravely injured and otherwise abused children talk in their sleep to a character named Mr. Wicker. But when they wake up, they don't remember him. And they don't remember their trauma."

Stunned, Alicia let the mystery swell within her. Perhaps what had happened was just a phenomenon, but she burned with the discomfort of her corrupt attraction to the broken, disgusting creature. She had always sympathized with the monsters in movies, even as a child. But the reality of this monster challenged that fantasy of compassion for the outsider. He had a power over her. Like having her secret name in a fairy tale, he had the secret that controlled her life. And this made him even uglier.

The psychologist leaned toward her. "You, however, very likely remember your trauma. And I was wondering if you know anything about that name."

A spasm of cold wracked her body as she spoke, and her jaw shuddered. Dr. Farron reached for a knitted throw by the couch and draped it around her shoulders as she broke into a fever. "Thank you," she whispered.

"You're an author, aren't you? Is he from a book? Or some movie I've missed?" Dr. Farron asked. He seemed puzzled and desperately interested. "Where does this Mr. Wicker character come from?"

Woman, shut the hell up. "I don't know."

"You didn't write about him by chance?"

"Absolutely not."

"I'm sorry. I just thought maybe there was something I should already know that I'm somehow not clued in about." He paused, as if still dogged by confusion. "Do you have any reason to believe you're missing a memory?" he asked. "Maybe you don't remember your trauma after all. Maybe it's from long ago."

She could not speak but instead stared at one of the dolls on the beanbag as it peered at her from glassy green eyes. "There's a lot from my childhood I don't remember. I thought that was normal."

"It is," he said. "But is it possible that a significant event took place that you've repressed?"

For the most part, Alicia had a relentless memory that exasperated everyone around her. No one wanted to be reminded of what they really said or did—especially not her ex-husband. But then, as she tried to focus on her sixth year of life, she found only a thick fog. "Anything is possible," she said. "But not everything is probable."

"True," he replied. "Well, it's controversial, but I've found that hypnotherapy can sometimes be effective at uncovering repressed memories. Do you want to try it?"

Alicia wanted nothing better than to run away—hard. An icy cataract of dread was now surging inside of her. Did she really want to know what was missing? "What if it doesn't work? What if this is a colossal waste of time?"

The gears seemed to spin behind his eyes for a moment. "Maybe it is," he said at last. He rubbed his neck, his eyelids heavy with exhaustion. "In fact, you don't have to do it. You can walk out of this office and never come back." He held his hand out toward the door. "It's up to you."

Alicia suspected that the burn of misery in her throat would never cool unless she retrieved that memory, and she had no idea how to return to the Library other than to repeat her bathroom shenanigans. She then felt anchored to the spot. "Do we have to talk about Mr. Wicker?"

"Not if you don't want to," he replied.

"I'm missing a rose garden. And maybe a lot more."

Her eyes closed, Alicia went limp and her head fell forward as she breathed deeply. Steadily. Down, down, down went the elevator of her psyche under the gentle and authoritative voice of Dr. Farron.

"Very good. Now, fully relaxed and aware, allow your mind to return to the experiences of your childhood. The memories are in your unconscious mind and can be remembered as I direct you back to them."

Unlike the bramble of Mr. Wicker's voice, the doctor's voice was soothing as it invited her into a familiar corridor lined with doors. Each doorway was a memory of her childhood, and at the end of the hallway was the door to the missing memory. She remembered being very young and wandering down the dark hallway of her parents' house toward the bathroom with the dim nightlight. The hallway created by her psyche contained several more doors than her old house in Los Feliz. Her grandmother once showed her pictures of the classic California bungalow her parents had bought when they first married. There was that one of her and her mother standing outside on Easter, and she was wearing some ridiculous yellow dress with angel wing sleeves as she clutched a stuffed white rabbit. A cowlick teased her hair into a rebellious curl on top of her head, and her missing front tooth gaped in the photograph. That morning her mother had stroked her hair and told her, *Someday, you'll be a rose, honey. Just not now.*

Someday.

Alicia reached for one of the burnished brass doorknobs. Her tiny hand touched the cool surface.

"So, how's the painting, Sam?"

Her father's voice. Grownup Alicia could not place the name "Sam." Who was he?

The walls hugged her shoulders, and her entire body folded into a tight, dark space. There was a presence in the darkness. Comforting. Loving. Feet touching...

The scene outside in the living room was familiar. It was the last time she had ever heard her father's voice in that house.

"Where are you?" Dr. Farron asked from somewhere outside.

"I'm hiding," she whispered in her little girl voice. "I'm at my gramma and granpa's house in Simi Valley."

Outside in the living room, her handsome father sat on her grandparents' golden crushed velvet couch in his black wool Yves St. Laurent suit. An expensive watch shined on his wrist as he gestured, a sleek ponytail gathered at the back of his neck. He leaned forward as he spoke with her grandfather, both smoking cigars. The smell turned her stomach. Her grandfather was just as she remembered him: big hands and bolo ties, an old cowboy. A bottle of seltzer water, a crystal whisky decanter, and two drained tumblers rested on the glass coffee table.

"Can't complain. Got a show comin' up in Pasadena next month."

Her grandfather's voice. Sam? She'd never known that was his name. Or, rather, she'd forgotten.

Cowboy boots. Leather. Paint thinner.

"Oh, yeah? How'd the last one go? Pretty good?" Her father again, his voice tense, the way it always is with her grandfather.

"S'alright. Sold some of the still lifes and one of the portraits of our little rose."

"That's terrific! Well, speaking of our little rose." She sensed the impending separation in her father's tone.

"Are you leavin' so soon, son?" her grandfather asked.

"Yeah. I better hit the road. I have to get over the Grapevine before nightfall."

About then, Alicia's grandmother entered.

"You're not leaving already, are you?" There was a clinking noise as her grandmother set down a tray on the coffee table. "Stay and have some lunch with us!"

"Have more scotch, son," her grandfather implored.

"No, I better get going. I'm supposed to be at Lisa's in Capitola by ten."

"Sounds like things are pretty serious." Her grandmother's words sounded more like condemnation than congratulation.

"Yeah. I guess so," her father replied. A pause.

Her grandfather called out, "Your daddy's leaving!" No response. "Stubborn as always," he said.

Her father spoke up. "It's all right. I know what to do." He called out: "Marco...!"

Timidly Alicia responded: "Polo!"

"Marco!"

His voice drew near to her in the cramped darkness.

"Polo!"

"What's happening?" Dr. Farron asked.

"He's leaving," Alicia replied.

"Where is he going?"

"Away. Forever."

The black wall slid back to cool air and sunlight. Alicia blinked in the brightness. Her father's handsome face loomed in the opening as he smiled sheepishly, guilt creasing his tanned forehead. The cowboy boots of Alicia's grandfather strode toward her, and he crouched down behind her father. "In the bar?" her father asked.

"Yup," her grandfather replied.

Her father took her hand. "I'm going away for a bit. I'll see you in a few days, okay?"

"Why do you have to go away?"

"Because I have to. Now, be good for Grandma and Grandpa, okay?"

Alicia withdrew her hand from his. Pressing it hard against the bar panel, she slid it back in place, plunging herself—and the presence—into darkness.

"Where is your mother?"

"Gone."

"What do you mean?"

Alicia was silent.

"I want you to go to another door, the one before this one you just opened. I want to know what happened before your father left you with your grandparents." Dr. Farron's voice was calm and patient. He spoke both to the little girl hiding in her grandparents' bar and the woman wandering the corridor of her psyche.

Alicia reached for another knob, one no higher than her chin. Light spilled out from under the door, over the toes of her pink bunny slippers. A draft ruffled under her nightgown. She no longer stood in the corridor, but at the door adjoining the family garage, the one her father had built so that no one would have to go into the rain to get into the Mercedes. A gruesome bellowing had awakened her from sleep; she'd slipped out of bed to pad down the hall. Beyond the closed door, a man wailed like an animal. She curled her toes inside the big floppy slippers and pushed open the door.

The odor of urine and feces flooded the doorway, gagging Alicia. Her father stood on the car hood with his shoulders hunched in a grotesque embrace around something she could not see, as if dancing with someone on the car. His hands worked with a fever, arms straining to reach the rafters, oblivious to Alicia's presence in the doorway. Her father's knee twisted, unable to keep his balance on the car as the hood buckled under his weight. Her mother's distorted face spun toward her. Tongue bloated and obscene, an electrical cord cut into her throat and one ashen cheek. A dark puddle of bodily fluids stained the concrete floor beside the car, a rivulet running down the slope of the garage floor. Alicia stood spellbound in the doorway as she watched her father wretchedly try to loosen his wife's dead body. Then, he caught sight of his tiny daughter, and he howled again with heart-piercing horror.

Alicia collapsed in the corridor and everything went black.

Chapter 6

"Good afternoon, Mrs. Rains. My name's Jimmy. May I help you with your bags today?"

The barrel-chested bellboy from Fremont greeted the elderly woman as he'd been instructed by his manager, who seemed kind of afraid of her and wanted her placated at any cost. The bellboy tackled her ten-ton Prada bags, and with a rakish grin, assured her that she packed lighter than most ladies. She bustled past him to the room, even though she knew nothing of the hotel's halls.

"I hate these hotels. I half expect to find a chunk of moldy cheese at the end!"

Streams of verbal bile showered the bellboy's ears as she continued to mutter under her breath. She had no fondness for anyone or anything that the bellboy could tell. He half listened, as he was thinking about his Nietzsche paper that was due for class. As she continued her diatribe against humanity, he told her which way to turn at each junction and her talk slid beneath the clever philosophizing in his brain.

Talking much about oneself can also be a means to conceal oneself, Nietzsche once said. What did she want to conceal?

When they reached the room, he slipped a hand between her and the lock, slid the keycard into the slot, and jostled open the door. The sun shone through the white sheers, warming the bed. As he pressed into the room from behind the old woman, the white whiskers of her hair bristled around her head. Pursing her pink-smeared lips and squinting her bloodshot blue eyes, she whirled around and nearly skewered his nose on her wrinkled fingertip. The bangles on her wrist jangled like wind chimes.

"And don't you think I have ever forgotten any of their ill treatment!"

The bellboy's eyebrows drew up into a fuzzy brown arch over his widening eyes. He'd tuned her out more than he thought! What was she going on about? He lowered the heavy bags to the floor, noting the Burbank Airport luggage tags. Of course she was from Los Angeles. While Bay Area folk could be snobbish and New Yorkers brusque, the most abusive people came from SoCal—particularly Los Angeles. So many pompous producers, directors, and studio executives came up north for either business or brief family visits. Hey! Maybe this cranky old woman was in the film industry! She could be one of those nasty-tempered old producers. This piqued his interest as he'd recently been toying with the idea of acting. Why not? He was a good-looking Asian dude. There weren't nearly enough of those in movies. And he had a more-than-decent memory for lines. He'd memorized those Nietzsche quotes for his paper. That was something!

Perhaps he should give the old woman an extra dose of service. He'd keep track of her as long as she stayed. This might well be the sign that he'd needed to make a firm decision about his future career. "Is there anything else I can get for you, Mrs. Rains? Anything at all?" He hoped that last bit didn't sound too groveling.

She flicked her wrist at him dismissively, shaking her head as her frail hand rummaged in her purse. Then: "Do you have a girl?" she asked.

"Excuse me?"

"I said, do you have a girl?"

"You mean a girlfriend? No, ma'am. I don't."

"Well, I'd set you up with my granddaughter, but she's in the hospital."

She retrieved a rolled up five-dollar bill and handed it to him like a piece of trash she wanted him to dispose of. He took it.

"Thank you. I'm sorry to hear that, ma'am. Will she be all right?"

"As long as she doesn't try to kill herself again."

It is always consoling to think of suicide: in that way one gets through many a bad night, Nietzsche once said.

An uncomfortable silence squatted between them.

"Thank you, Mrs. Rains. Have a good stay."

Chapter 7

This attraction, Dr. Farron thought, was what they called in the world of therapy A Bad Thing.

A fire crackled in his belly at the thought of her, but he cooled his passions with a cold handful of objective professional concern. While this attraction was potentially lethal to the therapeutic process, he could not imagine turning her over to someone who would not know the significance of Mr. Wicker. So they didn't find the rose garden per se in that first session—so what? They did explore some of the horrific family history that created a template for self-destructive behavior in her adult life. It made sense. Together they covered far more ground than either had anticipated—far more than Denise, her intake therapist, who had a talent for getting people to open up.

Alicia was to enter her first group therapy session since she had arrived and Dr. Farron was hellbent on observing the session. The trick was to get there early enough so that he could secure a seat in the observation room, the area secured behind the one-way mirror for training purposes. He wanted to see the way she walked, her affect, body language. Would she participate willingly in other aspects of the program now that she had his ear?

But did he really just want to observe her for professional purposes?

Come on, James. Are you really attracted to such a broken soul?

A commotion swelled behind him: voices, clattering of footsteps. He slipped into the observation room, closed the door, and settled into one of the padded folding chairs. Adrenaline flushed his system as the patients filed inside: withering specimens drained of hope, some laughing nervously, shuffling over the spotless white tile as if it were littered with balloons. It was one o'clock in the afternoon. Time to start. Dr. Ellen Gorman entered—a petite woman with short red hair and narrow reading glasses chained to her neck, carrying a clipboard for notes. She glanced back through the open door, checked her watch, and closed the door as everyone took seats in the circle of folding chairs.

Dr. Farron despaired; Alicia did not show. This meant that either something medically had happened that prevented her from attending (bad) or she was being uncooperative (also bad). He could tell she was very strong-willed, like Gina was. Strong-willed, imaginative, and highly expressive.

The door cracked open and Alicia appeared in the doorway with a guarded look. Dr. Gorman waved her inside. "Welcome! Have a seat," she sang with nauseating enthusiasm.

Alicia wore the lavender sweater over gray sweats and a loose T-shirt. She took a chair to the left of the circle. Dr. Farron could see her facial profile, but another patient partially blocked her body movements. He noted that her hair appeared freshly brushed; that was a good sign. When she'd entered his office earlier in the day, she'd looked like a wild thing with unkempt hair, blue-grey eyes gleaming with pain and suspicion. One of the nurses in ER had dry-washed Alicia's hair as she slept, but Alicia herself had shown no interest in grooming while under medical observation. That was normal. She now smoothed down the sweater sleeves as if to hide the white bandages on her wrists that protected her sutures. She had undoubtedly learned the humiliating routine of going to the nurses' station to ask for her clothing.

"Hi everyone. I'm Dr. Gorman. And I want to thank everyone for participating in this session. I think you'll find that, as you talk about what's happened in your lives, you have a lot in common. Maybe not with everybody, but sometimes knowing you're not alone and hearing that others have similar experiences to yours is very healing in itself. That way, you won't feel so isolated, which is where a lot of problems begin." She paused, gauging her patients' reactions. "And, please, as we talk, let's be courteous to others and not address what another person says. That's called crosstalk. Okay?" Several people nodded. "Let's start by talking about loss. Is there something you've lost in your life recently?"

A slight man in his sixties with a silver shimmer of jaw stubble spoke of losing friends in Vietnam and, a few months ago, losing his thirty-six-year-old son to a car accident. A young Hispanic woman in her early twenties described a loss of self-respect and family when her affair with her sister's husband was uncovered. Dr. Farron watched Alicia's face as she listened. She tended to look down at the floor with consternation, her mind working on an unseen puzzle as her toes wriggled in scarlet slippers. She looked weary. She probably didn't sleep well in the medical unit; it wouldn't be any better here. Watching these wounded, lethargic adults reminded him of why he had chosen to work with children in the first place. Children were a joy to watch unfold no matter how badly hurt they were. They still had a chance to build a life of happiness and wholeness. And, for a short while, they would shine with innocence that gave adults hope. As he had experienced with Jesse's mother, the adults were often the difficult ones to deal with, not the kids.

Mockery and boredom danced a sluggish tango in Alicia's expression as an overweight man named Charles described how he didn't belong in that room, that it was his wife—*the bitch*—who belonged in the "nut house." All he had ever wanted to do was to play his online computer game. She would not *shut the fuck up* about his games and how he never spent time with their kid. Shit, man, he'd forgive her if she ever got back in the sack, but she never wanted sex.

Dr. Gorman interrupted him. "So, what I'm hearing is that you've lost your wife's affections?"

"Yeah," he said at last. "I guess so."

Dr. Gorman lifted an eyebrow and looked around the room. She turned to Alicia.

"Alicia, is there something you'd like to share? Would you like to tell us about something you've lost?"

Alicia's lips parted—Dr. Farron inhaled and held his breath—but before she could speak, Charles spoke up.

"Fuck *me*! You're Alicia Baum!" he laughed, pleased with himself for his discovery. He leaned forward with a sneer. "Or is that bomb—B-O-M-B? Heh heh. I want my money back for that last book. Hoo-weee!" he said, pinching his nose.

Pele awoke.

With a screech of the chair legs scraping the tile, Alicia stood. Dr. Gorman started to lift a hand of caution as the angry woman walked around behind her chair. Now Dr. Farron could see her body as rage lathered her skin, scouring her cheeks scarlet. Her mouth held hard, she placed a hand on the back of the chair and looked around the room at each patient.

Hold on. He's just baiting you to feel better about himself.

Alicia then spoke with a controlled hostility that any Cold War leader would have envied. "I have lost a great deal. It's not what I have lost, however, but rather what I wish to lose—and that would be this obese fuckhole—"

Dr. Gorman raised a hand: "Alicia!"

"—who is so fucking stupid, he couldn't kill himself in a firing squad!" She shoved the chair at him. It spun into the circle, narrowly missing Charles's feet. "ANY LAST REQUESTS, YOU PORCINE PRICK?"

Dr. Farron leapt from his chair, but he couldn't leave. She would feel betrayed if she knew he was watching her in secret.

Dr. Gorman stood, voice even. "Calm down now or you'll be restrained." She leveled Dr. Farron a look through the one-way mirror.

Alicia streaked out of the room. Dr. Farron burst out of the observation room after her, dodging the chaos that ensued. In the hallway, he watched her disappear down the long corridor, past the nurses' station. A housekeeper, overburdened with a mobile laundry hamper, lingered at the threshold of the open white door with the glass window, security card in hand. She gawked at Alicia.

"It's okay!" he called to the housekeeper. He put out a hand to the orderlies chasing after him.

Alicia blanched at the sight of him, but then hardened her look. As Dr. Farron followed her to the elevator and stepped inside, Dr. Gorman came after him. He indicated everything was under control. The doors closed. Dr. Farron slid his card in the security latch and pressed the number to the children's ward.

"Wanna talk?" he said, leaning against the elevator wall. He reached into his pocket and pulled out some gum. He offered it to her. She gritted her teeth as she stared ahead. He sighed, slipping a piece in his mouth, and kept his eyes fixed on the elevator doors. In his peripheral vision, he noticed her watching him. He smiled despite himself.

"What are you smiling about?" she asked.

He just shook his head and let his smile grow bigger. There was something about her that made him feel like his heart was bouncing on a pogo stick. When the doors opened, she plowed out into the hallway as if escaping the plague. Dr. Farron followed Alicia, BlackBerry vibrating on his belt. He didn't dare take his eyes off her as she strode purposefully down a corridor into the ward where they brought children after ICU. He worried that she would see something too intense for her present state. Then again, perhaps she'd see something that would change her life.

Chapter 8

Huginn longed for Asgard. There, the sun shone eternally and she could soar above Valhalla itself. In the hall, she enjoyed the smell of blood when warriors arrived after dying in battle.

But no longer. When the other gods had abandoned Mr. Wicker, Odin pitied the librarian, giving Huginn and Muninn to him despite their cries. They hated their singed master, and keened so fiercely for Odin that they did not recover their voices for a generation.

Hundreds of years have passed since then. While she no longer hated Mr. Wicker, Huginn despised the shadowy repository with its blazing candles that threatened her wings. And she was beyond weary of the nasty-tempered ravens made by her master's foul magic. Although many of its visitors had died violently, the pain and suffering that entered the Library was not nearly as satisfying as battle blood.

She yearned for it.

She soared down the tunnel through the mists, wings dusted by the cosmos, until she found the glimmer of light that waxed to bursting and she dove in. The winds of the cosmos blinded her as they carried her into the mortal world. She emerged in an explosion of sparks somewhere above a large building. Invalids made their way through the front doors as shrieking red animals fled into an underground cave. Huginn reveled in the freedom, stretching her wings further as she glided under the delicious warmth of the earthly sun. Oh, to live! The flood of sensations! The fragrance of prey and tree pulp, spoiled only by the stink of humanity.

Find Alicia.

War drums rumbled in Huginn's chest as she was drawn to the white building. A noisy murder of crows jockeyed for the morsels that people dropped as they ate in the adjacent park. The crows bawled at her to mark their territory, but Huginn ignored them as she veered toward the glass. Perhaps she would find Alicia dead. Then she could perhaps savor a juicy morsel of flesh. It had been forever since Huginn had tasted that sort of earthly delicacy—the thing these beasts took for granted. Like her master, she never needed to eat due to her divinity, but that didn't mean she couldn't enjoy the pleasures of the world when offered.

A crow dove at her, beak open, talons raking her wing. Surprised and hot with anger, Huginn swept away but not far enough before she found herself in a raging storm of dive-bombing crows. Huginn felt the sting of her feathers being ripped from her body. The blackened cloud of wings hovered between her and that sprawling, guarded place where Alicia was. If she hadn't been compelled to follow her master's orders, she would soar up into the sun as far away as she could, enjoying the warmth on her back and the air in her lungs. But she couldn't veer from her order and the malicious crows doubled their fury, swarming in a dense cloud around her.

The pain ricocheted in her head and the sun dimmed. She would have to do something to preserve herself. Something unlawful.

The raven pulled her wings against her body and soared just above the murder. Drawing on her divinity, she focused until she found deep within her heart the thunderous voice of Odin, the strike of his hammer and the wailing of dying warriors. She then unleashed a cry that pierced the sky. A thousand needles of lightning scrawled from her mouth and through the air, striking each crow around her, felling them to the grasses below. In the shower of black corpses, humans pointed. Humans screamed. Humans ran.

But Huginn paid the carnage no mind. She collected herself and let her quest draw her toward the white towers. Toward the middle floors where both life and mind hung in the balance.

Toward Alicia Baum.

Chapter 9

Alicia's head pounded like a timpani as she passed each room in the hospital corridor. The maze of doorways and hallways swallowed her and she could not navigate quickly enough to escape Dr. Farron. Of course, this was his terrain. He knew it better than anyone. Jerk. What the hell was he doing? Was he just going to stalk her until she told him everything she knew about Mr. Wicker?

The stitches itched like crazy and the bland breakfast left her queasy. Alicia grew angrier as she walked, folding her arms in a protective sulk as she obsessed over the group therapy session. As a midlist author, she'd been nice to everyone. She'd stayed late at book signings to make sure everyone got a signed book. She'd answered fan mail. She'd been attentive to her fans at conventions, drinking with them, going to parties. She'd tried not to ever show any annoyance with them, letting her assistant or agent be the bad guy when she needed to say no to invitations and the like. At her core, she'd loved people, was grateful for her readers, and hated saying no to anything.

Now? Not so much. In fact, she hated everybody. And everything. She admitted to herself that maybe her reaction had been a bit over the top, but it was because for the first time in ages she'd let her anger turn from herself and God out to the world. The infinite damned world not only didn't give a shit about her, but it bred fuckholes like that guy back there. She hated everything with the burning of a thousand suns. Maybe even a thousand, thousand suns. Of course, the guy didn't know she'd been suffering horrific depression when she wrote that book, that she'd been contractually obligated to finish it, and that the publisher nearly didn't let sunlight touch the pages. He didn't know that, nor would he care. And that's why Alicia hated him.

Rurr-rurr-rurr.

A clattering and loud voices overtook the hallway behind her just over the *rurring* of heavy rubber wheels. She glanced back for the first time since she'd tried to ditch Dr. Farron and moved against the wall to allow a team of nurses to wheel a gurney past her. On the gurney slept a child, her head partially shaved and sutured. Her nostrils were caked with blood, lips cracked, face bruised, and long black eyelashes crusted with sleep. Something about the shattered innocence left Alicia standing there holding a monstrous bag of humility. They wheeled the child into a room just beyond. Alicia waited in the hallway as they worked. Eventually they cleared out, leaving an R.N. to take care of the last bits of business.

Cautiously, Alicia approached the room and peeked inside at the busy nurse who tucked and fluffed to ensure the child was as comfortable as possible. The nurse was short and lithe, light brown hair cropped above her ears. Her eyes brightened as she glanced toward the doorway. "Good afternoon, Doctor. How are you today?"

Alicia started, alarmed that she had not detected anyone behind her. It was Dr. Farron to whom the nurse spoke. And Alicia sensed more than professional courtesy in the woman's voice. *Oh, this guy must totally clean up around here. A not-bad-looking dude who works with children. He must draw women in sticky swarms. Another reason not to trust him.* Alicia hung out of sight in the hallway, pretending not to listen.

"I'm fine, thank you." A lackluster response with a polite smile. Not what Alicia had expected. Odd. "What's her story?" Dr. Farron asked, reading the chart.

They then exchanged unintelligible medical phrases.

He motioned toward the wall bracket. "May I?"

The nurse said, "Oh! You want to put up one of your recorders? Sure!" She then left the room but leaned back in. "Maybe we'll see you Saturday night at Bill's thing?"

"Maybe," he replied.

The nurse left, hustling down the hallway. Alicia entered. Dr. Farron's face softened when he saw her. "Are you all right? How do you feel?"

Alicia folded her arms again in a defensive posture. "I feel perfectly loony, thanks."

"Loony, huh?" Unfazed, he continued reading whatever was scribbled in doctor talk in the chart pages. "I'd say that was a pretty normal reaction. You're a bit raw, understandably." Alicia watched him suspiciously at first, but could no longer harbor negative thoughts about him as his eyes flitted compassionately between the child and the chart. He then placed it on the bed and withdrew a hand-held tape recorder from the pocket of his doctor's smock.

Curious, Alicia poked her head out of her rabbit hole of self-involvement. She padded over to the bed as Dr. Farron fingered a metal bracket that had been fastened to the wall over the bed, checking it for loose screws. The smell of antiseptic and thrush overwhelmed her as she suddenly realized she had never been in the hospital room of someone who was severely injured. She rounded the bedside opposite Dr. Farron.

"What's her name?"

He shook his head. "Can't tell you anything. It would be a HIPAA violation."

"Is she going to be okay?"

"Time will tell," he said, although he did not look remotely hopeful.

The little girl's injuries seemed significant. Black sutures like spiky caterpillars were stitched on the scalp above her ear. An I.V. fed her uninjured arm as she slept, while another tube snaked up into her nose. She was breathing on her own, at least. Her long dark lashes were as lush as what remained of her hair. A thread of maternal instinct wormed its way into Alicia's heart.

Dr. Farron placed the tape recorder into the wall bracket. It fit perfectly, with the "REC" and "Play" buttons facing up. "It's highly unlikely that she'll talk. But just in case."

"What's it for?" she asked.

"It's a voice-activated tape recorder. I turn them on at night," he said.

Overcome by a sense of protectiveness, Alicia reached out and took the child's fever-warm hand. The child's hand muscles immediately responded, gripping her fingers harder. Alicia inhaled sharply. "I thought she was unconscious."

"She is," Dr. Farron said. "It's just a reflex."

"Do you always do this?" She indicated the recorder.

"I try. I don't want to miss what they say," he answered.

"Does it work?"

"Not often enough."

As the fog of her own anger and embarrassment burned away, Alicia could now see the immense load this man was carrying. She felt sorry for him. She'd been swimming in self-absorption for so long, this felt like a new shore. As Alicia paused for the right words, the child stirred with a moan. Then, in a whisper:

"Mr. Wicker, who's Alicia?"

Dr. Farron's eyes widened as Alicia's heart did an Irish dance. She was certain they had not mentioned each other's names. This little girl must be in the Library! She must be speaking to *him*. Alicia wasn't quite ready to have her dream step into this world so concretely, but it thrilled her that she was not crazy after all. Or maybe she was extremely crazy and this was a hallucination, but she doubted that.

At first Dr. Farron could not look her in the eye. She could see his head was full of thoughts running bicycle races over what just happened.

But when his eyes met hers, his voice quavered. "Want to tell me about this friend of yours?"

Huginn tipped her head as she watched between the blinds. Everything she saw, Mr. Wicker saw, too. Undoubtedly, whatever drama was unfolding inside was his doing. Alicia and the man left the room. Huginn felt her master's panic about the man who seemed connected to Alicia in more than a passing way. He looked familiar to Mr. Wicker—not from this life but another, far more troubled time. He was displeased beyond measure that this man had anything to do with Alicia, much less that he had her ear.

The raven knew what cruelty her master was capable of and that he was about to do something desperate.

Chapter 10

Alicia and Dr. Farron walked together to his office. He locked the door behind her. She glanced nervously at the door and then at him. Was he sweating? Dr. Farron sat in his big black chair, biting his bottom lip again as he drowned in thought.

"Are you okay?" Alicia said, struck by the irony of this exchange.

Dr. Farron snapped out of some deep inner dialogue. "Yes! Please." He indicated she should sit on the couch.

Alicia instead walked over to the wall where Dr. Farron had been cleaning the day before. Propped against it was a large post-it pad the size of most easel paper. She tore off a piece, knelt by the wall, and stuck it to the surface. She picked up the Crayola box and scrounged around until she found the black one. Then, with a sore, unskilled hand, she tried to sketch Mr. Wicker's face. But when she tried to press the crayon to the paper, she gasped as pain tore through her wrist. She fumbled the crayon, nursing her wrist close to her body.

Dr. Farron stood from his chair and walked over to where she sat on the floor by the wall. "Would you like to describe him to me? I'll draw him for you."

She was at first dumbfounded. How could he reproduce Mr. Wicker any better than she could? She nodded and he picked up the black crayon.

He put up a new sheet of paper and centered himself in front of it. Soon it became apparent that she was much better with words. She recalled the exact slant of his nose and the general shape of his head. The fullness of his lips, she remembered very well. She described the strength of Mr. Wicker's jaw, the barely perceptible cleft. How his long head was vaguely heart-shaped, but the top of his head was egg-like. How his nostrils flared from an elegant nose that widened dramatically at the base. His prominent browline swept from his temples to the bridge of his nose, arching over the oval, cat-shaped eyes of sea green that sparked like the flames of the Inquisition.

As Alicia continued to verbally catalogue Mr. Wicker's features, she was astonished by Dr. Farron's skill. The composite portrait he drew from her florid descriptions nearly frightened her with its accuracy. What was he doing here? Why did he not pursue some career involving art? Alicia knew personally many great artists of fantasy and horror. (She then realized that they would kill her if they found out she had tried to kill herself.)

This child psychiatrist could have illustrated Gaiman's last work.

The best part was the way he settled into the task with a sly joviality. "Am I getting it?" he asked when he noticed she was agape. He knew he was good. The bastard was showing off.

Alicia nodded. "Oh, yeah."

He gave her a flirtatious, sidelong look that drew an unexpected *woosh!* of attraction from a place she had been certain was only hollow. She tried to pretend it didn't happen, but she knew from experience that forcing this particular feeling into exile was useless. Something warm slipped into her chest as she smiled.

"You're *really* good."

"Thank you." He glanced back over his shoulder at his desk skirted with crayon drawings. "I have great teachers."

"I bet you do," she said a bit more coyly than she meant to. She lost interest in Mr. Wicker for a moment entirely and let this wonderful thing unwrap itself at her feet as she relaxed and shared with him the experience in the tunnel, the lights, and finally what happened in the Library itself. He listened with a rapture that quickened the crayon strokes. Soon, the Library filled the blank space behind Mr. Wicker on the post-it paper.

He continued to ask her questions, but this time about her family.

"Can you tell me more about your family? Your grandmother, for example."

"So you've met her?"

"Briefly."

"Which means you've probably been bawled out by her. She's not what one would call pleasant. More like a Sherman Tank wearing Chantilly and Nikes."

"Is she still married?"

Alicia said nothing for several moments. Dr. Farron waited as her emotions ran a marathon behind her eyes. "Not any more," she said at last.

"So, we learned in your last session that you lived with your grandparents after your father left. How long did you stay with them? And what were they like?"

"Oh, man. I loved my grandpa—his big smiles and paints staining his wiry hands. I loved his country music and oil canvases. He taught me the alchemy of oil and brush to Gene Autry. Sometimes we played 'Marco Polo' in the house." She reminisced with joy. "He caught me early one summer morning, still in my pajamas, standing on the piano with my nose in the whisky decanter. I loved the whisky smell, probably because my mom used to rub it on my gums as a baby when I teethed. But he didn't get mad. He seemed to understand why I loved it. He slipped it from me with the softest admonition."

"What happened to him?"

"He left when I was six." She went on to explain that, before her grandparents, she'd lived briefly with her very busy and very handsome father in Malibu. Her father—in his dark Armani suits and black convertible—handled investment portfolios for celebrities. He was better at that than braiding hair and listening to long, impromptu stories about her dolls, the dog, and imaginary friends. Her grandmother could do those things and more.

"So your grandfather left your grandmother? Did they divorce right after you came to live with them? Or was that later?"

"You know, it's a big weird mystery, actually. He disappeared after they had this huge argument. And then the police showed up and took him away. My grandmother would never tell me what happened no matter how much I begged. Anytime I asked, she'd just say that he was a bad man—whatever that meant. I wasn't allowed to talk about him."

"You've never been curious? Ever look into what happened?"

"No. I figured he did something awful like hit someone with his car when he was drunk. My grandmother would make off-handed comments about his drinking. It only made sense. And frankly I just didn't want to know. I didn't want to ruin the good memories that I had of him."

At that, Dr. Farron sat back on his haunches away from the finished drawing. Talking about her grandfather, Alicia felt empty and wondered if she could sustain a connection with anyone. When was the last time anyone she was attracted to had any feelings for her except for what inspired the one-gun salute? Every man she had been with since Eric—and even before—was like Mr. Wicker. They devoured her body and soul. She gave them her art, her devotion, her passion. Yet she got nothing in return but heartache and disappointment. And this guy was her doctor, only interested in the mystery she could share with him.

Alicia regarded Mr. Wicker's portrait and once again lost herself in the beauty of those eyes that reached from death into her dreams. An illustration, no matter how brilliant, would never do him justice, but even this crude likeness elicited a hypnotic desire. She reached up and lovingly traced the Librarian's features, the waxy residue smudging her fingertips.

Dropping the crayon, Dr. Farron stood up abruptly. His face had lost its fire. He walked over to his desk, sat, and opened his laptop, fixating on the screen as he clicked around.

"What's wrong?" she asked.

"Nothing," he said. "We need to discuss your drug history." He barely looked away from his laptop as he spoke. He took a pen and pad from his desk drawer, popped off the cap with his thumb, and began writing.

Alicia continued to sit by the drawing, turning her back to it as she crossed her legs to sit on the soft carpet. The portrait loomed over her shoulder like a sentinel. "What do you want to know?"

"Have you ever dropped acid?"

She eyed him stonily. She knew where he was going. "Are you now going to deny what happened in that child's room? Try to squirrel it away between the pages of *Turn On, Tune In, Drop Out?*"

"Well, did you?"

"Once. In college. Many years ago."

"May I share with you some facts about death?"

"I would rather slash my wrists again, but go ahead," she said.

"When you die, your brain releases a chemical similar to LSD. It makes people see death images. Skeletons. Ghosts. The Grateful Dead's artwork is a perfect example of that. And that's what happens in a near-death experience. You see things. Like him. And given your rich imagination, I have no doubt you could conjure an entire experience like you described." He shifted in his chair as if to avoid a strategically placed tack.

What he said was possible except: "That doesn't explain what just happened with that little girl."

Dr. Farron opened a chart on his desk—presumably hers—and looked absorbed.

"I don't get what's happening here. We just got evidence that Mr. Wicker is real in some way. Does it make you more comfortable to think of him as a phenomenon rather than a real person? I think he's real. I think what happened between us was a miracle, a supernatural event that I wasn't meant to ever wake up from. But I did. And that's a miracle, too. No one should have known I was dying in that tub. No one. So how was I rescued? How are you going to explain *that*? With a handy psychological treatise cooked in some Ph.D.'s ass?"

Alicia wished he would spontaneously develop hemorrhoids. He'd *wanted* to talk about it, for Chrissake. It not only stung the tender palm of her pride, but panicked her deeply. She had an ally for a moment, but this development left her feeling abandoned and betrayed. She scanned the room as she considered how to counter him. Surely, there was something in this lively room that could awaken him.

Ah! On the stool.

Alicia grabbed the stool and stack of Rorschach cards. She placed the stool beside him on the opposite side of the love seat, putting him in the "patient" position.

Dr. Farron sighed, pushed his papers into pile, and then did a double-take when Alicia put the first card before him. And then a marvelous thing happened: his eyes widened with fear. He laughed nervously. "What are you doing?"

"What do you see?" she asked.

He waved his hand, looking away, down at his desk. "Just...I don't know...a dragon monster from the eighth dimension," he muttered.

"A what?"

"I don't know. What do *you* see?"

Alicia considered not letting him turn this back on her, but then inspiration seized her. She held his eyes with hers.

"I see a continent covered with swollen rivers and wandering orchards."

The upset melted from Dr. Farron's face and a subtle wonder misted his eyes. He said nothing. Alicia turned to the next card, lost in the rapture of her visions.

"I see a man, skin peeled from his flesh to air a weary, bleeding heart."

Dr. Farron's expression fell, as if he stood on the brink of an abyss.

"I see a woman, inhaling her lover like smoke—sweet, cedary, thick—swirling him about her tongue before she exhales him over her lips. To inhale him again."

Her eyes locked with his. He had stopped breathing, caught in her net, but she did not want to spill him on her deck and gut him. Instead, she just wanted to memorize the faint blush in his cheeks, the stray hairs of his eyebrows, and the speckles in his irises. He did not look away.

"You believe there is something much bigger happening here, don't you?" she said gently.

He hesitated before turning back to his desk and pulling out a pad of paper. "Believing in something doesn't make it real." He scribbled on the paper, tore it off and stuffed it in her file.

"What's that?"

"I'm increasing the dose of your Celexa."

Alicia dropped the cards on the floor and stood imperiously over him. She snatched the note and crumpled it in one hand.

"You need to calm down, missy!"

"You know what *I* don't believe? *I* don't believe I trusted you. Here I was, feeling frightened. And then a miracle happens! And what do you do? You deny it." She ripped up the note, scattering it over his desk like confetti. "Take your pills. Take your *Soma* so you can feel good while doing things you hate. Just don't treat me like a idiot." She stomped to the door and turned the knob, unlatching the lock automatically. "I want to go back to the lockdown."

"I'll have someone escort you back."

Was he really getting rid of her?

He made a phone call requesting that someone retrieve her. When he hung up, Alicia stood by the door, her back to him. The hot tears poured down her face, but she didn't want him to see them. Instead she just said, "I knew I should never have trusted a shrink." She didn't look at his face, but she sensed him tensing up behind her as the rustling at his desk quieted.

A moment later, the door opened to reveal Arnie. As soon as she stepped into the hallway, the tears came in a torrent, and she sobbed. She moved away from the door so that he couldn't hear her and collapsed against the far wall. Arnie was immediately at her side and led her back to the elevators.

"Aaaawwww, Ms. Baum," he said, hugging her like a baby sister weeping at her own birthday party. "Was it a rough session? It'll be okay. C'mon." He handed her a packet of tissue that she tore into and pressed the soft clumps to her running nose.

He led her to the austere cafeteria for dinner. The cafeteria was perhaps the size of a McDonalds, with acrylic sneeze guards over the buffets. A handful of orderlies moved along patients who had trouble focusing. Alicia was appalled at the greasy halfwits grappling with sandwiches and milk cartons. As the other patients shuffled and drooled with their trays, she stood in the middle of the room and soaked in her own helplessness.

Arnie walked with a young woman whom Alicia had not seen before today. Wispy blue hair bristled around her head in a thick mane, her milky gray eyes glistening. The faint line of an old cleft palate scrawled up to her nose. She stopped and looked at Alicia with such tenderness that Alicia thought her heart would break.

At that moment, the jackass from group therapy lumbered into the cafeteria. Licking his lips, he shuffled past Alicia as she tried to avoid eye contact with him. He swaggered toward the young woman and dug his meaty hand into her crotch. The girl twisted away, ashamed.

"Hey, motherfucker," Alicia growled. "Why don't you play with someone your own size? Oh...wait. 'Your size' is only two inches."

The man lunged at Alicia. She grabbed the cafeteria tray of a young man muttering to himself. But as she hurled it at her attacker, sharp shooting pains ripped up her forearms from her palms. She let go too soon. The tray's contents barely spattered him. Her head swam with white light from the agony in her arms. As Arnie called security, the man balled his fist and struck her in the chin—a sucker punch that made her head spin with pain. Another patient tried to hug her. She pushed him away. He then cried with rejection, which started a chain reaction of caterwauling.

Stocky men in hospital uniforms slipped past Arnie to Alicia, grabbing her from behind as they secured her upper arms and legs for a third nurse holding a syringe. She surmised that no one had seen his end of the attack.

"NO!" Alicia raged, struggling against the firm grip of the orderlies like a snake squirming from a flaky husk of dead skin. "Get *him*! He attacked me first!"

The stocky men carried her off to her room and laid her on the bed. Blood splotched the bandages where her sutures had come apart as they strapped her down.

They left her there alone, raging against her bonds, despairing that she would never feel right again.

Chapter 11

These days, Rachelle was so tired that the rumble of the BART train didn't bother her at night. That damned train could have leapt off the electric rail and she would have continued to sip her coffee as if the grandkids were squabbling in the back bedroom. Early that morning, she slid into the driver's seat of her old Lincoln, made its insides rattle and cough like a TB patient, and pulled into the back streets of residential Oakland.

Oakland. The Raiders. Jerry Brown. Lake Merritt. Jack London Square. Like much of the Bay Area, it was home to a vast population of mentally ill vagrants. This city had a nearly twenty percent poverty rate compared to the rest of the Bay, with over seventy percent of the houses built before 1959. It showed. The dilapidated Victorians crowded each other along the ill-repaired West Oakland streets. The city was bust long before the Silicon Valley boom and stayed that way until today in 2005. Rachelle had made it her home when she brought her mother and two young children here in the mid-1970s, all the way from Montgomery, Alabama. There were jobs in California. In the beginning, her mother had cared for Josiah and Taynia while Rachelle worked as a housekeeper to the wealthy families in San Francisco. She had ridden a bus across the Bridge every morning, often changing buses multiple times to reach her destination. The incentive to return to college and do something better with her life couldn't have been stronger.

This morning she had arrived at the hospital extra early, just after patient wake-up. She liked to get in about twenty minutes early to take the temperature of the ward, but today she'd slid in at seven a.m. to command the captain's seat of the asylum she called home away from home.

Could be worse. Could be a shot jockey at County.

Arnie greeted her as she slung her lunch/dinner into the kitchen fridge and they held a quick morning conference about who was scheduled to come in. Their newest patient was a woman named Alicia Baum. After deciding how Baum would be integrated into the ward, they'd settled into the morning insanity. Out of the gate, "Jesus" urinated in the patient cafeteria at breakfast and another patient tried to chew through her wrist.

Today was a double-shift.

When lunchtime arrived, Rachelle decided she absolutely had to take a break. She heated up her lunch, slipped her insulin from the refrigerator and put the steamy hot

Tupperware containers in a bag. She carried the bag downstairs and outside to the park where she could eat in peace. As she exited the side doors of the hospital, the fresh air washed over her. It had been much too long since she ever left that floor for something to eat. She felt alive for a moment as she inhaled the cool air, lifting her nose ever so slightly to take in the fragrance of freshly mown grass. Shiny, contemporary park benches were strewn at various points across the area.

Something was definitely wrong.

Rachelle approached an empty bench that stood just beyond a crowd of hospital personnel, patients, and other miscellaneous people staring at the ground.

"What the hell?" said one man.

"I dunno," a woman responded. "They just fell outta the sky!"

Rachelle's toe struck something limp, nudging it beyond her stride. She glanced down, thinking perhaps she'd struck a soggy, paper bag. Instead, it was a dead crow.

So strange.

Goosebumps raised on her arms as she scanned the grass. Dead crows littered the area, including where the crowd gathered.

"That's fucked up!" a younger man exclaimed as he shook his head. "Someone shoot them down?"

The crowd speculated as the woman continued. "Ah told you, they just fell outta the sky! I seen it with my own eyes. Theh was lightnin' and like a cloud or somethin' of electricity. And—BOOM! They jus' fell, like a rainstorm with black feathahs. I hate them noisy birds, but that ain't right."

Rachelle sat on the bench, listening, but she'd lost her appetite. An eerie feeling balled up inside her and her mouth tasted metallic. Never had she seen anything like this. She looked up: there were no power lines here that the birds could have struck. The power lines crossed the other side of the hospital. Odd. But more than odd. Scary. What could have killed these birds?

And there weren't just crows. Rachelle noted sparrows dotting the underside of a nearby tree.

The faint tang of ozone laced the air.

Rachelle's stomach remained knotted but she ate anyway. There was a time when she would have let such sights wreck her blood sugar levels by keeping her wound up and worried. But these days she couldn't afford not to eat.

When Rachelle returned from lunch, she found Dr. Mason Sark, Director of Adult Behavioral Health Services, standing at her desk with a pretty but slight woman who appeared to be a nurse. Dr. Sark towered over them both, blond hair swept back from his forehead as his gaze bore a hole in Rachelle's forehead.

"Rachelle! A word, please?"

The psychiatric ward was the 'hood of Headmaster Sark, a blue-blooded New England with a faux-Oxford accent and a fastidious manner even when he stirred his tea. Although Rachelle was the Mental Health Registered Nurse—supposedly in charge of staffing, meds, and the day-to-day business of the unit—Dr. Sark micromanaged her affairs to a ridiculous degree. He answered to only one person, Dr. Leonard Dulac, who was at least a decent man with a conscience about his practice. But if Dr. Sark had been diagnosed by one of his colleagues (and he often was from afar), an astute read would reveal a Cluster A personality disorder: a classic narcissist with histrionic overtones. Everything from his bizarre relationship with his mother—whom he alternately claimed to be dead on some days and living on others—to his overtly controlling yet subtly hostile approach to running the ward spelled a man short on ideas yet long on self-importance.

"This is Nurse Mindy Hannon," he said, as if they were at a cocktail party rather than in a psych ward. The young woman wore her black hair in two high, tight buns. "She joins the staff today. Mindy, this is Rachelle LaBeau, our Senior Manager of Nursing. You shall report directly to her. Any questions?"

"Oh, I got a question, Dr. Sark," Rachelle said, hands on hips, "but I'm gonna ask it in my office. With you. Alone."

A bit of air huffed from Dr. Sark's nose. "I'm already late for a meeting. Check my schedule online and make an appointment." He glanced at his silvery watch, making a face. "Nurse Hannon, good day and good luck."

Rachelle noted a sly, satisfied smile curling his lips as he turned on his heel and began whistling a measure from Vivaldi's *The Four Seasons*. No fan of classical music, she only knew that because he played and talked about that music all the damned time.

Rachelle tried to cap the steam rising in her ears but she let some escape with the annoyance in her voice. "Mindy, this is a bit irregular so I'm going to have to ask you a lot of questions. Now, tell me about your background."

In a squeaky voice, Mindy explained how she was recently licensed, had no experience whatsoever in an acute psychiatric inpatient unit, and was grateful to Dr. Sark for the opportunity to join his staff because she was "fascinated with psychology."

Rachelle stared at her in disbelief as she spoke. "How'd you meet Dr. Sark?" Rachelle expected that she'd hear of some acquaintance or even alumni pushing his advantage for Dr. Sark to hire his daughter or some such.

Mindy shrugged, a bit of color rising in her creamy cheeks. "Through mutual friends."

Oh, lordie. Rachelle suspected that there was so much more baked into this pie that she dare not break the crust with her thumb. She might have to talk to Dr. Dulac about this but that might bring repercussions she didn't want to deal with. Dr.

Sark's revenge often manifested in denying her critical family leave and making other unreasonable demands. The nurses at this hospital weren't unionized so he could do whatever he wanted.

That would have to change.

In the meantime, Rachelle gritted her teeth and decided to set Mindy to perform tech-level work rather than nursing until she could verify Mindy's credentials. As she handed off Mindy to the two techs on duty that afternoon, Rachelle was immediately paged to the next medical emergency.

Rachelle was tired and losing the ability to care.

For fifty-eight years she'd lived on Mother Earth and had learned the value of the human soul, no matter how wrinkled and soiled it might be sometimes. She'd raised four children on her own and they in turn gave her three grandchildren so far, with more on the way. She taught each one the same lesson: love each other more than your own self. The only way to survive this life is to protect each other like the Lord was never looking and, when the Lord did look your way, let Him use your hand to slap the fools that messed with you.

But for some reason the Lord never looked her way when it came to Dr. Sark. He wanted quiet in the psych unit at any cost. He even went over Rachelle's head and gave the nurses incentives for silencing patients by any means. Sometimes that meant locking up patients and neglecting them until they either passed out or, in one terrible case, died. The ensuing scandal barely touched him, as no one could finger him for the mistreatment. A nurse instead took the fall.

Dead birds. A crazy director who was, for all intents and purposes, a murderer. Everything looked especially ugly today.

For so long, she'd looked for a sign. She wanted to know that God was still listening to her. He seemed very far away, doing whatever it was He was doing. Rachelle believed in the afterlife. Her version of God wasn't strictly biblical but He was compassionate. He came from a lot of sources, those that gave her the most hope and then some. She was no stranger to miracles. She had seen amazing things happen in people's lives, as well as bizarre coincidences that could only belong to a master architect. God was in the details, someone once said. And that was all Rachelle used to see in her world. Details and God.

But lately, she couldn't find either.

"Damn you! I want my attorney! DAMN YOU ALL!" she heard Alicia yelling down the hall.

As Alicia's charge nurse had fifteen other patients to manage, chances were he was missing out on this action. Rachelle couldn't fill the gaps herself but she was particularly aware of Alicia because of both Dr. Farron and the fact that, well, she had loved Alicia's books. She'd especially enjoyed the early stuff, but felt the publishers were squeezing things out of her at the end. When nothing new had come out for a couple of years, Rachelle had kept checking Alicia's blog for updates that never transpired until she gave up.

When she saw Alicia's name on the incoming list, she wondered if indeed this was the same person. It was a helluva way to meet someone you admired. They had never received what anyone would call a celebrity. Alicia was the closest thing to it. Of course Rachelle had to serve Alicia some extra concern for the sake of Dr. Farron, but she was otherwise trying not to show her any favoritism. It just wouldn't be right.

But James Farron, now *that* man needed some looking after. When he'd requested to be on the Green Team as Alicia's psychiatrist, she'd had to swim big rivers to get him assigned because Dr. Sark hated him. She would do that for James. He'd been so good with her grandson Ezequial when he was having debilitating nightmares last fall; she thought the Lord had brought a true blessing to that godforsaken hospital.

He needed looking after these days, though. Sometimes life just up and strands us on muddy roads, taking what we hold dear with it. Just doesn't seem right, especially when it comes to people like James, who genuinely try to do good things for others.

He was a natural healer once. Life broke it from him and left him with an obsession that could have no good outcome. It only drove him further into isolation as fewer people understood what he was doing, or just thought it was entirely too strange. He insisted that the children were creating their own folktales, but the stories he relied on were told by only a smattering of parents and doctors around the globe. There weren't enough to support his theory. He just did not want to see it.

Denial. It ain't just a river in Egypt. We all raft it, though, from time to time.

During activities and free time, the patients were blocked from their rooms. They were only allowed back to their beds at bedtime and no sooner.

It was only lunchtime. Something was happening in Alicia's room.

Rachelle evaluated the situation at the station and, checking her watch, she judged she could leave for a couple of minutes. When she reached the tiny room, she found Alicia strapped to the bed, face cherry red and wistful.

"Alicia."

Alicia rolled her head slightly to the right and looked at Rachelle. "Hi."

"What's going on? You want to tell me?"

"Will it get me out of here faster?"

"I can't promise that."

Alicia sighed. "Dr. Farron's a fraud. He doesn't really want to solve his mystery."

"What mystery?"

"You know. The guy the kids talk to in their sleep."

Rachelle turned away. She couldn't discuss Dr. Farron with a patient. "Goodbye, Alicia."

Alicia called after her. "He's a better artist than a doctor. Maybe he should do that instead."

"Who says he doesn't?" Rachelle's nerves chattered a bit before she could think properly of what to say. She returned to the doorway and leaned against the jamb. "You wanna tell me what happened?"

"With Dr. Farron? Or the asshole in the cafeteria?"

"Let's start with Dr. Farron."

She was quiet for a moment, then: "He betrayed me, Rachelle," she said. "And that's all I can say."

Rachelle doubted that, but tried to look sympathetic regardless. Her sympathy was hard won these days.

"And what happened in the cafeteria?"

Alicia told her. Stunned at the bruise blossoming on Alicia's jaw, Rachelle ordered a nurse to bring ice for Alicia's chin, as well as some ibuprofen.

"I promise I'll look into the assault, but you need to worry more about yourself than anyone else right now. Tomorrow morning, they're gonna discuss your release and your behavior today won't look good. They've gotta know you aren't a danger to yourself and others, and you've not proved that."

"Who do you mean, 'they'?"

Rachelle opened her smooth, wide palm and counted on her short fingers: "Your medical doctor, your charge nurse, and Dr. Farron. Maybe even the director, Dr. Sark. And trust me,"—up went the hand and finger—"you do *not* want Dr. Sark at your evaluation, especially with any strikes against you."

"So, what you're saying is, even though I'm the one who got hurt, because of my outburst today, I can't go home."

"Dr. Farron will do his best for you, no matter what happens." Alicia looked doubtful. Rachelle laid a hand on her arm. "You are more important to him than you know."

Alicia's face relaxed. Rachelle could tell the fight had gone out of her and the sedatives were working. She unstrapped Alicia and let her apply her own ice bag.

"Are you a believer?" Alicia asked, blinking like a sleepy cat.

"Believer?"

"Do you believe there are things we can't explain?"

Rachelle's guard went up. Bonfires blazed in Alicia's eyes whenever she spoke. It was as if she had slipped into the rabbit hole and came back waving an open "Drink Me" bottle. And not like one of the regular patients. This woman was much too grounded—

especially for someone who had done to herself what she'd done. "I got my beliefs," Rachelle said. "We all gotta believe in something."

"It's just that—" Alicia laughed. "Actually, changing the subject, Dr. Farron said something about the eighth dimension." Then, a secret notion danced in her eyes. "Rachelle, can I use the phone?"

"Sure. But you've got to calm down—"

A dark movement at the window. Alicia had one of the few rooms with any natural light. Rachelle stepped gingerly toward the odd movement to find a glassy black eye peering at her from the window between the blinds. It was the biggest crow she'd ever seen in her life. The bird's size startled her badly, its weirdly intense focus giving her chills. Rachelle's heart raced as it sized her up with the boldness of a prizefighter.

"Or can you call the video store for me? There's something that Dr. Farron needs to see."

One of the nurses leaned in the doorway. "Excuse me, Rachelle. Dr. Bay is on the phone?"

"I'll be right there." She tore herself from the spectacle, wondering if she should shut the blinds or get over herself. She said to Alicia, "You promise to behave?"

"Witch's honor," she replied, her fingers straddling her nose from below in a V-shaped symbol, like Samantha Stevens on the TV show *Bewitched*.

For some reason, that gesture didn't make Rachelle feel any better.

Chapter 12

The playroom simmered that night with the emotional heat of the afternoon's session. Dr. Farron drooped in the big black chair behind his desk, staring at the drawing of Mr. Wicker that glowered at him from the wall. He could not bring himself to take it down. He wrapped up his paperwork for the day, put on his jacket, and then collapsed on the patient couch in a puddle of indecision.

He could not begin to address what had happened today. Had they really witnessed some kind of supernatural phenomenon? There was probably a logical explanation, but it wasn't forthcoming. It scared the hell out of him and he had no desire to look at it. He needed a vacation to regroup. He needed to see his therapist again. He needed to relax and get a grip—or something. Even the look on Alicia's face when she saw this drawing bothered him deeply. The act of drawing again felt amazing, like lying in the sun on the beach after a brisk swim. It had taken this woman and the insanity of the day to crack open the door to his art. Gripping that crayon awakened him to his long-neglected need to create. But he'd lost that desire with everything else in his life three years ago.

Was she attracted to this *character*? The exchange she'd described sounded fairly erotic, a disturbing attraction to say the least. It was just a dream. Just an NDE.

Or maybe it was something more. But what that might be, he couldn't fathom. He hadn't even totally discounted that she might be a cutter with a pronounced imagination, her missing memory probably related to sexual abuse as a child. He didn't want to "plant" memories in her mind, but he'd bring it up in the next session. The whole idea of the "rose garden"—sub-rosa activity. Dumped by her father with grandparents who may or may not have been good guardians. It seemed pretty likely that was what she'd forgotten about, especially given her rebelliousness and self-destructive behavior. Telltale signs of sexual abuse.

Dr. Farron felt as though he'd been asleep for three years and finally someone had torn open the blinds to let the sunbeams slash his pillow-smothered face. Everything inside him now woke up at once, and he felt afresh the pain that had put him into that stupor. This attraction, the cry of his soul to draw, the face of his nemesis…everything bit into him at once.

This was not what he'd envisioned when he signed up to be her treatment therapist—to have his sanity pulled taut like trampoline fabric and bounced on by some elephantine mystery. He had to hold it together, to fight the black waters washing over his head. He pulled open a desk drawer and reached inside, retrieving a medicine bottle.

Celexa.

The fear of needing the medication retraced an old path in his mind, leaving a residue of resistance. He recalled the reluctance when his own therapist recommended it. Despite his extensive education and training, despite everything he knew about the medication and how it had saved lives, the stigma stuck. Who cared about the research? He feared needing the medication for life, his biochemistry being unable to operate normally on its own. It might also kill his sex drive, although lord knew he wasn't using it.

Alicia seemed to have more of an intellectual bias against antidepressants than a fear, but he'd have to explore that with her to see where her reaction was really coming from.

Egg white guilt slid over him. He should not have been so cold to her. The combination of his overwhelming attraction to her, his absolute shock over what happened with the comatose Georgeta Martin, and then Alicia's story and response to the drawing was just too much for him to process at once. Still, he should not have shut her out. She's a suicide survivor, for Chrissakes. His personal crap had most likely set her back. Imagine what *she's* had to process in only a day.

He had to apologize to her. He would keep the focus off of Mr. Wicker for the moment. Maybe if he slept on it, things would be clearer by morning.

But he had to apologize. Immediately.

Yes, it was nine-fifteen p.m., but he needed to apologize.

He straightened his Powerpuff tie. And as he stood in the doorway, he grimaced at Mr. Wicker on the wall and slammed the office door behind him.

Chapter 13

"Morning or evening?" Brian asked.

"Evening," Rachelle replied wearily.

"Mick or Keith?"

"Don't you have work to do?" she asked.

"C'mon, Rachelle."

She sighed. "Keith."

"Really?"

"It's the skull rings," she replied.

"You like that dark stuff, dontcha?"

"Hell yeah. I like being scared. Why else you think I'd be in this job?"

Dr. Farron heard the exchange as soon as the elevator doors opened. As he approached the nurses' station, he saw a very tired Rachelle doing paperwork as Brian, a young male nurse, read from a *GQ* magazine that drooped over the desk as he squeezed a grip strengthener in one hand and sorted medications on a cart with the other. Threatened by every man in existence, Brian delivered a slicing glance at Dr. Farron, snickered, and pumped the strengthener harder. "Evening, Dr. Farron," he said more loudly than he should.

Relief and surprise tugged up a smile on Rachelle's tired face. "Now, what are you doin' up here so late?"

He ignored Brian's posturing. "I was going to ask you the same question! Why aren't you home?"

"Short-handed, as usual," she said. She looked exasperated at Brian. "What can we do for you?"

"I need to talk to my patient." He indicated up the hallway toward Alicia's room. As he stepped more toward the hallway, he noted that Alicia's light was on.

"She's asleep," Brian said, pedantic.

"With the light on?"

Brian leaned on the station with a bemused smirk. "She's terrified of the dark. Won't even sleep with a nightlight like the others. Has to have the full beam. You didn't know that?"

"Well...sure, it came up in session, but..." *Pants on fire, James.* "I'll just go take a peek at her, if that's okay."

Rachelle raised an eyebrow at him, but looked back down at her work and nodded.

"Knock yerself out, Dr. Eff," Brian said.

Dr. Farron rolled his eyes at Brian, who had no authority to say either way. He wandered down the hallway, his nerves crackling.

Alicia slept as she did when he first saw her, like she was slumbering under a giant toadstool in the grassy whiskers of a forest rather than the sickly fluorescent lights of the hospital room.

Sidelong would she bend, and sing a faery's song...

That Keats poem came back to him. He leaned back against the door for a moment, just watching her sleep. There was no way he could be detached or professional about her. Yet her evaluation was tomorrow morning and he was her psychiatrist. He would make sure that she left and assign her to another doctor for outpatient treatment. The mystery would remain unsolved, at least until she was willing to discuss it with him—if ever.

Turning away from her, he stepped through the doorway and flipped the light switch, dousing the room in pitch.

"Aaaaaaaaaaaaa!"

Dr. Farron scrambled for the light switch, flicking it back on to find Alicia sitting bolt upright in bed, hyperventilating as she seized the bedding with both hands. "Oh, my God! I'm so sorry!" he said.

Brian and an orderly jogged to the doorway. Dr. Farron shooed them away. Grabbing the visitor chair, he pulled it up beside the bed. "I'm sorry I woke you up."

"What are doing here?"

"I came to apologize."

"For waking me up?"

"No," he replied. "But I apologize for that, too. I wanted to say I'm sorry for being so uncompassionate today, not to mention unprofessional. I hope you will forgive me."

Alicia's face registered some shock. She never took her eyes off him as she adjusted her pillows so that she could sit up comfortably. "I'm kind of out of practice in the forgiveness department, but I'll give it a go."

"Thanks," he said. This was good. She hadn't blocked him out.

"So," he continued. "We've had some progress. I know you're a horror writer. You believe in Mr. Wicker. You don't believe in antidepressants. And you're afraid of the dark." He wondered why she just sat there watching him.

She closed her eyes and inhaled as if smelling the air, then exhaled.

"They flash a flashlight in your eyes every fifteen minutes, don't they?"

She shook her head and opened her eyes. "Don't have to. I keep the light on."

"What are you afraid of?"

"When you turn out the lights, what do you see?"

He shrugged. "Nothing."

"Me, too. I see the void. It reminds me of everything that's been taken away from me. Have you ever had everything that ever mattered to you taken away?"

Dr. Farron paused. He wanted to say *yes, more than you know*, but this was about Alicia, not him. "I need you to tell me about what caused this. How can I help you if you don't tell me?"

Alicia grinned and broke into her best Dr. Evil imitation. "Come on, people. Throw me a bone here."

"Be serious, please."

She picked at her wrist bandage.

"Let me see that," he said and cursed himself for letting her slip out of the question. He held her forearm in one hand and her fingers in his other to examine the bandaging. Dried blood bloomed darkly into the gauze. "Have you been scratching at your stitches?"

Alicia shook her head. "They gave me a shot today. They grabbed my wrists and worked the stitches loose."

"Why did they do that?"

"I exploded in the cafeteria."

"Exploded? Like in group therapy?"

"Kind of. I threw a tray at that jackass from group therapy when he molested some poor girl. And then he punched me." She showed off a bruise on the underside of her chin.

"Ooof! Are you okay?"

"Eh. You should have seen what I did to his ego."

"Who was the girl?"

"I don't know her name. She's just a young thing and he fucking just reached for her and molested her in front of everyone. I couldn't stand it. So when I goaded him to attack me instead, I threw a tray at him. Which, you know, was fucking brilliant, if I don't mind saying so, seeing as how I can't hold a fork much less a full tray of hot food. But I'm not here because I'm brilliant, am I?"

"That's the problem. You *are* brilliant," he replied.

Alicia blushed. She then looked at him squarely, her gaze permeating every layer of defense. The heat of her seeped into his hands and flashed through his body. Rather than pull away, though, he continued to examine her smallish palms and fingers with "wizard's knots" in the joints. His Irish grandmother had said they represented a thinker. With one of his own fingers, he traced a path from the base of her palm to the middle of her forearm.

"This," he explained as he drew, "is your median nerve. If you had slit that, your hands would be useless."

"My whole *body* should have been useless."

"True. It must have been very painful."

"I have a high pain threshold," she replied. He detected a flush of emotion behind that statement. "Besides, I looked it up in Gray's Anatomy before I cut. See the lines?" She frowned. "I didn't tell anybody what I was going to do."

He eyed the open door and worried for a moment about the lack of privacy in this impromptu session. Ah, screw it. She was talking. "Do you still want to die?"

Alicia's face brightened a shade. "Do *you* want to live?"

He frowned. "What makes you think I don't want to live?"

"Oh, nothing." She looked away, up at the ceiling, around the room, pursing her lips as if to whistle.

He needed a carrot. Something to draw her out. "Look, I can try to find out who called 9-1-1, but I can't guarantee we can discuss it. Suicide is a criminal offense after all."

"So was abortion, once upon a time."

"Point well taken."

"How will you find out? Do you have connections?"

"I haff my vays." He smiled. Like a brass chorus in his ears, something blared that he was holding her hand. And that she was holding his. Mortified, he let go and slid off the bed. "I have to go. Your evaluation is nine a.m. tomorrow morning, okay?"

"Okay."

Something fluttered in the window. Dr. Farron turned toward it, puzzled.

"What's wrong?"

He stepped toward the window with a sense of foreboding. As he approached, he peered through the blinds to find a glassy black eye angled at him. The great black bird stretched its wings and opened its thick beak threateningly. It would have been comical if the bird hadn't been so weirdly large.

It looked like a raven. But it couldn't be. This was Berkeley, not Britain. Or did that matter?

"What's out there? Rachelle was looking earlier. Is something wrong?"

"Nothing," Dr. Farron replied although his gut screamed that it was anything but. "Just a bird."

"What kind of bird?" A beat. "Is it a raven?"

He gulped.

"It's a raven, isn't it?" she asked, sitting up, eyes wide. "Fuck!"

"I—I don't know."

"You do know."

"I don't! It's just a crow." It had to be.

Then a plaintive voice called from the other side of the ward. "A LIGHT TO GUIDE THE GENTILES!"

Dr. Farron started. "What the heck?"

"Jesus is getting the flashlight in his face," she said, still distracted by the window.

"Jesus, huh?"

"JFC to you, pal."

He laughed. Her sense of humor felt stronger. She was coming back to the world.

"Goodnight," he said with a wave. She waved back. He turned to the doorway and reached for the light switch, but caught himself. Glancing back at her, he smiled sheepishly and curled his hand into a fist. Her weary face softened with an amused look as she lowered back down onto the pillow, never taking her eyes off him.

Out in the hallway, his mind started beating the inner tom-toms of obsession and anxiety. He was less anxious about the conversation with Alicia than he was about the odd bird outside her window—especially given what had happened that day. Being very conscious of the sound his footsteps made in the hallway, he forced himself to walk toward the nurses' station, even though he wanted to turn to the wall and beat his fists into it.

Bolting past the desk, he held up a hand in brief gesture to Rachelle.

"Hey!" she said as he passed. "I have something for you."

He slowed. "Where's Brian?"

"He's doing checks with Dean."

"Ah."

She reached under the desk, digging. "Did you see those dead birds today?"

"Dead birds?"

"Dozens of dead crows just dropped out of the sky in the park."

"That's bizarre."

"I tell you, James, I'm no psychic or anything, but I got a bad feeling about this."

"Did you see that bird outside of Alicia Baum's window?"

"The big black one?"

"Yeah."

"Just what the hell was that?"

He lowered his voice. "A raven, I think. Much too big to be a crow."

"You some expert? Damn, where'd I put that thing?" She found whatever she was digging for and pulled out a DVD, handing it to him like a traffic ticket.

Arched over by white Japanese lettering, the bright blue cover art depicted a Samurai in steel armor with a slick black face shield that obscured his features. Beside a silvery clad anime girl with wistful eyes and cinnamon brown pigtails that swept into the Milky Way, the cyber Samurai held a large blaster gun at an aggressive angle as he stood on the swollen black head of a horned dragon with blood running from frothy nostrils. Its tongue split into tendrils and fanned from a toothy jaw into the winds of space, grasping and crushing distant starships.

Dr. Farron gripped the case tighter as the dragon tickled his memory. "Where did you get this?"

"*I* didn't. *She* did." Rachelle gestured toward Alicia's room. "At some funky video store on Telegraph. Don't ask, I don't know."

Down the hall, a patient cursed Brian and the orderly, Dean.

Jesus was quick to respond to his fellow patient's outburst. "THE SON OF GOD IS THE TRUTH AND THE LIGHT."

"If ya don't shut up, Jesus, I'll bring the Romans," Brian yelled.

"She said that you should watch it again," Rachelle intimated.

"Again?"

"Like I said, I don't know."

With a sigh, he thanked Rachelle. "Good night, Rachelle."

And he went home. At first, he did not sleep. More than anything, he wanted to know who had dialed 9-1-1. So, he booted his laptop and emailed his friend Connie who worked in Emergency Services for Alameda County. If anyone could get a digital recording of the call and the readout from the PSAP, it would be her. When he clicked "Send," he hoped that it was Alicia who had called just before slitting her wrists. That kind of behavior wasn't unheard of.

He had a feeling, though, that the explanation would be anything but ordinary.

Chapter 14

Through the eyes of Huginn as she perched in that window, Mr. Wicker watched the exchange between Alicia and The Celt with increasing alarm. How The Celt examined her hands. How they spoke. Perhaps she would be the Librarian's undoing, but he wanted her close enough that she *could* undo him.

Worse, he had a moment of recognition. It happened rarely, as few of the people he'd known in life ever passed through the Library. But this soul he could not mistake. Mr. Wicker recognized a soul by the eyes. As these particular eyes drew close to Huginn, he could see that they were quite unmistakably the eyes of someone he hated more than his captivity.

Litu.

Most likely this man had no idea who he had been and what he had done. Yet the sum of his current and past lives determined what The Celt would do in this life. Or at least, what he was *trying* to do, anyway.

A volcanic rage roiled in the Librarian as the bitter memories of his long forgotten life flooded his mental landscape. Old, agonizing memories that he'd tried to leave behind with his death but could not. Ever.

The man who was responsible for his curse. For his imprisonment.

Mr. Wicker had to stop him, whatever his purpose this life. He had to out of sheer spite. The sweetness of revenge after centuries of suffering.

But how? He didn't even know what the man was about this time around. He didn't have a book. No one in his family did.

He had to bring Alicia back to the Library. If he could convince her to stay, then at least he had won half the war—the half that held his heart. Then if he could discover what Litu was about this life, he could prepare for the onslaught—if indeed one could prepare to counter destiny. And anything involving Litu returning to his life meant fate was afoot.

Mr. Wicker's eyes trailed up the towering stacks. Only the very worst memories made it to the Library. They had hardened him over the years. And now was the time to raise the curtain on his cruelty to let it strut proudly. While he had to lure Alicia back to the Library, the only way to bring her back for good would be to hurt her in some way, to widen the void so that she could fall into it once again and not be able to climb out.

There wasn't much left to take, but he had an idea.

This idea had already formed into a silent command. Muninn sailed to Mr. Wicker's side and dropped a slender tome before him. The shaggy hackles of the bird's black throat rippled as he cried and landed upon his master's shoulder.

Mr. Wicker laid a charred hand on the spine of the book he sought. The book need not be that thick. It could be as slim as a letter with one devastating memory. Or it could be as thick as an encyclopedia of pain. But this one could be carried by the raven alone. A feathered frenzy built between the book stacks. The air stirred with cruelty, raising a cry from the birds as if a fresh corpse had dropped before them.

The Librarian prided himself in drawing off the poison of people's lives, even if they often tried to kill themselves to be reunited with said poison. They would spend a lifetime pursuing those memories to feel whole again, but the contents of their book would elude them until death. Until they returned to the Library.

But if he annihilated that memory, they would never be whole. They would wander from lifetime to lifetime, a sick wraith in flesh. Always hungry. Never quite sane. It was a destructive power that They had somehow not yet taken from him. Perhaps it was to placate his rage at being imprisoned. Or perhaps it had simply been overlooked.

The Librarian held the book before the candelabra, opening the pages that stuck together from disuse.

The ink rose in a medieval chorus of voices that lilted above chords heavy with melancholy. A bell tolled. He tore one of the pages from the binding and a contralto wailed as she separated from her comrades, a solo voice that trilled with the strings of a mandolin.

Mr. Wicker held the page above the candle flame, the contralto shrieking as the fire devoured the paper. Under the shrill raven calls, the ink boiled on the page as it curled black and thin with smoke. When it shriveled into a mere whisper of charred parchment, Mr. Wicker flung it into the air...

Whoooosshhh!

The withered, blackened blossom sailed through the rafters, writhing as sinister petals of ash turned oily and bloody—a memory, a stroke of ink. A fledgling beak tore from the gory heap, wings convulsing as they ripped from the blistering, roiling mass. The newly born thing flapped and gyred through the air, its brothers and sisters dipping and swerving around it. Every moment another detail was teased from the blackness while the tarry throat stretched and rippled—*kraaa-kraaa-kraaa!*

Kraaa-kraaa-kraaa!

Chapter 15

Kraaa-kraaa-kraaa!

"Mrs. Rains?"

Jimmy the bellboy strolled into the lobby from the employee lounge, tugging at the leather hat strap that was cutting his chin, when he noticed Mrs. Rains in the lobby. Her skin was waxy, eyes fixed eerily on some point across the room. She wore glossy burgundy pajamas and slung her purse over her outstretched forearm as if she were about to parade into a high-end boutique. She also wore one white leather flat. Not a slipper but something comfy to scuttle around in when traveling. The other foot was bare, revealing her callused, bunion-twisted toes. The bellboy's stride slowed, a high-pitched ringing in his ears. The conspicuous juxtaposition of the old woman in her pajamas with her Italian purse standing against the lavish Art Deco décor of the posh hotel reminded him of a scene in a Fellini movie.

It was only six a.m., and the few people on staff at that hour milled behind the registration counter.

"Mrs. Rains?" he asked. "Are you all right?"

Her eyelids flickered as the orbs languidly rolled toward him. Her lower lip twitched.

Jimmy reached for her elbow. "Let me take you back to your room."

Her withered lips parted to release a deafening squall that rebounded from the domed ceiling and marbled lobby. A sick wave of fear washed up from the bellboy's shiny black shoes and into his chest. Then, the old woman looked straight up, pointing as she cried, and the skin of her face tightened into a death mask. The bellboy glanced upward, following her finger's accusations. His body went cold as he thought he saw a black bird streak across the mezzanine from one brass railing to another on the opposite side. A dreadful crash wrenched away his attention from the hallucination. At his feet, the elderly woman had collapsed, her twisted body forming a rosette of burgundy silk and mottled skin. The contents of her purse sprawled about his feet. He knelt beside her, blinking in shock as a colleague vaulted over the registration desk and rushed toward the scene. Everyone around him dialed cell phones, shouted, chattered.

A business card had settled among the detritus of her purse. The bellboy picked it up: *James Farron, M.D. M.F.C.C.*

Chapter 16

DAY 2—BAYFORD PSYCHIATRIC UNIT

The scene eerily flickered like a damaged film reel as Alicia approached a circle of roses.

Some stood as high as six feet tall, tightly surrounding a concrete arena about eight feet in diameter. Two blanching roses hung their blighted heads, Gog and Magog arching across the arena's entry. Their bowed stems crossed like pikes, thorns murderously cuspate. Like a fairy woods, the roses entwined above and below, a wild mass of commingling vegetation. In the background was the hiss of an unattended needle riding the dead grooves of an antique phonograph, dipping with a crackle into a deep scratch.

A cleaning machine rumbled over the linoleum of the hospital hallway, clacking as it crossed rubber runners in doorways. Awaking from the dream, Alicia rolled onto her back and let anxiety ransack her mind. He said the missing memory would explain everything. And someone—presumably her—had died because of it. Or them.

Someone? What did that mean? It sounded vaguely biblical. "Someone" died for your sins. If he was referring to her suicide, why didn't he say so?

Would she kill herself again? Perhaps. To see Mr. Wicker?

The answer fell into her stomach and burned it dry. What purpose had His Fucking Majesty of showing her the Library? Of plunging her into this great mystery with threats of death? God had turned her ultimate act of anger against her. He defied her. By some miracle, she lay awake and alive with desire when that was the last thing in the world she'd wanted just a few days ago.

But then, what future did she have if she did leave the hospital? How long before the void embraced her again, bit her cheek, and licked her veins dry?

Given the dream fragment, however, perhaps she and Dr. Farron could reach the missing memory through hypnosis. Was Mr. Wicker lying after all? Did she not have proof now that the memory was merely submerged and not catalogued separately in the Dewey Decimal System of the Damned?

The moment she'd stood in the Library, she'd stood in the center of the sun. The reality of it burned glyphs into her bones; she would never be the same.

She wanted to see that little girl again. If nothing else, she could hold her small warm hand and sit with her. She had no reassuring words about the sins of the world, no encouragement that life would be anything but disappointing. Hans Christian Anderson's Little Match Girl dies alone in the cold; his Little Mermaid dies in excruciating pain and never knows her lover; the Tin Soldier melts to a lump, alone and unloved. How could she say those tales were not true? But she could be there for the child in the silence of her coma when no one else in her family would. When God had gone, she might have a friend. And, meantime, Alicia might nurse her precious conduit to the Library and gain whatever the Librarian might pass to her through the child.

Her motives were mixed and she felt badly about it.

By six a.m., a mouse of a nurse was waking patients and rounding them up to the showers. Her tiny black eyes and compact figure supported a generous Shiseido-red mouth with swollen lips. Her hair was divided in two black buns, one on each side of her head. *Check out Minnie Mouse.* "Where's Arnie?" she asked.

"Oh, he'll be back," the nurse squeaked. Alicia had read somewhere that a grown woman with a little girl's voice was a classic sign that she'd been sexually abused as a child, as if the child inside had been bansai tied by the damage and could not grow.

"Would you know if Dr. Sark is here today?" Alicia asked.

"He doesn't come in until eight." A suspicious familiarity whetted the nurse's expression as she spoke of him.

Fuck a duck.

"My attorney. Malcom Shefter. He's coming, right?" She'd given his name to the admissions nurse when they filled out her paperwork.

"Oh yes," she said, brightening. "I spoke to him."

"What's your name?"

The nurse plucked at her badge. It sagged on her lab coat, out of sight behind her lapel and the elevator security card attached to her lanyard. She refastened it to make it visible. "I'm Mindy."

"Nice to meet you, Mindy." She wondered if Mindy made herself look like a cartoon character on purpose.

Nurse Mindy promised she'd be around for the day until Arnie arrived. She then left the room, Alicia's eyes trailing her far out of frame. She would need to make Mindy her ally as she seemed to have some kind of rapport with Dr. Sark.

Shortly thereafter, Mindy led Alicia to the showers, explaining that they'd have to tape plastic bags over her hands and wrists to protect her stitches. Alicia declined. There was no way she was going to shower with mumbling, drooling crazy people. Mindy made her dress and sit in a metal chair by the secondary nurses' station near the cafeteria until everyone was ready to eat.

After Alicia finished a breakfast of peeled hardboiled eggs, pre-cut fruit, pre-buttered toast, orange juice, and tepid black coffee—the entire meal uniquely concocted to be eaten without utensils—she decided to slouch about the activities room until her evaluation that morning. All except the sickest of the other patients avoided her these days, so she didn't worry that she'd be troubled. She growled at the most delusional ones and they recoiled. As she created twisted collages about her life from glossy magazines at the activities table, boredom beckoned her to get up and peer into the corridor.

Wearing a lab coat, a tall man with dishwater blond hair and wintry blue eyes swaggered down the hallway, a simper straddling his lips. He passed the secondary nurses' station where Mindy talked on the phone, motioning her to his side. When she saw him, she hastily ended her conversation, shoveled a few charts into her arms, and scampered after him.

Scanning the corridor for techs and other nursing staff, Alicia followed. Her footsteps barely whispered in red velvet slippers as she pursued the two. *Thank you, Grandma.* They moved down the corridor and turned down another hallway, headed toward the suite of offices at the southeastern corner of the ward through a door. She paced herself so as not to look suspicious, as if she were taking a self-absorbed stroll, crossing her arms and tilting her head forward.

The nurse and the man she suspected was Dr. Sark turned one more corner, exchanging banal words as he asked her how things were going on her second day and if there was anything she needed. Keeping just over a hall's length between her and them, Alicia knew this had to be the end of the line. She stopped just before the hallway ended, leaning her body flat against the wall, and listened to their *tete-a-tete.*

"So...how long until your next appointment?" Mindy asked hesitantly as he unlocked the door.

"Long enough," he replied and threw it open. They bustled inside and he closed it behind them.

Fuck a duck—for a buck!

Alicia waited several moments before she edged closer to the door. A plaque read "Dr. Mason Sark, Director of Adult Behavioral Health Services."

As her heart threw sidekicks at her ribcage, Alicia put her ear to the wall beside the door, standing closest to the hallway corner in case she had to escape. Ever vigilant to the scant sounds down the corridor, her ears were rewarded with the man's groans and directions to *lick, lower, suck, harder.* And more groans. Alicia leaned her feverish body against the cool wall, enrapt by the sounds of illicit intercourse, remembering the erotic thrall of Mr. Wicker when he ordered her to take off her robe and painted her skin with the wet brush of his gaze.

You don't seem to want life, but I do...

The groans gave way to more articulate phrases, Mindy's high-pitched chatter overrunning Sark's low voice.

Definitely Upper East Coast. New England, maybe. From "Assholechusetts," as her MIT pal, Doug, used to call it. But Dr. Sark didn't have the open, lingering vowels. Rather, he affected a faint English accent.

The voices jostled closer to the door. Startled, Alicia shoved herself from the wall and forced her legs to *move, move, move.* The door closed and the jangle of keys announced Dr. Sark was locking his office. The two then headed down the corridor after her. She had lingered too long, dammit. Scrambling in the velvet slippers, she skip-skidded down the slick linoleum of the corridor and disappeared around a bend into an adjacent hallway. Thing One and Thing Two (as she decided to call them) passed the adjacent corridor a beat later, nonchalantly discussing ward procedures. Mindy's buns hung a bit loosely and Dr. Sark's cheeks were flushed.

Alicia slipped from her hiding place, past the group therapy room, where the session had just started. As she passed the nurses' station, she smiled at Mindy who smiled back sweetly and answered a ringing phone. As Alicia ducked into the room, she slyly observed Minnie as she chattered. Something was wrong about her uniform. Her clothes looked less "busy." Mindy patted absently at her chest as she talked, uneasiness creasing her eyes.

Alicia retired to the back couch of the activities room, arms crossed defiantly. Whatever was wrong with Mindy's uniform nagged at Alicia.

She watched the young blue-haired woman from the cafeteria. The longer Alicia watched her emaciated form interact with the ethers, the more deeply she felt the edge of life's brutalities scrape and cut her own skin. But after several minutes she began to wonder if the woman truly saw something that Alicia couldn't. Who was the crazy one?

The young woman seemed to suddenly notice Alicia. The air thickened with the woman's sweat as she approached.

"Thank you for what you did." The woman wiped stray hairs from her mouth. A faint southern accent dusted her words.

"Any decent person would have done it."

"Not with hurt wrists."

"They'd try."

"I have a message for you."

"A message? From whom?" Alicia leaned back in the couch, amused at the suggestion. *Gimme more of the crazy. I can take it.*

"Lillian."

"And what does Lillian have to say?"

The woman paused, gaze brushing the ceiling before her eyes rolled up into her sockets. When the irises emerged, she stared at Alicia with unfathomable compassion, her eyes misted by some revelation. "She wants to know why you left her in the rose garden. It made her sad."

The caveman in Alicia's head began to holler, slamming a club against her hollow memory. *Lillian. Lillian.* Who was she? That name was incredibly familiar but no matter how far or widely it roamed, Alicia's memory could not place it in time and space. Like the word that falls out of a person's head as they age, Lillian the person fell into some chasm of memory that made Alicia quake. She'd have to ask her grandmother if she remembered Lillian. "Who told you this?"

"Lillian," the woman said.

"Where is she?"

"Over there." The woman pointed to the corner of the room.

Alicia saw nothing except sodium light spilling against the dayroom walls. How did this woman know about the rose garden? It wasn't possible she'd overheard something from her discussion with her grandmother because she'd arrived sometime after that conversation. Alicia also wondered what had become of her grandmother in the last twenty-four hours. It's so unlike her not to be involved at every opportunity.

"How do you know Lillian?"

The girl shrugged. "I don't. She just showed up over there. You can't see her?"

Alicia shook her head. *Oh, great. Sylvia Brown's in the house.* Alicia didn't believe in ghosts but now she had to wonder. In fact, she needed to recalibrate her entire supernatural belief system.

"What's your name?"

"Geri," she said. "Are you Alicia?"

"Yeah. How did you know?"

"Lillian told me."

"I see. What're you in for?"

"I get very sad," she said. "The voices told me to break up razors in my yogurt a few days ago. My family says I need to come here sometimes."

Alicia gulped, wondering what razors felt like on the inside. She decided she didn't want to know. In truth, she wanted as far away from this woman as possible, but she had to press on. "That's awful. Are you hurt?"

"They caught me before I could eat it. I just wanted to die. No one understands that. They think you're crazy when you want to die. When you just want to be free of the horrible depression. And the voices. I hate the voices." She hugged herself, eyes brimming with pain.

"I'm with you."

"Really?"

"Yeah. Not about the voices. But I totally get everything else."

Geri smiled shyly. "You're very nice."

Alicia felt guilty for her desire to bolt. "Thanks. So...how do you know Lillian?"

Before Geri could answer, Jesus dashed inside. He peeled off his white T-shirt and jumped up on the coffee table where two patients played cards. They cursed him loudly as he threw open wide his naked arms to proudly proclaim:

"I AM JESUS FUCKIN' CHRIST!"

Alicia rolled her eyes, annoyed at the Son of God for disrupting her interrogation.

"Hey, Ms. Baum!"

Arnie leaned into the room, working on a fresh piece of gum from the smell of it. The curly head of her attorney, Malcom, poked into the room alongside him. Malcom waved, his arm swathed in his usual granite suit.

"Hey, Mal."

"Hey, soldier." He shouldered a massive bag of briefs. "Let's get you out of here."

Alicia practically leapt from the couch. Malcom hugged her—gently at first, but then harder, and she reciprocated. It had been a couple of years since she'd seen him, but he still smelled vaguely like matzo ball soup and cheap cologne. They chatted for a few minutes in the hallway as Arnie kept vigil.

"So what's going to happen?"

"Just be cool. Don't exercise that wicked wit of yours."

"What wit? It's been bled from me."

"That's not funny. Look, the first certificate has been filed with the State Attorney's Office. They've only been legally able to hold you up to twenty-four hours. At this evaluation they can decide to file the second certificate, which will mean they can keep you here until the court hearing for involuntary admission."

"So basically we need this to go well or I'm fucked," Alicia said.

"Not permanently. Just for a few days until the hearing. Then we'll see."

Alicia felt panicked. "Shit."

"Don't worry. You're safe here, aren't you? Anything I need to know about?"

Alicia shook her head but she wanted to cry.

Malcom's face looked pained. "Why'd you do this, Leesha? Why didn't you call someone? Sara and I—we care about you, you know? Lots of people care about you. Don't you get that? I'm so sorry if we were bad friends. We really do care. Do you understand?"

Alicia's gaze fell to her shoes. How could she explain about the void? There were no people in the void. Well wishes brought no light, no hope. The moment that darkness flooded her skull and she took her life, her thinking was so twisted, it was as if nothing and no one else in the universe existed but her and her pain.

Arnie—who'd been standing a safe distance away to give them some privacy—motioned with his head. "Time for your evaluation, Ms. Baum."

Chapter 17

Feared.

Dr. Mason Sark sniffed and cleared his throat as he urinated.

Feared. And desired.

He sniffed harder, shook himself off, tucked his monster in his boxers, and zipped his trousers. As his habit, he washed his hands in tepid water with a good dose of liquid pink soap while examining his chin in the mirror.

Dashing. But not excessively so.

He dried his hands and opened the men's room with the damp paper towel he'd just used. He stood almost six-feet, five-inches tall, a full foot above the stream of medical personnel milling the hallways. Glacial blue irises drifted nonchalantly as he wiped a strand of hair from his high forehead. He was amused to hear that the nurses on the fifth floor called him "Hugh."

Waves of people parted before him. He nodded "Good morning" to those who greeted him and pointedly ignored those who did not, doling out his attention with papal grandiosity.

As in "Grant."

The door to the evaluation room loomed before him. He checked his watch. Two minutes before the nine a.m. evaluation for patient Alicia R. Baum—the one who so kept his ward in a constant state of turbulence. Absolutely flawless timing. The door stood ajar and voices filtered into the hallway. He pressed into the office without a word of warning, relishing the fact that his presence was not expected at the evaluation. The bland office contained a ring of chairs with various staff occupying them. Dr. Paul Stemmle, internist. Arnold Fleischer, R.N. (one of his own, chewing gum, a singularly disgusting habit). Olivia Hoenemier, the overly muscular social worker. Probably lesbian.

And the troublesome Ms. Baum. She sulked at the far end of the table, arms slung across her chest. He wasn't much for blonds, but he liked her look. Still, he felt her sort was best kept at arm's length. Too hard to control. Dr. Sark noted that Alicia was entirely too comfortable there with her attorney.

Where was that incompetent devil, Farron? He narrowly missed having to take Farron onto his staff. Under the halcyon wings of Dr. Dulac, he nested within the great children's hospital services where his failing performance could fester like a cracked egg in a forgotten bin. Thanks to the unmitigated negligence of the trustees who made the donation, the funds went to the children's hospital instead of mental health. *They* hired a part-time child psychiatrist, while M.H. laid off two more RNs.

"Good morning, everyone," Dr. Sark intoned. "Are we ready to begin?"

"James isn't here yet," Dr. Stemmle replied. The other participants shook their heads. "He called fifteen minutes ago from upstairs. He'll be here soon."

Just as Arnie scratched his head and offered to find him, Dr. Farron stepped inside the conference room and closed the door. Heavy lines on his face, he leaned back against the door and tucked a thick chart under his arm. "I apologize for being late," he said, out of breath. He sat at the table, acknowledging everyone.

Dr. Sark hated the histrionics of literary depressives. Without exception, they were attention-seeking whores with a sense of entitlement bigger than Mount Rushmore. She had two strikes against her—three if you counted how much he hated her attorney's hair.

"Alicia, I want you to meet the members of your evaluation team, some of whom you already know," Dr. Farron continued. He introduced each by name, including Dr. Sark, who noted her eyes lingering with him. Was she smiling? "So, Alicia," Dr. Farron asked, "how do you feel?"

"Alive," she said, looking directly at Dr. Farron.

"Can you elaborate?"

"I've had sort of a spiritual awakening these last twenty-four hours," she replied. "It's the beginning of a new journey."

Dr. Sark rolled his eyes. *Snotty artist manipulating the vocabulary of recovery and life coaching.*

Dr. Stemmle asked, "How about your wrists?"

"They're kind of sore and weak, but okay. Or at least they will be okay."

"You got quite a shiner there on your chin."

Alicia said nothing for a moment. "It's nothing. I was trying to defend a girl in the cafeteria and I was assaulted. I should have minded my own business."

Oh, you miserable failure, Farron. You look so disappointed. Clearly she's hoping to minimize her past behavior with the others. All the better.

Dr. Farron looked around the table. "Does anyone have any other questions for Alicia?"

Olivia spoke up. "Alicia, if we were to let you go home, who would you stay with? Or would you be alone?"

"I'd stay with my grandmother," she replied. "She's in town for a bit. I'm sure she'd want to stay with me at the house."

Dr. Farron looked uneasy.

"I've missed her," Alicia added.

"What about friends? Other family?"

She admitted that, while she hadn't much family in the country, she'd neglected her relationships, insisting that she'd start rebuilding connections right away.

Dr. Farron was strangely quiet. He let Olivia and Paul direct most of the meeting.

Dr. Sark grew impatient, bringing the session to and end. "Is that all, Dr. Farron?"

Farron slid Dr. Sark a patronizing look. "That is, in fact, all, Dr. Sark. You can go, Alicia. We'll talk later."

Alicia stood, thanked everyone, and left, saving her last glance for Dr. Farron. Her attorney remained behind.

Once the door closed, the rancor started. "Obviously, we agree on the condition of this patient," Dr. Sark said. "She's medically stable, she's prescribed Celexa, she's clearly unhappy in my ward and should be released to her home."

Dr. Stemmle nodded. "She'll have to return in a week to have the stitches removed, and continue with some physical therapy thereafter, but otherwise she's medically stable."

Dr. Farron looked to Arnie. "Arnie?"

Dr. Sark's glare settled on Arnie, who scratched his elbow nervously as he spoke. "Ms. Baum had two... incidents...yesterday." He squirmed as Dr. Sark leaned back, crossing his legs as if shutting a trap. "Um...one at dinner time." Arnie looked away from Dr. Sark and toward Dr. Farron, whose face reflected far more concern. "She seemed to have a real hard session with Dr. Farron just prior to displaying quite a bit of agitation and was aggressive with another patient."

In the slot of silence, Dr. Sark sat up straight in his chair to further settle the matter. "She can continue under your private care, if you wish."

"Well, I have to recommend that she stays," Dr. Farron said. Then, to Alicia's attorney, "She's not stable and she can't stay with her grandmother."

"Reasons?" Mr. Shefter asked.

"This morning her grandmother was admitted for three severe strokes. I can't believe she was even ambulatory when they found her wandering in the hotel lobby. She's in surgery as we speak. Dr. Gregg is her surgeon."

Dr. Sark folded his hands and leaned forward with a pedantic hunch. "And you think this has bearing on your patient's stability?" He knew he needed to make an appearance this morning. Arnold's observations alone would have guaranteed the woman's stay.

"She attempted suicide three days ago." Dr. Farron closed the thick folder. "Her grandmother was her primary caregiver from early childhood into her teens. So, sure! Yes! This has some bearing."

"Just remember that we do not cater to histrionic artistic types sniffing for sympathy," Dr. Sark reminded him. "This is the East Bay, not Beverly Hills."

"Oh, come on! If she finds out about her grandmother—"

"And your paternalism is *completely* out of line, Farron," Dr. Sark sneered.

Mr. Shefter looked skeptical. "How did you find out, doctor?"

"They found my card in her purse. They saw the M.D. and thought maybe I was her physician."

Olivia shook her head. "I'm not comfortable with sending her home just yet, either. She has no one to stay with."

"Correction," the attorney said. "My wife and I. We could take care of her. We're old friends."

"That's good. But she's having outbursts," Olivia said, making a note. "She needs more monitoring. James, has she been talking about this spiritual awakening in your sessions?"

"Oh, yes. I do believe that's genuine, as she reports having had a near-death experience. She truly is on a spiritual path. And we're making progress already. I think she's open to getting better. I just don't think home is the right environment at the moment."

Control over the room slithered from Dr. Sark's grasp, making him profoundly uncomfortable. "Well, Dr. Farron, perhaps Ms. Baum is not quite ready for release. However, if she continues to be agitated and engage in fights with other patients, I will recommend that she be transferred to county. Her insurance isn't going to hold up here." He paused as Farron registered the threat with precisely the level of distress for which Dr. Sark had hoped, judging by the way his eyes flickered as if he'd spotted police lights in his rearview mirror. Farron disliked being out of control as much as anyone. Further, Dr. Sark suspected from the way he looked at Alicia Baum that Farron was attracted to her.

Dr. Farron nodded as he recovered from the statement. "I'll continue to work with her until she stabilizes."

"I'm sure we'll do everything that we can," he said, squinting meanly at Arnie, which made him squirm. Dr. Sark, of course, was completely indifferent to the level of discomfort he had created among the team. Dr. Stemmle and Olivia excused themselves, following Arnie, who escaped Harry Potter-like under a blanket of who-the-hell-cares-about-me-anyway-ness into the hallway.

Mr. Shefter shook hands with Dr. Farron and the rest of the staff, crestfallen. "This scenario has already been explained to her."

Dr. Sark stood to leave, straightening his coat. But before he cleared the exit, Dr. Farron leaned against the door, eyes narrowed with the resolve of a mongoose taunting a cobra.

The director worked up a biting smile before he delivered his last and worst blow. "She looks a bit like Gina, doesn't she?"

And with that, he bid the doctor a good day, having just slaughtered Dr. Farron's peace of mind. As Dr. Sark left the evaluation room, he smiled to himself.

Invoke the murdered wife. Good call, Sark.

Good call.

Chapter 18

Alicia was pulled into yet another damned group therapy session immediately after her evaluation. She wanted to ask Rachelle if she could talk to her grandmother. Alicia was dying to ask her about Lillian. No matter how much the therapist tried to involve her, Alicia did not share what had brought her to these rooms, much less what happened in death. It was her precious secret. The therapist did not pressure her, thankfully. Alicia suspected that the therapist was glad enough for the author to slouch indifferently in the corner and not make trouble. Alicia studied each patient as they contributed a piece of personal agony to the pot. She imagined them as characters in a story, wondering what she could steal with impunity.

After the session, she ate a snack in the cafeteria. Dr. Farron leaned against the wall beside the doorway. She noticed him and an irresistible grin not only sliced through the sludge of her mood, but her entire body lightened. Curiosity about the results of the evaluation faded behind her sheer joy at seeing him. She liked a man who knew when to apologize—What woman wouldn't?—but his general good humor and caring nature charmed the snakes right out of her basket. He smiled wearily back at her, looking like he'd been beaten with a spiky stick. Today he wore a Transformers tie with Unicron's metallic orange bat-like wings cut off where they splayed beyond the border against a black background.

"How are you?" he asked as she walked with him to the elevator.

"Bored as hell," she confessed. "I take it back. Hell could never be so boring as this."

"I bet," he replied.

"Did you watch the DVD?"

"Not yet, but I promise I will tonight," he said. "What is it?"

"Not telling. Promise you'll watch it."

"Okay, I promise," he said.

They stepped into the elevator and weariness washed over his haggard face as he leaned against the back wall. When they arrived at Dr. Farron's office, Alicia stood instead of sitting in the loveseat. "I'm not going home today, am I?"

Dr. Farron hung his head for a moment. "The consensus is that you aren't quite stable enough to leave. *But*," he interjected, "I think you will be. You've just had too much to process in too short a period of time. It sounds like your subconscious mind is opening up. That's work we can continue after you leave."

"Why can't I go?"

"The team wants to see more stability. You've been to some dark places lately. They want to make sure that when you go home any further events don't make you spiral."

She doubted what he was saying for some reason as her panic for freedom silently shattered the air-conditioned stillness of the office. Paranoia shouted in her ear. Was he keeping her out of spite? But why would he do such a thing? Maybe out of self-interest? He didn't have the information he wanted about Mr. Wicker. The decision wasn't his alone, she assured herself. Yet she continued to wonder if he was trustworthy, acknowledging that she wasn't even certain how to test something like that again. "How much longer do I have to stay?"

"I don't know."

"You mean," she asked, sitting on the edge of the love seat, "I could be here indefinitely?" She felt her eyes heating with tears, but they were burned away with rage.

"No, no. We usually keep suicide victims for seventy-two hours and then if it's warranted we put a hold on someone, but they can contest it in court. Besides, your insurance will run out in twenty days."

"Twenty *days?*"

"Now hang on. You won't be here anywhere near that long, I'm certain."

"Dr. Shark made me stay, didn't he?"

"Where did you hear that name?" Dr. Farron asked, as if he knew exactly where she'd heard that name.

"I can't tell you." She suddenly felt protective of Rachelle.

Dr. Farron opened his mouth in a silent *aaahh.* That bruised look splotched his face again. "Are you okay? You can call your attorney if you need to."

"No, I'm okay. Are you?"

He smiled. "I'm fine. So, what else is going on?"

The moment arrived with a salute and a kick to the shins. She had to decide if she was going to trust this man. If she did, he might be able to help her retrieve what she so desperately wanted.

You left her in the rose garden.

"I had a dream about the rose garden. It's not really a rose garden, though. It's more like some tall rose bushes planted in a circle. It might not have anything to do with the real thing, but it definitely felt familiar."

"Really? What else do you remember from the dream?" He pinched his lower lip, puzzling over what she relayed. At last, he interjected, "It has to be there. We can definitely get it, but we have to keep trying. Are you in?"

"I guess." They say that men want to leave their mark on the world through either violence or art. Alicia wanted that as much as any man did, perhaps more so, and she had recently been robbed on both counts. No art. Impotent violence. What was left? "Besides," she said, "I heard something weird today. The girl in lockdown—you remember, the one I was trying to defend in the cafeteria? Geri? She told me that I'd left someone named Lillian in the rose garden. Can you believe it? I was dumbfounded."

"How bizarre," he said.

"It was very creepy. The things is, I don't remember anyone named Lillian," Alicia said. "And neither does Geri. She was just talking to the wall. But I have this terrible feeling that I should. Like someone Lillian-shaped has been snipped out of my memory, leaving a black shape where there should be a flesh and blood person."

"We can look for her, too. And don't forget, I'll be here if you go anywhere traumatic," he said.

The darkness came as before in gentle exhalations.

She found herself out of breath as her wee feet drove hard into the dry grass, hot winds glancing off the balding hillside that bowed far to her left. The sky sizzled with buttery light. Skinned knees burned when she fell in the field. She picked herself up and kept running.

"Where are you?" Dr. Farron asked from his big, safe nowhere-place.

"If I cry enough, they will melt from the top of my head," she replied in her little girl voice.

As she rounded the bend in the hillside, a chasm appeared to have been carved from the bulging earth. Dead grass bristled around the lips of the opening, eroded by the wind. Cool dirt walls enveloped her as she skirted the iron tracks that stretched into the blackness. Standing on the tracks, she pounded her fists into her thighs and let the sorrow choke her. Her disappointment in the God they talked about in Sunday school class led her deep into that black, soulless place where hope slept and never woke. Another slice of her soul blew away in the Santa Ana winds across the fields and hills of Simi Valley.

Tentatively, Alicia stepped farther into the chasm, rocks crunching beneath her Mary Janes. She clenched her fists harder. The heat retreated as the blackness of the tunnel embraced her, holding her cheeks with muggy hands as they invited her into the inky depths. Knees stinging.

Then, a pinprick of light winked at her from the nothingness. This time, she vowed. This time...

She choked on clouds of dust as the train rumbled forward. A cold beam of light broke across the tracks.

She stood her ground, eyes closed tightly. One...two...

The train horn blared, howling as it sped toward her.

...three...

Then, at the last minute, train horn blaring, deafening—Alicia jumped from the track. Sobbing, she hugged the tunnel wall as the train thundered past her. The chaos welled behind her, and she wished desperately that she had allowed it to tear away her bones. Crumpled like a dust rag against the dirty tunnel wall, she would not be noticed by the conductor. She wished so desperately not to be seen.

To vanish.

Alicia held her knees to her body as she doubled up on the love seat. The fever-grief snaked into the coils of her belly.

Dr. Farron folded his hands on his lap and watched her as she fought the outpouring. "It's rare for children that young to attempt suicide," he said at last. "Really rare."

She rested her cheek on her knees and bit down so no tears would come. "When I was in college, I read a book that really fucked me up, and now I know why."

"What was it?"

"It was called *The Last of the Just*. At one point, the main character, who's a seven-year-old boy, runs through the fields smashing insects into his mouth. He was pretending they were the children who bullied him. When he reaches his home, he throws himself from the upstairs bathroom window."

"He lived?"

Alicia nodded.

He looked beaten again, and her compassion went out to him rather than herself.

Soon, Arnie arrived and Alicia left with him. Grief gave way to sheer fucking annoyance as her situation grated on her patience. Unused to any amount of restraint, she mentally beat against her bars and shrieked inwardly in defiance. As they stepped into the elevator, Arnie reassured her that lunch was "pretty kickin'" today as he fumbled in his pocket for his security card. "Let's get this thing moving so we can eat!" He swiped his security card in the slot.

And then, the realization razed every synapse between her ears. She knew what was missing from Minnie Mouse's neck.

Her security card lanyard.

Chapter 19

Alicia brushed her hair until it fell in gentle wisps that curled around her chin and over her breasts. With some pain and trouble, she then dabbed on makeup that she had begged Rachelle to bring her from the downstairs pharmacy. Perhaps men don't notice that sort of thing, she thought, but they appreciate the overall effect. Lashes long and dark, a light pink t-shirt slit down the front worn with snug yoga pants that she folded down around her hips, the lavender sweater draped loosely over her shoulders. She even pulled off a trick with some lip liner and a slightly lighter shade of lipstick to give her those Angelina Jolie lips that Mindy had. It was nearly impossible to avoid both Rachelle and Arnie, but after Rachelle told her she'd not been able to reach her grandmother on the phone, Alicia executed Phase I of her plan: an afternoon of nervous pacing, disappearing into various halls to simulate isolation. An understandable reaction to the news she'd received that morning.

In Phase II, she skulked outside Dr. Sark's office after slipping past orderlies to reach the administration hall during one of Jesus' sermons. (She noted that they did not monitor that door very well in general.) At around three-thirty p.m., the long strides of Dr. Sark echoed in the hallway as he approached the office. He was alone. As she had observed in the evaluation, he seemed perhaps in his early forties and was definitely attractive. There was something predatory about him. *This guy's the one who's cleaning up around here, not Dr. Farron.* She leaned against the wall beside his office door, hands behind her back, thrusting her hips slightly forward. When he rounded the corner, he abruptly broke stride at the sight of her.

"How did you get back here?"

"Dr. Sark?" Just as he looked as if he would object, she coyly bit her bottom lip. "I've heard a lot about you."

Dr. Sark's cheeks reddened as she stroked his ego. "What do you want? You should be talking to your psychiatrist." He unlocked his office door. "Dr. Farron, isn't it?"

"Well, that's what I want to discuss with you," she said. "For a moment." Her tongue softly flickered over her lips as she fixed him with a hungry look.

After gauging her for a moment, he pushed open the door and held out his hand, inviting her to enter before him.

His pristine office menaced its visitors from every direction: a print of Degas' dejected absinthe drinkers hung on the far wall, while on another Goya's crazed Saturn devoured the bloody body of his son. Fuseli's haunting image of *The Nightmare* hung just above his uncluttered desk on the wall behind him. The cold, bald eyes of the stallion surveyed the imp crouching on the chest of the tormented female sleeper.

Somewhere in the background a stereo softly played a Vivaldi concerto, passionate violin strains warming the room. He crossed the room to the CD player tucked in a bookcase. As his back briefly turned, Alicia's eyes searched the spotless floor. Did Mindy already retrieve the lost security card? Or did it lie on the floor behind his desk, at the rolling feet of the massive black leather chair, where she most likely performed her "rounds?"

He switched off the music.

"No, please. I love Vivaldi," she said. "That's his *L'Estro Armonico*, isn't it?"

Dr. Sark blinked with surprise. "As you wish." He turned to the bookcase and switched the music back on. When he did so, Alicia slipped behind his desk and sat in his chair. She took a long, steady look at the floor as she leaned back.

The security card lanyard snaked from under the rollers.

"I love your artwork," she said, a sultry grin on her lips. "No one else here seems to have much imagination." She tipped the chair back slightly to survey the painting above her. "I saw that Fuseli at the British Museum. Sark's an English name. Do you have family there?"

"I must ask you to vacate my desk, Ms. Baum," Dr. Sark stated, voice wavering. "And I would be happy to hear your complaint." Clearly something about her both unnerved and intrigued him. Perhaps he was still weak in the knees from his early morning encounter? The fact that he let her in his office was highly unprofessional and dangerous—that much she guessed.

"Oh, it's no complaint," Alicia said. She bit the skin of her thumb and, with just her eyes, she stripped him to his boxers. She decided he was definitely a boxers kind of guy.

Transfixed by her, he took a step back and crossed his arms. "Then—then what is it?" he stammered.

Alicia enjoyed that slip of composure immensely. She stood up, keeping her eyes locked with his, smoke and burn. "I just want to know one thing."

She let the sweater slip from her shoulders onto the floor by the chair over the security card, pushed the chair back as she stood to release the lanyard from the wheels, and then circled around the desk as she moved toward him. Biting her lip coyly again, she halted just beside him. His cologne a rummy ghost in her nostrils, she whispered in his ear. "Who...do I have...to *blow*...to get out of here?"

He stared at her, terror and temptation flapping in his eyes. He opened his mouth to say something, but shut it just as quickly. Vivaldi spoke for him with firm downward strokes that ended in trembling, tenebrous chords. Clearly he was accustomed to being the one in control, and this situation threatened to unravel his dignity. He inhaled deeply, and then closed his eyes for a beat as he exhaled. When his eyes flickered open, she noted that he caught her cleavage, which she'd strategically placed beneath his vantage point.

A storm of adrenaline rained on her sternum as he took her by the shoulders, his large hands cosseting her. Alicia wondered for a moment if she would actually have to go through with this. She thought she would shake him up and maybe get herself booted into extra therapy, at the very worst. At best, she would find the security card and pray that it had not yet been switched off. But she then remembered that this man held an inordinate amount of power over her well being at the moment. *Stupid fucking girl. It's not worth it.*

The ice of Dr. Sark's eyes trickled under the swelling heat of his undisguised lusts. He raised his arm like a wing, inviting her inside, and put his arm around her shoulders—a fatherly gesture except for the way his strong fingers gripped her skin. "Ms. Baum, wherefore would you wish to leave our lovely ward? Is it not comfortable? Is it devoid of some...pleasure...necessary to your healing?"

A riot of emotions—mostly about Dr. Farron—burned and looted every ounce of her resolve to continue with her plan. "Perhaps you're right. I'm in a hurry to leave, and for what?" Flashing him a knowing grin, she turned her face to his and felt a faint rush of excitement at the idea of doing something so incredibly dangerous. However, the rush faded as his cheeks glowed again, this time with victory.

"Nothing. Absolutely nothing. Everything you need is right here." He clutched her shoulder to emphasize the last word. *Here. In this office. With me.* He then bent his neck to whisper into her ear. His breath was sour. Sulphuric. "Whatever it is, you just...have... to ask. And maybe, just maybe, your stay will go quicker."

The Lake of Hell lapped at Alicia's cheeks. "I'd best be back before they miss me."

Disappointment waved a hand over his face, and the intensity dissipated. His long fingers unwrapped from her upper arm, releasing her from his predatory embrace.

Alicia moved toward the desk.

"Ms. Baum!"

Alicia deftly gathered up the sweater over the security card, tucking the lanyard into the folds of lavender knitting. "I will—" she said, standing abruptly as Dr. Sark rounded the desk. The massive chair bumped the back of her knees and Dr. Sark loomed over her from the other side, his entire body radiating against hers. She clutched the sweater to her chest with one hand and, with the other, she pressed a finger to his bottom lip. "Ask, that is." That fingertip held back The Beast for a moment as he contemplated her touch. Terror and temptation. He then stepped aside, gesturing gallantly for her to pass.

Dr. Farron booted up his laptop and signed into Outlook. He already had an answer from Connie at Emergency Services for Alameda County:

hiya james!

how you doing? haven't heard from you in some time. no problemo with getting your patient's call. :) easy to find. really weird tho. you'll see what i mean.

lets have lunch next week and catchup. just name a time.

connie

He checked the attachment. No ACI printout. The file had a .mov extension. Probably a sound file.

really weird tho. you'll see what i mean.

Ah, Christ. Yes, okay. He loosened his tie. As he downloaded the file, the drawing of Mr. Wicker skulked against the wall, deriding him for not uncovering the mysteries lingering in his eyes. Dr. Farron could do nothing but clench his fists and pace the office until the progress bar indicated a full download.

When the longest two minutes of his life ended, he clicked "Open File" and watched Quicktime open a sound bar. He clicked the Play arrow.

Hissssssssssss

The female operator's voice crackled. "9-1-1. What is your emergency?"

Then, a voice dropped octaves into Dr. Farron's soul. Ancient. Inhuman.

"It's not my emergency. It's Alicia Baum's."

"What is the emergency for Ms. Baum, sir?"

"She has committed suicide."

"Where are you located sir?"

"Between the worlds."

"Could you repeat that?"

"No."

"Is she conscious? What's her disposition?"

"In the bath. Surrounded by blood."

"Sir, I want you to hold the line for a few seconds while we—"

Click.

"What the hell?"

Then, another voice. A male dispatcher.

"Shit, I couldn't copy any of that! What was his address?"

"No address on the API."

"Hang on...Alicia Baum. There's one in Alameda County. Five-two-two-five Pala Avenue."

"Ambulance is on its way."

Between the worlds.

The muscles in Dr. Farron's legs fought every impulse to bolt to the elevator. After sitting stunned for ten minutes, he dialed Rachelle's nurses' station.

"Rachelle! Hi—can I see Alicia again? It's urgent. Can Arnie bring her? Okay, I'll wait."

The time it took for Alicia to get there was the second eternity of the afternoon.

Chapter 20

Alicia feared that she'd been spotted coming out of Dr. Sark's office when she was soon thereafter summoned to Dr. Farron's office. She'd stashed the lanyard and ID card under the cushions of the couch in the activities room and slid the security card into her slipper. By the accumulation of detritus under the cushions, she surmised that no one would find it for some time.

Arnie deposited her just inside the threshold where she stood quivering as a disheveled Dr. Farron paced the room. If there had ever been any doubt, she now understood that something had taken root for this man. He stared at her a moment as if seeing her for the first time. He noticed she had cleaned up, as it were.

"You look great! I mean, you must be feeling better, right?"

Alicia nodded.

"Why don't you have a seat? I have something to play for you."

He pulled a swivel office chair right up next to his, tilting the laptop so that she could hear. She sat beside him behind the desk. And listened...

The voice—*his* voice—twisted her up so badly inside that she doubled over and held herself, yet she resisted any other reaction. She turned her gaze from the infernal drawing that still hung on the wall back to the Quicktime screen, biting her bottom lip until her mouth stung.

"Do you know who that was?" Dr. Farron asked her when it finished.

Alicia shook her head. She wanted to tell him—badly.

Dr. Farron studied her for a moment. "He doesn't sound like he's on a cell phone. His voice is really clear and there's no background noise. Except—well, I don't know. I think maybe he has a pet bird."

A raven. Or twenty.

"Is there any possibility someone got into the house?"

"Not really. The street below is too steep for random foot traffic."

His eyes narrowed with suspicion. "That wasn't a neighbor, then?"

"None that I know."

He replayed it, stopping it at one point. "Between the worlds? Have any idea what that means?"

Alicia had always been a convincing liar when she cared to deceive and usually was guilty of giving Too Much Information. She honestly did not wish to deceive Dr. Farron, but she could see no alternative. She would not alienate this man any more than she had; she wanted to be closer to him, not further away. And insisting on Mr. Wicker's existence caused arguments not agreements. Any more such discussions would distract from what she wanted to accomplish, which was to retrieve her lost memory. She reasoned further that, if she could somehow keep the peace and give him some evidence of her recovery, then perhaps they would let her go. But she couldn't count on that. The security card burned in her slipper against her sole. She was dying to be free.

"Does my grandma know I'm still here? I need to talk to her. She'll know who Lillian is."

Dr. Farron fiddled with the mouse, clicking and dragging things on the screen. "She's made no inquiries that I'm aware of."

"That's odd. She usually becomes overly involved in my life given half a chance."

He closed the screen to the laptop and looked at her. That "*whoosh!*" of attraction soared through her like a 1962 Riviera speeding over the Golden Gate Bridge. She gripped her chair seat, pressing her fingers into the fabric-covered cardboard stapled to the underbelly. The whole cushion seemed to widen and turn hot beneath her. The peppery stew of starch, sandalwood cologne, and salt sweat washed down her throat as she inhaled him.

He smiled. "I should take you back. I have to report to ER in a few."

Alicia couldn't stand it any longer. She reached out and wrapped her fingers around his Transformer tie.

"What are you doing?" he asked, an alarm clanging so loudly in his eyes she thought he'd drop-and-cover.

She suppressed a giggle. She wanted to pull him toward her and drink him like a chocolate shake, but instead she tightened his tie and tugged it straight. Digging a finger under his curled collar, she pulled it out and patted it flat around his neck.

"I'm just making you more presentable, Doctor."

He took her back to her ward and deposited her at her room. From then until the lights winked out in every room but hers, she masterminded her escape.

Chapter 21

Jay? Where'd you put the tape?

In the junk drawer!

In your junk drawer? Or mine?

His hand hovered over the open drawer as Gina's words lingered between his ears. When silence at last settled, he plunged his hand into the drawer and burrowed until he found the DVD connector that he'd put off replacing. He'd been living alone now for three years, so he could let things go like the bedroom DVD; the greasy mechanical detritus in the garage; and the dust swarming over the shelves of medical books. He shambled upstairs to the bedroom.

Even as a child, he'd excelled at obsession. Tonight he rehearsed this life skill by ruminating over the conversation with Alicia. What the hell? She knew who that was. Why wouldn't she tell him? This whole goddamned adventure was trying him on every level. He would have to commit countless acts of onanism in her name to escape the deadly undertow of attraction to her, just as he did today when he returned to the office.

As the runt of the family, he'd spent his childhood in books and sketchpads in the lengthy shadow of two older sisters—Amelia and Simone—who'd toured Europe by puberty as violin prodigies. The benefit was that he understood women better than most of his friends by the time he hit high school. The detriment? He might as well have been a haunt in the hallways. Despite his prodigious talents with ink and charcoal, as well as his relentless intellect, he never had the courage to pursue any of his female interests. A string of crushes kept him inspired but lonely throughout the early years as he trailed his sisters' reputations. Teachers compared his serious and sensitive nature to his sisters' unfavorably, even though the eldest was obsessive-compulsive and could not suffer anyone to crease a sheet of her music without throwing a tantrum. She subsequently memorized her music, including huge volumes of Paganini, memorializing herself with teachers and students alike. At the arts magnet school they attended, his four-point-five GPA meant nothing to anyone.

Then something changed his senior year. A scholarship. To Cal State Berkeley.

He packed up and left his stunned parents in Sacramento, the quiet capital of California. The day before he drove away from the house, his mother had taken him by the shoulders and exclaimed "You're leaving!" as if he had just announced his departure. What she'd really meant was: you're leaving *me*. He had always been her Rock of Gibraltar in the ocean of neurotic talent and marital discord.

"I'll just be two hours away, Mom. Don't worry." The truth was, she never did worry. Not about him, anyway. He kissed her, hugged his tall, withdrawn father, and climbed into the car with the secrets of his father's debts, his mother's resentment, and a thousand bruises in his ears from his sisters' neurotic banter.

In college, James Farron felt like an old soul in the midst of reckless freedom seekers, annoyed by the raucous parties and vapid conversations of his peers. He despised his dreadlocked dorm mate who donned a halo of pot smoke at breakfast and belched fine clouds of beer foam at night. He'd done the drinking thing in the middle of high school while his parents obsessed over his sisters' graduations and college admissions. It seemed childish to immerse oneself in it now, when one had to pay to be here. How stupid was that? Eventually he befriended the same kind of crowd he ultimately did in high school— the hyper-intellectual social outcasts. Not hard to find at Cal.

But when he started dating a redheaded rocket scientist with an Irish Catholic family, he not only rediscovered his roots but found that he loved the hoards of wee ones that drooled and wiggled around the grandparents' house during the holidays. In the endless hours of cartoons, play, crying, Cheetos, nap, rinse, repeat, he found the childhood he'd lost when managing the demanding emotions of his crazy but brilliant older sisters. Although he and the redhead broke up after two years, he was already diving into psychology books to understand the children. Child Psychology shouldered its way into a double major, as he was unwilling to give up his art. After graduation, he nearly killed himself and his social life getting through medical school.

He was still doing his supervised training when he met Gina, the woman he would marry. And with her he'd have the only supernatural experience he could ever recall—if that was what it was.

On a trip to Chicago for his friend Albert's wedding, he and several of the guys were celebrating at the Red Lion Pub. That's when he met the strawberry blond with marcasite eyes, apple red lips, and a mischievous look that reminded him of Maleficent, the bad fairy in *Sleeping Beauty*. She smelled like a field of orange blossoms. A very talented pianist, she had just recorded her first album of original jazz and mood pieces. She was to perform the next night at Blues, "the best blues bar in town," where Rosey the bartender would pour her free shots of Tennessee bourbon.

Thoroughly smashed, they entangled themselves for quite some time in one corner of the murky Red Lion. The low ceilings descended on the patrons' heads like the hands of a father blessing their debauchery. On every wall was a London Underground poster or an RAF aircraft—the British Empire proudly planted a single flag in the midst of Lincoln Avenue.

She grabbed his hand. "Let's go upstairs."

James dove in for a kiss. "Why?" His hand slid down under her soft round ass. She wore lambskin leather and a tight t-shirt torn across the cleavage. A large safety pin held the gaping hole somewhat closed just above the words "Fuck Fashion."

"Why? Because we're not supposed to, that's why."

"Do you often do things you're not supposed to do?"

"Whenever I can." She kissed him, her breath sweetened with raspberry Stoli. She then pulled back, her eyes indicating the darkened staircase on the other side of the English phone booth. She watched the bar for a moment until Mike the talkative bartender had turned his back to continue another patron discussion.

"Go!"

They scurried to the staircase.

A wave of insobriety crashed against his legs when they reached the top, and he reached for the wall to steady himself. Gina seemed to know where she was going and crested the stairwell, landing beside a murky bar. She strode past and flipped on a light in a room far to the right, past where the bar ended. Somewhere a door was open to the outside, and those infamous winds flung a frosty hatchet across the room, slicing through his sweater. Putting a hand on the slick wooden bar, James willed his eyes to sculpt some sense from the darkness. A number of black and unshaped things defied definition. The far left end of the room appeared to be a balcony closed off by a sliding glass door. Moonlight cast an almost imperceptible haze over a corner booth and an empty music stand. Gina leaned from the room.

"Bathroom! I'll be right out!"

The bathroom door swung shut with a metallic complaint, leaving James in the dark—and cold—once more.

From inside the bathroom, Gina continued to comment. "Ugh! Smells like cheap lavender perfume!"

He found a stool beneath the bar beside him and sat down. The hands of Padre Patron warmed his cheeks, but the heavy dew of insobriety was rapidly evaporating from his brow.

James.

He did not recognize the slight voice. Maybe one of his buddies was calling him from downstairs? It reminded him of stirring the ashes in the fireplace. And how the hell did that girl find the bathroom in the dark? His night vision had always been poor, but damn! He pulled the stool out farther to get a better seat.

Jaaaaamesssss.

Something stood up just beyond the lunar haze to the right.

Every vein in his flesh tried to uproot itself and flee downstairs, but he couldn't move. He stopped breathing, clutching the bar top. A child's hand raised in the moonlight, wriggling fingers that barely brushed the faded luminance.

THUMP!

The sound knocked James off his stool. His hands flailed for the bar and missed. The child thing lowered its hand and pointed at him.

THUMP! THUMP!

"James!" Gina cried. "The door is stuck!"

Stumbling, he found himself turned backward. He lunged for the wall to his left, hands searching desperately for a light switch. He dove for the other side of the doorway. He was rewarded. A hanging light bulb flared in the center of the room.

Frozen again, James watched the empty room carefully for signs of life. Nothing but empty tables scattered the space. Cherry wood booths lined the left wall. The balcony's bare trellis was planted against the far wall, past the closed glass doors.

There were no open windows. Or doors. The room was warm.

Gina continued to beat on the bathroom door.

"Coming! I had to find a light!" he called. He approached the ladies' room door and yanked hard before the door came loose. The bathroom gasped with a ghastly cloud of flowery perfume when it released Gina. By then, Mike the bartender was banging his way up the staircase.

"Hey! What are you *doing* up here?" he bellowed.

"Nothing!" James returned, indicating the bathroom. "The door was stuck."

"Aaaahh, so you got trapped by Sharon," he said. "You're lucky you got out at all, the way she's been acting lately."

"Who's Sharon?" Gina asked as they followed him to the stairway.

"A retarded girl who used to live here," he replied.

"I didn't see anyone," Gina replied.

"Well, that's good," Mike said, shutting off the light. "Because she's dead."

She's dead.

Chapter 22

Alicia lay in bed with nothing but a thin blanket to hide the rebellion fomenting in her belly. Hypervigilant, she monitored every sound in the ward as she awaited the changing of the guard at eleven p.m. Before she left, Rachelle shuffled toward her room and looked in on her. Alicia feigned sleep. It was a trick she'd learned when she was a teen, how to imitate the subtle rhythms of unconscious breathing in order to fool her grandmother so that she could sneak out. She'd fooled her boyfriends and ex-husband many times into thinking she was asleep when she didn't want them to think she had been up waiting for them. Hell no! Those bastards would never have the benefit of believing she worried about their absence. If they were so oblivious as to stay out late and not call, they didn't deserve to know it upset her. She was especially pleased with the notion when she walked out on them. She woke up one of them mid snore to say goodbye specifically because she knew he would hate it.

Rachelle shifted in place, and then turned to leave. "Sleep well, Angel," she said out loud. Alicia opened one eye. Rachelle winked, hefted her workbag over a stiff shoulder, and left Alicia to the glaring light and her dastardly plans.

She would escape this damned place. Even if she had to wander like a homeless person, she would get herself out. Maybe hitch a ride. Rachelle let her call her grandmother twice this afternoon, but her cell phone had been turned off and the voicemail box was full. Thoroughly bizarre.

"Rachelle, what's happened to my grandma?" Alicia had asked. "I thought she was going to visit me."

"Dunno, Angel. Maybe she got some business to take care of. Or maybe she went home. Don't you have anyone else?"

Alicia shook her head. No one else she wanted to call, anyway. She hated admitting she needed help. How could she start now?

Goodnights and farewells were exchanged at the nurses' station down the hall. Rachelle mentioned nothing about her being awake to Brian, the wannabe Jock Doc. He was alone tonight with just Dean the orderly, as they were short-handed once again. Three new patients arrived today: two more suicide attempts in worse medical shape than Alicia had been, as well as a woman who'd smoked pot until she turned herself schizophrenic. (That's what Dean said, anyway.) She had hovered in the hallways earlier that day, moving her hands around as if washing invisible windows. Brian would be making the rounds again shortly to the suicide watch with his Jedi Maglite. Alicia didn't have the reason or presence of mind to observe the timing of his rounds the previous night. She would just have to hope that her chance would come.

Voices down the hallway. A muffled discussion that might have been a bit heated. Footsteps going away toward the activity center. A door in the distance opened and shut with a delayed *bang*.

Another half-hour passed before Brian's high-tech high-tops squeak-squeaked in the hallway as they approached her room. *Strange. He was never alone.* The doorframe creaked as he laid a hand on it and leaned inward. Alicia's arm lay over the blanket top, the hospital gown covering her shoulder. Underneath she still wore the T-shirt from earlier that day with the yoga sweats. Icy clots of excitement pumped through her chest and arms as she tried to calm herself; it nearly wrecked her pretenses of sleeping as Brian stepped into the room. He stood there for a while, his presence radiating toward her with sweat and blood. Then it occurred to her that he could do anything he wanted to her. She was in a locked ward with a nurse who had shoulders like a quarterback and hands like a sawhorse vice. Sure, there was a technician, but where was he? What did Brian say to him?

He placed the flashlight on her nightstand. A scream crouched in the back of her throat like a runner waiting for the pistol shot. His clothing rustled ominously. Ropes of muscle in her already tense neck and arms tightened as she waited for him to move closer. More rustling, clicking...a strange *squish*. Then, the rustling stopped and he sighed with a low moan. For several moments, his breathing thickened and rough stroking movements accelerated steadily. She knew this sound from mornings when Eric thought she was sleeping. For months before he finally left, he flaunted his lack of interest in her. She punched him in the kidney under the covers one morning when she caught him doing it, and after that he must have taken his morning release into the shower. But now Alicia worried that this man was merely getting hard before he tore back the bedclothes and raped her. She would give this asshole the fight of his life.

A guttural gasping flapped in his sinuses as he came. Much to Alicia's relief he plucked some tissues from the box next to her bed. There was more rustling as his breathing thinned and he sniffed hard. When he finally trundled out of the room and down the hallway, Alicia wanted to fall apart right there, to sink into the very springs of the bed, piece by piece, and soak it with her bile. She wanted to be nothing at all.

Then, she heard a door open in the distance. Water running.

GO!

She heaved every bit of herself from the mattress and slipped from the bed sheets, the cool air of the hospital hallway stinging her eyes. The staff restroom stood between her room and the nurses' station. Unconvinced that she could make it to the egregiously slow elevator before Brian finished washing his hands, she raced past him to another patient's room. It was dark except for the nightlight. He wasn't due back for at least another ten minutes, which meant she could hide here for a few. Plus, the obese woman who slept here snored aplenty, hiding Alicia's nervous breathing. The only danger was if the orderly returned. Alicia pressed her back to the wall on the same side as the doorway opening, sliding as far as she could into the darkness. The round white clock hanging on the opposite wall read just after midnight.

When the water stopped running, the restroom door *shussed* open and Alicia held her breath. He lingered at the nurses' station for another epoch, pawing through meds and paperwork. To her complete humiliation, she realized he was whistling the old J. Geils Band song, *Angel is a Centerfold.* She balled her fists and swore she'd strangle him for terrorizing her if she got half the chance. Another five minutes passed as he whistled to himself.

Leave, you stupid bastard! Goddammit! Leave!

Brian walked away from the nurses' station, down the hallway to the men's beds with his flashlight. She held her breath again as he passed her room, listening for any signs that he noticed her vacancy. Alicia had not secured the bed sheets in any way so that the bed would look occupied. Silently she condemned her lack of presence of mind and felt the stab of panic until he moved past her room. Now, she just had to wait for her break—

"A LIGHT TO THE GENTILES!"

I love you, Jesus! Or, rather, Mr. Stern.

"COME TO ME, BRETHREN! TOUCH MY HEM AND BE HEALED!"

Alicia wrenched herself from hiding and fled to the white door. She kicked off the slipper to retrieve the sweaty card. Clenching her teeth against the pain, she swiped the card and grabbed the knob. But as she labored to twist it open, a pixie voice whispered behind her:

"Alicia?"

Alicia froze, turning to face Geri who stood in the hallway, watching the escape in progress with her doe eyes. Placing a finger to her lips, Alicia threw Geri a beseeching look.

Geri's eyes misted with what appeared to be disappointment.

Footsteps coming. Brian. Geri turned to face the sound. The young woman seemed torn between Alicia and Brian for a beat. She then ran down the hallway toward him.

"Brian! Brian!" she cried.

Alicia died inside.

"My roommate is peeing the floor! Please stop her!" Geri yelled, glancing back at Alicia as she rounded the corner.

"What the hell are you doing out of bed?" he bellowed.

And that was the last thing Alicia heard.

She bore down on the door and slipped in front of the elevator doors, punching the down button repeatedly until the metallic slats lumbered open. Ducking inside, she swiped the card and tapped the Lobby button. The hospital gown dropped to the corner of the elevator.

But the elevator was going up.

Chapter 23

"In a time and out of time, in time the ink shall sing."

Mr. Wicker stood before the arching lavender window, arms spread wide. The Library sat under the hand of darkness, all candles extinguished save the candelabra he held. On one shoulder sat Munnin.

"Blood and trust, they turn to dust, each secret that they bring."

A swarm of black feathers drifted over book stacks east, west, north, south, as ravens landed on tables, shelves, gargoyle fixtures. Solemnly Mr. Wicker watched the smoke swirl outside the glass as the ravens huddled, clawing nervously at their perches. Sea green eyes narrowed to lucent slits.

And he sang.

"Brooders weep and brooders keep their misery at hand."

Flames swelled ominously behind the rattling glass of the arching window. Mr. Wicker turned his back to the window and brought the candelabra to his lips.

"Let Mr. Wicker wash your sicker memories with sand."

He blew out the candle flames.

Like a cannon's blast, the window exploded with blazing bits of glass. Mr. Wicker felt the heat at his back from the eruption. This inferno could not dissolve him. Besides, this was no mundane conflagration. A thousand grains of molten light inundated a wall between two prominent book stacks, obliterating the iron gargoyle sconce that scowled betwixt.

The cataract of light poured forth before him and he prayed to the few gods who remained that it would carry her back to him.

Chapter 24

"SHIT!"

Despite Alicia's attempts to reroute the elevator, which involved hitting every button below the psych ward floor, the doors slid open four floors up.

At the children's trauma ward.

Alicia.

The whisper of a little girl's voice drifted into the elevator from the corridor.

A cold needle of dread danced up and down her spine as she stood in the elevator, doors wide open to the half-lit floor. No one seemed to notice her and the elevator doors did not close.

Alicia.

Drawn by the child's whisper, she stepped out. The nervousness of escaping the ward dissipated and freedom mellowed her movement as she wandered the hall, passing the nurses' stations. She passed a cleaning crew stuffing plastic bags of trash into a bigger trash can on wheels; a male nurse pushing the rumbling floor cleaner back and forth; a flashing light above one room that attracted the attention of a young Hispanic nurse; and several dark rooms with darker television screens that caught gobs of glare from the hallway lights.

She wasn't sure why she didn't turn around and go back into the elevator, but no one stopped her.

The hallway darkened a shade as she closed in on the little girl's room. Thinking the room was closer to the center of the floor, she made a couple of false choices, then realized that the correct doorway lay two or three farther downward, around the corner toward the dead end of the hall. The room swarmed with soapy, antiseptic smells mixed with a sour thrush of antibiotics farming her delicate flesh. The teddy bear had tumbled face-first into the footboard of the bed. Alicia plucked it from peril and tucked it under the child's hand. She was breathing on her own, but still feeding from a tube to her stomach as she remained unconscious. If the sleep crust had been cleaned from her eyelashes, the hard flakes had returned. A colorless antibiotic drip disappeared into her left arm. A second operation had been performed around her ear, the surrounding area swollen, sallow and purple. Alicia stroked her thin forearm and sighed, wishing good things for the precious one who had been so tragically hurt. The voice-activated tape recorder sat in the brackets mounted above her pillows. All Alicia would have to do is speak to trip the recorder. She could say what he wanted to say to Dr. Farron before she disappeared, and only he would hear it. Alicia smiled widely at the notion, and prepared a brief farewell-but-only-for-a-bit speech. The more direct the better, she decided. Screw it if he got scared, thought she was crazy, was embarrassed. She had to let him know how he had affected her and that the choice to escape was conflicted, not clear. Just as she leaned toward the recorder and opened her mouth to speak, the child spoke. Or, rather, sang:

"In a time and out of time, in time the ink shall sing."

The tape recorder gears ground as they snatched the tune. Her desire to connect with the Library blazed so fiercely that she recognized the profound danger. Another miracle, but not the save-me-Jesus sort that preachers waved at with palm fronds. Mr. Wicker's was a brimstone blessing that defied everything the world had ever taught her about sanity, about reality. She stepped back from the bed, transfixed by her otherworldly utterance, first sung to her by *him* when she entered the Library in death. But as soon as she reached the doorway, more tiny voices flooded the hallway in a nightmare chorus from the sleeping children:

"Love and trust, they turn to dust, each secret that they bring."

Every mounted tape recorder snapped on above their heads, a wave of mechanical clicks, as the children's voices reached an astonishing crescendo. Alicia stepped into the hallway, unsure which way to turn without stumbling into the abyss.

"Brooders weep and brooders keep their misery at hand."

And then the lights died throughout the hospital floor, leaving Alicia gripped in the black hand of insanity.

"Let Mr. Wicker wash your sicker memories in sand."

If anyone was panicking over the loss of power on the floor, Alicia could not hear it over the blood roaring in her ears. Her normal fear of darkness was amplified by the hell of lost bearings and potential psychosis.

You came here because you loved the darkness.

The Voice. She'd heard it on the 9-1-1 call recording. *Basso profundo.*

The dead end of the hallway cracked with a pinprick of light, a bright rivulet that grew steadily as it dripped down the wall. Awestricken, Alicia reached up and let the brilliance slice her palm with its warmth. The prickling of her wrist wounds was subdued as soon as she felt it. More and more pinholes broke through the wall and the dead end was rapidly eaten by knives of light slicing through from the other world. A child giggled somewhere beyond and others shouted to one another in some distant game.

Marco!

Polo!

At last the wall broke open and incandescence flooded the hallway, spilling into every child's room. A raven glided into the hospital hallway over Alicia's shoulder. As she glanced back to follow his inky trail, the effulgence swept beyond the hallway as if to herald his arrival into this world.

Heavenly. Breathtaking.

Alicia pressed into the radiance.

Chapter 25

Alicia emerged into a train tunnel much like the one after her death. However, this time the lights danced over her as she ran, the souls of children calling to one another as she chased after them down the tracks:

Marco...Polo!...Red rover, red rover, send Leesha right over... James be nimble, James be quick. James jump over the candlestick...

The exhilaration of release drew her deeper into the other world, oblivious to the miracle of transmigration. As the lights kissed her hands and cheeks, picking at her long strands of hair to splay them about her head, she stumbled toward a ragged hole of half-eaten wallboard with pieces dancing in the breezes. When she reached the blasted wall at the end of the tunnel, she leaned inside. The opening was lined with hundreds of books.

Reaching out to the book stack on either side of her, she let her fingertips brush the spines as she stepped between them, awe and wonder stinging her eyes. She did not doubt for a moment that she was not unconscious or dreaming, but that she had crossed some fearsome barrier. Something supernormal had happened in the hospital, she the focal point of the phenomenon. How could she not embrace it with her whole soul?

She had entered the Library of Lost Childhood Memories. And she was alive.

Not a single flame burned among the tables and shelves, but rather an eerie lavender light filled the place. Molten glass slithered upwards over the desk as the shattered pieces sculpted themselves back into a seamless pane. Alicia held her breath as she watched the spectacle; she started at the rustle of feathers.

Caw! Caw!

"Are you here?"

A thick white candle sunk firmly into an iron candlestick holder burst into a single flame in the center of the Library. Alicia's smile was so big her face almost broke with joy. "I want to see you."

Drawing veils of cool air over her body, the ravens darted to and fro in the rafters above. Then, another candle burst into flame. And another. A decadent silver candelabra on the centermost table gracefully lighted. One, two, three. All the while, the ravens swooped into an alcove that remained dark as the rest of the Library lit up. Were they fleeing? Had she spoiled their home by entering with her living body?

Before she could ruminate on the exodus any further, the abyss of the alcove erupted with a roar of black wings and hoarse shrieks. He emerged with a steady step. King of Shadows. Lord of Secrets. A raven sat on his right shoulder, while another landed on his left hand held aloft for the creature's perch. Every step he took closer to her freed her from the world she knew. She studied his body without shame. Magnificent broad shoulders hoisted arms so thick they could break a lion's neck, and his torso flared with smooth pectorals under the tattered robe. His stature reminded her of the Vikings in her childhood encyclopedias. But unlike the thick manes of the Nordic conquerors, not a hair graced his body. That lush char coated his lower legs, cheeks, arms.

He stopped only a few feet in front of her. "You are back. At last."

Alicia could not speak.

Without taking his eyes off her, he flicked his hand toward a book on the table. The cover flipped open and invisible fingers rifled the pages. The imperious scrawl of ink wavered on every page with a fiery waltz of piano, harpsichord, and strings. With his other hand, he reached out to her and the two ravens fled.

She took his hand, his velvet fingers grasping hers. He pulled her close, placing a hand on the small of her back. He moved one of her hands around his waist and the other up high on his shoulder. Her fingers and palm pressed into the dusty nothingness, yet she leaned into him just as securely as if he were true flesh. With the music's crescendo, he led her in a waltz about the Library. Her feet moved tentatively with his—back, side, forward, side. She had never waltzed before. The movement felt both foreign and familiar. Alicia was soon hypnotized by the music and his liquid movements.

He smiled fiendishly and drew her ever closer to him as they moved. "We're waltzing to someone's nightmare. Exquisite, isn't it?"

It was perhaps the most exquisite music she had ever heard. The clarity of the notes contrasted with the angelic tongues and the foreign lyrics. "Someone's nightmare?"

"The music of the ink that recorded their trauma—a trauma so severe they had to bring it to me."

"So, only the very worst memories come here."

"Correct."

"But there are people who live with some pretty shitty memories. Why didn't they bring them to you?"

"I don't know," he said. His sea green eyes softened to a willowy shade. "Their soul decides. Not me. And even then, I've turned away many."

"Why would you do that?"

His eyes twinkled. "I think you know why."

Alicia shuddered. An enchanting yet sadistic bastard who enjoys the misery of others.

"I'm pleased you came back," he said. "It's quite a surprise."

"Indeed," Alicia replied. "This was not where I planned to go."

"Where then? To Rome? Perhaps to the ruins of Pompeii or the cafés of Paris?"

"Home actually."

"Yours, I suppose, not mine. Were you not terrified when you saw the light?" he continued. "Did you not worry where it would take you?"

She shook her head. A big lie.

He raised an eyebrow. "We have to stop meeting like this."

They both laughed. He swept her around the main table, which stood over as many books as were stacked on top of it. The candelabra were balanced precariously among the books. Alicia worried about that for a moment before wondering if anything—the candles, the books—was even real at all.

"You're deathly curious about the Library. It haunts your dreams."

"Perhaps."

"I know it does," he replied. The waltz slowed. "I give you those dreams."

"Why not give me my book?" she asked. "I will never need to dream the rose garden again. It will only torment me until you do, and you know that."

"I cannot give you your book," he said. "Not unless you are ready to pass on."

"Then why am I here?" she asked. "How did I get here?"

"You are here because you wanted to be here. Here is where the most terrifying stories live. True pain and suffering for you to enjoy." He continued, *sotto voce*, in her ear. "Stay here with me."

"You send me tormenting dreams, and now you want me to stay with you?" Why did the bad ones heat her southern regions like a branding iron? She pressed her fingers into the silky warmth of his back. The char clung to her now, grinding into her sweater arms and t-shirt, smearing her hands. "I don't even know you and you want me to shack up. Tsk-tsk."

"If I told you who I am, would you stay?"

"That would depend on who you are and what sort of place this really is. And even then, I'd have to consider it. I sort of prefer make-believe pain to real pain, after all." That was a lie. The idea of staying in the Library was so weird that she couldn't get her head around it, much less consider it.

"You were eager to trade your life for the unknown a few days ago."

"Because anything was better than the pain," she replied. "But I'm not in pain any more. Things have changed."

"Because of this place. And because of me," he said, smug.

"In part...yes."

"Or because of *him*?"

Alicia nearly fainted at the reference to Dr. Farron. "Him?"

"You *know* who I mean. The Celt. He has been trying to divert the children from me. And now he wants to divert you, too."

"How do you know about him? And why do you call him The Celt?"

"The children," he said. "They tell me everything." As the enormity of the statement stooped into Alicia's already shaky frame of reference, Mr. Wicker continued. "Georgeta tells me about you. You think because she is unconscious she is therefore unaware, and that is not true."

"Georgeta? That's her name?" Alicia added.

"She adores you, you know."

The idea that that poor damaged baby adored her touched Alicia. "The last time I saw you, you tried to seduce me because you wanted to steal my skin and take my life for your own so that you could escape this place—"

"I wasn't serious. I couldn't really do that."

"Oh, really? Well, you want *something* from me and I don't think you're being honest about what it is."

"I am being as honest as I've ever been," he said. "And that's saying quite a bit given who I was when I was human."

Mr. Wicker looked away from her, as if catching a stray thought or sound. Alicia didn't believe him, but she succumbed to the hypnotic effect of his voice. She let go of his shoulder and touched the finely sculpted sinews of his neck, starting at the wide bone of his jaw, drawing her fingers down to his collarbone. They stopped dancing, and he motioned to the book with the singing ink. The pages closed and the music stopped. Alicia could hear nothing but her breathing and the flickering of oily wings somewhere in the alcove. Even the clocks had stopped. Mr. Wicker placed his hand behind her head and guided her to rest against his sternum. At first she was startled at the heavy beat within. She then realized it was not his heart but rather a distant war drum echoing across a valley.

She closed her eyes, and behind her lids, cornfields burst into flame.

HELVETIA, GAUL—58 B.C.

As his wagon approached the chaos, Drunos watched the twisting, spitting flames roll over the cornfields, the wind driving the fire across the valley. The roiling waves stretched to the feet of the hoary-headed Jura mountains and surely even to the silvery Rhine river. His eyes watered with the smoke and ash spinning in the sky like a blackened snow flurry. Hundreds of villages burned in the wake of a massive migrating caravan. Thousands of wagons, chariots, and horses rumbled west with his people, away from the land Drunos knew as a child.

"Stop!" he called to his slaves. "It's time to ride."

One of the slaves dismounted and, untying the mare from the wagon, he helped Drunos out and onto his beloved horse. The mare had carried him throughout the Isle of Briton during his druid training. It returned home with him, festooned in the ornate designs and complex wards of the druid school.

But instead of feasts and festivities, hostile Helvetii warriors soon greeted Drunos and his two slaves. Brass torques curled around their necks and bronze bracelets wreathed their wrists. Men and women alike wore brass helmets and brightly colored cassocks. They threatened Drunos with short lances, rattling a piece of tin at the base to intimidate the intruders. Long, flat shields covered in skins were slung across their backs.

"What is your business, stranger?" one of the female warriors demanded. "Tell us and be truthful or we will kill you now."

Drunos drew up in his saddle, angry. "I am Drunos, your druid returned from the Isle. In the name of Teutates, I demand to see Vercetillos or whoever is now the vergobret." If anyone should have greeted him, it should have been Vercetillos, as it was Drunos and his old mentor, Litugenalos, who had personally chosen him to be the tribe's high magistrate.

Unconvinced of Drunos' identity, the warriors pressed their captives onward, closely guarding them, while two riders separated to find their superiors. The other warriors returned after some time. Smoke darkened the horizon behind them, making breathing difficult. The blinding eye of the thunder god, Tara Nis, hung in the hazy sky. A mounted figure broke through the circle. Like Drunos', his white druid's cloak was spattered lightly with blue, red, and green.

"Hail Drunos. Old friend."

The rider pushed back his hood. It was not Vercetillos, but rather Litugenalos, the elder druid. He was a striking man, old enough to be Drunos' father yet still strong. At Litu's signal, the warriors apologized to Drunos, who in turn praised them for their vigilance.

"You almost missed the caravan," Litu said. "You chose a fortuitous time to return." He seemed different. Cold and distant.

"It was not my choosing," Drunos replied bitterly. "The Chief Astrologer said that Tara Nis had flung a fiery wheel across my sky. My studies were over, he said, and I must follow the wheel home."

"You were not initiated then?"

Drunos pushed back the sleeve of his robe to reveal the swirling brand of the oak tree on his forearm. Litugenalos' cheek twitched. Drunos drew his sleeve back over his arm and hunched under his cloak. His blood had thinned without the icy breath of the Jura on his cheek for the last five years.

"So you have."

"Why are we fleeing, Litu?"

"Ariovistus has been raiding our lands long enough. Last season, there was more bloodshed than ever before. He almost killed Vercetillos. So, at the last war council, we clasped hands with the other tribes and swore to leave. The Rauraci, the Latobrigi. Everyone is leaving."

Drunos exploded. "How could the Helvetii be so cowardly?"

"We have lost too much to Ariovistus! He will terrorize us no more. In seven nights, we shall meet the Boii and cross the Rhône bridge into Genava. The Allobroges have been fighting off the Romani. They'll appreciate help from our warriors."

Drunos brooded.

"I thought," Litu continued calmly, "that you of all the nobility might support the decision. We had good omens."

"Support what? That we become cowards? That we burn our lands and leave the valleys that have nurtured us? This brings us shame."

"What care you about fighting? You do not have to fight. You do not even have to pay taxes now. You have far less to fear than any other *celtae*."

"My mother, my father—my kin died for *nothing*," Drunos growled. "Teutates is dishonored. He'll punish us for this cowardice."

Children on horseback galloped past, taunting one another. Litugenalos said nothing for a while.

"I want a home, Litu," Drunos continued. "I want a fire, meat, bed. I want to *rest*."

"Ariovistus would give you plenty of rest." Litugenalos prodded his horse to a trot further up into the caravan.

Drunos released the slaves and wagon to return to Briton, taking what supplies they could spare. Just before dusk, a lean teenage boy with long, lime-streaked hair rode to him. A pretty girl of about twelve summers who looked much like him shared the horse. "Drunos! Uncle, you are home!" she cried happily. She stood on the steed as it neared and leapt to Drunos, her brother tossing her by the hips. The druid caught her in his arms and settled her on the padding before him. She wore *bracae* on her legs like her brother, thistles and foxtails snagged in the wool of the pant legs. Over a bright green shirt, she pinned a square cloak of crimson and black wool.

"You have started throwing women since I left, Lucos?"

"Aye! Because they have been throwing *me*," the boy laughed.

A long blade with an intricate boar's head hilt swayed from his gold-plated belt. The sight of real weaponry on Lucos infused Drunos with pride. He remembered his nephew as a boy with a wooden sword, howling like a Helvetian warrior in nothing but his boots.

He kissed his niece on the top of her head. "How do you fare, Little Bear?"

"My name is *not* Little Bear," she responded indignantly. "It's Arctosa, remember?"

"I remember your name," he said. "You are named after the goddess who took the shape of a bear. You may be a bear, but you are still a *little* bear." He mussed her hair. She *harrumphed* and turned in the seat to look at him with eyes the soft blue of birds' eggs. Her fingers patted at his gold earrings, as well as the beard covering his chin and lips. "Did the Britons steal your moustache?" she asked with astonishment.

Drunos smiled for the first time since he had returned home. "Druids are clean shaven during their studies. Look." He pulled back his hood to reveal a thin layer of soft blond hair covering his scalp. It had grown in a bit over the last month of travel, but it was by no means the ragged mane he wore when he left for the Isle. "It's growing back. Soon I will look as I did before."

They rode together, the two children plying him for stories about the gods, the Isle of Briton, the Romani. "The Romani are like dark ants," he told them. "They have tiny, straight swords and big shields to protect their weak bodies. To hide their puniness, they wear their sails for clothes, draping them around their shoulders."

"How do you know this?" Lucos asked breathlessly.

"I saw them," Drunos explained. "Roman ambassadors were embarking on the Isle as I left. But let me save some stories for the fire, eh?"

When blackest night came, the wagons, chariots, and horses halted in a valley formed by two hills giving way at the shoulders. Lucos brought Drunos to some of his kin toward the front of the caravan, and they struck camp together. He clasped hands repeatedly with Medudorix—the round-bellied master craftsman who designed the exquisite hilt of his son Lucos' sword, as well as the hilt of every warlord. He then kissed Medudorix's clever, willowy wife, Rosmerta. She had been married to Drunos' brother before he died. Drunos was glad to see that Medudorix loved her now. She appeared ill, her face bloated. His uncle and fellow nobleman, Suros, was camping with Vercetillos the vergobret. By the time eating, drinking, singing and swordplay had finished, and tales of the tiny Roman soldiers petered to punchy jokes about ants and boats, heavy clouds rolled over the encampment and showered the ground until it muddied. Thunder broke in the sky in deafening bursts.

Medudorix called to Drunos through the flaps of his tent. Inside, Arctosa wept uncontrollably in Rosmerta's arms.

"Explain to her, Drunos, what the great noise is," Rosmerta pleaded. "She will not listen to us. She would listen to Litugenalos, but he sleeps closer to the vergobret than the people these nights."

"Shhhh! Little Bear," he whispered, squatting beside mother and daughter. He stroked her hair as he spoke. "The great noise is just the voice of Tara Nis the Thunderer. He always shouts during times of change." Arctosa's sobs subsided. Drunos looked up reassuringly at Rosmerta, whose face wrinkled bitterly, and then to Medudorix, whose brow was crushed with stress.

"Can you see anything in the clouds besides the wet, cousin?" Medudorix asked.

Drunos paused before answering. "That is for Litugenalos to divine."

Rain sprayed the tent's leathery dome. Drawing Drunos aside, Medudorix lowered his voice. "You are wise not to openly cross Litugenalos. Do you sense it?"

"I do," Drunos answered. "But why?"

"After you left, he argued strongly against having sent you to the Isle to become a druid."

"Truly? For what reason?"

"Plenty, you fool! Listen!" he said. "One voice to the gods. One voice to the councils. One voice to the Romani." Lucos stirred in his bed, whispering for his parents to sleep now. Medudorix hushed him. "His family grows stronger every day, while ours...this is all that remains."

Suspicion sunk painful roots into Drunos' bones as he considered the implications of his mentor turning against him. Gentle Litu, they'd called his mentor. His name literally meant "the fire that sleeps." The druid line typically stayed in noble families, but Litu's mother bore only an idiot son besides him. Some thought perhaps his mother had been behind more than one druid death and was cursed. Several druids had been killed through plots and misfortunes over the years before Drunos was chosen from the line of royal craftsmen. Despite his appeal to women, Litu himself had had no fortune in producing children, his seed withered.

"Vercetillos says the Allobroges are weak and that they will yield the bridge over the Rhône. What do the augers say? Will we be safe?" Medudorix pressed.

"Who needs augurs?" Drunos replied at last. "This whole migration is madness. It will yield nothing but death."

The tribe awoke to the blaring of a ram's horn. Drunos had not slept well. The crush of his tribesmen, the cold, and the duress of the migration ripped Drunos from the arms of his dreams. As the caravan lurched along the valley floor, Drunos studied the black cloud formations on the horizon. They had not changed since the night before despite the rain and the winds that shortly followed. More bad omens.

The Helvetian vergobret, Vercetillos, found Drunos and greeted him warmly. His stocky warhorse lumbered beside Drunos' white mare.

"I hear that you will press us through the Allobrogian territory," Drunos said. "Why so dangerous a route?"

"Because the Jura pass admits only one wagon at a time," the vergobret replied. "We will not settle by summer's end if we take such a tedious course."

"But what of the Allobroges and their allies? Will they allow us to cross the bridge? The Sequani pass is quite defensible. I rode that route to and from the Isle."

"The Allobroges are easy to overcome. We need only say we mean to take the bridge by force and they will surrender." The warlord bragged of the standing forces, the strength of the people, and what the mighty Helvetii could do in the lands to the southwest—even if the lands had to be cut from the feet of their enemies.

"I thought we sought peace for once, not war."

"If we must give Teutates his due to find peace, then so be it. What else concerns you, Druid? Your wisdom was not weighed in debate."

The warlord was testing his allegiance and ambition, Drunos thought. He rode for a few moments before breaking his silence. "I would have better wisdom to offer if I knew the current disposition of the Allobroges. Should we not send ambassadors to them first to see what agreements can be made before our arrival? And what about the Boii? Are they meeting us as agreed? Or have they met difficulties? At worst," Drunos offered, "we will have to backtrack for two nights to the pass."

The vergobret answered to the Druids; Drunos and Litu were the only two Druids in the tribe. With a grunt of acquiescence—"I will send them with haste"—Vercetillos then made a surprising order. "I will provide you with slaves and guards for the duration of the migration."

Potential spies from Litugenalos. Drunos almost protested, but since they were natural markings of his priestly rank, he accepted graciously to avoid suspicion. He would have to watch his mannerisms and speech, trying not to contradict

Litugenalos. But Drunos' mood did lighten a bit to know that Vercetillos respected his wisdom.

Drunos sought out Medudorix and discovered that Rosmerta had taken to riding in the wagon with her head covered. "She's sick," Medudorix explained.

"From the incessant rumble and sway of the wagon, no wonder," Drunos offered. "I could prepare something for her—"

"It's not just the wagon," Medudorix countered. "She's pregnant."

Pregnant. Rosemerta had not been fertile for some time.

Children on horseback suddenly crowded around Drunos and Medudorix, who winked at the druid as the children begged sweetly to hear stories about the Isle.

The Isle. Where the Britons live and teach *celtae* how to be druids.

"The Britons speak much like we do," Drunos explained. "And our gods speak to them, as well. They live in the mists, near the mounds where the gods dwell beneath the oak roots. The Danu nurses her Children with abundant crops and herds. They do not eat the hare, or even the dog, as these are sacred to the Danu. I saw the stones laid by the thousandfold fathers in the fields. I heard the fearsome groans of war harps on the cliffs as the great god Tara Nis breathed upon the strings. I learned the secrets of herbs to heal dying warriors and bring sacred dreams to see the future of kings. I witnessed the passing of a soul from one dying to the lips of a babe being born. I fell in love with a witch with long red hair from the north. I lit the fire of sacrifice for Teutates, our father of war, and sang hymns as criminals and animals burned in a towering man made of branches."

"Where is the witch?" a boy asked. "Would she not be your wife?"

Drunos winced. "That is a story for when you are grown."

Before the sixth nightfall, the ambassadors returned from Allobroges, and Vercetillos requested Drunos join the council. A thousand fires burned in the camp. Drunos followed his slave's torch to the massive tent of Vercetillos. The domed ceiling passed far above even Drunos' head, the sloped walls embracing the company of several vergobrets and nobility from the tribes. Litugenalos smoked in the far corner as he listened to the men argue. The ambassadors sat beside Vercetillos, faces bleak with hard travel as they dug fingers into wool cloaks. Several other noble families were present, including the many-times grandmother Dirona. Slaves replenished the food and Grecian wine. Drunos took a seat near Litu.

Suros stood as Drunos entered. His beard cascaded like white drifts over the rain-carved stones of Jura's cliffs. They clasped hands and his wrinkled face reddened. "Drunos, welcome! What make you of these fools?"

"I will first hear everything," Drunos replied, glancing to Litugenalos. "And then we will consult augurs, because wisdom comes not to men but through the gods."

Suros wiped the spittle from his mouth and pointed to the addled ambassadors. "The Boii have not kept their promise and the Allobroges have joined the Romani. The Roman king, Caesar, has taken residence within Vienne. We should not seek the bridge."

The Allobroges are indeed easy to overcome, Drunos thought. And this time not by the Helvetii.

Vercetillos slammed down his cup. "We have no other choice!"

"We could go the pass," Drunos reminded him.

Dirona sat forward, her fat gray braids ratted like wool ropes draped against her round, splotchy cheeks. She put a knotted finger forward, emphasizing each word to Vercetillos. "I will *not* see our children freeze on those cursed cliffs! Nor will I see them buried when the winds bring avalanches!"

"The pass is controlled by the Sequani," Drunos reminded her. "We need only request aid from Dumnorix—"

"Dumnorix is power hungry and would betray his own people," Suros said.

Litugenalos withdrew his pipe and spoke. "We must make concession to Caesar's desires so that he will consider our case."

Drunos could not believe that Litu spoke out of turn. The druids were not to interfere in the politics of the clans unless addressed directly. Plenty of nobles had opinions on the matter that needed to be sifted through. The older druid never looked at Drunos, but kept his eyes fixed on Vercetillos, whose face sweated with the resolve to fight.

Suros asked, "Concessions? Such as?"

"Hostages," Litugenalos said. He puffed on the pipe languorously and looked to Vercetillos. "Or whatever they demand—within reason, of course. And we send our finest as ambassadors to Genava." He pointed to two young men whom Drunos had known as well-considered citizens even before he left; they were now finely attired in *bracae* and cloaks black as midnight, with golden torques on their necks and wrists. They received the elder druid's recommendation with great poise. "Numeios and Verudoctios. You go to the Roman king and plead our request. Ask for his consent, tell him we are not of hostile disposition. If he resists—"

"We take the bridge by force," Vercetillos said.

The slighter of the two ambassadors spoke, cheeks pinched pink from the brisk ride. "But my lord, the legions of Caesar have formed considerable allies—"

Dirona waved off the word *legions*. "And *I* have the head of Lucius Cassius in a trunk!"

Everyone laughed raucously, slamming wine cups together. Drunos shrugged his cloak over his head and stepped between the flaps, his slave after him. The clouds broke overhead to admit the deepest blue mysteries. Drunos looked for even one celestial outpost, the faintest indication that the plans within held some hope for his people, but he saw nothing beneath the shapeless mask of night.

Suros abruptly left the tent and stood with Drunos. Gazing up into the mystery, he held his cloak tightly about him. "My lord, I for one eagerly await the augurs. *Your* augurs."

"Will it matter?" Drunos replied. "Or will the council do as it pleases?"

Suros hung his head as if shamed by the druid's question.

The slave lit his torch, standing at command. Drunos ordered him to move to a farther tent before he addressed Suros. "I looked to the sky. And, although there was a break in the storm, I saw no signs of salvation."

"Why do you say this to me and not the assembly? It does me no good."

"Because there are dangers if I contradict Litu."

Suros nodded. "Many and more than you suspect. But do not doubt that the council dreads your magic. I will do my best to honor the omen you alone have witnessed, upon Teutates I swear."

Drunos returned to his own tent, where he wept with exhaustion and fear until, starved of wood, the fires died and the winds spun them to wraiths on the horizon.

"Drunos!"

Drunos awoke with his chest burning with sadness. The dampness from the fog seeped through his tent as the horses stomped impatiently outside.

"Drunos!"

He wrapped himself in his cloak and left the tent. Suros stood outside with Numeios and Verudoctios, horses prepared for the journey to Genava.

His uncle took the bridle of one horse as he spoke. "Drunos, it has been requested that you ride with Numeios and Verudoctios to speak with Caesar. If you accept, you must leave at once."

"Who requests this?" Drunos asked. The mists reminded him of the Isle, and for a moment he thought he heard the distant chant of a woman as she worked enchantments in the grove.

"I requested it," Suros said. "As did the young men." The two ambassadors nodded to one another and then respectfully averted their eyes from Drunos.

"But what good would it do for me to stand before Caesar when I'm not committed to the course proposed?"

"You are committed to the tribe's safety," Suros replied. "And you judge wisely."

Drunos sifted through shards of shattered sleep to find his thoughts. When tribes send ambassadors to other tribes, they never send druids. Teachers, priests, judges—while they are the most eloquent speakers to be found, druids are never used to create liaisons between tribes, much less nations. "You don't think Caesar will take offense? That he will feel threatened?"

"The Romani fear our druids more than our swords!" Suros replied. "But when they see *you* are peaceful and sensible, he will know we are of the same mind."

Neither convinced nor dissuaded, Drunos agreed to the journey because he wanted to do anything rather than settle squabbles and tell stories under the eye of Litu. Suros probably surmised as much.

A young man not much older than Lucos had packed Drunos' white mare with provisions and some spare comforts demanded by nobility. Drunos recognized him as Bratu, one of Lucos' friends. Bratu explained that he had chosen to become a servant to pay off a debt of protection.

The druid felt better about his travel with Bratu. He'd be almost as loyal as kin and his family had always cared well for the warhorses.

Fed and washed by his slaves, Drunos saw the sleeping camp from the height of his steed and was stung by the sheer number of people in the miles-long caravan. Tens of thousands marched toward Genava. His responsibility weighed heavily upon him.

At once, the riders struck out across the budding valley between the Alpina passes that guarded Genava, the richest and most pivotal city in Gaul. The Allobroges alone controlled the Alpina passes, allowing travelers through for a toll. They were commerce savvy, if not military minded. Drunos let the two ambassadors lead the flight down the narrow trade route into the southernmost reaches of the Helvetian basin until the Genava lake raised a glittering blue shoulder just over the horizon. The Alpina mountains eclipsed the west like a monstrous battlefront of blackened, petrous warriors, crushed by cloaks and helmets of solid ice. The dramatic falls and swift currents of her many rivers reminded Drunos that the goddess of the mountains had the power to eradicate them every moment of their lives. Knowing the full forces of the earth were at her command, the Helvetii might try to conquer other men but never her.

The four camped in a grove by the lake off the route, protected from the spring winds that slit through their cloaks like the haft of a newly whetted *falcata*. No doubt the Romani saw the smoke from their fire; they rested three hours from the city. But no one molested them. They ate and drank in good spirits. Numeios was more conversational, lacking in the hubris that characterized the Helvetii, which allowed him to elicit ideas from other Gauls. Verudoctios was more charismatic, with strong features and a confidence that radiated the profound courage of his people. Quiet Bratu turned out to be ailing from a sore tooth. Drunos made him some tea from medicinal herbs brought from the Isle. But that treatment aside, the three cared for Drunos as if he were king, cooking and serving his food, pouring his libations, preparing his tent before their own. The attention still made Drunos uneasy. His family had always had slaves, but never had freemen of his own kin shown him this kind of obeisance.

Wolves bayed with the winds of the lake for hours. Drunos fell into terrible dreams. He stood on the lakeshore in the crippling cold as an abandoned war boat drifted toward him on the still black waters. A man's head rose from the water before the war boat, his white shaggy locks heavy with dampness and debris clinging to his face. He held a rope over one shoulder as he dragged the boat to shore. As he emerged, he wore a druid's robe that dripped from the large sleeves, clinging to his emaciated frame to bring every rib and ripple of flesh into stark relief.

Drunos backed away from the drowned druid as he staggered onto the shore. With a groan from its hull, the boat crawled over the edge of the land and lodged in the sand. A flock of ravens descended on the boat, ripping and tearing at the floorboards. Drunos' gaze traveled up the sails. Blood sprayed the sallow leather. The large black birds shrieked, viciously pecking at one another as they fought over the grisly contents of the boat, claws and beaks glistening with gore.

The old druid continued toward the woods and dropped the rope on the grasses. His robe sloshed with each step.

"Where are you going?" Drunos asked. "Why have you brought this to me?"

Breathing hard, the old druid halted unsteadily as if he still treaded through waves. He coughed, water gushing from his mouth and nose in filthy sluices that spilled onto his bare feet. He threw back his head and opened his mouth, a thousand voices keening in despair. Drunos heard Rosmerta wailing, Medudorix cursing, and Lucos shouting the war chant.

"Arctosa?" Drunos asked as his hope crashed, pierced and struggling, from the storm-addled sky. "*Arctosa!*"

The old druid turned to him, mouth open to expose the stump of a cut tongue that wagged furiously to utter cries not his own. The voices crescendoed into an otherworldly squall that forced Drunos to his knees, palms pressed against his ears. His bones, guts and gristle resonated with the terrible god sound. Drunos screamed as it threatened to unthread his spirit from flesh.

Drunos awoke with the burden of god visions. As dreadful as the night had been, the bleak awe of the divine fortified him. But as to what he should do, he could not decide. Teutates demanded human sacrifice by drowning, and he sometimes required a druid. But they were not at war; the god would not call for such a sacrifice to avoid one, nor would he to start one. The ambassadors packed for the last three hours of travel while Bratu prepared the horses and asked timidly for more "tooth tea." Drunos gave him some of the herbs and showed him how to prepare them himself.

As noon approached, the halcyon surface of the Genava blinded them as they moved away from the *Alpina*. A large flock of swans descended to the lake surface, but Drunos lost sight of them when the trade route veered into the rich groves of beech and holy oak that thickened the basin floor. Pines bristled over the slopes of the *Alpina*. Wooly herbs dusted the bosky ground, with clusters of golden, lavender, and lapis pansies. Wandering streams sloshed under hoof. Bratu called for a stop to water the horses and themselves. The sky had cleared to a bluish brilliance, lightning crowning the white heads of the *Alpina*.

The ancient buildings of Genava jutted from the earthen promontories of the *Alpina* like broken teeth as they rounded the mighty southward bend in the lake. Beyond, the Rhône swayed and slithered as traders' ships rode its reckless back to the southern ocean. However, much of the city was tucked between the shore of the Rhône and the edge of the lake, surrounding a sprawling plaza where traders from various countries set up shop. Wine. Oil. Weapons. Ceramics. Linen. Jewelry. Drunos detected at least three different languages as they approached: two dialects of Gaulish, Latin, and Greek. What startled him was not the heavy commerce, for the Allobroges were prosperous in trade and husbandry, but the queer sight of four towering *celtae* in blue *bracae* striding toward them with spears and wearing the bronze breastplate of the Romani.

Numeios hailed them and explained that they were returning to negotiate terms of passage over the Genava bridge with Caesar. As Numeios spoke, the four watched Drunos with obvious distress. Before the *celtae* could respond, a Roman soldier approached with a statesman not much older than Drunos. The ambassadors hailed the statesman as Quintus Metellus and thanked him for his intercession. Quintus introduced himself to Drunos in unbroken Gaulish and explained he was an administrator for Caesar. His dark hair was cut close to his head, his face shaven, and his skin oiled with a faint perfume. He looked close to Drunos in age, maybe twenty-three years. He wore a wool tunic with red stripes, over which he elaborately wound an off-white fabric with a stunning purple border. Drunos noted how the Roman kept his left arm close to his body; the druid could not decide if the Roman was guarding himself or holding the pleats of his robe in place where they met in a complex interweaving at his waist. His wore an intricately carved gold ring, but no other jewelry. This lack of adornment rendered him stark yet regal at once.

As Quintus ordered the *celtae* soldiers to stable the horses, the ambassadors assured Drunos that they would be brought with haste before the Roman king.

"My friends, Caesar is not a king," Quintus explained, leading Drunos' company from the plaza into a long thatched building built from the white stones gathered on the promontories. Three Roman soldiers stood guard at each side of the doorway. "He is our *proconsul*, merely a governor of the land. In some ways like your vergobret."

Quintus entered what appeared to have once been an Allobrogian vergobret house, but the entrance had been converted to a floral room with a hole built into the ceiling over a stone well. Some of the more vibrant flowers grew indoors in a striking mosaic of delicate mouths yawning with violet, white, and blue lips from trellises and wooden boxes. Allobrogian slaves removed the visitors' shoes and washed their feet, and then ushered the four into a smaller room filled with skins and pillows, wherein Quintus urged them to rest. More Allobrogian slaves brought in large basins and urged them to bathe their hands and faces in the cool, scented waters. Drunos gingerly dipped his fingers into the basin. He disliked the effeminate smell and let the water roll off his skin. Bratu sat against the far wall, sweating as he scanned the room. When the slaves brought food, the boy sniffed like a hare in the grass and waited until Drunos invited him to eat from the tray. Numeios and Verudoctios ate and engaged in terse conversation, reclining among the skins like favored guests in a dining hall. Pork, spelt grits, and some leafy vegetables Drunos didn't recognize made a very satisfying meal, which they washed down with honey-sweetened wine. It was unlike anything he had eaten the last five years and he thoroughly enjoyed it.

The Allobrogian slaves returned with more basins of scented water. By then, Drunos had relaxed somewhat and washed despite the way the blooming smells tickled his nose. No one came for them and the room warmed as the stone house soaked up the afternoon sun.

When Quintus returned that afternoon, he seemed in good spirits, clasping his hands together as if about to lead a song. "Proconsul Caesar wishes to see you now," he said. "Come along."

Leaving Bratu in the room to sleep, the two Helvetian ambassadors immediately followed Quintus out of the room and into a large dining hall, somewhat bigger than Vercetillos' tent but not as large as a Helvetian stable. A tile mosaic depicting a battle between mortals under a watchful god lay underfoot in a labyrinth of pigments in glossy stones. That was when Drunos realized that they had been dining in Caesar's home.

After passing through a lengthy hallway, Quintus entered a room where statues greeted the occupants with upraised arms and cups. A complex mosaic pebbled the back wall, depicting an old god bearing a young woman from his head. The gods overwhelmed the mortal man who sat on one of the couches surrounding a low table in the midst of the room. Drunos glanced back to find two Roman guards standing at attention on either side of the doorway. He and the ambassadors stood over a full head taller than the rest of the men. The guards watched him with curiosity and hardly noticed the ambassadors. Drunos pushed a dour look their way that turned the delicate stems of their legs as rubbery as rotting blossoms. In soured unison, they leaned on their spears and threw their gaze to the man on the couch.

Drunos watched the man whom Quintus addressed as Gaius Julius Caesar. Self-assurance lighted his eyes as they examined his newest guest, a great sloping forehead suggesting an avalanche of thoughts. The Romani were shaven from neck to ears, Caesar even more so with neither scratch nor scar. He held a slender iron stick with one sharp end while the other was circular and flat. The instrument was not large enough to be an effective weapon, Drunos decided. At some suggestion of Quintus, Caesar stood as he addressed the Helvetii in quite passable Helvetian Gaulish. "Salutations, my honored guests. Sit with me please?"

The three Helvetian men took seats around the low table and that is when Drunos saw it: Wooden *tabulae*—tablets—lay open before Caesar, each with a shallow recess covered in a thin layer of black wax. The tablets seemed to be fastened together in pairs; a set of five tablets sat together at one table corner. Lettering was etched into the wax of the tablets, scratched by the stylus in Caesar's hand. Drunos had seen some Greek lettering from the transaction records carved on wood between Greek traders and the Helvetii, but never had he seen such a profuse use of letters in one place. He wondered what this Caesar could be inscribing at such length. That was when he noticed in the far corner of the room a bundle of parchment stored in an ivory cabinet with one door standing open; tiny amphorae on bronze tripods perched atop the cabinet beside a cedar box about the length of the stylus Caesar held. At least one of the parchment bundles had been stained with strong black strokes.

Writing.

Caesar spoke to Quintus, who translated the discussion. The Roman proconsul's voice reminded Drunos of a wind striking the thickest string in a war harp.

"Caesar understands you wish to bring the entire Helvetii tribe over the bridge. Are you prepared to negotiate terms?"

"We are," Numeios responded. "Let us discuss your terms and what we are willing to offer."

Quintus relayed this to Caesar, who spoke readily. "He says he requests three conditions to your crossing."

"Speak them," Numeios said.

"The first," Quintus explained, "is that the Helvetii pay a tribute to the Romans as insurance against mischief wrought against our people by wayward citizens of your tribe as you enter our territory."

"How much?" Verudoctios asked, squinting suspiciously at the Romans.

"Five hundred amphorae of wine," Quintus answered.

Verudoctios looked with uncertainty to Numeios, who continued. "We can pay three hundred."

Caesar nodded. Quintus smiled. "Three hundred," the translator offered.

Numeios conferred with Verudoctios, who said, "Three hundred is fair. What is your second term?"

This time when Caesar spoke, Quintus paused before translating. "Caesar would like ten hostages."

"Ten hostages?" Verudoctios asked. "That, too, is fair. What is your third condition?"

"That one of the hostages be your druid," Quintus said.

Caesar looked to Drunos and the druid's throat tightened. A dire connection sprung between the two men that the druid had not guessed possible.

"Drûis," Caesar said, enunciating the Gallic syllables. Somewhere he had learned the Gallic word for druid and used it as a title.

Verudoctios stood, his face flushing with rage. "I will not on my soul permit such a thing!"

"Verudoctios," Numeios said. "Sit. Please?"

"I will not!" the brasher Gaul cried. "This is not a point of negotiation! You are not just demanding royalty!"

Numeios turned to Drunos, faint with his own outrage. "Do not agree to this, Drunos. This is negotiation. There must be another way." He turned to Quintus as Verudoctios silently fumed. "Is there no one at Vienne to whom we may appeal?" Numeios asked the statesman. "Have our cousins no longer any say in matters of state?"

Verudoctios exploded. "We demand one of royal state in return!"

"There is no negotiation on this point, I'm afraid," Quintus inserted calmly. "The druid was decided upon as you ate. If you do not accept our terms, you must seek another route over the Rhône. Possibly," he added, "you might not find one at all."

Be taken as a hostage and save thousands of lives? Or refuse, knowing that the Helvetii will engage in mutual slaughter with the Romani? Drunos held up his hand, never looking away from Caesar's inscrutable eyes. "I will go," Drunos offered. "But take me alone. I am worth ten thousand of my kindred."

Quintus leaned forward. "We have not forgotten what happened to Lucius Cassius."

"Neither have we," Drunos replied, his lip curling derisively. "The deal is struck." He held out his hands to the ambassadors who reluctantly clasped them.

"I do not like this deal," Verudoctios lamented, as if it needed repeating. "But I understand. I will take care of your kin, Drunos. You have my oath."

Numeios withered, clasping the druid's hand. "As will I." For him, the negotiation was a failure and he clearly feared the fallout from Suros. Vercetillos would be all too happy, however, as would Litu. Especially Litu.

Quintus and the Roman guards escorted the ambassadors from the meeting room, leaving Drunos alone with Caesar. The proconsul paced around Drunos as if inspecting a bear for the games. Drunos' attention was divided between the intriguing man and the *tabulae* scattered on the table. Caesar noticed Drunos' interest in the *tabulae* and offered him the stylus.

Drunos shook his head. "I am forbidden."

"Forbidden?" Caesar repeated, letting the Gallic word slide around his mouth like a sliver of ice. He stood at least a head shorter than Drunos and wore a different tunic than Quintus. His off-white toga with purple trim was wrapped loosely about his body. "So, it is true." Regarding the druid with pure astonishment, Caesar sat back down on the couch and placed his hands on his knees. He spoke again, but this time to himself in Latin. Then, he gave some order to the Roman soldiers at the doorway and they cautiously surrounded Drunos. Caesar watched with undisguised amusement. Drunos did not resist, not even when the soldiers led him by the elbows toward the door. He stumbled as he tried to match his longer strides to their shorter ones.

The march back through the house was not nearly as pleasant as the one into it with Quintus. Once they stood in the plaza, an open cart drawn by an ass came to them in the company of several soldiers on horseback. They seated Drunos in the cart and locked the low gate. The soldiers surrounded the cart, chattering in hushed Latin as they drove it out of the plaza and to the outskirts of Genava. The winds lashed their faces as the cart rumbled down the main road over one of the Alpina passes that led to the Allobrogian capital, Vienne. Drunos tried not to think of his painful circumstances, but instead compared them favorably to the difficult ride from the Isle to his beloved Jura valley.

The Jura valley, which he would never see again. He spent those years training to be a druid, and now he'd be a Roman citizen. He could hardly believe it.

The Genava lake spilled to the North in a great silvery sheet, the mighty Rhône writhing westward along the pass. Drunos positioned himself so that he could greet the sway of the waters as the convoy ambled forward. The coveted bridge lay just beyond the short bend.

Drunos raised himself to see better. A dark swarm of Romani seethed below the pass. Soldiers mingled with lower class Romani and slaves in muddied, unbleached togas as they hitched massive blocks of wood to horse teams. The chaos of disassembly sputtered and lurched as numerous horse teams, carts, and bonfires dispatched stone, plank, and pylon—

"Great Teutates," Drunos whispered.

They've razed the bridge.

The druid cried out to the sky of his great Tara Nis. Bowing forward, he began a terrible chant. The cart shuddered. The wood siding ripped apart, spitting splinters that gored the soldiers' flesh.

Although he heard the horse's hooves, Drunos did not notice the soldier ride up behind him before the sharp sting of darkness felled him.

VIENNE, GAUL

Drunos awoke in a wide bed warmed by lush animal skins. On a table at his bedside sat a plate of fruit and olives next to an urn. He sat up, the back of his head still throbbing. Clearly the soldier had meant to render him unconscious—which he did, briefly—and not dead so that they could bind him.

A hostage would never be treated so roughly, he thought. *They must have greatly feared me.*

He sniffed inside the urn and drank the honeyed wine within. A Gallic god face was painted on the side. The work of the Aedui, whose land lay to the west. Drunos lay down again, a heavy anchor of depression crashing deep into his chest. The meaning of the dream unfolded behind his eyes, the ravens tearing at the boat's bloodied contents. His people would perish.

Or would they? The Helvetii were superior warriors. Normally they were the ones who took hostages. If Litu made the proper sacrifice—a drowning—they would be certain to win. The dream must have been a warning. If Teutates were not appeased, the Helvetii would suffer a grim defeat. But if Litu had had the dream as well, he would heed it.

For the rest of that day and into the evening, Drunos was tended by slaves who washed his hands and brought more food—at last, some salted pork. A physician examined his head, applying cooling salves. Later, Quintus paid him a visit. The statesman's face puckered with worry as slaves placed a chair beside Drunos' bed.

"Where am I?" Drunos asked.

"You're on the north bank of Vienne," Quintus replied. "Caesar was alarmed that you were hurt. He ordered the soldier to be punished."

"He should have rewarded that soldier," Drunos replied. "Those men would have been dead in another moment."

Quintus laughed. "Most certainly."

"You don't believe me. Did you see the wounds on those soldiers?"

An awkward moment of silence. "Caesar believes in the power of the gods of Rome, yet just as much in the intellect of man. He would consider anything else...*superstitio*."

"*Superstitio?*" Drunos repeated the Roman word carefully.

"It means to worship false gods."

The next day, Drunos had bathed and dressed before Quintus arrived to take him to the forum, where he instructed Drunos on the glories of Vienne being a Roman province. "The architects are now developing an aqueduct for the city." He rubbed his hands together as he relayed the project details—how they would build an underground network of tunnels that followed the sides of the hills. Drunos half-listened as Quintus laid bare the mammoth design of the numerous conduits that would first bring water to the public and then to private houses. Little more than a busy village, Vienne meandered to the west, stooping at the edge of the Rhône. Already the Romans were building districts on the embankments on both sides. No doubt the temple that shaded them in the forum would soon be dedicated to Caesar "Son of the Divine" instead of to Lugus of the Long Arm, the Shining One, Chief Lord of the Tuatha De Danaan.

Quintus caught him staring at the temple in misery. "You are worried for your people."

"My gods will break your gods, Quintus, and my people will kill you. If luck is with you, they will drown you in the Rhône. And, if luck is *not* with you, they will feed you to the wicker man."

"You seem certain of your people's victory," Quintus laughed.

"Caesar's treachery will be for naught," Drunos replied. "We once defeated the Romani. We will do so again."

The next day, Quintus retrieved Drunos and tutored him on Roman law, philosophy, gods, and circuses as they strolled through the concourses teeming with Allobrogians in commerce with neighbors and foreigners alike. Winding into the more pedestrian district in the southwest, Drunos noted that they conducted business out of the front room of their houses. The drafty avenues of the district seemed almost exclusively civilian; few soldiers, or even Romani for that matter, patrolled this suburban part of the city. Quintus explained how some of the wealthiest merchants had hired Roman architects to install a heating system under the floors of their homes.

"I suspect the tax collectors were the first to acquire such luxuries," Drunos replied dryly.

"Taxes, Drunos, allow us to develop many civic projects and maintain a standing army."

"Which is why we will defeat you. Our men and women fight because they love their tribe, not because they are paid or forced by a king to defend it."

"You did not defend your land, Drunos. You left it to Ariovistus, did you not?"

Morose, Drunos would not speak again until the evening, when Quintus brought him to dine with the Allobrogians, former nobility that were now Roman administrators. The diners pulled dripping joints of boiled pork from massive pots. Drunos sat with his distant kinsman, who shied from talking to him directly as they spoke, yet they seemed to defer to him in discussions.

"Where are your druids?" Drunos asked when Quintus excused himself to use the lavatorium. "Your priests? Who hears your oaths? And what of your *bardos* and *weledâ*?"

"Druids, seers and singers we have no longer," the biggest Allobrogian explained. His was the bushiest beard and mustache, while the others trimmed their facial hair more like the Romani. "They will soon be forgotten altogether."

"Vienne is a Roman province now," a frailer Allobrogian offered. "When the rebellion failed three years ago, Caesar reinforced his hold over us."

Another Allobrogian interjected. "I, for one, am glad you came here, Drunos, for you will be spared."

"Spared?"

The big Allobrogian wiped his mouth on his sleeve. "He intends to extinguish the Helvetii if he must to set an example to the other tribes and get revenge for what happened to Lucius Cassius."

"How do you know this?"

"Caesar has recruited several more legions." He leaned closer to Drunos, eyes scanning for Quintus as he spoke. "And they will meet your people at the bridge." He clasped his hand with Drunos'. "Believe me, there are many who despise the Romani. We cannot offer you oak and scythe because our gods have been proscribed, but we can give you our faith and ask that you remember us when you purify and bless others at moon time."

Moved by the man's oath, Drunos plucked a cluster of grape stems from an empty plate and dipped them into the perfumed water. The man closed his eyes, his forehead wrinkling in pious reception. Chanting under his breath, Drunos sprinkled the man's brow. The others did the same and Drunos purified them, droplets beading on their lashes and beards. He then blessed each man, drawing the symbol of an oak on the forehead with his thumb.

Other Allobrogians gathered about his table. "Bless us, too, *Drûis*," they asked in whispers. "Cleanse us and make us right with the earth and sky."

Then the first man Drunos had blessed spoke, his voice rising dramatically. "How will you ever learn Latin if you do not speak it, *Drûis*?" His eyes flickered like fish in a pond, indicating the approach of Quintus. Everyone scattered.

Quintus approached the low table and held his toga in place as he reclined beside them. "I have not tried to teach him Latin, Correos." Plunging hands into the silver bowl, he cleaned himself thoroughly before reaching into the pot once again. "And I suspect he would not have my lessons."

Learning the language might bring him occasion to hear news about his people that he might not otherwise. For a short while he might even be able to eavesdrop on conversations until everyone knew he spoke the language.

"I would learn," Drunos said, idly fingering an olive in his bowl. His appetite had fled at the news of the legions, and to see his cousins spiritually starved almost drove him mad. "Why do you wait?"

"Good," Quintus said between bites. "Then we begin tomorrow morning."

The next day, they began a lesson in Latin in the terrarium of the house. Infinitely more relaxed, Quintus started by explaining that he knew quite well that Drunos' tribe used Greek letters to record merchant transactions—that writing itself was not entirely forbidden. Drunos admitted that was the case. "Would you suffer learning Latin letters?" Quintus asked.

"Perhaps," Drunos responded. "But I will not write."

The druid learned Latin as a fish learns to swim, drawing Quintus into digressions about the battle at Genava whenever he could. Quintus assured him he would give him news when it came. But, for now, would a discussion of mathematics interest the druid? Quintus was an excellent mathematician, but he was a better Latin teacher and expressed amazement that Drunos could so quickly memorize the inflections, conjugations and declensions. Drunos used the mnemonic devices he had learned on the Isle to memorize vast chants and stories to acquire a workable vocabulary in a short period of time. The Latin vocabulary was not that wide, it seemed, yet the nuances of how words were used varied.

"So, one can manipulate the order of the words in the sentence, yet it means the same," Drunos realized almost at once. "How convenient to emphasize some ideas over others...or to delay delivering the truth."

Quintus smiled. "Who is the barbarian here?"

Each day they studied from first hour until sixth, when Quintus would visit the makeshift baths and let Drunos explore the market and forum. He attempted to talk with some of the Allobrogians to get news of the battle at the Lake, but no one knew anything yet and many had not even heard that the bridge had been dismantled. A handful of the Allobrogians from the dinner recognized Drunos, but he politely refused their requests to conduct ritual in the forests or at the shore of the Rhône. The hills that surrounded the city were forbidden and well patrolled by Roman soldiers.

After three weeks of tutoring, Quintus seemed anxious to show off his protégé at the next feast of delegates. However, with each passing night Drunos grew more despondent over separation from both his tribe and the forests where he should observe the next moon. The morning after the twenty-first night, Drunos refused to leave his room. A fever shook him in the coldest hours and he sweated into the skins. Quintus entered with slaves carrying food, wine, and new bedding. "Today is a great day, Drunos. We have important visitors from Rome. My wife is with them. It would benefit you to greet everyone."

Drunos sat with his back to him on the floor, sweat beading his scalp. His chin bristled with thick blond strands as it began to sculpt itself into the bushy Gaulish cascade that would soon brush his chest. One of the slaves brought him a razor, mirror, and bowl, which he shoved violently to the floor. "What of my people, Quintus? What happened at Genava?"

The young administrator pressed his lips together and the hand at his waist clenched into a fist. "You would believe me?"

"I believe you would honor us both with the truth."

Quintus ordered the slaves to leave and sat in the carved chair near the door, sighing. "They were turned back at the bridge."

"How many lost in battle?"

"There was no battle, Drunos. They were at a disadvantage and they retreated."

"Where are they now?"

"They are invading the Aedui." The Roman paused, as if trying to build an argument before it started. "They're overrunning them to commandeer passage over the Rhône."

"We have invaded the lands of your allies, which means..." Drunos said, prodding Quintus.

"We had no choice. The Aedui asked for our help."

Drunos said nothing.

Quintus left Drunos to consider what was happening. His people had kept their bargain, but now they chose a route that the council never considered at all. Why overrun the Aedui? Why not send ambassadors and work out a trade? Of course it was not always the Helvetian way to negotiate. The Sequani, who were on good terms with the Helvetii, hated the Aedui. Cornered by the Romans and unaware of the strength of their allegiance to the Aedui, the tribes perhaps felt that they could persuade the Sequani to squash the Aedui if they objected to their occupation.

As his temples buzzed with pain, he dropped his forehead to rest on his knees. If he could somehow flush this anxiety with prayer and ritual, he would have the strength to deal with the Romani. He did not want to appear weak, but neither did he want to appear insolent. Although it was Ariovistus who was notorious for threatening to torture his hostages, Drunos did not want to antagonize the Romani.

Drunos ate a bit and went back to bed, where he slept off feverish dreams. In his visions, his beloved Sirona lay beside him like she did that morning when she dreamt of the flaming wheel of Tara Nis, the skins thrown from her bare skin in her sleep. Her hands were pulled up in front of her face as if fending off an attack. He grasped her hand and kissed the back of it, crushed lavender perfuming her fingertips from a ritual the night before. He would never forget that scent, nor how the distress beaded on her neck as she whispered the dire prophecy of her dream. Drunos had to return to his people, who were suffering. He was to play a sacred role in the dreadful days to come. Anxiety yielded to desire as they made love in the hazy light of early morning. She swore she would never tell the Arch Druid, who would certainly send him back to the Helvetii. Although everyone revered Sirona's dreams, Drunos fought the prophecy. He didn't want to leave. His studies weren't half over. And his heart was here. Here, with his redheaded witch. Here, where the gods lived.

For days afterward Sirona remained silent but haggard. At last, the Arch Druid called her to him and she betrayed Drunos by relaying her dream. A careful judgment of the stars by the Chief Astrologer bore out the dream message. Sirona's wailing cleaved through the canopy of the grove as she followed the company that led him to initiation—his formal release from the college—and then off the Isle. She cursed herself and begged Drunos to forgive her for his expulsion. Enraged at her betrayal, he never looked back at her and hoped he would never see her again in any lifetime.

Yet, in this fever sleep he blessed her for her honesty. He would love her for eternity.

When he awoke, he dressed and made himself presentable to the delegates at dinner. Quintus received him coolly in the private feasting hall wherein slaves skirred in every direction as they prepared the tables for the arriving guests.

The elaborate dinner commenced when an ox-bellied, grossly dimpled man with arms plucked smooth of hair arrived with two lovely young men of undetermined status and relation. Quintus introduced him as the *censor*, Marcus Licinius Crassus. Thereafter entered Metella, the impeccably coifed wife of Quintus. A thousand auburn ringlets snaked over her round head; fine jewelry covered her ample chest, strong arms, and graceful neck. Her long tunic was fastened at the shoulders with golden and garnet-encrusted fibula. A faint dusting of freckles spread over her cheekbones like constellations. Drunos stared at her as he slowly realized that Quintus had married an Allobrogian.

Quintus introduced her to Drunos, whom he described as a formal hostage of Caesar. Her eyes widened. "*Drûis?*" she asked.

"Really, Drunos. We must dress you like a Roman," Quintus sighed.

"I'd like to see you try," Drunos threatened with a smile.

Unlike a noble woman at a Gaulish feast who would have offered both conversation and argument, Metella sat wordlessly beside Quintus as Crassus the Ox droned on about a great many subjects that Drunos followed in part. He gathered that Crassus was very wealthy and had considerable military victories, albeit he no longer had the physique for such valor. The druid languished as he considered the dire implications of Roman men marrying Celtic women until Crassus addressed Drunos directly. He could not understand what the censor said except something about death and men. Quintus interceded.

"Censor wishes to know your beliefs about death, Drunos," Quintus explained in Gaulish. "In Latin, please."

Drunos shifted on the pillows as he struggled to string the words together. "We believe not in death. We believe the soul of man passes to the body of a babe when he dies. Perhaps even a tree or an animal."

Crassus sucked at the bird bones. "An interesting man, Quintus. You say he knows mathematics, astronomy, and religion. Perhaps this is the reason we find no druids in Gallic government matters. They are the most civilized of all the *gallia comata*."

"*Gallia comata?*" Drunos asked Quintus. "What does that mean?"

"It means...long-haired Gaul," Quintus replied. Drunos detected faint traces of moisture budding at the neck of Quintus' tunic. The two beautiful young men snickered as Crassus noisily licked his fingers.

"You think we are barbarians?" Drunos narrowed his eyes at Crassus. "You who sleeps with men?"

Crassus snarled at Drunos, his crowded bottom teeth jutting from his lip like a boar. "Quintus could have you *killed* for what your people are doing! But he won't because of Caesar's *clementia*."

Drunos glanced at Metella, who ate daintily at her husband's side, eyes cast downward. Her resignation crippled Drunos' faith in another Allobrogian revolt. They had been crushed during the last attempt and Caesar now splinted their broken souls with his version of civilization.

"But then killing you would not prevent their mutiny, would it?" Crassus added.

"*Nullo modo, nullo pacto*," Drunos replied.

By no means...

Months passed like ice floes breaking reluctantly from frigid shores.

Quintus permitted Drunos to attend plays to improve his Latin, engage in games of chance, and attend feasts. He caught rumors about the war as they slipped down alleyways, into wine cups, and out of the occasional pocket. The legions pursued the Helvetii and the tribes who joined them across the Aedui territory toward the Saone. And Caesar had named Ariovistus a "Friend of the Empire." But Drunos heard nothing of the battles or losses on either side. Quintus appeared genuinely uninformed about the efforts of Caesar to crush the Helvetii in their migration. A capable teacher in every subject, he instead offered Drunos long discussions of philosophy and law, supplemented by reading sessions of political and philosophical tracts. Quintus exclaimed that Drunos spoke and read Latin almost as well as a Roman.

One especially elaborate feast held in Drunos' honor on the Day of Mercury took place in the home of Medumara, a very wealthy Allobrogian landowner on the shores of the Rhône. Scar pocked and snowy haired, Medumara grew his beard in tufts, denounced philosophy as Greek propaganda, and confounded Roman fashion by wearing the brightest colored toga he could fashion from imported silks. His family owned several choice pieces of land near the river and elsewhere. As an aristocrat in the burgeoning Roman province, he supported one of the more ridiculous construction plans—namely the bath proposed by Voccio, an Allobrogian tax collector appointed by Caesar. The bath would benefit from the aqueduct that Quintus so passionately anticipated. In this way, Medumara bought favor with both Voccio and Quintus, and thus widened his berth for impropriety.

"Medumara, have you forgotten?" Drunos said. "Today is *Aidrinijâ*. We should be celebrating Lugus, the winner of the harvest and lord of spears."

Medumara and his kin fell silent.

"*Drûis*," he answered at last, "you learned much on the Isle. The many chants. So very many words..." The wild-haired man held an imported fig and examined it before tucking it between his whiskered lips. "The time has come to forget."

That night, Drunos awoke just over an hour before daybreak to a keening between his lobes that burned at his temples. A faint rasping came from the far side of the room. Drunos lit the candle at his bedside and the keening faded as if carried away on a swift current.

At the base of the open door, a large bird hopped into the room. Its tiny tongue worked in its mouth. *Click. Cluck. Click.*

A boduus. A raven.

Drunos watched with fear as the carrion eater approached him. On the Isle, the raven belonged to Badb, the goddess of war, but also to Bran—the god of songs and death. He then knew his people were under the sword, and he wondered if this was another druid in shape shift or if Badb had come to enlist him to confuse the enemy with magic. Almost one hundred miles away, he had heard them in his sleep. Their voices pierced his heart. Pure and valorous.

"Litu?" he asked. Then, more fearfully, "Or are you one of the gods?"

The bird *kraaawed* with a low, throaty rasp. It turned a glassy black eye at Drunos and hopped forward another step.

Drunos sat naked on the floor with legs crossed and, holding hands out to his sides, he raised his palms to the heavens and chanted. Lowly, darkly. With the unbroken patter of the rain. He chanted to Teutates, the god of war, the one-handed one who would bring them victory, and the raven leapt onto his wrist. Into the morning hours, the druid continued to chant. Legs numb. Hands icy. Claws pricking his skin. Where his *anatîjâ*—his spirit—went he could not say, but it walked the wastelands of his chanting, a shade on the bleak moorlands, lending strength to his people. A giant man of flames collapsed on the horizon. Teutates?

Teutates!

The slaves were whispering to one another at the doorway when Quintus arrived. They grasped at his arms and hands, begging him not to enter. Quintus brushed them aside, but when he reached for the door, a layer of ragged frost coating the door singed his fingers. The frost continued up the door and a rivulet of crystals encrusted the ceiling above. With the awe of a believer, Quintus backed away from the door. "Leave him be for now," he said, not taking his eyes off the anomaly. "I will return later."

As the sun set once again, the raven erupted from his perch and soared out the door into the hall. Faint shrieks from the slaves discharged somewhere in the belly of the dwelling. Drunos rocked his body until the nerves in his hips awoke and his veins flushed with fire. He rubbed life back into his stiffened arms before attempting to stand. The room blurred until the druid's eyes adjusted to this world.

A rap on his door. "Drunos?"

"Come in, Quintus."

The young administrator entered. Drunos saw in his eyes that something had happened while he chanted. Something that drove fear into the man's soul. "Are you hungry?" Quintus asked. "Would you like another candle?"

Drunos' stomach burned with hunger. "Yes. Both."

Quintus left and returned with a platter of food. He set it hastily on the table by the bed and started toward the door.

"Where are the slaves?"

Quintus froze. "They refuse," he said. "They will be punished."

"Why are you afraid?"

Drip.

Drip. Drip.

Drunos looked up for the first time since awakening. As if the Jura winds had breathed on the surface, blades of frost crisscrossed the ceiling, creeping out to the walls of the room above where Drunos chanted. The edges beaded and dripped as they thawed.

Quintus swept back from Drunos as if the water would singe his sandals. "I don't know what you have done here," Quintus said, eyelids twitching, "but it is an abomination!"

"My gods are in the water, the grass, the hills, and snow. Not marble. Not temples with sculpted columns—" Quintus fled the room as Drunos shouted into the hallway after him. "And *not* men!"

A fortnight passed before Quintus summoned Drunos to the terrarium in the house one afternoon. Outside, thousands of footfalls invaded the city. The servants and other inhabitants called to one another throughout the house.

Caesar had arrived.

The legions remained elsewhere with their baggage train whilst he traveled with a convoy of almost one hundred officers and some cavalry back to Vienne.

But what could he want of Vienne? Drunos wondered as he entered the terrarium.

Quintus fingered some of the purple blooms that climbed a finely carved trellis. Even as Drunos approached, Quintus let his hand wander over the flowers. He wore a bright white toga that caught the white strands in his curly hair. "I was away in Lugdunum," he explained. "I was very harsh with you before I left," he said. "I should not have been." Sore news hung at the corners of his mouth.

"Why has Caesar come back to Vienne?"

"He wishes to tell you himself."

The Gaul and the Roman walked side by side to the forum, where the Allobrogian temple had been transformed into an elaborate Senate, holy mosaics defiled by the installation of Roman seats and tapestries. Every wealthy or ambitious Allobrogian clamored with his neighbor for audience with Caesar. Prostitutes threw Drunos solicitous looks from the porticoes, while the poorest Allobrogians reached for him with grimy hands, begging for coin. The masses roiled like maggots in carrion. The ugliness burrowed under Drunos' skin as Quintus parted the crowd and they ascended the steps to the temple.

The mirth of the Allobrogian administrators startled him. Had his people brought the Romani the promised destruction? Is that why Caesar returned with so few cavalry?

Skin glistening with bathing oil, Caesar sat in the widest seat surrounded by his officers. Quintus walked Drunos to the edge of the audience and waited until Caesar looked up from his writing table. The wax tablets were covered in scratches but Drunos was not close enough to read. Those eyes once shaped by self-assurance now bore the glint of determination. Caesar motioned to Quintus and stood balancing a tablet in his hand. "Ave *Drûis*," he said. "Were you were treated well?"

"I was given much respect, care, and education about your people, Proconsul Caesar," Drunos responded in perfect Latin. "But I was denied reports of my people. Was it because of your shameful defeat?"

Caesar dropped his gaze from Drunos to the tablet in his hand. "We surprised your people as they attempted to cross the River Saone after raiding the Aedui," he said. Then, more gently, "Of the two hundred and sixty-three thousand..."

Grief hammered Drunos before Caesar could speak the words.

"...only sixty thousand survived." He closed the tablet and handed it to one of his officers. "We sent them home, Drunos," he said. "You may follow them or you may stay here with us. Quintus and many others speak highly of you. I embrace you as a brother."

Blackness. Shadows, passing. A thin light.

Chapter 26

He stopped the story there. He couldn't bear having her know the true end.

The end of his humanity.

Chapter 27

Alicia buried her cheek in Mr. Wicker's chest as she fought tears for Drunos.

"No, no." Mr. Wicker stroked her hair. "I am no longer human. I no longer cry for these things." He snapped his fingers at another book. It flipped open to a chorus of piano and violins, and he began to sway. Alicia clung to him, reluctant to open her eyes and leave the fantastic ancient world. She did not want him to see her cry, although he already knew she was weeping because her tears soaked his chest. She worried he would think she was weak and maybe sympathetic to his offer. She had to be strong. But she related to his being a hostage. His loss of freedom affected her. And to be betrayed by a lover...her husband had ejected her from the life she'd loved. Those wounds were opened anew at the telling of this tale. And the very idea that he'd been forbidden to write— writing was the thing that kept her alive for so long.

"Litugenalos betrayed me. All along he was allied with the Romans like his Aeduan counterpart, Diviciacus. But these things are, quite literally, ancient history."

The gentle swaying gave way to a brisk waltz. The two moved about the Library as before, sweeping between large tables as the music rose from the book's ink-streaked pages. Just as her body relaxed into the hands of the rhythm, white light tore through the far wall.

Alicia didn't want to anger the Librarian, especially not after he'd opened up to her like this, but she felt powerfully defensive of Sirona. She opened her mouth to speak, but nothing came out. She cleared her throat to make way for words. "But you said Sirona betrayed you, too."

Mr. Wicker looked surprised. "She did."

"Are you sure? Just because she told the Arch Druid about that dream? I know it had dire consequences for you, but maybe he'd threatened to kill her if she didn't tell him what she saw. Or maybe he'd forced her to tell him through magic. I don't know. I understand Litu betraying you, but it sounded to me like Sirona truly loved you. In fact, I wouldn't be surprised if she threw herself off the cliffs after you left." She hesitated. "I would have," she whispered.

Eyes welling with bloody tears, Mr. Wicker kissed her. A kiss holier than a thousand mosques yet dirtier than a million brothels. She plummeted into his whisper softness and then he spun her closer to the light. Alicia fed him one last glance before uncurling her fingers from his as the light engulfed her.

And as the radiance pressed a warm hand against her back, Alicia suddenly realized there was someone on the other side waiting for her. Someone very important. Dead? Alive?

Who?

SMASH CUT TO:

EXT. GALACTIC FORTRESS—NIGHT

The GALACTIC FORTRESS winks and shimmers like a Las Vegas hotel in space. Brassy lights bubble up and down the metallic pillars. Tiny space pods randomly float in and out of unfolding iris holes in the surface. All the while two VAST SPACE FLEETS hover around the fortress: one SILVER, the other BLACK. Both poised for battle.

ON ONE GLINTING SPACE PLATFORM: the meaty villain RAFARIUS BART wears glossy black armor, Samurai hat, and something resembling a white hockey mask with an eye slat. A comically large KATANA is strapped to his back.

He faces off against an ADVERSARY on the slick platform.

RAFARIUS

Did I not defeat you once? Must I crush you again and again? Foolish Son of Zarquat!

The foolish Son of Zarquat—also known as the GALACTIC AVENGER—wears a silver cape, gloves, and Zorro-style mask. He holds one hand behind his back.

GALACTIC AVENGER

You will not win this time, Rafarius Bart! For stealing the woman I love and my
Galactic Fortress, I will make you suffer in this duel to the death!

Peering out of a SPACE WINDOW, the PRINCESS KOMENGEDIT waves her arms at the Galactic Avenger, her neon pink braids bouncing with enthusiasm.

PRINCESS KOMENGEDIT

Galactic Avenger! Save me from this evil man!

Rafarius Bart squats like a Samurai and draws the katana.

RAFARIUS

No more good guy/bad guy posturing! Now—you die!

He lunges at the Galactic Avenger, who pulls his hand out from behind his back to reveal a REALLY HUGE LASER GUN.

The Galactic Avenger pelts Rafarius Bart with LASER BLASTS, the gun rattling like Jesse's toy space gun. The laser blasts are merely miniature golf park balls that Rafarius Bart deflects with his sword, making MARTIAL ARTS MOVES and WEIRD KARATE SOUNDS, like Wonder Woman in a hockey mask with a katana.

CUT TO:

Dr. Farron wiped away tears of laughter with his palm. As the battle heated up between the two cartoon heroes, his phone rang. Clutching the remote and punching the mute button like a Star Trek phaser, he rolled over twice on the rumpled California King to snatch the phone from the receiver on the bed stand. "Hello?"

"*Farron,*" Dr. Sark barked, "you don't answer your cell anymore, do you?"

A momentary flash of panic heated his skin as Dr. Sark spoke. "Crap!" He patted down the bed sheets, the nightstand. "It must be in the living room." He usually kept his cell phone by the bed. The day had definitely gotten to him.

The news was bad. Really bad.

Alicia was missing. And she did not appear on any security camera.

Hospital security had combed the ward, and now they were searching the rest of the hospital. They suspected that she had somehow escaped, but wouldn't contact the Alameda County Sheriff until they were certain she didn't just fall asleep in a janitor's closet somewhere or, worse, do some harm to herself in another ward of the hospital.

"You know what this means, don't you?" Dr. Sark dropped the statement like a bowling ball. But Dr. Farron was so panicked about Alicia that it rolled past him. A gutter shot.

"I'll be right there."

The scene at the hospital was hushed on the lower floors, but security officers in bulky blue nylon jackets spoke into bleating walkie-talkies as they blearily scoured each floor. Dr. Farron stepped into the elevator and pressed the floor button for the psych unit. When he slipped his hand into the pocket of his white doctor coat for his security card, a burning in his solar plexus told him to bypass the floor. His finger hovered over the button to the children's ward and he pushed it deliberately. He pushed it again when the elevator stopped at the psych unit so the elevator would jump past.

The doors slid open with a ring. He inhaled deeply and stepped into the corridor. The night nurses greeted him with surprise and inquired if he was working late.

"Yup. How are you all this evening?"

"Oh, *fine* since the power failure earlier," one nurse said, weary. "The emergency backups didn't work as they should."

"A complete power failure? Jesus, is everyone okay?"

"Scared the be-jeezus out of *us*, that's for sure!" another nurse offered. "But everything is okay now. Miraculously."

"Good to hear." Dr. Farron excused himself and said he needed to check one of his tape recorders. If Alicia was in darkness for any amount of time, there's no telling what she might have done. But how did she get out of the psych unit? *Especially* if the power had failed. The elevators would have been inoperative. Perhaps the failure was limited to a certain area?

Where the hell could she be?

As Dr. Farron invaded the ward, he passed room after room of sleeping child. He leaned into doorways that exhaled gusts of soap, blood, and anesthetic. Tape recorders were mounted above most of the beds, but he only taped the children he suspected had been abused. When he reached Georgeta's room, he entered heady and flushed as her stertorous breathing tore through the silence. From the rattle in her chest, it sounded like she was due for a visit from the respiratory therapist.

Her father had been driving drunk with Georgeta in the passenger seat—the murder seat, as the Sheriff calls it. The mother died on impact. How anyone could put his family in harm's way was just totally beyond Dr. Farron's understanding, even if it was his job to understand it. Even knowing that alcoholism was a disease did not assuage his anger toward the father.

Shadows burst past the doorway. Dr. Farron spun toward the opening and froze, uncertain of what he had seen. He approached the doorway, placed a hand on the frame, and peered out.

The linoleum dimly reflected with the lights from around the hallway corner. The hospital corridor yawned with boredom until it reached the dead end.

Dr. Farron stepped into the middle of the hallway—

KRAW! KRAW! KRAW!

As the raven dived at his head, Dr. Farron covered his face with his arms, swatting at the bird as it dogged him. It didn't seem bent on hurting him, though. The carrion eater merely screeched as it fluttered.

Then he felt the warmth on his back. He turned to greet the heavenly light that flooded the hallway from the dead end. Stunned, he shielded his eyes with his hands, as if to push the glare back into the wall as the raven flew into the light. A dark waltz echoed with sweetness into the hospital. Then, he saw her:

Alicia danced from the light and caught his hand. She swung him into a quadrille, silhouettes against the infinite.

She smiled so peacefully that he wondered if she was asleep. Black smudges caked her cheeks. Her chin. Her lips...

At first he wondered why her face was covered in black charcoal, but then: "He kissed...?" Dr. Farron sputtered. "You...kissed...?"

Alicia stopped dancing. She slipped her hands under his arms and, pressing every curve of her body against him firmly, she kissed him so passionately that he thought the light would burst through his eyes and chest.

Everything dissolved into an opalescent haze as the powerful emotions pulsed into his fingertips and her warmth sank into his flesh.

...in a time and out of time...

Chapter 28

DAY 3—BAYFORD PSYCHIATRIC UNIT

Dr. Farron awoke to the ringing of his cell phone. He sat up abruptly, the rush of blood to his temples stealing his balance. Body wavering on the brink of sleep, he slowly realized that he sat in a chair beside a hospital bed. Daylight stung his eyes from the open blinds. He glanced to his left to see Alicia crashed out almost face-first into the pillow, turned toward the window. He checked his phone. Dr. Dulac's number appeared in the missed call window.

His fingers were dirty. Grimy. He shuffled into Alicia's narrow restroom and sleepily washed his hands. What was the last thing he remembered?

The light...

Oh, shit.

Dr. Farron dried his hands and briskly left the room. As he passed, she looked at him strangely. "Good morning, Dr. Farron," she squeaked. "Are you okay?"

He nodded. "Good morning," he said, swiping through the white door to the elevator. Once inside, he ran his card through the reader and pushed the floor button for Dr. Dulac. As soon as the doors opened, he punched out into the busy hospital hallway. A surge of joy lifted him, like endorphins after a run. He could not remember when he last felt happier. He hummed a waltz as he strode. It was a new melody. What was it called? Come to think of it...when did he hear it?

"Good morning!" he said, to nurses and orderlies, therapists and administrators. "Hi! How are you?" But they greeted him with worried looks and blank stares. *Some people sure got up on the wrong side of the bed this morning,* he thought. But as it persisted: *What's wrong with everyone this morning? Was the outage that bad?*

As he approached Dr. Dulac's office, he slowed to check himself in the mirrored, gold-veined panels. His hands automatically reached for his tie again, but they stopped mid choke.

A black streak smudged his lips. He pushed his lip up with one finger. His *teeth* were smeared black.

Fear widened his eyes and he turned his head. A wide smear of ash streaked his neck from ear to collar. Ash also blackened his clothing and dusted his arms.

Dr. Farron stumbled backwards against the far wall, staring at his disarranged clothing, palms turned upward.

Ashes...ashes...

Chapter 29

This time she could feel the wind on her face and everything around her rippled in its fingers.

The scene eerily flickered like a damaged film reel as she approached the circle of roses. Some stood as high as six feet tall, tightly surrounding a concrete arena about eight feet in diameter. Two blanching roses hung their blighted heads, Gog and Magog, as they arched across the arena's entry. Their bowed stems crossed like pikes, thorns murderously cuspate. Like a fairy woods, the roses entwined above and below, a mass of commingling vegetation that faintly reeked of perfume. Throughout, the hiss of an unattended needle rode the dead grooves of an antique phonograph, dipping with a crackle into a deep scratch.

Also this time a voice. Tender. Small.

Help me, Alicia? Help me do it.

A deep fright launched Alicia from her pillow.

Lillian.

Breathing hard, she blinked, felt the heaviness of exhaustion beckon her backwards, and then twisted back to fall face-first into her pillow. But when she saw the black smears on the white case, she caught herself and scrambled back toward the end of the bed. More ash stained the sheets. Sitting up, she held up her hands.

Alicia shook uncontrollably, her breath coming in short, quick hiccups. Her legs unfolded deliberately beneath her like metallic cranes as she stood up dizzily, the enormity of what happened pulsing megawatts through her frail nerves. She touched her lips. Her fingers came away dirtier than before.

Mindy happened by the door that moment with a tray full of med envelopes and shrieked, the medication crashing to the linoleum. "How did you get here, Ms. Baum?" she squeaked. "Ms. Baum...?"

"Mr. Wicker!" she whispered. She raised her soiled hands in the air. Triumphantly, she cried, "Oh, my god! I was *with* Mr. Wicker!"

A round robin of howls from the other patients began, a mock chorus of mad revelation echoing throughout the ward as every patient hooted the Librarian's name.

Mindy backed away and shouted for the techs. Within seconds, a five-man takedown team swooped into the room, surrounding Alicia with restraints and needles. One orderly tried the needle spray, a thin stream arcing into the air. "This isn't gonna hurt a bit, Ms. Baum. Just relax, okay?"

"What are you doing? I'm fine!"

The men grappled her down to the bed. Terrified, she shrieked as they bruised her ankles and arms.

"Wait! You don't understand! Come...ON!" She sobbed, anguish knotting in her heart.

"Get off her! NOW!"

Dr. Farron pushed through the takedown team and began to loosen her straps. The orderly interrupted. "This is Dr. Sark's order. She escaped last night and..." He eyed the black smudges. "Dude, what's up with your clothes?"

Dr. Farron winked at her as he unbuckled her restraints. Tears ran cold on her cheeks at the sight of ash streaking him. She threw her arms around him and he held her, his presence immediately soothing.

"I think it's pretty obvious that Ms. Baum never left the hospital," Dr. Farron replied. "Which doesn't surprise me since Dr. Sark is the biggest inmate of the ward." He spoke to her directly. "Let's go back to my office and talk about this, okay?"

Alicia sensed that he meant to talk about the night before, not about what just happened. She nodded.

He escorted her out, shooting a dirty look at the team as they left. Mindy seemed distressed. "I'm so sorry, Dr. Farron," she cheeped ruefully as she hopped after them like a harried rodent. "Rachelle is coming in soon. Do you want me to have her call you?"

Dr. Farron stepped into the elevator with Alicia, who wiped her running nose on her lavender sweater. "Yeah, I would," he said, swiping the security card. The door shut and they were alone. Alicia reached out and touched his stubbly cheek, wiping the grime. It was real. Incredibly real. He stared at the elevator door and sighed deeply.

Tears of awe ran down Alicia's cheeks as they walked silently to his office. She sat in the black overstuffed leather chair as he paced. "This is so fucked up. I don't have to tell you *how* fucked up this is, do I?" One hand lay on his forehead as if taking his mental temperature. "Oh my god! I'm dropping f-bombs!" He seemed genuinely disturbed by this.

"It's fucked up," she said, "but now at least it's fucked up for both of us."

"Well, before we get into the weird stuff...tell me how you escaped."

"You said yourself that I never left."

"You left the ward. I know. I saw you."

"I can't tell you."

"You can't? Or you won't?"

"Are you kidding? I'll never get out of here if I tell you!"

"You won't be held for that. It's a hospital security problem. Not your fault. Tell me what happened!"

"You don't care how I got out. But you do care how I got back."

"Well, *yeah!*" he exploded, throwing up his hands. "Hell *yeah!* But you've got to tell me how you got out. Like I said, it's a hospital security thing. Not every patient is like you. Some of them if they escaped could be dangerous. So, come on."

Alicia sat for a moment as she weighed her next statement. "I found Mindy's security card."

"Found? Or snatched?"

"Found!"

"Okay, okay! Found."

"She lost it. I found it on the floor. I simply failed to return it."

"So, we've got security issues," he said, digging through his desk. He procured a box of child face wipes and offered the pack to Alicia. They both took one and began cleaning their faces. "And?"

"And?"

"How did you...you know...get...ashy?"

"The light came for me when I was with Georgeta."

"The light," he said, exasperated. He planted himself on a child's chair and massaged the bridge of his nose. "Wait—how do you know her name?"

"Yes, the fucking light. You know? The light that comes for you when you die. Except this time I didn't." She lowered her voice. "It took me to the Library."

"Oh, no!" he whined. "I don't want to hear this!"

"Mr. Wicker told me everything, James," she said. "Even Georgeta's name."

"From your book?" he asked more hopefully.

"No. From his past," she replied. "Who he is. And James...oh, my god. It is an unbelievable story. *But* it rings true with what I know about that time period." She told him briefly about the Gauls, Caesar's war, and how Drunos the druid suffered.

He slumped on the chair. "There's got to be an explanation. I'm sorry, but there *has* to be something that—"

"What *the hell* is wrong with you?" She stood, pointing at him. "Look at you! Look at me! Ash! Everywhere! I don't know how this happened, but I know that it did!"

His eyes shined. He looked like he was going to cry.

Resigned to taking the reins of this conversation, she set aside her anger and knelt before him as he sat on the small chair. As she tenderly stroked his cheek, he did not cry but he spoke to her as if for the first time, his eyes flicking from hers to the floor.

"This is a lot," he said. "You take a man who's a golem—just a lump of mud, moving around to please other people. But you, you come along and he feels human again. Not just alive but like there's something more to being alive. Alive, after years of death."

Alicia could relate too well. "When did you die?"

His hands shook. "It was summer, and we were in D.C. visiting her family. We took a stroll out onto what they call Tourist Alley one evening, just looking at the monuments. I left her alone on a bench to get some water. And she was pregnant, so..." He sighed deeply again, as if something had flown from his open mouth, and faltered. "Witnesses say that sonuvabitch demanded her purse, but he took her life."

"Both lives?" Alicia asked, astonished.

He nodded, eyes dimmed.

"Oh, god. I'm so sorry, James. Truly, truly sorry," she said.

"Thanks."

"You talk a lot for a golem. That makes you considerably less golem-ish."

A smile hooked the corner of his mouth.

A moment of silence.

Alicia ached with stupidity. Yes, life had shat on her, but it had not stolen from her something as precious as this. A wife. A baby. A happy life of love and hope gone in a flash of gunpowder. And here she was judging this guy, punishing him for not getting caught up in the ecstasy of her so-called revelations as they tore his world apart in some terrible new way. At least he'd been listening to the children. At least he knew something had been going on. Yet she criticized and scolded him like he was every other man in her life. Clearly, he wasn't.

And here he opened up to her and she hung onto her stupid secrets like Monopoly money in a Hello Kitty purse. Maybe it was time to let it go. Take a risk. She wondered if this was how people learned to trust one another—drowning in the same sunk bag when together they could swim and save themselves. She wasn't sure why talking about Mr. Wicker had been easier than her life before the Library. But after a moment of consideration, she knew exactly why—

"Can I tell you a secret?"

He nodded.

"I feel really stupid when you ask me why I hurt myself. It's like what Winnie the Pooh says—you know Winnie the Pooh?"

He nodded officially. "We speak Pooh here."

Alicia smiled. "Well, like Pooh says, I have this very thingish thing inside of me but I'm afraid that once it's outside of me, it won't be so thingish. And then I'll feel even more very stupid for hurting myself."

"But it must have been pretty thingish. In fact, there were probably several pretty thingish things that happened, one right after another."

Alicia broke her look with him briefly, summoning her courage. "In fairy tales, things come in threes. In my life, things left in threes. The first thing to leave was my career. My last two books did poorly and I then became blocked for the first time in my life. Nothing of any worth could possibly come out of me. At least, that's what it felt like. And when I couldn't write, I couldn't save myself from the world. It was how I coped with everything. Which leads to the second thing to leave: my husband, Eric. We were married five years and he left me for another woman. Me! He left *me*, when he was the one who was violent and moody. He could be incredibly charming when he wanted to be, of course. I was much better off without him. Still, I felt like someone had torn open my chest and knuckle-punched my heart. We had taken out a second mortgage to pay off his expensive habits. Drug habits."

"Heroin?"

She nodded. "The house is in foreclosure. I'll lose it any day now." Alicia paused. She remembered how badly the weight of this had been crushing her. "The third thing to leave was my health." She tried to fight the tears, but it was just no good. "They found another lump. I'd had one a few years ago. It was brutal. I narrowly missed having to have a mastectomy. This time, I might not be so lucky."

After a moment of her silence, he said, "That all sounds very thingish to me."

He hugged her and she sank into him. He received the weight of her completely.

"Okay, before you jump to conclusions about the lump, you need a diagnostic mammogram. But one step at a time. I need your total cooperation," he said. "I've got major dragons to slay."

"Dr. Sark?"

"Yeah. Although Dr. Dulac might be harder to deal with."

"I don't know who that is."

Dr. Farron explained that Dr. Dulac was the Chairman of Psychiatric Services at the hospital. He was his mentor and a good man, but not very understanding when it came to breaches of professionalism.

"Oh, give me a fucking break! You know Minnie Mouse is sucking off Dr. Sark, right?" she said. "I heard them carrying on in his office." As he started to react, she added, "And that Brian guy? He thought I was asleep, so he jacked off next to my bed! Fuck this place. Dr. Dulac is AWOL."

Dr. Farron looked shellshocked. "Are you sure?"

"You have *got* to get me out of here," she begged. "I'm afraid of Dr. Sark. There's something about that guy that's very wrong."

The office phone rang.

"The dragon," Dr. Farron said and answered it.

Chapter 30

Dr. Farron hit the tension in the room like it was a rubber wall when he saw Dr. Dulac and Dr. Sark conferencing. The stalagmites of paperwork on Dr. Dulac's desk showed no evidence of thaw, but Dr. Dulac had moved some to the floor for the meeting. Dr. Farron had scrubbed himself as best he could, put on a polo shirt with an embroidered logo from the last hospital fundraiser under a hooded sweat jacket from his locker, clipped his hospital I.D. to the zipper, and ditched the lab coat. He looked clean, if not entirely professional.

"James, Mason has recommended that we transfer Ms. Baum to a facility," Dr. Dulac explained. Alicia's chart was lying open on the desk before him. "He says she escaped last night, is violent, and needs at least a month of in-patient treatment."

"She is *not* violent," Dr. Farron said.

"She is totally out of control!" Dr. Sark countered.

"Your staff tried to sedate her when she discovered someone had played a mean joke on her."

"Are you suggesting that my staff would allow such a breach of conduct?" Dr. Sark sneered.

"I'm suggesting that your staff might have been the perpetrators!" Dr. Farron asserted. "Ms. Baum reports that one of your nurses masturbated beside her bed last night when he thought she was asleep. What do you have to say for that, Dr. Sark? Do you normally run your unit this side of a lawsuit?"

"I will not bear one more accusation!" Dr. Sark responded, more to Dr. Dulac. "Not unless Dr. Farron can explain how he slipped past my night nurse into Ms. Baum's room and left this morning covered in some noxious black substance. We've a half-dozen witnesses to that, whereas not a one to these other baseless assertions other than the accuser."

"Look, here's the story," Dr. Farron said, hastily pulling on his bullshit gloves to K.O. this piss of a man. "Last night Dr. Sark called me when they couldn't find Ms. Baum. I had a hunch that, if she was missing, she was definitely somewhere in the hospital. So I checked the one place that she had expressed a desire to go, and that was to a child she had seen one day during a walk after our first session. Sure enough, there she was. I walked her back to her room and sat with her until she fell asleep. The problem was," Dr. Farron intimated, spreading it on as thick as he thought they would eat it, "that I was exhausted myself and I fell asleep in the visitor's chair, making sure she stayed put. You know I'm on medication, Leonard."

Dr. Dulac nodded.

"I realized when I got back to my office that some kind of stunt had been played on us both. Now, do you want to talk about credibility? Or do you want to discuss a formal complaint against your unit? Because no one was checking her that night when she was supposed to be on watch. I know. I was there."

As Dr. Sark coldly absorbed the story, Dr. Farron wondered for a moment if that concoction was not the truth. The swift hand of guilt stifled any desire to rationalize what had happened or deny the phenomenon he had witnessed in the children's ward. *Phenomena*, he corrected himself. She didn't show up on the security cameras, he reminded himself. Another point for the Twilight Zone. And why hadn't anyone found them both before morning? He definitely had one cheek pressed against the window of insanity, but the rest of him remained comfortably indoors with reality.

"Well, Mason?" Dr. Dulac said, folding his hands on the desk. The disapproving look Dr. Dulac now wore for Dr. Sark came out of some dirty steamer trunk Dr. Farron had never before seen opened.

"I don't know what happened, but I will investigate, Leonard. I promise." His barely guarded hatred reached between the bars of his professional façade and swiped at Dr. Farron. "As for Ms. Baum, her very presence in this hospital is a liability. I said so at the evaluation and I stand by that assessment."

"How is Ms. Baum's grandmother, James?"

"Not great," Dr. Farron said. "She had another stroke yesterday." He held back the information about her mammogram results. One more day and they could tackle that problem, too.

Dr. Dulac raised his frosty eyebrows and sighed. "Do you think Ms. Baum is almost ready to receive the news?"

"Very close. This morning's shock aside, her mood has stabilized considerably. She even told me why she attempted suicide." He registered Dr. Dulac's approval. "That's a first. That's big."

Dr. Dulac paged through the chart. "How did she get a security badge, Mason?"

"I haven't the slightest notion. But we need funding to prevent incidents like this. The staffing caps have us hamstrung."

Dr. Farron stifled an urge to make a crass remark about Dr. Sark spending his budget on nurses instead of whores, but he decided to stop while he was ahead on this one. "Ms. Baum told me that she found Nurse Hannon's lost security badge. It hadn't been reported lost or deactivated."

"Christ! Mason, this is unacceptable! You have enough funding to hire competent people. I expect to see major changes in personnel and protocol." Dr. Dulac then closed the chart and handed it to Dr. Farron. "Ms. Baum stays here for one more night under observation. If you feel her meds are on track in her appointment tomorrow morning, we'll discharge her. She can report to the outpatient clinic."

Dr. Farron thanked him and ducked out of the office. In the hallway, he resisted launching into an ecstatic series of hip-thrusting, Jim Carrey-like, *yes-yes-yes* gyrations. Instead, he sighed as if a thousand sins had been pardoned, sailed out of the hospital, and prepared for a final session with Alicia by visiting the U.C. Berkeley library.

On the way there, he called Jesse's mother. He had an idea of how to get through to him that just might work.

Chapter 31

Alicia watched with agony as the soot sluiced into the drain just feet from another patient who spoke in strange, slippery sentences that went nowhere. Under the tepid torrent, the Librarian slipped away from her as she washed. She could have refused to shower but she feared the repercussions. She just wanted to leave. That meant cooperating, even if she had to let go of everything most precious. To her art, she had always been dedicated and disciplined. She summoned those qualities for this present emergency.

Besides, some things they could never wash away, the bastards.

She left the shower, peeled off the plastic bags taped over her hands and wrists, dried off, and dressed before they dragged her to another suicide-proof breakfast. Arnie gave her a clean gown and a band to tie back her hair. Every day was like Victorian high tea with these finger sandwiches and pre-cut fruit. Well, not so much high tea as high apple juice. They did let her have tea with breakfast, but it was tepid.

During the meal, Alicia observed Rachelle's shoulders and mouth sagging as if she had been battered. The head nurse shuffled past the cafeteria several times as she worked. Alicia stung with a profound suspicion that she'd missed something important. Rachelle circled back past the cafeteria and met Arnie near the secondary station, where he prepared afternoon medications with another nurse. The three spoke in hushed voices.

Arnie wheeled the medication cart into the cafeteria. "Hey there, Ms. Baum!" he said. He handed her a cup of pills and a slightly larger cup of water. She took them, as part of being newly sworn to cooperation.

"Hey," she said back. "Is Rachelle all right?"

"Oh, is something wrong? I didn't notice."

"I don't know. It sure looks like it. She seems sad."

"Don't worry, Ms. Baum. It's just Dr. Sark has been in one of his moods." Arnie rolled his eyes and leaned into his cart. "See ya!"

Yeah, she could imagine that Dr. Shark was in a "mood." A really vile mood that oozed alien sludge like some kind of Lovecraftian nightmare. She wondered now what he would do. Alicia was definitely afraid of him. He was so brazen. It suddenly occurred to Alicia that Dr. Sark probably took out his ire for her escape on Rachelle.

Sore with guilt, Alicia scuttled toward the nurses' station. Rachelle glumly talked on the phone, one hand with a pen making notes on her pad. Alicia waited until Rachelle hung up.

"Arnie will take you to Dr. Farron as soon as he's finished," Rachelle offered.

"I just wanted to tell you something," Alicia said. "I'm sorry if I got you in trouble. You and Dr. Farron have been really good to me, and I hate the thought that you might have suffered because of something I did."

"Angel, you don't have to apologize."

"I do," she said. "I never dreamed this would hurt anyone other than myself."

"Now you don't worry about me," Rachelle said. "You make sure to take your meds and do what Dr. Farron says. But..." Rachelle's face brightened. "Thank you, Angel," she said with a weary smile. "I appreciate your concern."

"You're welcome."

"Why don't you talk to Dr. Farron about it?"

"I will," she said. "But there is something else I need to tell you. Am I the only one who's afraid of Dr. Sark?"

Rachelle leaned in, brows furrowed. "Why do you say that, Angel?"

"I can't say, but I'm afraid. He really scares me."

"Can't say or won't?"

At that moment, Arnie appeared to escort her to Dr. Farron. "Well, hey there, Ms. Baum! Are you ready?"

"Make sure you talk to Dr. Farron about that this afternoon," Rachelle said. Alicia nodded and let Arnie lead her to the elevator. Something about the way Rachelle stared at the telephone console made her wonder if the head nurse was debating an overdue call.

MEANWHILE. WITH JESSE.

Jesse stood before the big stupid doctor door, his space gun hanging at his side. His mother had wandered off down the hallway, talking on her cell phone. Her new dusky sunburst tattoo rode up on her back just above her low-riding yoga pants. That guy made her get it. He hated that guy. But for now, he had no choice. He had to go inside and talk to the big boring doctor who would show him cards and stuff. Well, he was the Galactic Avenger. He did whatever he wanted to. He would show the big dopey doctor what for.

He laid a hand on the doorknob. A voice boomed from within.

"GALACTIC AVENGER, HAVE YOU COME TO RECLAIM YOUR GALACTIC CASTLE?"

Jesse quivered in awe. He pushed open the door and slowly entered, eyes wide.

"Raffabarf?"

The office was dark except for a nightlight from somewhere behind the dopey doctor's desk. Suddenly, an immense figure rustled in the far corner of the office.

Rafarius Bart stood before him. Black plastic garbage bags were tacked around his legs, torso, and arms. A newspaper folded into a Samauri hat cut a sharp bow over a white hockey mask. Rafarius Bart lowered a humongous, Conan-the-Barbarian glow-in-the-dark toy sword and pointed it at Jesse. "ARE YOU, OR ARE YOU NOT, THE GALACTIC AVENGER?"

Stunned, Jesse shut the door. Emboldened by the threat of his arch nemesis, he slipped into his fantasy. "Raffabarf! What have you done with my doctor?"

"I ATE HIM. NOW WHY HAVE YOU DARED TO COME HERE?"

"I have come for the woman I love, Raffabarf! Bow before my Lasers of Death!"

At that, Jesse lifted his ray gun and master-blasted Rafarius Bart, the big plastic gun rattling and flashing.

Rafarius Bart "deflected" each shot with his sword. He jumped with each shot like a crazed tennis player and made vague martial arts sounds. "Heeya! Hooya!" When his Samurai newspaper hat slid off, he caught it and put it back on. Abruptly he stopped and pointed the sword at Jesse.

"YOU HAVE FAILED TO LAY ME LOW WITH YOUR LASERS OF DEATH, GALACTIC AVENGER. DESCRIBE THIS WOMAN YOU SEEK—OR SUFFER MY DRAGON MONSTERS!"

Jesse thought that was the most ridiculous request, but he decided to go along with it because maybe Rafarius Bart had forgotten.

"She's the Galactic Princess! She's powerful...and...smells good...and," he struggled as the feelings kicked at each other. "And...she makes the best peabutt-nutter sandwiches in the world." Jesse's lip quivered. His space gun drooped at his side. "I don't want you in my castle anymore! I want Daddy!"

Rafarius-Farron slipped off his hat and mask, and knelt beside him. "What am I doing in your castle?"

"Mommy doesn't love Daddy anymore and it's all your fault!" Jesse shouted. "I hate him! I HATE HIM!" Jesse dropped to his knees and threw down the gun. "I...HATE... HIM!" As he cried, he tore off the silver mask and wiped his eyes with the back of his hand.

"Hate who, Jesse?"

The name came through in pieces between his sobs. "Al—al— bert!" It was that guy's name. The guy his mommy loved now instead of Daddy.

Dr. Farron let him cry for a few moments. "Can you do something for me, sport?"

Jesse wiped his eyes. "What?"

"Wanna draw?"

Chapter 32

Mr. Wicker sat at his desk, cheek propped on hand as he scowled out the lavender window. Muninn perched on one shoulder, preening himself in oblivion to his master's brooding. He squawked into his ear, the edges of his wings splitting and bristling.

"Huginn has work to do yet," he said, his *basso profundo* voice threatening to dip below human hearing. Under his hand sat the still-blank book of Georgeta Spinosa. That morning she came to him. She stood mutely at his elbow for about five minutes, her one good eye welded to the movements of his hands, before skipping back into the light. "My dear bird will bring down this whole charade and Sirona will see that she belongs back here with me."

If only Dr. Farron didn't know about the Librarian. It wasn't that Mr. Wicker was afraid of Dr. Farron getting through to the occasional child. Or even many children. He couldn't possibly take them all away. They came to the Library from the world over and the doctor's reach was limited. But if Dr. Farron began to publish articles in psychiatric journals, then a problem could start. Granted, it would take great acceptance from the psychiatric community worldwide before anything would change, but it could. But for now, there were only a few nurses, a doctor or two, and maybe a few parents who had heard the children speaking to him. Yet no one communicated about it. So, no one understood.

Except Dr. Farron.

Mr. Wicker pushed away Georgeta's book and picked up Alicia's instead. The heady burn of obsession warmed his eyes and expectation hung heavily in the air. Perhaps he could shake this dream of her as his racing thoughts dragged his sore desires over the cobblestones of disappointment. He would open his hands Christ-wide and let the stones scrape his back and legs. He would lose her in rips, in bits of flesh, in crimson drops. Every bit of her. If only he were so fortunate.

No, Mr. Wicker wasn't afraid of Dr. Farron taking away the children. He was afraid of him taking away Alicia. Sirona. Alicia, who warmed him in ways that no one ever had since her betrayal over two thousand years ago. Alicia, who appreciated who he was and *what* he was as no one ever had.

But no worry. If Huginn and the other raven out in the world did their work, Alicia would be back.

Soon.

IN THE CAFETERIA. LUNCHTIME.

Dr. Farron dragged his lunch tray from the cashier to the table where Rachelle sat poking a long spoon in a thermos of milk. She crumbled fat pieces of homemade cornbread into the thermos as she worked the spoon up and down like an oil drill. The tray scraped the booth table and clattered to a stop. Rachelle glanced at the miserable cup of chocolate frozen yogurt, bag of chips and huge cup of coffee. "That ain't lunch," she said. "More like culinary self torture. Your stomach is going to hate you for weeks."

The doctor had already leaned over the table, a fist digging into his cheek as one hand poked the frozen yogurt with a spork. He said nothing.

"Nothin' like comfort food," she continued. "We were so poor, we used to eat cornbread and milk sweetened with honey. Had chicken on Sundays, if we were lucky. You look like you need some comfort food." She dipped her spoon into the thermos, shoveled out some soggy cornbread, and stuck it in his face.

Dr. Farron grimaced at the heap of cornbread.

"Suit yourself." She shrugged, eating with gusto. "Are you going to kindly tell me then what happened last night? 'Cause I got the chewing out of my life from Shark this morning. Lord, that man can't take responsibility for anything!"

He withered. Then, under his breath, lyrically: "Let Mr. Wicker wash your sicker memories in sand."

Rachelle leaned forward and stage whispered, "I already think you're the craziest man on earth. And you are not disappointing me."

Dr. Farron sighed. "Rachelle, what I have to tell you is crazy enough that it could jeopardize our friendship."

"Our friendship is already in trouble, James." She wadded the plastic wrap from the cornbread in a ball with her napkin. "But if you don't feel like talkin' about it, I can't make you. I can say that whatever happened last night got me in more trouble than I ever care to be in."

"I'm sorry. If you knew what was at stake, you'd understand, but there's patient confidentiality." He paused as his feelings for Alicia momentarily rioted. He wished he could tell Rachelle exactly what had happened with no preface or postscript—exactly what transpired in the hallway, what he witnessed, what he felt—but even just that slice of the whole bizarre pie would taste like insanity. Still, he couldn't have Rachelle mad at him. He felt terrible that she had gotten the brunt of Sark's narcissistic chastening. "Rachelle, do you believe people can...go places...in their dreams?"

Rachelle lowered her spoon, seemingly entirely by the question. "I suppose. That's what dreams are supposed to be. Your soul travels around to distant planes and things. They say a silver cord connects you to your body. That's in the Bible."

He speared the yogurt with the spork and let it stand. "In the Bible?"

"Mmmm-hmm! Old Testament. In Ecclesiastes."

Wriggling his jaw in place, he considered the strangeness of that. He and his über-talented sisters were raised as Easter-Christmas-Catholics. When he grew older, he seldom gave Christianity another thought, believing it to be outdated and arrogant like so many other religions that thought they had a monopoly on truth. Although people were free to believe what they wanted, it seemed downright unhealthy. This tidbit made him wonder if he ought to have read more. "But...well, that's too weird."

"You can't tell me anything too weird," Rachelle said, resuming her excavation of the thermos. "But it better get back to the original topic, if you know what I mean."

"What about real life. Waking life. I mean, can people physically go places... maybe the same places they go in dreams?" The excitement of the idea crackled in his spine and fingers. "I don't mean, can they really go. I mean, can they go...as in...you know... theoretically. Like in the old myths and legends."

"Honey, that's called 'transmigration.' Remember your Sunday school? When the prophet Elijah was taken away in a chariot to heaven? But all the major religions believe in that. Not just Christianity or Judaism. It's *not* a new idea, I guarantee."

He must have had the words OH FUCK sandblasted across his forehead because Rachelle eyed him strangely.

"You thinkin' of goin' somewhere?" She raised an eyebrow as she shoveled the last of the cornbread into her mouth.

"If I tell you what's been happening, you wouldn't believe it," he said, rubbing the stress from his eyes and temples. "That, *I* guarantee."

"Look, I know Mindy lost her badge," Rachelle said. "But that man said you blamed my staff for a practical joke and now I'm on the carpet for running a shoddy ship. I figured you were in a tight spot to say such a thing, and that I don't mind. I don't even mind if we need some disciplinary action. But I gotta know what happened, James. I gotta know what I'm dealing with."

"I wish I knew," he replied. "And I wish I could promise you that it won't get worse. But I can't."

Rachelle stood. "When you're ready to discuss this, you know where to find me." With that, she left without a look back.

I'm an ass, Dr. Farron thought. *A great big jerk who's about to lose a good friend.*

He had one more visit to make before heading to the Cal library for a bit of research. He sailed up the elevator to the seventh floor and solemnly approached the hospital room of Alicia's grandmother.

"James!" Dr. Gregg called. "How's it going?" Looking like a young, hip ad for a gymnasium franchise, Dr. Gregg was a black neurologist in his late thirties. Even at Bayford he stood out, but in the best possible way, James thought.

"It's going," Dr. Farron answered as they walked into the patient room. "How are you, Mrs. Rains?"

Alicia's grandmother sat catatonic in a wheel chair, one eye patched over. The other eye vacantly stared out the window to the deep green Berkeley Hills. Dr. Farron pulled up a chair and sat beside her as Dr. Gregg reviewed her chart.

No answer. Dr. Farron looked to Dr. Gregg.

"We're having a lot of trouble getting her stabilized. She had another stroke yesterday."

The child psychiatrist placed his hand on hers. Her wrinkled, spotted skin was so soft it melted away under his warmth. "Good news, Mrs. Rains. Alicia is close to being released."

Alicia's grandmother frowned and continued staring out the window. "Alicia!" she admonished. But she wasn't talking to Dr. Farron.

"Alicia!"

Claudia had taken great care to prepare the portrait area for Samuel. She had vacuumed, dusted, and arranged the prop walls and sheets just so. No, she would do it right and only once. This painting would fetch a few overdue dollars from her father for certain. Why they had ever agreed to take the children was beyond her. When the money was good, she had no objections. But when the money stopped, they had to make ends meet, plain and simple.

Alicia sat on the wooden stool in a red velvet dress with white frills and white tights, with slick black vinyl Mary Janes binding her china doll feet. Her long blond hair had been curled into long loops. She squirmed like a dog in heat. "I want to play with Lillian."

"Be still!" Claudia yelled at Alicia. She half upraised a hand. The child froze. "Are you purposely trying to upset your grandfather? Your grandfather loves you, you know."

Alicia shook her head almost imperceptibly.

Her grandfather smiled with that easy-going cowboy grin. "Now Claudia, just relax and don't be so hard on the little rose. It'll be all right. I just need a few more moments and this here paintin' will be done soon enough."

God, how she hated him when he undermined her like that.

Alicia's grandmother continued to bark at the hospital room window. "QUIET, I SAY! QUIET!"

"She's suffered too much hemorrhaging. I don't think she even knows what year it is." Dr. Gregg made another note in the chart and closed it. "Are you okay?"

Dr. Farron nodded and sighed. "Yeah. I think it's time to let Alicia know what's going on." He looked down at Mrs. Rains' arms and realized for the first time that they were bare of their shackles of jewelry. Out of curiosity, he took her hand and turned over her wrist.

It was streaked with glistening scars.

Chapter 33

When Dr. Farron returned to his office, he realized he didn't have time to go to Cal before Alicia's session. Just parking on campus and getting into the halls of the university library was going to take just under an hour each way, not leaving him much time to sink into the subject he was hoping to uncover.

Instead, he opened his laptop and stewed a few ideas in his brain juices as his machine awoke from hibernation. What did he want to find exactly? In particular, he wanted to find out what had happened to Alicia's grandfather. Dr. Farron wasn't certain he should even be digging into his patient's history. He'd never been tempted before, nor had he ever needed to burrow into their private lives. That wasn't how therapy worked.

But Dr. Farron was not a bad armchair detective. He'd searched for many things online for his friends and colleagues. He took pride on numerous occasions in finding missing china pieces and special musical venues for his wife. He'd even outed her best friend's boyfriend as a married man and drunk driver. (From the get-go, no one had liked the guy with his vulgar sarcasm and abundant gray chest hairs prancing out of open shirt collar.) He knew his way around online public records, although it sometimes took a while.

What would he do with this information? He decided at that moment he would share with Alicia anything he found. He already felt guilty for his paternalism about her grandmother. He couldn't continue that pattern. It wasn't right. Now he really wondered if there was some pattern of sexual abuse in the family—suicide attempts from one generation to the next. Perhaps her grandfather had attacked her and, as a result, her grandmother finally got up the nerve to have him hauled off? Sometimes what women wouldn't do for themselves, they'd do for their children. But not often enough.

Under hypnosis, Alicia had mentioned his name was Sam—Samuel Rains perhaps? And they lived in Simi Valley. As soon as his browser opened, he first tried searching for "Samuel Rains" and got almost four hundred hits. The first few pages of search results yielded nothing interesting. Alicia seemed to have not even remembered his name until the hypnosis session. Was this even the right name? He forced himself to click through every search result page, scanning everything.

There were lots of guys named "Samuel Rains" who were not only dead—dead was a possibility of course—but also dead too long or dead having lived in the wrong state. There were also lots of living people named "Samuel Rains," but they mostly seemed too young. The genealogy websites took him to some interesting states—Arkansas, Oklahoma, even Montana. States from whence he might have gotten his cowboy persona. Yet nothing that felt like a definite connection with Alicia. Dr. Farron decided these must be her maternal grandparents. Despite the limited number of results, hunting through them was daunting. Even if Alicia had been curious, she wouldn't have even had the resources to find him until very recently. And even then. He needed another search term. Something to narrow it down. He typed in "Simi Valley" and clicked "Search" again, but this time he received no results at all.

Crap.

He also tried "Samuel Rains" combined with "artist" and even "painter," but found nothing remotely promising.

Out of curiosity he entered just "Alicia Baum" and dredged up thousands of hits about her books, stories, interviews, reviews. It was overload and he didn't like seeing her this way, depersonalized and dispersed in a million electronic droplets. So, he shut down that search and stared at the background of his laptop—a lush full-screen photo of a mauve country house, framed by lapis and ivory flowers, as well as some green foliage he couldn't name. Very striking. So beautiful it couldn't be real.

He mused as to what Simi Valley must be like as he typed in just that name and searched for photos. Not impressive—dry, rocky, rambling. Perhaps if Dr. Farron had been a fan of the desert he would have appreciated what he saw. However, he wasn't, which is why he set up his life here in the San Francisco Bay Area. He preferred soggy and foggy over sandy and smoggy any day of the week.

Simi Valley.

Just searching on "Simi Valley" turned up some solid information pages. Since time was running out, he decided he had nothing to lose just reading up on this place, the early home of Alicia. Nothing about it seemed attractive—not even the Ronald Reagan Presidential Library. The city website trumpeted that it was one of the Safest Cities in America. He also noted that this was where the officers who'd beaten Rodney King had been tried and acquitted. A very white population—at least three-quarters Caucasian. Even the city website had a WASPish feeling to it. Sparse, organized, a cultural calendar full of old musicals and Elvis impersonators. Nothing the least bit edgy.

There were links to several banal news articles. Dr. Farron hovered his cursor over them to see the link addresses. They led to a Ventura County newspaper. He clicked and the whole screen gave way to the conservatively designed website for the Ventura County Tribune—"Delivering News Since 1962." The website could have been a raucous, multi-million dollar tabloid for all Dr. Farron cared because he saw something he hadn't anticipated: a link named "ARCHIVES."

He clicked the link and groaned to see that it cost seventy-five dollars a year to have access to the brand new digital news archives. Just installed within the last year.

Screw it. He'd pay it, even if there was nothing there.

He fumbled with his credit card, entered the payment information, and dove in.

Searching on "Samuel Rains," he found something he seriously wished that he'd not found at all. But it explained everything.

And now he'd have to tell Alicia.

Chapter 34

Alicia squatted on the floor of Dr. Farron's office in her freshly laundered sweats and shirt, snipping with a pair of scissors at a piece of folded black paper. A hot shower and good breakfast made all the difference. And she felt better for having apologized to Rachelle. She grinned at Dr. Farron, who sat in his chair, lost in thought. She had just been telling him about her father, the expatriate who lives in Vienna. She hadn't heard from him in at least five years. She sent him a copy of her last book, but he didn't reply. She wished that she could know what she'd done to drive him away.

"I'm sure his emotional and physical distance have nothing to do with you," Dr. Farron assured her.

"That's what every therapist says," she said, "but I don't believe it's true." For years she was a tremendous troublemaker, she explained. The schools even put her in special education because she was so troublesome they thought she might be mentally handicapped. Perhaps she'd been such a pain that she finally wore thin what little love he had for her—thinner than the paper she was cutting.

"I challenge you to make better paper dolls." With a flourish, she drew apart the paper edges to reveal a whole line of Mr. Wickers.

Dr. Farron stirred. "Oh, yeah?" He lowered himself to the floor and scrambled to her side, snatching a large piece of white paper. As he carefully folded and snipped, he grew around her like a Sendak forest—wild, impelling, distracting. He twisted away dramatically, as if to call attention to the fact that he was hiding something from her.

"What are you doing there?"

"Just one…more…cut." *Snip.* "Okay." He turned back to her and pulled apart the paper. A row of plain white paper dolls.

"Um, that's great," she said sarcastically. "Paper dolls. Original."

"Touch their heads."

She tapped the head of the center doll and a split divided its head—that last *snip.* "Oh! Lobotomies! That's brilliant!"

Dr. Farron grinned proudly.

That's when she pounced. She merely let the tractor beam pull her toward him. But he dodged her. She landed in a heap of nothing when what she'd wanted were his mouth, hair, cologne, and hands. He rolled away just out of reach onto his knees and pitched himself up off the carpet.

"Stop it! Now! I won't have you jeopardizing my practice any more than it has been!"

Alicia smiled wickedly. "But you want to, right?"

"Just...*stop it*! You can't be under my care any more."

"What? That's ridiculous!"

"There's a lot more going on than you realize, Alicia. And it's dangerous for me professionally to smear these boundaries. It's absolutely unacceptable and you've got to respect that!"

"But who else can I possibly talk to about Mr. W?" Sitting up, she sank her hands onto her thighs. "Besides, I don't want to be without you. You're the only one for me." Which was not how she'd meant to phrase it.

"Am I?"

He snapped the double-entendre at her like a wet towel. She wasn't even sure of what she'd heard until he looked away as if bitten by some revelation that slithered away into his vast underground network of emotional insecurities. She then recalled the ash that covered her lips when they kissed and she knew exactly what he meant. Or had he heard about what had happened with Dr. Sark? Oh, god. This was messier than eating a Cadbury Easter egg in an earthquake.

"Yes."

This seemed to soothe him. "Just please stay out of trouble tonight. For me and Rachelle, if not for your own good?"

"Of course I will," she said. "And if Mindy loses another badge I'll turn it in to Security ASAP. How's that?"

"Perfect. And so you know," he added, "I had to do some fast talking today to get both of us out of trouble."

"I'm sorry," she said. And meant it.

"Which included trying to get Rachelle on the same page."

"What did you tell her?" Alicia asked, nervous.

"Nothing," he said. "Nothing that I didn't tell Dr. Dulac and Dr. Sark. I can't tell her what really happened, anyway. It would violate patient-doctor confidentiality."

"But you had to say something."

"I told her I found you in Georgeta's room and that I walked you back to your room, where I fell asleep in the visitor's chair. As for everything else, I had no explanation except that someone else blackened us up as a prank." He leaned forward, determined. "This is the part where, if we were, like, ten years old, we would cut our palms, spit into them and rub our hands together. You understand?"

"Blood brothers?"

"Something like that."

He then looked haunted as he sat in his chair and spoke. "Alicia, do you want to know what your grandfather did?"

Alicia drew her legs up in front of her. "You know what happened? How do you know?"

"Answer my question. Yes or no."

Alicia let the question simmer. What the fuck? Her grandfather! She'd told herself over the years that it didn't matter. He was clearly dead or else he would have contacted her long ago. But he didn't. He'd just vanished like everyone else in her life. Even her grandmother was now pulling a vanishing act.

And she was damned tired of it.

"Okay," she said. "Yes, I want to know."

"Because I know what happened. I checked the newspaper archives online for Simi Valley."

"I didn't think they had such a thing."

"I wouldn't have thought so, either, but more and more newspapers who have microfiched their archives are now putting scans online. And not just scans but searchable papers."

"Jesus."

Dr. Farron gathered up some papers from inside the drawer of his desk and handed them to her.

With a weird sort of anxiety that felt like ants spreading over her skin, Alicia examined the printouts of the newspaper scans.

Samuel Rains Charged with Murdering Grandchild

Alicia frowned. What grandchild? She wasn't dead. She was very much still –

Oh fuck. FUCK FUCK FUCK FUCK FUCK –

She read some more. The tears came in a torrent. Bizarre. Unbelievable. Yet here it was. Her name wasn't in the news report—she was a minor then—but her grandparents were both named, as well as Lillian.

Lillian Baum.

"This can't be right."

"Why not?"

"It says that he was arrested for killing his grandchild. By strangulation. Not me but—"

"Lillian."

Alicia stared at the news article.

"You don't remember having a sister? Maybe a stepsister? Or a cousin?"

"No," she croaked.

"A younger sister. About a year your junior. You have no memory of her."

Alicia shook her head. She hated crying. She hated this weak feeling like everything was being pulled out of her through her belly button. Dr. Farron brought her the box of tissues and set it beside her. She yanked out a handful as the deluge started.

"Did you wipe out that memory of her somehow? Did you give every single memory to You Know Who?"

"This is completely off the hook insane. There has to be a mistake."

"There might be. This is what I found with just a couple hours of research online. I don't have any other information to back it up. You'd have to hire a P.I. and make some family inquiries. Maybe call your father, even if it's a hard call to make."

"But they're definitely my grandparents. Right here. Claudia Rains of Simi Valley. And...well, I didn't remember his name until our session, but Sam is right, I think. Samuel Rains. And it's right around when my grandfather left. I just can't believe..." She sat there shaking a moment, wondering when the world would swallow her. "He drank. My grandmother made lots of derogatory remarks over the years about him being a drunk."

"Why didn't you ever look him up? Weren't you ever curious?"

Alicia thought for another moment. "Grandma told me so often that he was a bad man and a drunk that I gave up any thought of him. Seriously. Between not remembering his first name, not knowing how to find him, and not having the money or the resources to pay someone, that was that. Grandpa exited the theater of my life. Exeunt. Gone."

Dr. Farron handed her another printout, this time an article about her grandfather's conviction. "Is it possible that you witnessed the murder? They hint at it but they never come out and say it."

She shrugged. Anything was possible. She'd never seen baby pictures growing up. Just one or two that her grandmother claimed to have salvaged from her father, ostensibly photos of just her but they could have been separate snapshots of either her or Lillian. It would explain her father's distance. Guilt, bereavement, reminded daily of her absence by the visage of his other child. He must have been a mess.

She marveled at Mr. Wicker's surgical precision in excising her memories. She couldn't conjure even the faintest image in her mind's eye. Not a breakfast, not a playtime, not a single moment with her.

Her sister.

Someone knocked on the door. Dr. Farron grimaced and checked his watch. "It's probably Arnie. You've got a medical evaluation after this with Dr. Stemmle." He stood and approached the door.

"Are you going to still be my doctor? I promise to behave." The thought of not seeing him again felt like a knife twisting in her chest.

"I don't know."

She slid in front of him and flattened herself against the door. "If not, will you be anything else?"

The smell of him. His skin. Everything so close, yet...

"You need to get through this before you think about those things," he said.

Another knock thudded against her back. Louder.

Alicia felt the singe of loss but was determined not to let it get to her. She stepped aside.

Crestfallen, Dr. Farron opened the door. "Hi Arnie. She's ready."

Chapter 35

These days, Arnie was feeling pretty darned good.

Sure, the drugs were giving him the trots and drying out his mouth, but they were better than the alternative. He started chewing gum and drinking a lot of water. That worked pretty well to get him drooling again. It masked the initial thrush, too. God! The thrush made him feel less sexy than the virus itself. Kiss me, baby—ew! A spongy white tongue carpet was definitely not how he wanted to greet a lover. But that was gone now. Finis!

And—hooray!—his depression was lifting. The initial diagnosis was probably the worst moment of his life. That's when he discovered that the so-called stages of grief were total bull. He went through the stages out of their supposed order, sometimes two or more at a time. He'd lost a couple of friends to the virus—who hadn't?—but they weren't people close to him. In fact, he'd been really blessed and hadn't lost hardly anyone in his life. Not to death, anyway. To ostracization? Yep. But not death.

After a long run of heartbreaks, he had decided to date only positives, as the neggies rejected him time and again. He tried to not take it personally. They were rejecting the virus, not him. But it still beat him up emotionally. The major depression last year made him reach out to the community and his friends for support. Definitely, only positives from now on, he swore. And that changed everything. For one, it took the guessing game out of when to disclose, which was great because he wasn't about to *not* disclose right away. That just didn't seem fair. But immediate disclosure to a neggie brought with it drama followed closely on the heels of shame. The other day, he bought a navy blue muscle shirt with a big red "plus" sign across the pecs. On the back it read, "Take the shame out of the game." It both emboldened him and shocked him with its courage and honesty. He got such a supportive reaction from his friends that, with much trepidation, he wore it to his local bar last night. As frightening as it was, he got quite a draw and met potential lovers who were also positive.

Now he was, like, *really* out. And it scared him shitless.

Arnie was not a courageous guy, but he was learning something about life. About how some things he had to do would always be scary, so he just had to do them scared. This was one of those things, yet he could manage. He was really good at taking his meds, of course, and knew a lot about nutrition. But his meds had side effects, in addition to the emotional strain, financial concerns and social pressures of having the virus. While Arnie was more afraid of getting hit by a bus than dying of the virus, the daily struggle to not let the virus define who he was and how much he enjoyed life was overwhelming at times.

Like today.

The drugs also gave him nightmares. His CD4 count consistently clocked in at a goodly number, which meant the current antiretrovirals were really working for him. So he had been reluctant to change, even when the dreams turned bloody. Last night he had weird dreams about domestic animals that were the victims of vivisection. When Rachelle asked him to take the extra shift tonight, he did so gratefully, not wanting to go home and sleep right away even though he was definitely tired.

Arnie straightened like a rabbit that just caught whiff of a hound. He could sense when evil—that is, Dr. Sark—was at hand. Sure enough, Dr. Sark swung into the ward from the elevator as Arnie sorted the next day's meds. He'd always assumed Dr. Sark was one of those who was on the "DL"—that is, on the "down low," a supposedly straight guy who secretly had sex with men but who did not claim to be gay or bi. It was just a feeling Arnie had about the doctor. He also thought Dr. Sark was attractive in a scary sort of way. He used his temper like a scythe, which would have been the kind of power thing Arnie liked if it weren't for the fact that Dr. Sark had sidestepped a murder accusation some time ago. Dr. Sark was a tsunami in Arnie's pond in more ways than one.

Everyone was in bed and the day was over. Soon he'd start the flashlight rounds. Tonight an extra orderly had come in to beef up security and replace Brian's muscle. Arnie had never liked Brian, who oozed homophobia in a stereotypical way that had sometimes proved lethal to gay men in the past. Arnie was kind of used to it. He didn't feel too threatened, just actively disliked. He could handle that.

"Well, heya there, Dr. Sark! Aren't you working kinda late?"

"What are *you* doing here?" Dr. Sark's eyes were slightly dilated. Sometimes Arnie wondered if Dr. Sark had a drug problem, the way he was grandiose at times and manipulated people, but that could be caused by a number of things. Tonight, Arnie smelled something wrong.

"Rachelle asked me to stay an extra shift."

"Don't."

Arnie finished smoothing a new name label onto a cup. "Sure, Dr. Sark. Anything you say." He pushed the cart aside and braved the next question. "So, who's taking over this shift?"

At bedtime, Alicia didn't feel like lying down. Her mind worked feverishly over the last session. Over Lillian. She'd read the articles over and over, scraping every last clue from the printouts. Her grandfather's confession was the most difficult to read about. He'd *confessed* to killing her sister. She wondered what Malcom would've said about that. His specialty was family law but he had an opinion about every case that crossed the headlines. Curiosity about her grandmother's whereabouts bloomed under the constant attention of her thoughts. How could she have not talked about this? They were another generation, sure, the ones who didn't talk about WWII, the ones who even clenched the horrors of the Korean and Vietnam Wars in tight, suffering fists. But her silence was unprecedented—or was it? Her whole family seemed experts at minimal communication. Hell, they were fucking mimes and that was only when they gave a damn to press a couple of flat palms against the air in front of them, which was almost never.

The meds cart rounded the bend into the room. She perked up, thinking she'd see Arnie, but the last person she ever wanted to see was pushing the cart.

"Hello, Ms. Baum," Dr. Sark cooed. Wearing a white doctor's coat, he plucked a cup from the cart and offered it to her. "You look well."

"Thanks," she said, taking the cup. Something felt very wrong about this.

He pretended to dust a space on the bed. "May I?"

"Sure."

As he sank into the mattress, Alicia's body tensed like a granite breadboard. She swallowed the meds and handed him the empty cups.

"So," he said, a statement unto itself. Dr. Sark's lips pouted slightly as he leveled those glacial irises at her. "I just wanted to say that I'm sorry you needed something that you could not ask me for," he said.

"Oh?"

"What I'm saying," he said, "is that I thought we had an understanding. When you denied me the opportunity to do something for you, you denied yourself the opportunity to do something for me."

He laid his hand on her leg. An oily dollop of revulsion dropped into her stomach.

She pretended to hunch contritely. "Sometimes it isn't easy to think clearly in the excitement of an unexpected opportunity. I hope you won't fault me with negligence as much as impulsivity. I did not forget your generosity. I count it one of the greatest assets of this hospital."

A thin smile stitched across his face. "Of course not," he said. He patted her leg, then massaged it briefly. Just as Alicia prayed to everything she never believed in, he placed his hands on his thighs and declared, "Well, I won't keep you. Good night, Ms. Baum."

"Good night."

He slid off the bed and plunged his hands into his coat pockets. He smiled and strolled toward the door as if leaving a cafe.

Alicia laid down in bewilderment. The whole conversation stank. What did he want? To make a point? It felt strange.

The subterranean parking garage was slightly damp, even on the third level. Arnie zipped up his leather jacket as he walked to his car. Something about Dr. Sark and the way he looked bothered him. Brian was suspended, so he couldn't have called him in; Mindy had worked twelve hours (last he checked the schedule, anyway) and was not scheduled to come in until tomorrow; and one of the other relief nurses had the flu. The staff were spread far too thin. Dismissing him was highly unusual.

Arnie stopped between the cars next to his Honda. A *wrongness* burned a forest fire in his gut. He immediately strode to the elevator, slipping his cell phone from his jacket pocket. Before last night, he would have been too scared to report something out of line. He would have feared retribution on a grand scale. In fact, that's what happened before—when that patient died. He'd feared reporting Dr. Sark's odd behavior the two days leading up to the isolation and death. That soul-scoring guilt was what drove him to that drunken night where he slept bareback with that guy and caught the virus.

But now, things were different. Now he knew he could do scary stuff, even if he had to do it scared. And after the investigation, he'd realized that he alone was not responsible for what had happened. He'd just done as he was told and, beyond his keen intuition, hadn't any reason to think or do otherwise. That knowledge had cooled the guilt somewhat.

As soon as he reached the lobby and got a signal, he scrolled to his contact list and dialed.

About fifteen minutes after Dr. Sark left, Alicia felt heavy. A smooth emptiness swelled behind her eyes. The air thickened. Her breathing slowed. Alicia gripped the sheets and pulled them taut up under her chin as she attempted to focus. But the strength drained from her fingers and she let go of the sheets, arms and legs sinking into the mattress without her. As she lost control, panic spiked her throat.

The Library bled into her dimming vision. Mr. Wicker read from a book with his feathery, *basso profundo* voice.

Come into the garden, Maud, for the black bat, night, has flown...

Alicia pressed her lips together to form an "M," but her facial muscles disobeyed. *Mmmmmm.*

Her fingers bent with muscle spasms as she desperately pawed at the nurse's button. And still, his voice:

...Come into the garden, Maud, I am here at the gate alone.

Whether it was his voice or her imagination summoning him as she drowned under the influence of a narcotic, she could not tell. The veil between the worlds had grown thinner each moment since she'd first met him.

A figure in the doorway. Tall. Menacing.

Mmmmmm, she said. *Mmmmmmmiiiisssterrrrrr.*

A cloth strap slid over her wrist and tightened with a tug. Alicia strained to focus on the face in her narcotic haze. A tremor drilled into her gut as she recognized the man who stripped the blanket from the bed and strapped her ankles to the corners of the bed frame. Two other, bigger men assisted him, but they soon left. The room door was closed, the world's eyes shut to her.

Mmmmmm!

"According to my report, you became agitated and lashed out at me tonight, repeatedly suggesting that you would take your life again, and not a moment before you had taken mine. This threat required that I use both chemical restraints and mechanical," he said, his voice a low boil. He tugged the leg straps to ensure they were taught. "Tomorrow morning, I will send a request to the court that you receive forced inpatient treatment for another month." He circled the bed and bowed close to her. His lower lip grazed her cheek as he whispered in her ear. "But not before I make your life a living hell."

MMMMMM! She yanked and the wrist restraints painfully cut into her stitches.

The door opened.

Dr. Sark nodded at the doorway, where the burly jackass from group therapy stood, rocking on his slippered heels. Dr. Sark motioned him inside. "I believe you two are friends? Or perhaps not. Pity. Why don't I leave you alone so that you can reconcile?" The smile that bled across his face was so chilling that Alicia forced a sort of throttled scream from her throat, the sort that she often tried during "old hag" dreams when she half-awakened in naps to the thing sitting on her chest. She'd learned not to panic during old hag dreams, but simply try to relax and go back to sleep rather than fight the suffocation and paralysis.

This time, there was no relaxing. No waking up. The drugs folded thick wooly hands over her eyes.

The mattress buckled and a sharp pain stung her legs as the jackass climbed over her and crushed her legs. His stinky breath wafted into her face as he growled at her.

"So, cunt. You gonna apologize for what you did to me?"

Alicia could barely breathe. His fat knee dug into her thigh, making her wince with agony. She couldn't speak articulately even if she wanted to. Instead, a garbled groan escaped her throat instead of the well-placed verbal barb with which she wanted to gouge his balls.

"All right then. You get what you deserve, bitch."

His meaty paw slapped her so hard that the pain knocked out a bit of the cottony feeling in her head. He hit like a girl, slapping her again and again, bruising her breasts and busting her lip before he got the gumption to drive his fist into her abdomen. Alicia coughed, winded, pain blossoming in her belly. Blood dribbled down her chin as he laughed. Her head rang with anguish as her face, torso, arms and legs throbbed. Her wrists and ankles stained the bonds with blood from struggling to escape every blow, the skin scraped raw. Judging from the pain in her neck and right shoulder, she'd pulled a muscle or worse. She couldn't tell if the searing in her side was a broken rib or bruised innards.

Like it mattered at this point.

Little more registered in her medication haze except that now the asshole was yanking at the drawstrings on his sweats, loosening the wide band that hugged his overabundant waistline. He managed to unhinge the pants waist from his greasy hips and shoved them down around his ass, revealing a half-erect hairy cock bulging under his sagging, stretch-marked beer belly.

And it wasn't much bigger than the two inches she'd suggested.

Injuries scalded Alicia's entire body as he crawled up between her battered legs. She fought the sick welling up into and scorching her throat, terrified of choking on her vomit. He wrapped his hands around her neck, crushing her larynx. Every ugly pockmark on his face loomed over Alicia, spittle working its way over his lips. She couldn't breathe! Oh god! Worse than an old hag dream. Waves of blackness washed over her eyes as his hands dug into her larynx.

Dr. Sark stepped into the room, hands dug deeply into his white lab coat pockets. The two orderlies flowed into the room before him and peeled the man off Alicia, who choked and gasped. They dragged him away as he protested. "You said I could do whatever I wanted! You said!"

"My goodness! I never said such a thing." The smug lie lit a rage in Alicia that burned away some of the chemical influence. "Someone as deluded and violent as you, sir, belongs under heavy chemical restraint." To the orderlies, he said, "Please put him in room 4-E?"

When the orderlies hauled Alicia's boisterous, flailing assailant out of the room, Dr. Sark remained and nonchalantly shut the door.

"Oh, dear, Ms. Baum. You no longer look well at all."

His voice spoke behind a thick glass wall—faint, distant. But he was right there, those cool irises examining her face. She could feel the lid swelling around her left eye, pressing her eye partially closed. Her breaths came in long, belabored gasps.

"You look so unwell, I suspect they will have to put you back under medical evaluation. But before I alert security..."

A tear leaked from her eye and rolled wet into her ear. *Nightmares and narcotics.* He stroked the hair from her eyes and crushed his lips against hers. His breath tasted sour. *Sulfuric.* A white blade of terror slipped between her eyes as he ran his large yet slender hands over her bare legs, drawing up her nightgown as he slid his hand up her thigh. He loosed his pants, letting his long, hard penis escape from the opening. Unlike her previous assailant, he was nearly hairless with just a sprouting of graying hairs from the base of his cock. His smug face dipped into hers again, his hand separating her jaws so that he could press his tongue between her lips.

Alicia bit down. *Hard.*

The doctor shrieked into her mouth, beating her head with his hands and pulling her hair, but much less effectively than he could have if the tender muscle between Alicia's teeth wasn't in the most intense agony. Alicia held on, the coppery juices sliding down around her teeth and gums, lacquering her throat. *Fuck you, you sonuvabitch*, she thought. *I will fucking eat you alive.*

...the steady pounding of ancient Norse drums...

...shrill explosion from the window...

...slivers of glass...

...cold air blasting the room...

...a rush of black feathers...

...Dr. Sark tried to wrench himself around to fend off whatever was diving at his head. Something thicker than water spattered the blankets, Alicia's hair, even her bandages as the smell of blood bloated in the air.

...*click*...

...*whooooosh.*

A handful of security guards charged inside the room, feet crunching in broken glass from the ruptured window. Alicia relaxed her jaws in the bedlam of howls and handcuffs as they dragged Dr. Sark off her and hauled him away like one of his patients.

"What the hell is that thing?"

"How'd it get in here?"

"Jesus Christ! What the—?"

Alicia watched groggily as whatever it was swooped out of the room cawing so loudly that everyone scattered in its wake as it soared down the hallway. Her synapses were so soggy with the drugs that it took a moment for it to register that perhaps what she was seeing was a raven.

Alicia spent the night in another part of the hospital with Rachelle holding her hand. Portly nurses with kind eyes visited her at intervals as she sweated and vomited from the drugs, reassuring her as they applied ice, antiseptics and bandages to her wounds. They changed her soaked sheets and cleaned her mouth several times before she finally passed out from exhaustion.

She sensed at one point that someone else was holding her hand. She squeezed back best she could as she faded back out of consciousness.

As she slept, the words of Tennyson's poem drifted from the darkened porticoes of her subconscious into the brighter parlors where her dreams gathered.

Come into the garden, Maud,
I am here at the gate alone.
And the woodbine spices are wafted abroad,
And the musk of the rose is blown...

Chapter 36

With her powerful beak, Huginn wrenched off the vent cover of an air conditioning duct and scurried deep into the bowels of the hospital ventilation system until she found a place she could huddle.

As the dark ducts rumbled with blasts of warm air, she bore the winds and listened to her master's furious, grieving voice:

You should have been at the window!

I am weakening here. I needed water.

You should have never left that window. She has been harmed and it is your fault.

Huginn did not respond, but instead pondered her predicament. She had to return to the Library. Soon. She was starting to feel things she had not felt in centuries—not since her first master snatched her from the nest and brought her to live at the top of the tree with the Aesir and Vanir.

She'd wanted to dive out the broken window that she'd just shattered, but couldn't avoid the humans. She did not wish to hurt anyone else and could not risk injury herself. That did not matter to her master. Alicia had been hurt.

Huginn would have to atone for this terrible lapse in her watch and guardianship. But how?

Chapter 37

DAY 4—BAYFORD HOSPITAL

Alicia awoke in a strange room to the brisk movements of a nurse, a tiny Filipino woman twisting a plastic cover over a fat electronic thermometer. She stuck the apparatus under Alicia's tongue and began to take her blood pressure, grinning with crooked front teeth. "Ah! Seventy over one-ten, Ms. Baum," she announced as she unwrapped the gauge. "How do you feel?"

"Like a crunchy lump of toaster cheese," Alicia replied behind a fat lip.

The nurse snorted with laughter. "I'll get you some breakfast. Toast? Tea? Or you feel like more?"

"Toast and tea is great. Thanks."

The nurse brought in a light breakfast ten minutes later. How old was she? Thirty? Forty-five? Over fifty? Alicia couldn't tell. Her cheer contrasted starkly with the gloom of the psych unit—except for maybe Arnie. He seemed happy. Alicia took the food, sipping hot tea for the first time in many days. She drank it black, leaving the sugar and cream packets unopened. The dry toast was good, too. Her appetite was greater than she'd anticipated from such a horrendous night.

Then, a police officer came. He took a statement from her about what happened.

"Will you press charges?" he asked.

"Definitely," she replied.

As they wrapped up the statement, Dr. Dulac entered. "Well, if it isn't the illustrious Ms. Baum," he said with a newfound sparkle in his eye. "I'm Dr. Leonard Dulac, the Chairman of Mental Health Services."

Alicia beamed at him. He seemed less stiff than James had described. But then she wondered if he was being nice to her because he feared she'd sue the hospital. He shook hands with the officer, who excused himself. "I'm pleased to meet you," she said, and he shook her hand, too. He seemed like the serious but caring grandfatherly type. He pulled up a visitor's chair and sat with her.

"The pleasure is mine, Ms. Baum. As deeply saddened as I am, I don't think there is any way for us to adequately apologize for what happened. We are waving your bill and the next six months of prescribed outpatient treatment, if you agree to some kind of arbitration."

"Here's my attorney's number," Alicia said, handing him a scribbled note. Malcom had put her in touch with a killer personal injury lawyer.

Dr. Dulac took the card and sighed. "Dr. Sark's been let go from the hospital," Dr. Dulac said. "And we've given you twenty-four-seven security."

"Dr. Farron has been great. You should know that. He's a great doctor. A real healer."

"I appreciate you saying that." He smiled. "Good luck, Ms. Baum."

"Thank you."

Dr. Stemmle arrived next to check her wrists and other wounds. "Not bad. You avoided reopening the wounds," he said. Earlier that morning, an orderly had taken her to x-ray, where they determined her rib was not in fact broken, but badly bruised. They x-rayed her shoulder, skull and ankle, as well. A possible rotator cuff strain, but nothing broken.

Dr. Farron arrived just as Dr. Stemmle was leaving. "Hey Mike, how are ya?" Over his denim dress shirt, he wore a wide Justice League tie with Superman's "S" bursting from the silk.

"Nice tie, James." Dr. Stemmle waved to Alicia. "See you at follow up."

As soon as they were alone, Dr. Farron proffered a paper bag. "Your things?"

Alicia flashed him a jagged smile.

She changed into a sleeveless, peach silk dress, but not the lavender sweater. It was sealed in a plastic bag, soiled with soot and badly in need of dry cleaning. She slipped on a pair of sandals she hadn't noticed before that sat at the bottom of the bag under the dress. Entirely too sunny, but of course part of her grandmother's crusade to change her wardrobe. Her grandmother had forgotten that the Bay Area isn't nearly as warm as Los Angeles. As she left the room, Dr. Farron was waiting for her.

He beamed. "You need a ride? 'Cause you know, Superman doesn't have any citizens to save for a couple of hours."

"Sure," she said, happy. "Can we say goodbye to Rachelle first? And I want to thank Arnie."

He shook his head. "We can't go in the ward, but this is from her." He reached in his pocket and withdrew a card.

Alicia tore open the envelope and glanced over the Hallmark schlock to read Rachelle's writing at the bottom. *Good luck, Alicia. And be careful when you go home. Memories have a habit of walking around like they own the place.*

Turning the card to him, she showed off Rachelle's turn of phrase.

"That's Rachelle. A budding Rimbaud," Dr. Farron said.

"She's great," Alicia said. "You think she'd adopt me? Or not so much?"

"I think she would." He grinned. "They're talking about promoting her somewhere higher in the hospital administration, but she told me this morning she's got bigger plans."

"Such as?"

"She's applied to Stanford's psychology graduate program. I think she's got a good shot at getting in."

"That's amazing! She can do it. I know she'll get in."

Dr. Farron shifted. "Alicia, there's something I have to tell you before—"

Raaa! Raaa! Raaa! Raaaaaaaa!

A greasy cluster of feathers and claws plunged at Dr. Farron from nowhere. "Jesus!" He ducked, swiping at the attacker. A line of blood wept from his cheek.

Alicia stared awe-stricken at the raven as it glided down the busy hallway toward the opening elevator. The river of hospital staff and patients parted as Alicia madly dodged people to keep on the raven's tail.

Raaa! Raaa! Raaa! Raaaaaaaa!

"ALICIA!"

The raven dive-bombed a nurse waddling alongside an elderly man with a walker. She screamed as her hands flew up to protect her face. Alicia slid past them, following the raven into the open elevator beyond. But as Dr. Farron charged toward them, the doors rolled closed on him. "Shit!" he yelled as he slammed the "Up" button repeatedly.

Fluttering and cawing, the raven pecked the seventh floor button and Alicia shrank against the metallic back wall.

The elevator groaned to a stop with dreadful finality and the doors opened to a draft that stank of sickness and antiseptic soap. The raven erupted into the hallway and silently careened down a dull white hall of hospital rooms. Televisions flickered and buzzed with talk shows as Alicia passed each room. Coughs. Rasps. Moans. Phone conversations.

"Quiet, I say!"

An elderly woman's voice shouted from a room at the end of the hall. The raven sailed into that room and out of sight.

Alicia knew that voice.

Dr. Farron emerged from the stairwell at the other side of the ward. "Alicia!" He reached out to her. "This is what I was...trying...to tell you."

Alicia stopped at the doorway. The raven landed on the shoulder of an old woman who sat round-shouldered in a wheelchair as she gawked out the window at the deep green Berkeley Hills, blanketed by storm clouds. The window's reflection told Alicia who the sentinel was.

"Grandma."

Dr. Farron skidded to a stop at her side as she entered the room. He didn't try to intervene but rather watched as Alicia approached her grandmother.

The raven cawed loudly in the old woman's ear. Her upper eyelid twitched and her withered lips parted, but nothing more came. Alicia looked to Dr. Farron. "You knew about this."

"I started to tell you downstairs, but this—*bird*—beat me to it."

The raven shrieked at him, the hackles of its throat bristling. A nurse entered the room. "What is going on here? Doctor?" Her eyes widened with alarm. "Oh, my god!"

"Call animal control," Dr. Farron said. He glared at the raven, more than delighted to see it put to sleep.

The nurse nodded and reeled back out of the room, never taking her eyes off the pest. A muttering crowd of nurses and patients gathered outside the room in the hallway, peering inside to see what was afoot.

Alicia wasn't sure she believed him. "What happened?"

"She's had several strokes," he said, avoiding her eyes. "I'm sorry."

Alicia covered her mouth with one hand as she took her grandmother's in the other. "Grandma?" She pressed her grandmother's frail hand to her cheek. "Oh, poor Grandma."

Leery of another attack, Dr. Farron watched the preening raven as he approached Alicia and put a hand on her shoulder.

"She's in really good care here, Alicia. Dr. Gregg is the best. We can talk about it over lunch. Unless you want to stay here—and I totally understand if you do."

Chapter 38

As the white Lexus wound into the Piedmont Hills, Alicia's head lolled miserably against the car headrest, eyes burning with depression once again as she contemplated her future. The heater was on full blast to warm her bare arms and sandaled feet.

"I wanted to tell you about your grandmother—in fact *paternalism* is a big no-no in the psych unit. But as a therapist I don't give patients bad news unless they're stable enough to hear it, and not right after a suicide attempt."

"Right after?"

"Yeah. It happened the day after your admission to the psych unit."

"Just after we met." *Bastard*, she thought.

He shifted the direction of the conversation. "We wouldn't have met at all if it weren't for a certain 9-1-1 call. By the way, I know it was old barbeque butt."

"I couldn't tell you because I didn't want you to think I was crazy. I just wanted to cooperate, to stop arguing with you so that we could be closer." She paused. "I'm really pissed. I can't believe you knew and didn't tell me."

He said nothing for a moment. "I understand you're angry. I'm so sorry. I wanted to tell you. Honest."

Alicia's head lolled his way as she inspected him. Despite her current anger and uncertainty, he was still the man she'd pounced the day before. She unfolded one of her arms and reached up to touch his cheek, letting her fingers brush his face until they met his lips. Her bandages lightly scratched his jaw. He grasped her hand and deposited it by his side.

"I wonder how he made that call. He isn't real—like a person. He's more like a demi-god or something. Right?"

Alicia raised an eyebrow.

"I don't know," he said. "It's been a lot of years since I played Dungeons and Dragons. What would *you* call him?"

"He doesn't have a classification. But he does have a phone."

"Really? Like, a cell phone? A cordless phone? A box on the wall that he cranks to reach earth?"

"More like a phone from the nineteen-forties that sits on his desk."

"Oh, right. I should have known. Well, at least he can't text. Yet."

They drove on in silence until they pulled up in front of Alicia's dying lawn. Leaves scattered the dead grass as storm clouds drifted heavy and dark across the sky. The "For Sale" sign swung on its hooks in the wind under the soulless eyes of the dark windows.

Dr. Farron's Lexus drew up to the curb. He peered past Alicia and out at the spooky house. "Here we are. 1313 Mockingbird Lane." Slivers of raindrops began to streak the car windows. "Stay there a sec."

He climbed out of the car and went around to the trunk to retrieve an umbrella. They huddled together under the emerging downpour as they headed for the front door, the empty driveway a stinging reminder that her car—with her good credit—was gone forever. Or, at least, it felt that way.

Dr. Farron retracted the umbrella as they passed the wilting violet ginger lilies crowding the walkway. He halted just short of the wide, flat steps leading up to the art deco door. It had a burnished nickel knob and deep blue, geometrically patterned, stained glass. Even the mail slot toward the bottom of the door was polished nickel. "Wow. This door says 'Welcome!', doesn't it?" he said.

"It's my favorite part of the house." Alicia paused as she realized she was going to be away from him now. The idea seemed to wrap around their ankles and hold them both there on the porch.

"Don't you have a friend or someone who can be with you?" he asked.

"I don't want to be with anyone for a while. I need to write. I'm pretty tired of reality. I want to create a bit of fantasy for a change. To sort of soothe myself."

"That's great!" he said, a flicker of excitement in his eyes. "But—seriously—it's not a good idea to be totally alone."

She just looked at him, too angry still to kiss him, the attraction stoking the fires of her rage. After a beat or two, the burn of passion turned back to depression in her chest and her stomach soured. She placed a hand onto his chest as if carefully pushing away and smiled wanly. "Doesn't Superman have some citizens to save this afternoon?"

"Yeah," he said, sounding reluctant. He produced his wallet and fingered out a card. "I want you to call me later tonight. Tell me you're okay."

"I will." She played with his Justice League tie. "Just be careful going back. One wrong turn and you'll end up in a dangerous part of Oakland."

Alicia waited until the white Lexus was nowhere in sight. Then, and only then, she turned the nickel knob of the brilliant door—the door she had custom designed and installed so that, no matter what awaited her inside, she felt glad to be home. She never locked her front door. Never needed to. And her house had waited for her as houses do, patiently and vacantly. The mailman fed it mail every day, but no one loved it on the inside.

Nothing affects you, you sullen, frigid bitch. Eric's voice. She heard it as she entered the house and kicked aside new bills lying on the floor under the mail slot. Bills blackened by boots when trammeled by emergency crews as they rescued her. She closed the door and leaned back against it, squeezing her eyes shut for a moment.

She headed for the living room where she bleakly surveyed the wreckage. A wingback leather chair had fallen beside a half-burnt heap of manuscripts in the fireplace. Hardback books littered the floor, pages bent as if someone were rubbing their prose into the ground. And melted candle wax hardened over the ruined surfaces of her furniture.

Overwhelmed by the damage, she picked up the fallen chair and sunk into it before dropping her face into her hands. What a horrid, stupid, sickening display of violence. *We are ultimately powerless against God. Not only is He apathetic to our losses, He lets us shit on the floor and generally make a mess of things without lending a hand to clean up after His spiritual neglect.*

Those Sunday mornings sitting on polished pews in a Baptist church with her grandparents summed up her snapshots of God. He made her miserable and uncomfortable, yet He was the great giver, responsible for everything good if not evil. Evil was our fault. Our fall. God was this shapeless fourth family member who hovered over the dinner table and pressed Himself against the walls, staying out of sight yet often referenced in conversation as if he were *right there.* Alicia could now begin to see that most of the losses she'd blamed on Him were the result of bad choices on her part. But how could she have known? And what about her grandfather? If God was in control, what was that about? Her life had been too synchronistic, too guided in so many ways to not believe that this, too, was the product of relentless divinity. Clearly something was at work. The events of the last week were undeniable. She could pronounce Salieri's prayer, declare God her enemy, but she could not imagine what her weapon against Him would be. She'd tried to take her life, the last thing that could be used against her, but even that option was denied to her.

The philosophical wheels boring into familiar ruts at a steady speed, Alicia headed for the kitchen to make some tea.

She halted at the threshold when she saw the couple fucking in front of her refrigerator.

Ashes, ashes...we all fall...

Dr. Dulac bowed his head, hands folded as if in prayer. He'd pushed the file toward Dr. Farron, watching. "I hate to say this, James, but it *was* poor judgment on your part to advocate violence with that child."

The child psychiatrist sat dumbfounded on the other side of the chairman's desk. "Leonard—I had a breakthrough with that kid! And when did it become not okay to role play in therapy?"

"You put a weapon in his hand!"

"His *mother* forced me to take him into session with a toy gun, Leonard. I asked her not to, but she wouldn't listen." Bolstered by the reality of his success, he slid forward to the edge of his seat. "Look, if I hadn't used the approach that I did, I would still have no idea why that boy was so withdrawn and defiant. His yoga-going, cell phone–*blathering* mother didn't bother to tell me anything, even on questioning. And do you know why? Because she'd moved her lover into the house after she'd kicked out her husband. Brilliant, huh?" Dr. Dulac started to interrupt. "It's a free country. She can take her child to another therapist if she doesn't like my techniques—there's no law against that—but she's not angry because of a plastic gun. She's mad because I suggested that what she'd done was having a negative effect on her child. She's pissed off and she's threatening me, when all I did was point out the source of her child's unhappiness. The very thing she'd wanted to know." Dr. Dulac seemed to listen now, albeit Dr. Farron knew he wasn't completely on board. "You *know* there's nothing we can do when the parents are more screwed up than their kids. I can't be held responsible for that."

The older doctor sighed. "She's reported you to the medical board. I wish I could dictate human resource policy based on your reports, but I can't use those alone. I have to go by feedback from patients and parents. This..." he tapped the report with his finger tips, "...is just as important. And I don't have enough of these."

Dr. Farron let the awful truth about his practice slither into his brain and coil up somewhere profoundly uncomfortable.

"James, you did very well with that woman. She's going to be fine. You should be proud."

"Which is why I'm suspended and not fired, right?" Dr. Farron stood and extended his hand to Dr. Dulac. "Goodbye, Leonard."

Dr. Dulac shook his head slowly. "Think about where your true calling lies."

"I will."

He drove home as water poured down on his windshield, the thrum of his wipers as sluggish as his heartbeat. He examined the shards of his career. Never in his life had he failed at anything, much less his work. Not anything.

Crossing the bridge into Alameda, he considered briefly calling his own therapist, Stanley, but thought better of it. It was too much to explain in a very short period of time. To have lived it was enough to know it was real; to describe it to someone else would thin its impact—and if he wasn't believed, it would be crazy-making. Then he'd have to add resentment to the emotional laundry pile. Now he understood why Alicia was reluctant to tell him that it was Mr. Wicker on the dispatch. He had not even gone into any detail with Rachelle, figuring it was best that she think of Alicia's condition as involving potentially potent spiritual and psychological factors. Of course, she knew he was bullshitting her, but he had no choice but to beg off telling her the full story until he was in a better place to explain—if ever. He considered calling one of his many friends for sympathy about his suspension, most of whom he'd graduated with from Cal and not med school. Derrick, who now practiced occupational therapy in San Jose, was too busy with kids and wife to be available for any lengthy discussions; Donald the audio engineer for Thomas Dolby had fourteen girlfriends and three jobs; Ahmed, who lived in Marin but drove to Mountain View three times a week to play Silicon Valley corporate psychologist, would be too exhausted, especially with his bad health; Natisha and Ben were both teaching down at UCLA, but they had a newborn child who shrieked from two p.m. to eleven p.m. every day.

Isolation was best for now anyway, he thought, as the white Lexus glided into the garage of his house on the Isle. He loved Alameda, the island burb in the middle of the Bay. Gina had been particularly taken with the award-winning Christmas decorations on the houses at holiday time. They'd strolled in the frosty streets with dozens of other families that Christmas when visiting her friends. Spectacular webs of light had been laid by some Christmas spider over the roofs and trees. There were elaborate electric displays of reindeer with light bulb hides, and even bright pink flamingos pulled a sleigh spilling over with a "Divine" Santa. It convinced them to buy a house there and stage their own PG&E diorama come the following holiday season.

He sat for several moments in the dimly lit garage before sliding out of the leather seat and making his way into the house. He stoically wrestled off his tie and dropped his pocket contents on the kitchen counter. Soon, the cappuccino machine burped out some rich dark brew into a yawning cup that he filled with whole milk and heaping teaspoons of sugar. His drug of choice to chase off depression.

The television flickered on to some college basketball game that gabbled in the background as he leaned against the bookcase and stared at his books.

Creative Therapy with Children and Adolescents
Handbook of Art Therapy
The Applications of Play Therapy
Drawing On the Child's Creativity
Contemporary Art History
Early Medieval Art

Archaic and Classical Roman Sculpture
The Art and History of Egypt
Renaissance, Mannerism, Baroque
The Art of Faery
Fantasy Art: Techniques and Illustration
Dreams: The Art of Boris Vallejo
Second Slice: The Art of Olivia
The Encyclopedia of Fantasy and Science Fiction Art Techniques
Struwwelpeter: Fearful Stories & Vile Pictures to Instruct Good Little Folks

Small, framed pictures cluttered the shelves. Formal portraits with his family from ten years ago. Candid shots of him and Gina at parties together. (She didn't look anything like Alicia, contrary to what that pompous ass said.) A graduation picture from his last days at Cal. He had taken the wedding pictures and shunted them away in a box up in the attic.

Large boxes of his life lurked in the attic, several versions of him lying in cardboard coffins to decay in memory. If only he could discard them once and for all. For some time he hadn't the courage to creep up there and converse with the dusty haunts. Intensely introspective this evening, he decided to make the journey up as he downed the last of his coffee. Something new had entered his life and he was ready to move on, even in the face of uncertainty about his career. Setting the empty cappuccino cup on a bookshelf, he switched off the TV and gathered the rest of the photos of himself and Gina from the bookshelves. He passed the fifty-two-year-old mahogany baby grand that he kept shut and polished since Gina's death, the French doors that gracefully framed it from behind streaked with rain. Even with that musical sarcophagus sprawling in the living room, the house felt twice as empty as ever. He strode back to the kitchen to go out to the garage, which also suffered a sort of lingering neglect by housing a rotting bicycle and a number of half-finished house projects. Dr. Farron found the attic door, switched on the stairway light, and ascended into the cedar-scented murk.

He yanked on a thin chain hanging from the beam above the stair landing. *Click!* A weak light from a dusty, exposed bulb flooded the 1500-square-foot attic. The rain roared against the roof, just inches from his head as he stooped inside. Where normally bits of daylight would probe into the attic from the perimeter, the powerful bouquet of dampness wafted through. Dr. Farron's steps stirred a storm of dust motes as he paced between the neatly packed boxes crowding the space. Their contents were scrawled hastily in black marker across the top flaps and along the sides, but the bulb was too dim to read them. He pushed the boxes this way and that with his foot to expose their sides to the light until he found the box he was looking for.

"Wedding Photos."

Dropping to his knees, he placed the photos from the bookshelves on the floor and pried open the flaps. The white satin photo album was cool to the touch. He resisted a faint urge to look inside and started layering over it with the other photos.

From the open attic door, piano music rose eerily behind him.

Phantoms of Alicia and Eric. Naked and sweating, passing ice cubes between their lips as their hands stroked moisture from each other's necks and shoulders in front of the refrigerator. Unmailed wedding invitations spilled from the counter.

At first, Alicia's hand flailed for the doorjamb and clung to it. What the hell was happening? How had Rachelle's admonition come to truth? Had Mr. Wicker's *touch* altered the way her memories manifested?

She shivered.

The phantoms continued to sigh and giggle as she opened the cupboard and retrieved a box of tea bags. Phantom Eric moaned as Phantom Alicia lapped his nipples with her cold tongue.

She tried leaving the kitchen and returning to the family room to start picking up books, but Phantom Eric was fucking Phantom Alicia on the deep burgundy velvet couch. Alicia left the family room and passed Phantom Alicia moaning as she leaned against the wall, Phantom Eric kneeling before her, his face burrowing into the sweet, soft dampness between her legs. Exasperated and tired, Alicia returned to the kitchen and, grabbing the kettle from the counter, thrust it under the water dispenser in the refrigerator, inches from Phantom Alicia's naked ass. She set the kettle on the stove and turned on the burner. As the water steamed, she paced out of the kitchen and back in. As soon as the kettle whistled, the phantoms disappeared.

On the counter, she found an envelope marked, "Just In Case." Her grandmother's handwriting. The envelope was full of hundreds and twenties.

Thanks again, Grandma.

She poured the steaming water over a crumpled tea bag into a mug. As she leaned against the counter, coaxing clouds of tea from the bag with her spoon, she remembered names and faces. And conversations. Mostly conversations. Copious notes from her editor. The rejections of outlines and proposals for future books. Her agent's letter announcing her termination. The last royalty check sliding into an ATM envelope.

Can't you at least clean around here? Eric's voice again. His phantom threw dishes he'd pulled out of the dishwasher, his face carved with rage. Alicia's phantom tried to dodge the flying dish. Alicia herself stood her ground, watching him this time instead of screaming. Instead of throwing her hands over her face and twisting away. Instead of folding to her knees in the porcelain debris as her chest heaved with anguish. Alicia just wanted to hold herself, her phantom. She hated seeing herself so gutted, especially by the undeserved hostilities of this terrible man.

Somewhere outside, a dog barked as she cried. And then it was silent.

The loss of her mother, her father, Eric, her grandfather, her career, the loss of her life. She'd watched it all drop away, like brittle leaves snapping from grizzled trees, fleeing from autumn breezes into an endless winter.

The grand piano faintly trilled with a music box waltz. Dr. Farron froze, the sound running over his arms and neck with a thousand nibbly feet. The music swelled as hands ran up and down the keys with the precision of a master pianist. Dr. Farron slapped shut the box flaps over the pictures, but the piano continued to natter.

Did someone break in?

Dr. Farron glanced around for a weapon, but the boxes were full of things entirely useless against intruders. He crept down the attic stairs to find something in the garage, trying not to let the steps squeak as he descended. As he grabbed a tire iron from the garage wall, the music broke for a moment. Except for the beating of his heart, the house sounded empty. Then, as he entered the house, he heard a sprinkling of notes—a reworking of the last passage he'd heard as he searched for his weapon. The music swirled around that passage and then picked up momentum, launching itself into another phrase.

A phrase he recognized from the last piece of music Gina was writing before she died.

Who could be so cruel? And how did they enter his home to commit this brazen act of inhumanity?

It didn't matter. He was going to rip the pianist's fucking head off.

He plunged into the house, iron ready to swing into the first skull he met. "Whoever you are, you're fucking *dead!*" he shouted, charging into the living room.

The grand piano stood open, lightning ripping behind the French doors beyond, brilliance skittering across the polished mahogany. Slender arms moved up and down the keys, attached to delicate shoulders covered in a blue knitted shawl. And then her sharp chin dipped below the slanted lip of the baby grand, red curls sliding down her cheek. Dr. Farron held his breath. Many years ago, in that pub in Chicago, he'd written off the ghost to lager logic and had forgotten it as the romance reached a fever pitch. But now he could not deny what he saw. Gina moved as if she lived, petite and pregnant, her hands moving skillfully over the keys. Music paper and pencils covered the piano top.

Suddenly she left off playing and picked up a pencil, scribbling on one of the papers as thunder rattled against the French doors. "James!"

Dr. Farron stopped when he heard her say his name.

"James," she called again, laying a hand on her belly. She was five months along. They were leaving in a few days to go to DC for a brief vacation and to see her family.

And then his brain sizzled when he heard someone else—himself—reply.

"Coming, your majesty!"

The sleeves of his sweatshirt rolled up over his elbows, another Farron, a phantom, carried a tray of food from the kitchen to the living room. The sweatshirt was stained with daubs and drips of colorful paint. Phantom Gina gathered up the music paper so the Phantom Farron could set the tray of food on top. "Thank you, sweetie! You rule." He scooted onto the piano bench with her and she kissed him, her fingers noodling a few sweet, silly notes.

Dr. Farron gripped the tire iron, his insides boiling with torment. He backed away slowly and then dodged into the hallway opening, peeking around the corner into the family room. He was too frightened to question how this was happening. It just *was* and it hurt like hell.

The Phantom Farron reluctantly slid off the piano bench, grabbed a sandwich, and winked at her.

"So can I see?"

"Nope, not yet."

"But when? It's been forever!"

"Some day," he said.

"Oh, come on!" she pleaded. "We wanna see!"

"Uh-uh," he said. "Not until it's ready."

That Phantom Farron, already stuffed on happiness, bit into his sandwich as he headed into the hallway. He stopped inches from Dr. Farron, who pressed his back against the hallway wall, as if that would keep the Phantom Farron from noticing him. Phantom Farron grinned at Phantom Gina. "All good things to those who wait."

Phantom Gina pouted and played a dark jig—her own version of "The March of the Marionettes"—as the Phantom Farron continued into the hallway.

Dr. Farron followed the phantom down the hallway and around the corner to where his study was...

...but instead entered a vast canvas of forest and fantasy. The Phantom Farron picked up a palette and brush, evaluating a section of the wall where he had left off fleshing out the multicolored foliage in which a pearlescent unicorn lay awake. The mythical beast resembled the medieval tapestry of "The Lady and the Unicorn," which he'd seen at the

Musée de Cluny in Paris. He'd jokingly called it the George Clooney Museum. Gina had wanted Paddington Bear, but Dr. Farron had wanted something more special. He'd instead depicted Pooh and Piglet holding hands as they peered into the face of the ancient unicorn from the leafy pile. A nice juxtaposition of old and new stories. The unicorn was sitting above the bassinette her parents had given them. The colors of the mythical forest fell around him like autumn. Lots of primary colors with some rust and subtler shades to soften the overall effect. In time, baby's eyes would appreciate them all.

Overwhelmed with memory, Dr. Farron ignored Phantom Farron and approached the mural. But as soon as his fingertips touched the brilliant brushstrokes, rivulets of white ran across the wall as if his touch caused the paint to bleed. In a flash, the wall went white.

The palette vanished and the piano fell silent. Dr. Farron dropped the tire iron and climbed on the desk as he his fingers dug into the wallpaper's edge. With a tentative tug, he peeled back a portion of the covering to reveal leafy hints of the mural buried beneath.

Daylight faded and the kitchen would soon be glutted with murk. It was time to begin Alicia's ritual. One by one just before twilight, she would flip on the house lights, starting in the kitchen and ending in the bedroom. This childhood fear had resurrected itself a year ago, the night Alicia came home and found Eric's goodbye note. He had abandoned her, the house (in her name), and the bills, and left like a houseguest who had to catch an early flight, quickly and quietly. She had always been afraid of the dark. Having another person in the house somehow disarmed the nightmarish prowlers, but with Eric gone, the creatures of her imagination were free to swipe at her ankles from the shadows with their sticky, bristling limbs. She almost wished her grandmother was well enough to stay with her, but she knew the old woman wouldn't stay here even if she was that well. Not in the house where her granddaughter had tried to kill herself. And not with the person from whom she'd hidden so much her entire life.

Alicia placed her mug in the kitchen sink and reached for the switch on the kitchen wall. Before her finger could touch the plastic cover, the light died. She frowned and toggled the switch.

Click. Nothing.

Alicia ran as her world dimmed, flipping switches. The living room. Den.

No lights.

The retreating sunlight dimly lit the foyer, falling through the rippling glass pane of the front door and spilling across the bills she'd kicked earlier. In the mess of paper she saw the words "Final Notice." She picked up the envelope and held it to the light:

her electric bill. A strong wind stirred the large evergreens around the house and a cloud swallowed the last of the sun.

She dropped the envelope and heard it slip to the floor.

They told her at the hospital she should call someone at times like these. Dr. Farron wanted her to call. She hadn't told anyone her phone line had been disconnected.

She could go to bed, but the darkness did not suggest rest. Vague hands pawed at her vulnerable body—not the limbs of outré creatures as she'd expected, but the familiar fingers of shame and defeat. It was her fault what happened with Dr. Sark. Had she not egged him on in his office, he would never have done what he did. She knew he was a rattlesnake. And if James ever found out, how could he ever love her? James. If she could ever conquer her anger at him for deceiving her. Besides, he would leave her like the others. How long had she known him? Four days? Please. What was she thinking?

In that moment, between the darkness and the violation, she felt like nothing, as if at the slightest movement the seams of her flesh could unbaste, utterly unmaking her.

The bathroom and the razors. They could free her from the shame and defeat.

Brooders weep and brooders keep their misery at hand.

The thought suspended in her mind, dangled by self-power, but held back by a thread of self-preservation. As she stepped toward the staircase, her intentions tumbled over one another, hands to ankles. Bed or blade, bed or blade...

Let Mr. Wicker wash your sicker memories in sand.

She could hear him singing as she climbed to the top of the stairs, stumbling twice on weak legs. When she reached the top stair, she stopped. In the thickening dusk, the void stretched its arms before her, larger than she remembered and far more loving. Her rational mind recalled that, if she would just reach out beside her, she could feel the wall, perhaps a painting hanging from it, but she kept her arms close to her body and let the void embrace her.

Then, she heard the soft patter of the rain. And his voice.

You slipped into the light because I wanted you...

The bandages on her wrists fell to the floor.

...and because you love the darkness.

Bed and blade. Dream and death. She could have both with Mr. Wicker. But it would mean the end of her life. Forever.

A whisper of movement, a clicking sound behind her in the hallway. Every hair on her arms and neck prickled.

Alicia slowly turned to look.

A raven hopped up the last step and shook its wings.

"What do you want?" she asked, throat tight. Every injury to her body throbbed as adrenaline razed her veins. She felt more insane at that moment, talking to the bird, than she had ever in her life. The animal must have worked its way down the fireplace flue. It was no stranger to ash.

The bird rose with a flap of its wings and soared over her shoulder, swimming in slow motion toward a pinprick of light that appeared at the far, far end of the hallway where the bathroom should have been. Was she imagining the light? Had the bird summoned it? She could now think of nothing else but the Library as she moved toward it, her feet dragging on the carpet. Her rational mind said a bathroom was there, not a library. Not the souls of children, but the brittle glass of the shower door.

She ran.

The light waxed and shifted, howling toward her as before, this time with the raven's body in sight. Two realities fought for her mind.

Light and glass. This world and his.

Chapter 39

Dr. Farron's cellphone rang. He let go of the wallpaper and clambered down as he answered. "Alicia?"

"Not remotely," Rachelle answered.

"Oh, hey," he said. He knocked aside the chair and dropped into it.

"Sorry to disappoint you," she said. "I got your message."

"Yeah, I wish I didn't have to leave it."

"I'm still pissed at you, but I'm going to miss you around here."

"Me, too—you, that is," he said, distracted. Two of the most important people in his life were now mad at him. Great.

"You know," she started, voice lowered, "you haven't turned on your recorders."

"Yeah," he said. "I didn't even want to think about the grant."

"Do you want me to have someone do it for you?"

Alicia's feet hit gravel.

Exhilarated, she threw open her arms and tears of joy streamed over her cheeks. She laughed, running faster to meet the children and the light. And him. He was waiting for her. He was real, and she was free from the void.

"You're a tattletale!" "...sitting in a tree, k-i-s-s-i-n-g." "Ummmm-mum-mummmm, you're in trouble." The vapors drew over her like veils, covering her with their happiness as she ran toward the greater warmth blazing beyond. "Ring around the rosie, a pocket full of posies..."

He, indeed, waited for her on the other side of the light. She passed through, her skin damp with sweat from exertion and excitement. She still wore the clothes her grandmother brought her. The peach silk clung to her curves. His eyes—luminous, excited—softened when he saw her.

A dark-haired little girl stood at his side, one eye clouded with broken blood vessels, bone fragments prickling from her head, coated with slick hemoglobin that shone like freshly sucked Tootsie pops. A white thrush from the antibiotics fleeced her tongue.

Alicia recognized her. "I know you." She kneeled between the book stacks and held out her hand. "What's your name?"

The girl shambled toward her and smiled grotesquely, missing a front tooth. "My name is Georgeta. Are you Alicia?"

Alicia nodded. "That's a pretty name. How'd you get it?"

"It was my grandma's name. My mommy's Romanian and my daddy's from Brazil."

"It's a beautiful name. So, what happened to you, sweetie? Why are you in the hospital?"

Georgeta frowned. "My daddy had been drinking when he made our car go into the other cars. I was really scared. I think my mommy died."

Alicia clasped the child's sickly warm hand. "That sounds terrible. I'm really sorry."

Georgeta continued, "I heard the nurses say my head is hurt pretty badly and I'll never be okay again. Do you think I'll be okay?"

The truth bit viciously at Alicia's stomach, which was already sensitive to the grotesqueries of the child's injuries. "Of course, honey. Don't listen to what grownups say."

Georgeta's good eye focused on Alicia's hand. "You hold my hand, don't you?"

"Whenever I can," Alicia said.

She threw her arms around Alicia, who thought, of all the nightmares she had created, none were as moving as this.

A wall behind Alicia hummed.

Alicia's back warmed as the light shone against it, bleaching Georgeta's face with the infinite. "I gotta go," she said and limped into the blinding whiteness.

Now they were alone.

"You shouldn't have come here," Mr. Wicker said. He approached her and she reached out to him, the backs of her fingers lightly brushing his soft cheek. His eyes closed and his breath slowed as he succumbed to her touch.

A blue nylon backpack slung over his shoulder, Dr. Farron slipped past the front desk to the elevators. If anyone asked, he was cleaning out his office, even though he wasn't going to do it until Saturday. The security staff changed guard at seven p.m., and they often did not communicate with the previous shift. It was now about eight thirty p.m. and he could move freely up to the children's ward.

The night nurses greeted him as before. Word had not traveled, it seemed. He continued down the hall and swung into the first child's room. Starting with the empty bed, he flipped open the tape recorder and flicked the tape out of the slot before slipping it between the teeth of the backpack zipper. As expertly as a London pickpocket, he filched the tape from the recorder over the head of a wispy-headed, eight-year-old boy who snored through his nasogastric tubing.

Room after room, he repeated the sleight of hand, removing the numerous tapes without even a yawn from the bed occupants. The labels were marked in black felt pen with the current patient's names and date of admission. The ones where the tape had moved forward concerned him. Had they been talking to *him*? Or had the night nurses been gossiping as they worked?

Toward the end of the ward was the last room he wished to visit. Georgeta, his bloodied cherub. His only other link to the Library. He threw his sports coat over the chair and sat watching her breathe as he contemplated the weird events of the last three days. Some bizarre logic must be at work, but he could not fathom why it chose to invite him into its *machina*. He felt the brittleness of his spiritual mind cracking and spewing dust from disuse as the revelations bucked against its walls.

Georgeta slept soundly in her not-death. He opened the tape recorder and withdrew her tape. It had rolled forward significantly. As Dr. Farron excitedly dropped it into the backpack, Georgeta moved for the first time. Her feverish body shifted toward him and her chin tipped backwards as she whispered through a mouthful of thrush.

"She's pretty, Mr. Wicker."

That name. He hunched closer, because maybe for the first time he would hear for himself what she told the Librarian instead of any human being.

"I heard the nurses say I'll never be okay again. Do you think I'll be okay, Alicia?" Georgeta whispered more airily through her enflamed esophagus.

Dr. Farron's thoughts spiraled into chaos.

He staggered from the hospital into the visitor parking lot under the crushing downpour and threw the soggy backpack into the passenger seat of his car. He strangled the wheel of the Lexus as he fled the lot. The car roared under the unrelenting pressure of his foot as he madly sped from Highway 580 to Park and scrambled up one steep hill after another with alarming speed into the labyrinth of narrow streets. His deepest fear was that the house was empty, that the void Alicia so feared had swallowed her, that she had retreated to the Library—and not in one piece.

As he slid to a shrill stop in the wet driveway, the headlights angled at the front door, he threw open the car door and shouted at the top of his lungs. "Alicia! Alicia, are you there?" The entire house was dark inside. He ran back to the car in the rain and retrieved a mag light from the trunk. He then approached the elegant front door, pounding on the doorframe. No answer. He even pulled up the metal flap for the mail slot and shouted into that, training the light into the opening. Through the flap, he saw nothing except more darkness and a wall. No signs of life.

Then, inspired by the rescue team's entrance, he turned the doorknob. It gave way with ease, the door's bottom brushing through a thick stack of unopened mail. He swallowed. "Alicia?" He swept the light over the entrance. The light caught an unusual ink drawing on acrylic paper hanging on the foyer wall: a bald man sitting on a stone, draped in crosses with a bandaged hand and a knife for an erect penis. Clive Barker, unmistakable, although the signature gave it away. Beneath it, a light switch. He flicked it on. Nothing. Dr. Farron wandered carefully into the family room beyond, the spotlight in his hand illuminating the fireplace, the books strewn over the floor. Coated in cobwebs, the ceilings were entirely too high for his tastes. He felt both like an intruder and the only person in the world who belonged here. He located a lamp. No juice. The melted wax and burned manuscripts unnerved him as he surveyed the home of what was—and might now be—a dead woman.

He resisted the urge to make a pre-emptive call to the authorities or ambulance. He'd call if he found her in any state other than breathing.

A wooden banister threw back the mag light's glare. Dr. Farron abandoned the living room and, although terrified of what he might find, approached the stairs. His footsteps grew heavier with dread as he landed on each step. He pictured her lifeless, bloodless body crumpled in some bathroom or on her bed. Success in death at last. As the hallway floor met him at eye level, the light skittered over the white gauze strips. Stunned, he let the light drop center stage on the bandages. She had taken them off here, probably just prior to slitting them again.

A flicker of light from the hall's end. He raised the flashlight beam to catch the glimmer. One of those beveled glass shower doors. As he drew the light over the walls— more portraits, including one of Barlowe's hellish parades—and then that flicker. He brought the light to bear on the shower door once more.

The rain was punishing the roof. Deafening. He knelt and picked up the bandages. He could look through every room—and he did, to be certain—but he knew that she was gone from this world.

And she did not even say goodbye.

Mr. Wicker took her wrist and brought it to his nose, inhaling the grotesque bouquet of her stitched wounds. His long arms closed around her waist and hers around his neck as he kissed her. His lips, softer than silk, pressed against hers in a tender hush. He then held out his hand toward the table and one of the books opened, a darkly romantic waltz of piano and sweet sopranos ringing from the blotchy pages. "You chose me over life," he said. "Let us celebrate." Taking one of her hands in his and pressing his other to the small of her back, he led her in a waltz around the book stacks.

Alicia smoldered in the green flames of his eyes, never fearing that she would misstep as she sank deeper.

"You say this music is someone's nightmare," Alicia said. "So this music really is, in fact, evil."

"Can anything this beautiful be, in itself, evil?"

"Can anything ugly be good?"

"Oh, yes. Yes it can," he replied.

"Even when I was in grade school, I was partial to the monsters in movies."

"I would have never guessed."

They kissed. After a moment, he drew her down onto the ancient hardwood floor. They continued kissing. Death and dream. Eros and architecture. The lingering candle smoke trailed across the repository ceiling. His fingers found the cloth-covered buttons that closed her dress up the front. He loosened every one, the flaps falling back to bare her flushed chest and waist. Then those scribe hands, fleecy and firm, moved slowly over her skin.

She tensed up. She didn't want this. She'd wanted freedom and to escape the darkness, but now she had neither. How could she now say no? The word fell between the blackened cracks in the floorboards and imbedded itself in the otherworldly dust. The clack and whirr of the clocks on the wall grew more pronounced by the second, plucking at her attention.

Help me? Alicia. Help me do it.

Lillian?

"Is something the matter?"

Alicia looked into his eyes. Sea green and flames. "I heard a voice. Did Georgeta leave?"

"Georgeta is gone," he whispered in her ear. "You could not have heard her."

"But I heard someone. Can you check?"

He reluctantly stood up, those robes swishing about his ashen ankles, and strode to the far end of the Library, peering into the book stacks.

Help me, Alicia.

As her hand reached out for a table leg for leverage, her fingertips scraped the sharp edges of unevenly bound pages. Her hand grasped again and this time stroked a cloth cover. She cast her gaze aside.

Her book. It lay with several others beneath the table in a heap.

She twisted under the table as she reached for it.

"No! You mustn't!"

He ran to her and lunged for her waist. She grasped the table leg firmly, pulling away from him. The table groaned, its frame crumbling under the weight, and then it crashed, the precarious tomes and candelabra tumbling. Thick candles rolled across the floor, wicks licking the wood as they sought kindling.

"Damn this!" He gave up his grip on her to chase the flames.

Alicia reached in the pile and worked her book free. She snatched it up, holding it hostage to her chest, and scrambled to her feet. The light broke between the stacks, warm and fluctuating, humming to announce its arrival. But when she tried to leave, Mr. Wicker blocked her path.

"Don't do this," he pleaded, those whispering hands stretched out toward her. "You mustn't, *mustn't* do this."

"All my life things have been taken from me," she said angrily. "I can't bring back any of it, but I can bring back *this*."

"Perhaps, but there is a terrible price," he replied. A blustering wind rattled the window glass as he spoke. The smoky lavender landscape turned slate. "These memories were vomited by your soul for a reason. Reading the book could have a devastating effect on you, and I can't let that happen. Besides," he added sadly, "if you take your book... you can't return."

"You don't mean it."

"You foolish woman," he said. "I don't make the rules."

Silence.

"Would it matter if I told you what you meant to me?" he asked, his eyes blazing.

Of course it mattered. She could not say it, but her face surely betrayed her true feelings.

"I've already died once, Drunos," she said, passion flattening to fact. "What worse could happen to me?"

The passage shined behind him, those eyes emptying two thousand years of pain at her feet.

Every part of her ached horribly for him—he had suffered so much—but she could not change her mind. For the first time in her life she felt whole and uncorrupt; not just because she had the book but because she was listening to her intuition, to her own needs and no one else's. Wordlessly, she walked past him, clutching the book. At the edge of the light, she turned and looked back. He wasn't going to stop her.

Holding a victory in her arms—and love for him in her soul—she stepped into the light.

Chapter 40

The Lexus skidded and fishtailed as it sped down the treacherous hills away from the house.

"How could you have left her alone?" he berated himself. "What the hell were you thinking? But..." The inescapable fact that she chose Mr. Wicker over him drove an ice pick into his chest. He wanted to die. How was this happening? Mr. Wicker was...he couldn't say. A specter? A creature? How could she possibly go to that creature in her need and not him? Was she really that sick? She must be. But just because she loves—loves?—something so horrific doesn't mean she's horrific herself. Or does it? That...that *quote* from the movie *Adaptation*... If true, it means that he's falling in love with—or, at least in serious lust with—a crazy woman, which makes him a crazy man. *No.* That can't be it! Because then what does that make her because she loves a creature? A female creature? And then, by extension, does that not mean he becomes a creature for her being a creature because she loves a creature?

The windshield wipers blasted away at top speed, swishing away each miserable thought so forty more could rush to take its place. The parade of self-castigating remarks marched back and forth between his ears and sometimes they became words he shouted at the windows. He lost himself in a tsunami of guilt as the Lexus squealed onto the 580 onramp.

Or, what he *thought* was the 580 onramp.

My potential girlfriend disappeared into another dimension. How fucking lame is that?

Rain clung to the windows, slinging this way and that as the car slowed. Dim lights dripped from the crumbling rooftop of a liquor store. A derelict car sat up on cinder blocks, wheels locked. Homeless wrapped in dirty, ripped sleeping bags huddled in doorways. A marauding band of hoods and baggy pants spilled over the sidewalk, shouting at the car. And everywhere the P-funk was beating.

"Dem wheels is phat, yo!" "Wazzup, G!" "You'd best be gettin' yo whitebread ass out the Oaktown, crackah!"

A loud whistle cut through the window glass, startling him like a fire alarm as he peeled past the hoods. A *thunk* as a rock hit the side of his car. And then another. He flinched. Even though every bit of prejudice had been schooled out of him by life and literature, everything he knew was eclipsed by the reality that he had entered an economic and cultural war zone. He, the privileged white man in a Lexus.

Dr. Farron scooted down in his seat. Everyone looked his way as he passed. He wished for not the first time that he'd gotten his navigation system fixed. He drove around, thankful that at least the rain had abated for the moment, but nothing looked familiar as the Lexus rolled deeper into the outerlands of his own home. Barred windows. Graffiti. Laundry rope stretching from roof to banister, whipping back and forth in the rapidly mounting winds. San Francisco was one of the most racially integrated cities in the world, ten square miles of melting pot, simmering in the heat of geographical claustrophobia. Yet the Sacramento boy in him reared behind his eyes and rattled with fear, worried he'd be carjacked. Or worse.

The streets continued grim and grimy as the fuel gauge slipped dangerously close to E. A house party bounced and flashed to the rhymes of old skool masters. He vaguely remembered that Rachelle lived somewhere in Oakland, and then realized that he had never been to her house. He flipped open his cell phone to call her and found there was no reception. "Oh, for crying out loud!"

As he turned toward what looked like a freeway overpass but wasn't, a green neon sign flickered over the roof of a building that squatted across the street from a closed corner grocer and taco stand. The Castle Rock Bar. The door was propped open, revealing a moderately well lit dive with a number of patrons inside. Adjacent to the bar sat a wide parking lot with one tall light that hung over the faded white lines. He parked under it amidst a dozen battered sedans and dirty compacts.

Under the low rumble of the bar patrons, 2Pac encouraged his listeners to *be strong* from a jukebox tucked in the corner of the room. Although the room was smokeless, a dim haze clung to the tables. Dr. Farron stepped in and paused to survey the scene. Several people elbowed their neighbors, jutting their chins at him—most likely not just because he was a stranger but because of the Superman tie. He flipped it over his shoulder to stifle its scream.

Behind the bar stood the bartender in a tissue-thin tank top that stretched over a grand landscape of sculpted muscles. To his left sat a scruffy guy who was watching a fight on the television hanging above. A skinny redhead with a cauliflower nose, he slouched in his dingy gas station uniform, leaning on one elbow as he gritted his teeth every time one of the fighters took a punch.

Dr. Farron approached the bar and stood next to Mr. Gas. "Excuse me," he said to the bartender, "but can you tell me the way back to the freeway?"

The bartender scowled as he picked up an icy beer bottle, twisted the cap, and slammed it down on the bar in front of Dr. Farron.

That wasn't the answer he'd hoped for. It wasn't even the answer he'd expected, given his reception in the streets. He took the bottle reluctantly. It had been years since he had had a drink. Not since that night at the Red Lion. It seemed he was now knee-deep in haunts without the assistance of alcohol. So, he might as well indulge.

Mr. Gas struck the bar top with his fist as he hollered for the guy in the red boxers—or was it the guy in the gold boxers who just got six-packed by the ring floor?—on the tube. Dr. Farron wondered if perhaps when the round ended this fellow could give him directions. He sat on the bar stool, hunched over his beer, and feigned interest.

"You see that, brah?" Mr. Gas said, pointing at the screen. He barely looked at Dr. Farron, but kept watching as the fighters resumed their slug-and-hug fest. "Daaaaamn. He got right back up, too!"

Dr. Farron nodded and wondered if he should put the beer bottle to his lips. His back prickled as the eyes of other patrons continued to prod at him. As Mr. Gas continued to invest his interest in the fight, Dr. Farron bided his time by mulling over his predicament but felt more self-conscious the longer he sat there not drinking. At last, the bell rang for the second round and Mr. Gas turned to him.

"So, brah, you a fan?"

"Yeah," Dr. Farron responded. "Although I'm more of a basketball man myself."

"Lakers, brah, forever," he raised his beer bottle, which Dr. Farron took as his cue to clink green glass. As Mr. Gas swilled his brew, Dr. Farron put the bottleneck to his lips and took a sip. The bittersweet yeast of the Beck's lathered his tongue. He swallowed, setting down the bottle with an emphatic not-doing-this-again thud, despite how good it tasted.

"Hey, I'm actually just passing through," Dr. Farron said. "Can you tell me how to get back to 580?"

Mr. Gas bristled. "Whatch y'all in such a hurry for? Ya got a woman on yer ass to get home or somethin'?"

Dr. Farron sighed. No, he didn't. And why was he so afraid? No one was threatening him. Sure, he was a fish out of water. So what? He focused on the beer sweating in his hand. And how good would it feel to slip on a mild buzz? The guilt jangled inside him like a lung full of razors. He almost didn't survive the last time he felt this way. "Nope. Just tired is all."

"Brah, ya gotta watch the fight," Mr. Gas said. "It's all messed up, this guy knockin' down Clark and him gettin' up and shit."

"Oh yeah?" Dr. Farron said.

The bell rang again and the next round started. As Dr. Farron watched, he put down the entire beer in two more rounds. His long sobriety opened him readily to the sway of the alcohol. As he set the empty bottle on the bar, the bartender slammed down another at his elbow. And so he continued until he had downed almost three beers. He recollected that he had not been asked for money or given a credit card to keep a tab. Maybe this place was so casual, they just assumed you had a tab and made you pay up before you left. That bartender could make anyone pay up with no more than a hard stare.

When the bartender planted the fourth on the bar and cleared away the empties, Dr. Farron was gesticulating in harmony with Mr. Gas at the tube. His tie slipped back into place, but Dr. Farron no longer cared. He also failed to notice two young wannabe gangstas draw up next to him at the bar, exchanging rough words in a street slang Dr. Farron failed to understand. The featherweight fight then ended and the ring personnel prepared for the middleweight contenders. Mr. Gas took this opportunity to turn to Dr. Farron.

"So, no bitch, brah? A slick guy like you?" His eyes flickered up behind Dr. Farron's head, as if gauging something going on behind him.

Dr. Farron shook his soggy head.

"Them bitches ain't worth it, brah. I got me a wife once back when I was in Maui. She was a nutty one, too. All over my ass for everything, and you know what? Bitch left. But I ain't mad. No sir. It's better that way. More TV dinners and shit, but hey. Can't have everything. Where would ya put it?" He pulled on his beer and his whole body seemed to nod.

"I lost her."

"Whaddaya mean, ya lost her? Ya mean, to another brah?"

"Sort of. If you can call him that." Under his breath: "Charbroiled bastard."

Mr. Gas waved his hand in protest. "C'mon, man! You're a player, I can tell. Smart, good lookin', and hey—" he said, gesturing to the goofy tie, "ya got the threads. This other guy can't have much on you, Super Dude. What's he like? Do you know?"

Dr. Farron swilled his beer, wiped his mouth on his arm. The beer had foamed up his brain pretty well by now. "Well, he's tall...and..." he rolled his eyes, "...he's a good dancer...and...and...I don't get it because," Dr. Farron lowered his voice, not wanting the whole bar to know he was crazy. "He's—he's covered in black!"

Mr. Gas eyed him. "You mean he's black?"

"I mean—"

One of the brothers who had been listening to the exchange kicked his stool out from under himself and stood so close to Dr. Farron that he nearly pressed his chest into his face. A compact wad of angst, he placed his hands on his hips and stared down at Dr. Farron. He chewed a piece of gum like it fueled his perpetual anger machine. Behind him loomed a brother who could have been mistaken for a slab of Stonehenge if it weren't for the Ray-Bans. He crossed his arms and watched Dr. Farron from over the shorter man's head and shoulders.

"Yo, wonderbread," the shorter man said. "You dissin' a brutha?"

"Excuse me?" Dr. Farron said, unsure if he heard correctly.

"Ah said, Ah heard you jankin' a brutha—crackah," he said, pushing a finger into Dr. Farron's face. "Less you 'pologize fo yo janky mouth, I be sendin' this muthafuckah mandingo to mess wit yo comic book shit."

Dr. Farron squinted at the men through beer goggles. The only bit he caught in the swell of words was "comic book" and he wasn't certain he'd even caught that. Just as he realized that he had been staring a moment too long, he said at last, "Could you please repeat that?"

The man grabbed Dr. Farron by the tie and yanked him off the barstool to his feet. He appraised Dr. Farron's clothes, shoes, and tie. Dr. Farron frantically looked to the bartender, who daintily dried a shot glass with a massive towel.

Mr. Gas, however, showed some interest. "Hey, hey, hey! Tryin' to watch the fights here, brah! Show some respect for the locals."

The man licked his lips and stared hard at Dr. Farron. "Mah name is J Money and this's Amp. You know why he called Amp? Cuz he talk so loud."

Amp nodded mutely, his neck so thick that he could barely move his head. He palmed a large fist armored with gold rings.

Devil alcohol bowed to devil fear, clearing Dr. Farron's head enough to realize he was in real danger. "Look," Dr. Farron said, "I don't know what this is *abooout*." The last part of that word spiked in his throat as J Money choked up on the tie.

"Hey hey, knock that shit off, will ya?" Mr. Gas pointed to the TV. "It's the ninth round, fer Christ's sake. Let's finish one fight before we start another, huh?"

"Check dis muthafuckah with his bitch body, yo," J Money sneered, addressing Amp. His eyes seemed to snap Dr. Farron's bones everywhere his gaze landed. "Sucka betta come correct, or I'm gonna smacka cracka. You feel me?"

The patrons started making room for whatever was going down by the bar. Dr. Farron then grasped that, when complaining about Mr. Wicker being in "black," he had been seriously misunderstood.

"Oh, I get it. I'm sorry. There's been a misunderstanding," Dr. Farron managed to stage whisper. His neck was burning where the tie was cutting into his jugular as he shuffled on his tiptoes to stay erect. Unfortunately, the beer spoke. "I went to Cal Berkeley. I can't possibly be prejudiced."

With that, J Money planted a solid punch across the bridge of his nose. Blood flooded warmly over his upper lip and a flash of pain seared his skull. He fell toward one of the tables, which skidded under his weight. As he splayed on the table, Dr. Farron felt the wooden surface dig into his gut. At first, he didn't care. They could come beat the hell out of him. But... Pushing himself up off the wooden tabletop, he leered at them as he bellowed: "BEWARE MY LASERS OF DEATH!"

J Money cocked his head slightly in confusion. "Say what?"

And then Dr. Farron rushed him. He drove his shoulder into the hood's stomach like a linebacker. J Money tumbled back against the barstool. He crumbled as it dug into his kidney.

Amp pulled a large silver milli Glock from his pants and leveled it at Dr. Farron's head. He spoke in a voice that would have rattled a subwoofer: "Hol' still or I'll put you underground."

Dr. Farron felt as though someone had dumped ice water on his head. A woman screamed in the background. Everyone cleared the bar in two seconds flat, along with Dr. Farron's will to live. "Just go ahead and blow my brains out. I don't care," he said. The blood ran from his nose into his mouth and down his chin.

J Money considered this for a moment. Then, something large whizzed toward his head. In a single blurred movement, Amp twisted and shot blindly toward the chair sailing in his direction from the surprisingly strong arm of Mr. Gas. The noise cracked like thunder in Dr. Farron's ears.

The raspy cock of a shotgun slid over the bar and the barrel landed in Amp's direction. "Gimme the gun! Cain't have you killin' my customers," he said. Amp sighed and laid the Glock on the bar top. He held up his hands and stepped back. The bartender picked up the gun with a dishtowel and put it under the bar. He then ordered the two thugs onto the floor facedown where he kept them at bay.

Dr. Farron took a few deep breaths to get his body back, but noticed Mr. Gas lying bleeding on the bar floor. He immediately checked his breathing, which was shallow. The shot seemed to have torn deeply into his abdomen, just below the left breast. "Call an ambulance!" he yelled, grabbing a bar towel to staunch the bleeding. "Hang in there, man," he kept saying. He threw his sports coat over Mr. Gas.

"What're ya, a doctor, brah?" He gasped as he clutched Dr. Farron's arm.

"Yup."

Mr. Gas held his arm even tighter, fighting as the blood loss threatened to drag him into the abyss of unconsciousness at any moment.

"Stay with me! What's your name?" Dr. Farron asked, trying to keep the man conscious.

"Dan Foster."

"So, tell me, Dan, where are you from? Maui?"

But with each moment that passed, Dr. Farron lost faith that the ambulance would arrive in time. He remembered how reluctant the medical crews were to enter these neighborhoods.

As he waited, he got encouragement and help from everyone around him.

"Hold on, man! We gotta get you fixed up so you don't miss the next fight."

Mr. Gas smiled crookedly. "Brah, you just gotta go get 'er okay? I'll be alright."

"Get who?"

"Get yer woman. Bring 'er back, brah. That's what I shudda done."

The ambulance siren sliced through the air, but it was too late. Dr. Farron had seen people die, but this was the second time someone had died in his arms. The agony of losing a patient and the despair of losing Alicia drew and quartered his heart.

But he didn't show it.

The next thing Dr. Farron knew, he was standing outside the bar with a dishtowel on his gushing nose as he spoke to a police officer. The flashing lights of the cop cars were the only illumination for what seemed like miles around. When the interview finished, he wandered out into the empty parking lot.

Empty being the operative word—

"Where the hell's my car?" he shouted. He turned, and turned, and swiveled back to stare at the ground where he had parked it under the dead light. A black metal box with a squid of wires on the asphalt caught the glare of spinning police lights. He squatted beside the curiosity and poked at it:

It was his LoJack.

Dr. Farron sat down on the curb and drooped with misery, the adrenaline still shaking him like a martini. Every bit of him hurt and he just wanted to go home.

After taking a theft report on top of the assault report and testimony to the shooting, the police cajoled a cab driver to pick up Dr. Farron, as none would come to that part of town. Dr. Farron soon found himself striding toward his front door, the cab pulling away with a wad of cash for the long drive.

How grateful he was to be home. Home. Where memories had a way of walking around like they owned the place.

LSD. Droppers. Ash... The ash! Could it have worked like a drug, affecting his memories and perceptions?

A fresh round of rain drenched him as he strode to the door. He was not in a hurry. The rain felt like a natural baptism of sorts. Something fresh and icy to wash away the bad night. He had yanked off his tie in the cab, unbuttoned the top of his shirt, and rolled up the sleeves. Now he was wet, flesh and fabric.

He slammed the door behind him, his face throbbing, and all he wanted was to take some Advil and fall into bed. But then, as he entered the dark hallway to the bedroom—a faded, plastic Big Gulp cup of water in hand—something glimmered from the hall's end. Dr. Farron stopped dead when the memory jumped up in front of him. He knew that a portrait of him, his dead wife, and the rest of her family hung at the end of that hall. Some light from the kitchen maybe, or from one of the room windows, must be hitting it.

Another glint. As if very far away and moving closer.

Run toward the light. It will receive you.

No way, he thought. *It couldn't be...*

He pictured Dan the Gas Man, blood brimming his lips. *Brah, you just gotta go get 'er okay?*

Fear knuckled his insides as everything she meant to him shouted in his ears. She meant more than anything or anyone had in a very long time. He dearly hoped that whatever had started between them would last far beyond this current nightmare. Deep down, however, he did not believe in letting fairy tales force his actions—not even the nasty, life-stealing one that was now ruining his life. It was too much to ask after what he had been through tonight.

He took another sip of water and stepped forward.

She'll die if you don't come.

The words rolled before him and retreated like a riptide into the darkness. His will got caught in the undertow and he could not resist the plea.

Dr. Farron put down the water cup and sized up the hallway, the portrait glimmering. Forget sanity. *Eat me. Drink me. Vomit me. Scorch me. Love me. Remember me...*

He ran.

Chapter 41

An arm thrown up over his head, he hurtled forward, sounds from another world seeping through the walls as the light exploded and he tumbled into incandescent chaos.

Baa, baa, black sheep, have you any wool? Five for silver, six for gold, seven for a secret never to be told.

The cold blasted him as soon as his feet hit the gravel and he stumbled from the shock. The tiny lights swarmed around his head, further confusing him. *I'm here. Dear God, I'm here!* But where? It was not a library, that was for certain.

Giggling and bouncing, the tiny orbs flashed at him playfully and continued dancing down the tunnel. *Monkeys made of gingerbread, and sugar horses bleeding red.* He examined his feet: gravel, metal and boards. Train tracks.

The ground shook.

The howling pumped terror into his skull. A pinprick of light in the distance was coming at him faster than he could calculate, the tunnel winds drubbing him as he stood mesmerized. Just as Alicia had described.

He clenched his fists and closed his eyes. *I will not die*, he told himself. *I will not die.*

Shrieking, moaning, shaking, the sharp glare of eternity collided with his body. The impact swallowed him, pricking his skin with fiery pins. He fell to his knees, holding his head as the screams sliced and diced his cortex. Just as every square inch of his flesh was ablaze, the heat dissipated. A cool stillness held him. After a moment, he convinced himself to open his eyes.

Edward Anthony Brust.

Dr. Farron had no idea who that was, but the name was inked in black on the spine of a book on a dusty bookshelf before him, amongst many, many names and threading book spines. Some were in languages he did not know, so he could not be certain they were even names, but he suspected they were. The book in question was wedged between others in the middle of a row. The shelves had wooden backings so he could not see to the next row behind it like he would in a normal library. An endless number of rows stacked atop one another to what he could barely make out as a raftered ceiling. A rustle of feathers. Something darker than the shadows flapped over the stacks.

The Library.

He crouched between two book stacks. At the end to his right was a stone wall, a gargoyle holding an oil lamp at about his shoulder's height. Why was it so dim? And it smelled of smoke. The stacks opened to his left, revealing a narrow slice of the greater Library. A large table was piled high with books. A candelabra sitting on a stack cast a thin sheet of light as far as the gargoyle on the wall.

No sign of the Librarian.

Stepping into the Library center, he looked around. The wall of clocks clicked and clacked at him. A raven perched just above him on one of the stacks and cawed. A palpable presence lurked in a darkened alcove. Dr. Farron couldn't look away from it, sensing Someone was within. All five candles leapt aflame on the candelabra. Startled at first, he plucked it from the table and proceeded to explore the Library. The lavender window churned with a heavy smoke. It caught Dr. Farron's breath as he realized something—*someone*—lived beyond that window. A very big Something or Someone. Maybe multiple Ones. Strange energy, to say the least. As soon as he noticed the big black phone on the desk beneath it, he was struck with both dire curiosity to pick up the phone and utter dread of what lay beyond the windowpane.

"Where is she, Drunos?" he called out, sweeping the candelabra in front of him as he scanned the tables. "What did you do with her?"

Silence.

Dr. Farron surveyed the limits of the Library and a profound sadness struck him. The Librarian was a prisoner. While the good doctor was surrounded by sickness and despair in the hospital, he was also around beauty, healing, and life. Here wasted the mysterious ex-druid in his ugliness and isolation. He had no one but a handful of screeching birds, his steady flow of damaged children, and the parade of dissipated souls who came to retrieve their books. In fact, his only hope of company was that these people came back. This was the other side of the world: where Dr. Farron worked in the light, Mr. Wicker worked in darkness. But the difference was, Mr. Wicker had no choice.

Or did he?

"You must be lonely here," Dr. Farron said. "Maybe if the children talked to me and others like me, you might be free from this place. I bet if you refused to do it they would have no choice but to let you live. And you can live, you know. There are great things out there: basketball and sunrise and pizza and sitcoms, and...man! I can't catalogue the world for you. It's too big and great. Maybe you should put down your pen and try it."

Silence, except for a tremendous rustling in the alcove. Dr. Farron could not bring himself to enter it.

"It's not right, you know! She has a life to live and things to do yet! You shouldn't keep her here and tell her lies!"

"She is not here."

The voice rolled from the alcove like a boulder. It was the voice on the 9-1-1 dispatch sound file. If he did not believe before, Dr. Farron did now. "Then where is she?"

"She took her book," the voice said, plaintive. "She is in very great danger."

Feeling a bit braver, Dr. Farron took a few steps closer to the alcove. "But people remember things," he said. "They can deal with bad memories and heal themselves. Surely this has happened before. You've lost books, right?" He held the candelabra before him like a crucifix to a vampire, hoping to catch a glimpse of the Librarian.

"Not these memories," the voice replied. "These are the ones they are never meant to remember. She is not meant to remember what happened. It will destroy her."

No wonder they had been hitting walls with the hypnosis. But Alicia did report some kind of repeating dream about a withering ring of roses. She must remember something about it. Then he wondered who else he knew had books here. His parents? His sisters? His colleagues?

Did he?

"Why didn't you stop her?"

"I tried. I truly did."

Dr. Farron sighed. He could hear the love in Drunos' voice. "I'm sure you did," he said at last, knowing too well how stubborn Alicia was. "On second thought, it's best that you didn't. It's best that you stop trying to protect people and let them deal with life." Hey, black kettle? Pot calling. He spoke as much to himself as to Mr. Wicker.

Another moment of silence.

"You must help her, Litu—" the voice said.

Litu? Confused, Dr. Farron edged closer, the light of his candelabra stretching into the alcove. Mr. Wicker's cat's eyes flashed like broken glass as they caught the candlelight.

"—NOW!"

A thousand black wings and needle-sharp claws erupted from the alcove. Dr. Farron dropped the candelabra. He ran for his life toward a humming light that bloomed between the book stacks. The murder of ravens howled at his back, ripping his clothes and tearing his hair as they chased him. Before he lunged into the incandescence, he dared a glance back to see a terrible sight.

Mr. Wicker picked up another book and lit it on fire.

Chapter 42

Brooders weep and brooders keep their misery at hand.

She awoke, her face half-buried in the pillow, his brambly voice caroling in her head. Her bedroom window rattled from the blustering winds, the open drapes revealing high morning storm clouds. She exhaled heavily with relief. She must have survived the darkness by choosing bed over blade. Or had she? Given that she was in bed, it must have been a dream. *A very sad dream.*

She sighed again, pushed herself up from the bed, and then stopped: black soot smudged her white cotton pillowcase. Her hand wiped her chin, both smeared with black ash. It was no dream! Delirious with joy, she clambered out of bed, still wearing her soiled, unbuttoned peach dress, and discovered that everywhere his hands had touched her (*everywhere*) that delicate black char smeared her. The light must have carried her exhausted body straight to bed. She touched her fingers to her tongue and tasted him in the char. Her eyes rolled up into her head as the memory of him burned her mouth.

The book! Where was it?

She tore apart the bed sheets and found nothing. Alicia even looked under the bed. Still nothing. Her eyes next scanned the shelf that ran along the ceiling where Eric kept his god-awful business administration books and Westerns. She pulled down every book, but couldn't find it. The house was huge. If it was here at all, it could be anywhere. If only it answered to its name...

With the excitement and wit of a child, she got an idea brimming with magic. She cleared her throat and stood on tip-toe, her voice carrying out of the room. "Marco."

Then, faintly, a reply: "*Polo.*"

It was her voice. Her little girl voice.

Thrilled and spooked, she tried again. "Marco..."

"*...Polo.*"

She followed the voice down the hallway. "Marco..."

"*...Polo.*"

It rang from the bathroom. She approached the dark room uneasily, and then whispered inside. "Marco..."

"*Pooloooo...*" Mocking and singsong, the voice echoed against the porcelain. The book rested on the cold, bloodstained tile.

Alicia picked it up carefully and retreated into the hallway. The tome was as long as her forearm, a foot wide, and three fingers thick. Some gothic calligrapher had written her name, Alicia Baum, in gold on the black, cloth-bound cover. With the exhilaration she'd felt in the tunnel, yet with that same fear she'd felt in the dark foyer, she returned to the bedroom and climbed over the dirty sheets with her treasure. She placed it on the bed, hands shaking, and opened it.

A beautiful drawing in sepia inks filled the inside cover: A cross-section of a fairy woods revealed myriad tree roots sinking into the magical soil. In gold ink, words wove among the roots. "In my father's house, there are many libraries. W-"

Alicia drew the comforter around her. The twisted biblical quote worried her.

The cover page was blank and yellowed with age. She turned the page.

Nothing. She turned the next.

Nothing again. Irritated, she turned blank page after blank page, marking each with black fingerprints.

She shuffled through the pages so rapidly that she almost missed it: a crude treasure map sketched by a child with a thick-leaded pencil. Below the map, her eight-year-old self had scribbled a description of how to get to the prize. The map outlined her grandparents' backyard, including a significant landmark she did not remember: a large circle drawn in the upper right-hand corner of the page, surrounded by pencil swirls depicting flowers. Roses. Within the circle at its edge the pencil marked a deeply etched "X."

Alicia felt sick. It was the only written page in the book.

She took the envelope of cash from the cupboard and stuffed it in her purse. After a shower, she walked to the elementary school down the hill to make the toll-free call at the payphone.

"Can I get a cab to Oakland Airport?"

Ring around the rosie, pocket full of posies. Ashes, ashes, we all...fall.

Dr. Farron emerged from his deep sleep. He did not open his eyes. He had been dreaming after all, which was both reassuring and alarming.

Not only did his nose throb but his hand hurt. It was tightly clenched, a pronounced cramp stinging his fingers and palm. He shifted uncomfortably. Neck pain ran from his shoulder to his temple. The bar fight must have busted more than he thought. His head rested on his arm, he on his side. As his head tried to find a better, softer place on the pillow, he realized that he was not lying on a pillow at all. The length of his body was curled tightly into a fetal position on an unforgiving surface.

Dr. Farron's eyes snapped open. The carpet of his office stretched inches from his nose. His office in the hospital, that is.

The shock of lying in his office was worse than finding himself in the tunnel after flinging himself at a wall. He was stretched out on the carpet, his hand twisted into a grotesque grip, his fingers smeared with something red. He would have stayed there a few more moments, just processing, but the pain in his hand was too awful. Breathing deeply, he opened his hand a finger at a time, begging each to relax. A red crayon stub rolled from his palm onto the carpet. The paper had been peeled away, the end rubbed to almost nothing. His palm and fingers were stained red.

As Dr. Farron propped himself up, his eyes panned the walls. He staggered to his feet.

On the office walls surrounding him were drawn red roses. The continuous mural formed a circle of withered blooms bobbing, swaying, and mocking him. It was clearly his style and shading, yet he had absolutely no recollection of committing the Crayola vandalism. And in his handwriting with a thick black line were scrawled the words "HELP ME."

His clothes were tattered and barely scabbed gouges covered his arms where he'd rolled up his sleeves in the cab. Talon slashes.

He checked the clock. It was 1:51p.m. He had no idea when Alicia had returned to this world. But he did know one thing:

She wasn't long for it.

Chapter 43

Mr. Wicker huddled in the miserable chaos of the birds and books. He had never told anyone in the Library about his past. And even with Alicia, he'd kept the final chapter of his history a secret—that which transformed him into the creature he was. He had not thought about it for some time. He wanted so badly to forget. But now he could do nothing but remember.

After Caesar pronounced the genocide of his kin, Drunos became sick, as if a black hand gripped his heart. Quintus came to check on him. He stood in the folds of darkness by the door, his arm still pressing that ridiculous wad of cloth against his body. After a while, he moved to the chair and sat for a long time. A slave brought him wine, of which he drank an entire amphora as he watched the druid.

Drunos opened his eyes but did not look at the Roman. "Quintus?"

"Yes?" the Roman answered, suddenly roused. He slouched forward, inebriated, and rubbed his eyes.

"Would you bring me something?"

"Anything."

Drunos burrowed his fingers into the skins. "A calamus," he said. "An amphora of ink. And parchment."

For the next two weeks, Drunos dipped the reed into the tiny amphora and drew letters he knew so well from his reading.

And he wrote. Chants. Songs. Laws. Rituals. Stories. Everything he could remember from the Isle but had hidden in alcoves of memory. He knew the Romani would not stop until they had slaughtered or conquered every Gaul from the Isle to Acquitaine. Every drop of Gaulish blood would feed the ground and stain the feet of Caesar's soldiers.

He envisioned the souls of his people indwelling the next generation of Romani. Perhaps that was the plan of the gods, but it offered no solace to Drunos. Who would pass on the stories of his people? How would the gods be remembered so that the people could repent and rejoin them? The arrogance of his tribe, of his entire race. By keeping the sacred traditions in memory to enlighten the elite, they had made themselves vulnerable to obliteration. As the ink bruised his fingers, he understood how the old laws were those of man and the new laws must come like desperate oar strokes driving a sinking boat toward land.

Quintus secretly supplied Drunos with as much parchment and ink as he desired, at great personal expense. Parchment was preserved for literary undertakings, while the wax tablets were used for general correspondence and legal contracts. One morning, Quintus slipped into the druid's room as Drunos rested, head in his arms at the table. Quintus held his breath when he realized that Drunos had filled over five hundred sheaves with the laws, theology, and rituals of Gaul. Not only had he written everything down in a legible hand, but he had also catalogued the parchment sheaves using some cryptic system the Roman could not decipher.

Drunos examined Quintus blearily. Lathed with buttery streaks and threads of silver, the druid's hair and beard lay in shaggy shanks about his head. Drunos noted the amazement on Quintus' face as he examined the cataloguing. "It is not half finished."

"So that's why the numbering is so mysterious."

"I don't mean the catalogue."

"You mean—?"

Drunos nodded and sighed. He coughed noisily, his lungs soaked with rheum.

"Drunos, I cannot afford any more parchment. If you would like wax tablets, I can arrange for those." His eyes locked with the druid's and guilt dampened his eyes. "Caesar is very interested in what you are writing. He would supply you with more parchment, but he wants to know what has spurred such blasphemy."

"I am in deep gratitude to you, Quintus. But I shall never give Caesar the pleasure of knowing," Drunos replied. And then the Jura rose behind his eyes, its rocky shoulders draped with a thick fleece of clouds and snow. At the feet of the Jura stretched thousands of acres of burned Helvetian farmland. An endless sea of ash. "I must return home," he whispered.

"It is time."

Drunos suffered those days as he crossed through the Sequani territory on his way back to the Helvetii. Tara Nis showered him with early winter rains that numbed his face and feet. The baptism of exile. Drunos accepted the cleansing and humbly licked the droplets from his lips. Before bedding for the night, he checked the hundreds of parchments tightly bundled in lambskins to keep out the lament of nature. His precious *athenaeum*. Keeper of memory.

His Sequani cousins gave him no trouble as he passed. The speckles of his druid robe attracted offerings of food and passionately sworn *lugjoi* of devotion. Drunos accepted the offerings and oaths. Everyone asked what the druid carried in his cart, but he responded that he brought back personal belongings of Gauls lost in the battle at Genava. This they believed readily as many of them were already corrupted by the Roman consumerism: the need for *things* to define life rather than the simplicity of nature.

Drunos knew what a dangerous situation awaited him if he returned with the blasphemous cargo. But who would know what the parchments contained? Who could read, much less decipher Latin? Thousands of lines had been transliterated from Gaulish to Latin letters. Still, not a soul would know. Nor would he tell them. But could he lie? And would they feel betrayed by his Roman writing in the face of their defeat?

Where else would he go? A wanderer with cursed luggage. No rest. His precious parchments to be pillaged by rival tribes. No, he must return home and convince his tribe of their imminent extinction.

The druid's cart rumbled into a blackened field, the razed cornstalks crackling under the heavy wheels. Smoke drifted in vague patches over a village at the far end of the valley. Drunos guided his horses toward it in the autumn's early morning. Three young women on white mares rode out to greet him, the horses' hooves silently cutting the burnt ground. Spirits of *Eponâ*. Goddess of fate. Guide of the dead. As they approached, faces and hands dissipated like candle smoke. Even the flesh of the mares dissolved in the winds.

The village was inhabited by about fifty survivors of the migration. They recognized Drunos and offered him what wine they had left. A young woman made him a place to sleep in the corner of one of the larger huts. "I need to see Litu," he said to her. When she placed an icy hand on his cheek, he realized that a sickness boiled under his skin.

"Litugenalos?"

He nodded, half faint.

"You sleep," she said, returning to the fire where others sat and talked. "We will find him."

He reached out to her. "And my cart—please."

"*Drûis*, what would you have us do with it?"

The world dissolved in his eyes like the earth spirits.

For the first time in his life, Drunos could not tell how long he had slept. His body no longer kept the hours. Nor the nights. When he awoke, hard hands seized his shoulders, arms, and legs, upending him from the bed. Someone pulled his robes over his head and yanked them from his body. Rugose, scarred faces with filthy beards and red eyes leered into his as someone twisted his arms behind him and wound heavy ropes around his hands. Feverish numbness gave way to the clarity of danger as Drunos struggled against the mob. Once they had properly bound him, they tied a rag over his eyes.

They carried him from the hut into the darkness and heaved his body into a caged cart. Drunos fell into the straw and his shoulder struck a board with an ominous crack. The cage door swung shut like a thunderclap before someone dropped the iron pin in the lock.

The cart rumbled for some way before it shuddered to a stop at the edge of a massive gathering. The Gauls' voices blurred into an indistinct rattle of conversation as the tang of freshly cut wood spiked his nostrils.

Not just wood. Wicker.

Over the chanting of the sprawling crowd, Litu censured Drunos for his blasphemy and his crimes against his people. Two stout Gauls carried him up a steep staircase onto the narrow scaffolding. Chickens, hares, pigs, and other animals squawked and shrieked as they frantically battered cages with wings and snouts. A wicker door creaked open and Drunos was heaved forward into a wooden box. He scrambled to his knees. Someone tore off his blindfold.

Welts swelled across Medudorix's deformed features. A deep scar swept from his forehead into his withered eye socket and thinned at his jaw line. "The Romani fattened you while Rosmerta and Arctosa died from rape and torture. How could you betray us? How could you give them our sacred words?"

"I did not betray you, Medu! I swear with my blood!"

Medudorix spat on Drunos' cheek. He slammed the wicker mesh door and the other Gaul dropped the lock pin into place. So many times had Drunos witnessed criminals burn to death in the towering wooden cage with its faceless head, the legs and arms crowded with sacrifices and kindling. Dry wood heaped around the feet of the giant wooden man.

"You are isolated here, Medu!" Drunos shouted after him. "Our people are dying! Our tribes are vanishing." Drunos stopped as Litu stood below him, using his a ceremonial staff to bless the sacrifice to Tara Nis.

I bless the face.

I bless the mind.

I bless the breath.

I bless the flesh.

I bless the bone.

I bless the blood.

I bless the soul.

He pointed the staff at Drunos. "But you—I *curse*. Yet no curse can cast you far enough from mercy."

"Litu, you condemn me with no trial! You would kill me for power!"

"May you be a keeper of the most baneful memory—"

"I DEMAND TO SEE THE COUNCIL!"

"—a prisoner forever removed from the journey of souls."

He laid the tip of the ceremonial staff in a slave's torch and then touched the woodpile with the staff. Soon the crowd behind him was illuminated by the flames of condemnation, revealing more druids from the Sequani and Boii standing with hands raised in sacred pleas to Tara Nis. A council of sorts had gathered during his fever and condemned him. *In absentia.*

So few remained. As the smoke climbed the lattice of his prison, Drunos remembered the morning that he mounted the mare in the caravan camp, thousands of Helvetii forming a river before and after him. Arctosa standing on her brother's steed and jumping to his arms.

Little Bear.

The great noise is just the voice of Tara Nis the Thunderer. He always speaks during times of change.

Drunos collapsed back on his haunches and howled until the sound hollowed his soul. Flames blistered his cheeks and lips. As smoke engulfed his convulsing body, Drunos wept not only for his family, but for the death of Gaul. In the swirling cinders, he had visions of Roman legions that swarmed like angry bees as they steadily crushed one uprising after another until all of Gaul had been consumed by Caesar.

Gaius Julius Caesar.

Chapter 44

It was early evening by the time Alicia's flight landed at Burbank Airport. As far as Alicia could tell, Los Angeles never grew dark. Autumn was green trees, coral-covered rooftops, and grainy hillsides faded with the haze of damp and dreams.

She wore almost no makeup as she trudged through the compact airport. Her eyes found people of every shade, but none like her angel of cinder and secrets. She wore a black sweater and jeans, her nails filed down. Her overnight bag sagged heavily with the book. She didn't plan to stay long.

She drove between the legs and over the bellies of sleeping, grassy giants as she made her way down the highway toward Simi Valley. She felt the embers of his passion, a burning seed blown from the hand of Death to her dry lands. Desire was turning her bones to ash and leeching reason from her wits. She would drink the poison of his sweat. It was no sane thing, but neither was playing Marco Polo with a book. She saw from the highway a train tunnel boring into one of the giant's verdant hips and her fingers once more felt the softness of his cheek, her soul the pain from those pale green eyes.

In time the ink shall sing.

In her childhood, roads were a fiction, something only adults saw and used. But now, as she drove up that old hill to her grandparents' house, she realized that children don't really see roads as much as they feel them. She felt the road and the driveway and the house face itself, and put names to those feelings that she hadn't before: chaos, warmth, horror, love, and despair. The gravel road rolled beneath her rented compact and she pulled into the circular driveway before a large Spanish ranch-style house. The driveway cracked with age and quake as if one of the sleeping giants had lifted a lazy finger beneath. The house rested alone against the hillside. Elm trees in the front yard bowed to the strong Santa Ana winds. A "FOR SALE" sign loomed on the lawn.

The sprawling, green field from her hypnosis sessions adjoined the house's open lot. The nearest neighbor was about a quarter mile away. In the distance, the deadly train tracks rolled into the hillside.

She sat in the car gathering her courage. She missed Dr. Farron. But she had done so much alone, she could not imagine having help. That's just how you get yourself through things: alone. Men are useless. Family members are absent. Doctors are unreliable. And love? She'd never had it when she'd needed it most. Not from her father or her husband, and certainly none of her miserable lovers. (Why do people call them "lovers" when it's just lust?) And there was no chance James would understand what had happened with either Dr. Sark or Mr. Wicker. Even if she already felt something deeper for James than she could admit—something more real and palpable than her interactions with the Librarian—he would not understand. Could not. She would face only his rejection.

Alone. She definitely had to be alone.

She didn't bother to lock the car. Simi Valley was still provincial. With a bag slung over her shoulder, the Book inside, she went to one of the windows and peeked through the curtains.

Her almost-seven-year-old self danced in the living room. A vivid phantom of memory. Little Alicia pranced out of the living room toward the kitchen in the back. Alicia tried to see more of the living room through the curtains. Some of the furniture had changed, and so had the carpeting. But the white stucco walls, from foyer to family room, were covered with oil paintings. Alicia wished she could examine every sweep and swirl of the bitter, dry landscapes lapped onto these canvases.

Her grandfather's paintings.

Had they always been so dark?

Alicia wandered past the garage to the side of the house. While walking down the side alley to the backyard, she noticed the kitchen window was open. The phantom of Little Alicia sang with her much younger, thirty-years-ago Phantom Grandmother. Alicia marveled at how happy her grandmother looked, how fresh compared to what she remembered from the last ten years or so. Grandma clutched a bowl of half-mixed potato salad at her waist as she sang alternate lines of the song.

"N-G-O!"

"B-I-"

"N-G-O!"

"And Bingo was his name-oh!" they sang together.

"Yay!" Little Alicia cheered, clapping and spinning around.

"Now," her grandmother said, "why don't you go play outside with your sister while I finish making lunch?"

Alicia's heart seized mid-beat as she bowed over the edge of the chasm of memory, arms out, on tiptoe.

Little Alicia nodded and skipped toward the sliding glass door that led out to the patio.

Alicia wondered where her grandfather was. The workshop in the garage! She doubled back and found the dirty window. She had passed it, thinking it too dim and knowing that Little Alicia would not go in there. Oh! Her grandfather. The bittersweet thought of seeing his phantom seized her with regret. Perhaps this was what she needed: to see him as he used to be.

The window was so dirty; Alicia wiped it with her palm. She cupped the sides of her eyes and placed the edges of her hands against the glass, blocking out any glare. His paintings and works in progress hung or were propped up around her Phantom Grandfather. He sat painting, sipping scotch from a tumbler. He looked relaxed and introspective, putting the finishing touches on a painting of her that she'd forgotten about: Little Alicia wearing a rosy dress, surrounded by blooms. He must have sold it—although, given the way he gazed at it and lovingly attended to the details, he surely mustn't have wanted to. It must have been out of necessity.

Alicia turned from her grandfather and the grime on the window to see if she could spot the rose garden. Just as she thought of it, Little Alicia was sliding the patio door closed as her grandmother said, "I'll call you two when lunch is ready."

"Okay!" Little Alicia said, and then bounded outside. Cupping her hands to her mouth, she called out, "Marco!"

Dr. Farron drove straight to Oakland Airport and got on standby for Southwest, as they had flights leaving every fifteen to forty-five minutes. It took five minutes of internet sleuthing to find Alicia's grandparents' address. A location website sold him the skip trace for a reasonable fee. When he got the Alamo rental car, he sped off as fast as he could, relying on the general laxness of the Los Angeles County police to patrol the freeways. Highway 5 was crawling even at six-thirty p.m., which made him sweat until he reached Highway 118. He knew it would be a long, slow waltz over asphalt until he reached Simi Valley itself. He tried everything to slow down his mind as it raced. He wondered if he should have called the police. He wished he'd thought of it because the local police could have gotten there much faster than he ever possibly could. He could still call. But what would the police do? There had been no crime and she was not a missing person.

Perhaps it was meant to be. Maybe Mr. Wicker told him to help her because he was the only one who could.

That is, if anyone could.

Alicia gauged the backyard territory. Everything was as it was labeled on the treasure map, including what had escaped her memory so completely:

The circular arena of roses.

Come into the garden, Maud.

She heard his voice as she held out the book, the pencil scribbles tracing her path as she took childlike steps toward the circle of roses in the corner of the yard. There was no string of memory that she could tie to her ankle to find her way back. Little Alicia had disappeared. As Alicia approached the circle alone, the stiff stems of two blanching roses hung their blighted heads, Gog and Magog, as they arched across the opening to a circular concrete arena. Their stout stems bowed toward one another as they crossed like pikes, thorns murderously cuspate, preventing casual entry. Like the fairy woods in her book, the roses entwined above and below, a mass of mingling vegetation.

As she approached, her grainy dream intercut with her vision of the rose garden. She realized that her dreams were never memories about the past at all, but rather visions of the future. Of this very moment unfolding.

"...Polo!" she heard from within. A child's voice.

Holding the book against her with one hand, Alicia grasped the head of Magog and pulled the watcher from its post. The sentry fought her, like a child turning from its parent's hold to seek some forbidden wonder, but she snapped its pulpy arm down at the base with her foot. She crushed the rose head in her palm, releasing its sickly perfume. She dropped it and, watching Gog, slipped beneath the sylvan girdle.

Ring around the rosie, a pocket full of posies. Ashes, ashes...

She entered a rippling circle of wildishness and found Gog and Magog had marked both entry and treasure. October breezes rifled the blossoms, ripping their silken skirts from bare waists, as the aging blooms wove a tattered tent around the concrete where a young girl with mousey brown hair sat, humming as she posed her half-naked Barbie dolls. The roses' fragile faces sagged from stiff necks, nodding at her as they wept petals.

Squinting at the sun, the child upturned her sweet face to Little Alicia, who was filled with both sibling love and competitive rage as she knelt on the concrete and placed the book beside her. "Lilly! Gimme my dolls! They're not yours!"

The book pages waved on the cement behind her and the parchment blotted words from the air onto the numerous blank pages. A dark waltz began. Piano and sweet sopranos. Alicia realized with alarm she was no longer the obedient audience of memory but prisoner to the scrawls frantically scratching the book's pages. She had become Little Alicia again.

"You don't play with them," Lillian answered, her silvery medical alert bracelet dangling from her wrist. She was prone to seizures. Not as classically pretty as Alicia, her eyes were more deeply inset, her face broader and fatter. One eye strayed just a bit starboard while the other focused directly on Alicia. "You left them by my bed."

"I didn't mean to," Alicia said. "I –

(a puff of smoke in her eyes)

—want them—

—BACK!"

Alicia stopped breathing. Grainy TV patterns appeared before her eyes as she felt herself go faint and slump to the ground, the hot cement banging her bare knees and scraping them like a thousand pins. But this time she didn't fully lose consciousness the way she did when she was a baby. She was a big girl now, the doctor said, and she wouldn't suffer what he called "breath-holding spells" much longer. She'd been having them since she was two years old, and even suffered a bad one when she'd discovered her mother's body hanging in the garage. The doctor said they weren't her fault. They happened in-volun-tarily. (Alicia had memorized that word.) But soon, they'd not happen at all.

The strain wrung her fragile body like a washrag. She let her body go limp.

Lillian dropped the dolls and crawled over to Alicia's prostrate body, the rip in her pink corduroy jumper yawning across her kneecap. Her head blotted out the scorching sun as she peered down at her older sister. The winds were picking up, as Daddy used to say. "How do you do that?"

"Do what, stupid?" Alicia gasped, the blood slowly flushing her gauzy head. While she thought her younger sister was kind of stupid, she was deeply attached to her. Alicia had taught her to walk and draw letters and everything—usually, though, by saying, "It's easy, dummy. Just..." Fill in the blank. That was all it took to inspire Lillian, who did not want to be thought stupid or weak by her pretty and smart older sister, whom she let do the talking whenever any adult was speaking to them. Even grownups thought Lillian was slow. And Alicia could not dream of doing anything without her sister—the one person who had been there for her through the awfulness of losing both Mommy and Daddy in the space of a few months. They had held each other and cried so many times she couldn't count. And Alicia could count pretty high for her age.

"I wanna hold my breath," Lillian said.

"It's easy, dummy. Just go like this..." Alicia sat halfway up, leaning on her elbow, and sucked in air until her cheeks bulged like a trumpet player. She let out the air.

"But I want to hold it longer than you," she said. "Let's see who can hold it longer. Let's try."

"Okay." Alicia orchestrated with her index finger. "One, two, three."

The two girls dramatically inhaled and clamped their lips shut. The stillness of the incandescent summer air impregnated the bower for a few moments as the two stared at each other, not breathing, not moving. Alicia felt too uncomfortable as the fiery swells pulsed through her chest. Without her wanting it to, her mouth opened and the air rushed out. Lillian did the same, and they giggled.

"That wasn't very good," Lillian said. "Will you help me, Alicia? Help me do it. For, like, a minute. Or two minutes. You can hold your breath for two minutes, can't you?"

"I dunno. I guess."

"Then help me do it longer than two minutes."

"Okay. One, two—"

Lillian inhaled as before. Alicia counted out loud. "One one-thousand, two one-thousand, three one-thousand…"

When Alicia reached fifty, Lillian's face blanched and her eyes quivered like the worms in her grandfather's fishing bucket. Alicia kept counting despite the obvious distress on her sister's face. Just as she was sure Lillian would give up, Lillian pointed to her mouth and slapped her hands over her mouth and nose, holding on.

"…fifty one-thousand, fifty-one one-thousand, fifty-two one-thousand…"

During the second minute, Lillian grabbed Alicia's hands and slapped them over her mouth and nose. She sagged to the ground as Alicia continued to count. Her legs kicked in the air, which made Alicia giggle. "Stop—one-thousand—*moving*! one-thousand—" As if challenged by her sister's resistance, Alicia—the stronger and sturdier of the two by far—planted her hands over Lillian's mouth and nose more firmly. She dug her fingers under Lillian's chin to keep her mouth shut as it tried to work open. One of Lillian's hands worked free from the strangle but rapidly lost direction, at first flailing toward Alicia and then falling to the side, her medical alert bracelet tinkling against the pavement.

When Alicia reached a minute and a half, Lillian had stopped moving, but she kept counting, her sister's body slackening beneath her hands.

"—and sixty one-thousand! Two minutes! You did it!"

She lifted her hands from her sister's rubbery lips with triumph, somewhat annoyed that Lillian had made it but also pleased with herself for helping Lillian master something new, even if for not as long.

Lillian's lips parted to emit the startling stench of vomit that had filled her mouth. Her head fell to one side, the deep bruises from Alicia's fingers darkening on her pale throat and cheeks.

"Lillian? Lil-li-*aaan*!" Alicia sang, poking her sister. "Come on. Stop pretending to sleep. Come—on!"

But Lillian didn't move. Strange red splotches dotted the whites of her eyes and splayed over her face like bloody freckles.

Confused and alarmed, Alicia drew back from her sister until the threatening thorns caught her hair on the other side of the circle. She wanted to cry for her mother, but keen sorrow rather than words stung her tongue. What had happened to Lillian? Why was she lying there that way?

"Lillian? Little Rose?"

Her grandfather, but almost thirty years younger. Just as she remembered him. He grasped Gog and pulled it back effortlessly as he stepped with a slight sway into the sanctuary.

"What's holdin' up the show here? Yer grandmother's been calling you for lunch."

Alicia's eyes caught her grandfather's as they locked on Lillian's lifeless body. "Lillian! LILLIAN!" He knelt beside her and cradled her head, noting the bruises and other marks. The fumes from the whisky he'd been drinking ripened in her nose as he spoke, smearing with the odor of Lillian's vomit.

"She asked me to help her hold her breath the way I do when I get the faints. She wanted to do it better," Alicia said.

In the distance, Alicia's Phantom Grandmother opened the patio door and called out. "Leesha! Lillian! Lunch is ready!"

His eyes watered in a terrible way as they widened and he turned to look at Alicia. "Run!" he whispered harshly.

"Why?"

"Run, child! Run! You never saw this! You never set foot in this circle, you hear me?" Tears bled from his red eyes and scrawled his leathery cheeks. "GET OUT!"

The song of the book's ink fell silent.

Free from the vision but not its trauma, Alicia knelt where she fell in the memory, vomiting into the soil at the base of the roses. She hadn't died in the bathroom but in that circle of roses with her sweet innocent sister. And all her life she'd walked, death and decay, blossoms dropping from rot. Her grandfather whom she had loved had taken the onus for her unspeakable act; she could not bear the memory.

Run!

She crawled beneath the thorns, scraping her hands and arms on the cement. She then staggered to her feet and ran to flee the filth, the guilt smearing her skin so thick the stench caught a scream from her throat and flung it to the winds unfurling above her like dry white sheets. Balloons and birds belonged there, in the air, not her guilt. Not this tsunami of agony. And there was no God to hear it.

Dr. Farron's car screeched to a halt in the driveway next to Alicia's rental car. She had to be here, dead or alive.

Alicia burst from the yard like a bird. She tore across the adjoining field, which Dr. Farron recognized from the descriptions of her hypnosis sessions. He wrenched open the car door. "Alicia!"

She didn't seem to hear him. Rather, she ran across the large green field as she cried. The tall grass whipped against her legs. He chased after her. The roaring Santa Ana winds stole his voice whenever he tried to call her name. She ran across the field and into the train tunnel.

Dr. Farron stopped. There was no way he would follow her. If she wanted to die, he must let her. Judging by the newness of the Amtrak signs, the track was active. He could not risk himself any more than he had. But he dropped to his knees in the grass and called to her. "Alicia! I care about you! I'll help you through this! I swear!"

He heard the distant blast of the train inside the hill.

Alicia entered the tunnel, time slowing until she felt like she was barely moving, arm up over her head. This time she would not jump aside. She would meet death head on.

As if an answer to prayer, the approaching train rumbled, its unbending beam of light flooding the tracks and tunnel. She opened her arms. Christ-wide. The train light baptized her on the tracks.

"...I care about you! And I'll help you through this! I swear!"

The words broke her conviction. She torqued away from the light, toward his voice, and ran. The train bore down on her. She did not want to die. She did not have to die. And she remembered why.

But it was too late.

Huginn alighted at the tunnel opening, the brutality of mortality fraying her senses. Still, she saw.

She told.

And he knew.

Mr. Wicker, who did not know time. He stood outside of it yet kept it rolling forward like a man pushing a barrel full of heaven's finest wine.

He bent his head in the Library before the arching lavender window with the light he so loved and abhorred. For what it brought. And for what it took away.

He bent his head with a single candle in hand, hoping for this one favor. And he blew on the flame.

The train tunnel opening exploded with flames. They swallowed Huginn as she flew back home.

Dr. Farron hit the grass, covering his head with his hands.

In the field...

　　　　...in the smoke...

　　　　　　　...in a searing plume of light...

...Alicia appeared...

　　　　...running...falling...onto the grass.

　　　　　　　　　　Gasping for breath.

"James!"

He grasped her with all his might and life.

And she did likewise.

Chapter 45

Mr. Wicker knew Georgeta had entered the Library before he saw her broken features. The girl's feet dragged against the floor. She did not look him in the eye, even when she stopped beside the table where he stood. She laid a hand on the surface and hung her head.

Holding up Georgeta's book, Mr. Wicker asked, "Is this what you want?"

Georgeta nodded.

"Do you mean to pass on?"

Silence.

Mr. Wicker gave her the empty tome. She had given him nothing, yet she wanted it anyway.

"Are you afraid?"

Georgeta nodded.

"Come here." He pulled two chairs from the table and brought them together. He sat in one and Georgeta sat in the other beside him, hugging her book. "When you go into the light, life goes on. You may come out a tree, or a kitten, or a river. But most likely you will find yourself to be a new girl. Or perhaps a boy."

Tears rolled from the corner of Georgeta's one good eye.

"Why the sorrow? Either way, you will re-enter the circle of life. Old Mr. Grumpy Pants can't even do that." He paused. "That's me, by the way."

Georgeta wiped the tears with her fingers. "I miss Alicia, the lady who used to hold my hand. Where'd she go?"

"I don't know. But she is well, I suspect." He missed Alicia more than anyone could know. "Well and happy." He sensed Georgeta was not pulling out of the funk, despite this news. He honestly had not expected Them to free her in the tunnel, but They did. And it cheered him, even though now she most likely lived with the Celt. He knew that the love they were meant to share would not die. "Would you like to see her again?"

Georgeta nodded vigorously.

He hunched slightly and whispered in her ear: "I will put in the good word and see what I can do. Perhaps in the circle of life you will rejoin them."

Pulling back her shoulders, Georgeta swelled with hope. She hugged him. Her warmth buzzed through him with an auspicious strength. It reaffirmed what he'd resolved to do once she left. To think, he'd worried that Sirona would expel him from his world when it was Litu. The one who'd imprisoned him now wanted to free him. He'd already said goodbye to Huginn and Muninn, letting them return to their Norse master. The other ravens had fled after them to swarm the great halls of Valhalla. Without them, his bones weakened and the ink faded on the page.

From between the stacks, the radiance hummed invitingly. Georgeta slid off her chair. She turned to him and gave a little-girl-bendy-finger wave before she skipped into the light.

"Goodbye, Georgeta."

Mr. Wicker set down his quill for the very last time and the Library was quiet.

Chapter 46

Dear Grandpa Sam,

I know this letter must come as quite a surprise after all these years. I'd somehow blocked out the memory of what had happened that day—the day you gave your life for mine—and since then believed Grandma's admonitions to never contact you. Now that I remember what happened, I want to write to you. When I found out you were living in Montana, that you'd taken up drug and alcohol counseling as a community service when you got out, I thought I'd send you a note.

I was having a difficult time in life when I remembered. I was sick with breast cancer. The good news is that the lump was encased in a fibrous sheath that they were able to remove with ease. I had some radiation treatment but that was all. Pretty amazing, eh? A hospital in Berkeley took care of my treatment gratis. Unfortunately at that time, Grandma passed away. She'd suffered several strokes. I don't know if you know much about me, but I'm writing again and that seems to be going very well. And I'm engaged to be married. He's an exceptional man. A real-life Orpheus.

The guilt, though, was eating me alive. I went to the police in Simi and talked to old Sergeant Rogers of Homicide. He'd been a regular cop when Lillian died. I told him about the breath-holding game, how I was really the one who accidentally took Lillian's life. He wouldn't even take a statement. He talked about how you'd served your sentence, the justice system had played its hand, and that the only person who could challenge your conviction would be you. And if you hadn't by now, you probably never would.

Be that as it may, I couldn't stand the void of real justice. I want you to know how much I love you. There isn't a bigger place in my heart for anyone as there is for you. I know that probably doesn't mean much after the terrible things that have happened. I'd understand if you threw this letter right in the trash. But I couldn't go another day without saying it. And any time you feel like saying something—anything—I'm here for you. Because you showed me there is something worth living for in this world, something I had when everything else had been taken from me: I had your love.

Thank you, Grandpa.

Love,
Your Granddaughter Alicia

Acknowledgements

Some stories take years to slither into the light. *Mr. Wicker* is one of them. I'm grateful for Neil Gaiman's input on the original novelette and his reminder that, in fairy tales, "things come in threes." It made all the difference.

The story had such haunting visuals that I had to adapt the novelette to screenplay. Screenwriters Adam Campbell and Sean Dickson, actress Elyse Ashton and industry friend Kelly Brice read the adaptation. Their feedback and encouragement were priceless. When the script became a quarterfinalist in The Don and Gee Nicholl Fellowships in Screenwriting, I knew I had a great story. Despite numerous meetings, Hollywood wasn't ready for it and I had more to say. So, I adapted it to novel.

In hindsight, taming wild weasels would have been easier.

My gratitude goes to Dr. Jen Thompson for sharing with me her experience working in a psych unit. (I wish more professionals would have agreed to being interviewed.) I'm also grateful for my readers: Devi Snively; Susie Putnam; Elyse Ashton; Bret Shefter; the Dark Delicacies writers' group, in particular Jodi Lester, Lisa Morton and John Palisano; and the late Rebekah Owen. A big thanks goes to Jeanne Cavelos and Theodora Goss at the Odyssey Critique Service for their invaluable help. My copyeditors Faryn and Beverly are amazing people.

But it is to Dr. Maurice James Moscovich, professor emeritus in Classical Studies from Western University in London, Ontario, that I raise a large Grecian urn of honeyed wine. Thank you, kind sir, for taking me under your wing and teaching me about both Roman hostage-taking practices and the Gauls. Et merci mille fois for critiquing Drunos' story.

Most of all, I deeply thank John and Jennifer at Raw Dog Screaming Press for believing in me and Mr. BBQ Butt.

Lugus bless you all.

About the Author

Maria Alexander writes pretty much every damned thing and gets paid to do it. She's a produced screenwriter and playwright, published games writer, virtual world designer, award-winning copywriter, interactive theatre designer, prolific fiction writer, snarkiologist and poet. Her stories have appeared in publications such as *Chiaroscuro Magazine, Gothic.net* and *Paradox*, as well as numerous acclaimed anthologies alongside living legends such as David Morrell and Heather Graham.

Her second poetry collection—*At Louche Ends: Poetry for the Decadent, the Damned and the Absinthe-Minded*—was nominated for the 2011 Bram Stoker Award. And she was a winner of the 2004 AOL Time-Warner "Time to Rhyme" poetry contest.

When not wielding a katana at her local shinkendo dojo, she's being outrageously spooky and writing *Doctor Who* filk. She lives in Los Angeles with two ungrateful cats and a purse called Trog..

Explore her website: www.mariaalexander.net. You won't regret it.